THE RING OF STRAW

The Ring of Straw

A Novel. By LADY NORAH BENTINCK

Author of " The Ex-Kaiser in Exile," " My Wanderings and Memories " :: :: :: ::

LONDON: HURST & BLACKETT, LTD.
PATERNOSTER HOUSE

TO THE MEMORY OF

WILLIAM THE SILENT,

PRINCE OF ORANGE.

CHAMPION OF RELIGIOUS TOLERATION.

MURDERED BY A RELIGIOUS MANIAC IN 1584.

"Creeds are millstones round the neck of truth."
—Henry Van Dyke.

"Ne'er yet by Force was Freedom overcome."
—James Thomson.

" He that will not reason is a bigot.
He that cannot reason is a fool.
He that dares not reason is a slave."
—SIR WILLIAM DRUMMOND.

" And religion pure and undefiled before God is this—to visit the widows and the fatherless in their tribulation, and to keep oneself unspotted from the world."

" . . . and because iniquity shall abound the love of many shall grow cold, but he that shall endure to the end shall be saved."—WORDS OF OUR LORD JESUS CHRIST RECORDED BY ST. MATTHEW.

" In the early days of the Inquisition a certain Jean Teisseri, summoned before the tribunal of Toulouse, defended himself by exclaiming : ' I am not a heretic, for I have a wife and I lie with her, and I have children, and I eat flesh, and I lie and I swear, and I am a faithful Christian.' "—GUILAL, Pelliso Chron.

vii

This book "is not pickt from the leaves of any author,
but bred among the weeds and tares of mine own brain."
—(*Religio Medici*, SIR THOMAS BROWNE, 1605-1682.)

CONTENTS

PART I

RENUNCIATION

CHAPTER						PAGE
I.	A CHANGE OF MIND	-	-	-	-	19
II.	TRANSMUTATION	-	-	-	-	29
III.	THE DUKE'S LETTER	-	-	-	-	46
IV.	THE HEART OF ROME	-	-	-	-	56
V.	LOVE AND HATE	-	-	-	-	71

PART II

MARRIAGE

VI.	" WHOM GOD HATH JOINED TOGETHER . . ."				-	103
VII.	DOUBT	-	-	-	-	109
VIII.	THE UNSEEN LURE	-	-	-	-	122
IX.	THE SHADOW OF THE DEAD HAND			-	-	134

PART III

TRANSITION

X.	THE MIND OF QUENDRED	-	-	145
XI.	THE PSYCHOLOGICAL WIZARD	-	-	160
XII.	" ON THE MOUNTAIN-TOPS IS REST . . ."	-	-	171
XIII.	THE HEART OF QUENDRED	-	-	190

xi

PART IV

THE PULL OF LOVE

CHAPTER   PAGE

XIV. " . . . LET NO MAN PUT ASUNDER " - - 207

XV. MADDALENA'S " AMARI ALAQUID " - - 214

XVI. MY " LOVE " OR MY " CHURCH " ? - - 237

XVII. SIMON SPEAKS UP - - - - 255

PART V

SACROSANCT

XVIII. BITTER-SWEET - - - - - 265

XIX. FRA GIOVANNI - - - - - 279

XX PARSIFAL - - - - - 290

XXI. " . . . BUT THE SPIRIT GIVETH LIFE " - - 300

The Ring of Straw

PROLOGUE

AT the outbreak of the Franco-Prussian War a fair young man was seen leaning over the taffrail of a Channel boat, gazing with thoughts far away, into the swirling waters beneath. His name was Stephen Fitz-Urse.

It was a wonderful September night, and a full moon shone upon the still waters. Looking upwards to the calm skies where grey clouds fluttered tremulously, he felt like a modern " rich young ruler." He could not help certain thoughts coming to his mind, and he was extremely conscious of his great position and wealth, in this his hour of agony. Young as he was, the turning point in his life had been reached, and he knew that he had to choose now which road he would follow : the one indicated—as he thought—by Christ's shining finger, or the " primrose path of dalliance " all ready and prepared for him, which everybody expected him to take. But he felt that should he pursue this path the voice of conscience would never be still, and that there would be no possible peace—either mental or spiritual—for him in the world any more.

Ullcombe Towers was the home of the Fitz-Urses, and in the great hall of the Barons hung a picture of a woman which was held in a certain kind of awe by each generation.

It was a strange picture, about which little was officially known, but tradition said that this was the famous " Rose of the World " Rosamund, daughter of the mighty Lord Clifford and mother of the still mightier and wise William Longspee, Lord of Salisbury. In her day this lady was renowned as the mistress-piece of Beauty of England, and she was the beloved of King Henry II. In the language of his love he called her " Rosemouth," and " Rosemouth " she is named on her picture at Ullcombe.

It was from her that the family's looks were supposed to

have been inherited, for a descendant of hers had married a Lord Athelston, and had brought the picture of her famous ancestress with her.

" Rosemouth " had chosen to be limned as Diana, bounding down a green glade, her golden bow hanging from her hand, her quiver slung across her back, while from between her scarlet lips youth laughed.

Round the frame was scrawled, in uncouth lettering :

> " If Rosemouth hang in the Castle Hall
> No evil shall Fitz-Urse befall.
> If Rosemouth fall or movéd be,
> Fitz-Urse, Fitz-Urse shall surely die."

Those words—written by an unknown hand far back in the dim centruies—had been the foundation of a tradition which had grown stronger and clung closer as the years rolled by, and each succeeding generation held the belief—superstition perhaps —that evil would come to their family should any harm befall their beautiful " Rosemouth."

The history of Ullcombe itself was curious. It had once been the home of Offa, King of Mercia, and Quendred, his queen ; but in the course of long years of fighting and wassailing it had fallen to ruins ; two short, thick towers and a crazy, ivy-covered wall being all that remained of it in the twelfth century. The Stephen Fitz-Urse of the day had cast his eye upon it and, being rich and mighty, he resolved to rebuild it and make it into a splendid stronghold, where he could withstand the king's enemies.

The house had had good fortune, and the family were inherent and unconscious lovers of beauty. All through the centuries no fire had ever touched its walls, no thief had robbed its treasures, and no ruthless spendthrift had scattered its beauties to the winds. Each Fitz-Urse had added something beautiful, historic, or precious, to his adored home ; the only home, excepting a London house, that they had ever possessed. For nearly eight hundred years all the love, wealth, and taste of the Lords of Athelston had been lavished upon Ullcombe. Nothing ugly was ever kept, nothing beautiful or precious was ever sold. The house was full of the best examples of every art, of every age, and of every land. One great gift which this family had seemingly borne in them was that of being well served ; no trusted servitor had ever been false.

" They're made to be loved," an old woodman had once said of them. " They 'ave a sort of something ye can't well explain that draws everybody after them." And this charm, so strong in them all, was especially noticeable in Stephen.

Tall and slender he was, with beautiful hands and feet. Dull gold-coloured hair rippled over his small head, and from under straight, delicately-marked eyebrows, almost as fine as a girl's, his large grey-blue eyes looked earnestly into the world. The unusual expression in these—almost that of a visionary, a mystic—gave a thoughtful look to his fair face, and made him appear older than his twenty years. His soul seemed to hover in his eyes.

Stephen Fitz-Urse, Earl of Athelston, was as nearly pure Anglo-Saxon as it was possible for an Englishman of the nineteenth century to be, and he looked it. His family could trace an unbroken male descent from the reign of King Stephen, hence his name, for that monarch had been sponsor to the son of the Lord of Athelston of the day, greatest and richest of his courtiers, and since then every eldest son born to the Fitz-Urses was named Stephen. Round this custom had again grown a sort of superstition that, should there cease to be a Stephen in the family, the Fitz-Urses would wither and die.

A tall, clean-limbed race were they, with well-shaped heads set on necks like columns, and well-shaped ears placed close against proverbially fair hair. " Fair Fitz-Urse " they were always called.

Stephen's father was the Duke of Seyntleger, and one of Queen Anne's Dukes, a point by which they did not lay so much store as the romantic fact that, in 1589, when there were only seventeen Earls in all England, the seventh Earl of Athelston was one of them ! Added to this he was one of the richest men in Europe, possessing coal mines in Wales, oil in Rumania, forests in Russia, and streets in London.

To-night then, the heir to all these immense possessions leaned over the taffrail of a Channel boat, and gazed, with thoughts far away, into the swirling waters beneath.

His mind went back across the rolling centuries behind him, and he was not ashamed of his forbears. The women had been lovely, winning, wise ; the men good-looking, chivalrous, brave. Not a page in England's glorious story but some Fitz-Urse appeared on it with honour. They were in Jerusalem and France with Cœur de Lion, in France again with Edward I.,

Henry V. and Henry VIII. One comforted poor old Henry II. at Chinon when forsaken and forgotten by all his relations and friends. In Flanders and Germany they were with Marlborough : in Spain and Belgium with Wellington : and Stephen's only uncle had led the Guards during part of the campaign in Crimea. It was a proud heritage, and one which few families in England could equal.

Capturing his flighting thoughts, Stephen brought them back to the pulse of his life—his father. Now he not only admired his father, but he loved, revered, and trusted him. To Stephen, he was the symbol of all that was right and upright, splendid in English, and he knew deep down in his heart that the reason the old man would have given for being what his son knew him to be, was that for four hundred years his family had conformed to the state religion of England. This thought gave Stephen the acutest discomfort. How well he remembered past conversations—words dropped, though not bitterly, in all the casual talks of their home life during the years of his adolescence.

"You can't be a really good and useful English citizen if you're a Roman Catholic," the Duke had often said in Stephen's hearing. "The basis of the system doesn't allow it. The Roman idea is to separate you from the rest of the community, not to mingle with it, which is the essence of good fellowship and all social and useful life. It's a very curious system built on typical continental—that is, Latin—lines, and never did and never will suit free-born, island-bred men. Even in the days when England *was* Catholic, most of her kings kicked against the power of Rome, and inwardly resented her obvious desire to encroach on their far-away, sea-girt land."

It was because he knew his father's heart and feelings so well, that Stephen felt especially sad to-day.

"How angry he'll be, how weak and emotional he'll think me, how he'll despise me." The boy flushed at the last thought, for to be despised by the person he honoured and admired most in all the world was indeed a bitter fate.

A sudden scampering was heard on the deck and the sound of men shouting caused him to realise, like one waking from a wild, distorted dream, that they had safely reached England at last.

PART I

RENUNCIATION

CHAPTER I

A CHANGE OF MIND

All Creeds I view with toleration thorough
And have a horror of regarding Heaven
As anybody's rotten borough.''
—THOMAS HOOD

" What strong mysterious links enchain the heart
To regions where the morn of life was spent.''
—JAMES GRAHAM.

STEPHEN'S father sat in his favourite sitting-room at Ullcombe.

The walls were lined with cedar wood by which the air was faintly scented. On the floor lay a pale blue Chinese silk carpet, and a Stephen Fitz-Urse, painted by Titian, gazed haughtily at his descendants from his dark gold frame above the exquisite carving of the stone mantelpiece. Huge logs lay upon a heap of soft silver ashes, from which glowed a ruby heat and, as the wood occasionally fell together, millions of sparks danced away up the cavernous chimney, making tiny kaleidoscopic designs upon the iron coat-of-arms at the back of the fire.

The Duchess, with her only other child, Rosamund, was in Scotland and expected home in a couple of days. Rosamund and Stephen were twins.

His wife was much younger than the Duke, who had married her when she was twenty-two and he forty-five, and stories about her life with her extraordinary father were still rife round Conyers Castle, her old home in Yorkshire. She was the only child of the last Lord Condicote, whose wife had left him soon after the birth of the child on account of his brutal habits. He had firmly refused to let her have the little girl, not because he liked the poor, wee creature, but merely to annoy his wife, who had married him—so her friends said—to get away from a young and detested stepmother. She was thin and white and had pale yellow eyelashes.

" A poor, pale, puny thing," her lord had described her in his cups to his equally intoxicated friends.

And the child grew up amongst the grooms.

Her father was a monster of selfishness, and a miser to boot. Although he spent endless sums on horses and servants, and feasting and wine, he let everything else go to ruin. The house was in a state of utter dilapidation : the brocade of the drawing-room walls was hanging in ribands, and water poured through enormous holes in the roof. Nothing new was ever bought except horses and carriages, and poor Elizabeth's clothes were a perfect sight. The housekeeper used to buy her a few garments at the local shop, so that the girl should be at least decently clothed.

As for his own personal appearance—it was notorious! His lower lip was unkempt and bristly, and when he kissed his daughter he made her chin bleed. His London clothes were green and shone with age and dirt ; most of the seams were split somewhere, and the soles of his boots flapped away from his feet as he walked. His beard was like a last year's bird's nest.

Out hunting he wouldn't wear pink, saying that as red was the King's livery it was incorrect to wear it hunting with any hounds other than His Majesty's buckhounds ; so he appeared in a bottle-green coat, brown buckskin breeches, black top-boots, an extremely old and battered top hat, and a black silk handkerchief tied in a wild knot under his left ear—at least, it was generally there at the end of the day !

He always smoked a pipe and swore oaths which no one but himself could even pronounce. His stud of thoroughbreds were the finest " leppers " in the kingdom, and nobody before or since had been known to ride across country like he did.

He died at eighty-one, from the result of a fall from making his horse jump a low fence on the way home after one of the grandest runs of his life. He had practically led the field for an hour and twenty minutes.

For three weeks he lay in his great black four-poster, dying. No one was allowed to touch his shaggy beard or his hands—and those looked like grimy claws as they lay on the coverlet.

He commanded that Elizabeth should be brought to him. At the time she was seventeen ; tall and roguish-looking, with small brilliant teeth, and a distinct " come-hither " in her pansy-coloured eyes.

" Thank Satan you're not like your mother," said he, casting his wicked dying old eyes over her young form. " I suppose you'll have to go and live with the fishy creature when I'm in hell. But take my advice and don't listen to her babblings. Get married quick and have a rollicking time, that's what the old world is meant for, my girl. Do just what you d—— well like, and don't care a curse for anyone. Rot my bones, rot my bones," and he rubbed his skinny old hands together as he muttered his favourite oaths in a hoarse rattling voice.

" Father ! How can you say such things ? Don't you know that Mother has been dead for years ? "

She looked with fear at the old man, nearly lost in the immense bed. Since his fall he seemed to have withered to nothing, and now he looked like an evil mummy shrivelling away before her eyes. There was a fearsome silence for a few minutes, and the girl wanted to scream and run away, when suddenly he shot forth a skinny claw and gripped her by the arm.

" Bend down," he whispered ; " nearer, nearer. I've got something to tell you—a secret ; nobody else must know—nobody else, nobody else," and he pulled the girl towards him with what seemed to her superhuman strength in such a very old man. He then fumbled in his breast with the other claw, and at last held out a key.

" Take it," he whispered, his half dead eyes glittering again for a second. " Take it, but, rot my bones, don't let anyone see it. Now, be quick. There's no time to be lost. Quick—quick. I hear a step outside. Press your finger on that black wooden knob in the panelling above my bed."

She did so, quaking like an aspen leaf. At the instant the whole of a large panel flew back and revealed an immense iron box. She looked round and, to her horror, she saw the old man had turned and was sitting on his haunches facing the box, chuckling with demoniacal laughter.

" There it all is ! Ha ! ha ! He ! he ! he ! and nobody ever knew ! I had it behind my head all these years and nobody ever knew but me ! Ha ! ha ! Rot my bones, but it's a d—— good joke. Well, my lass, it's all for you. Every month since I was twenty I've put two hundred sovereigns into that box, and if you're good at your books you can tell me how much is in it now."

He was becoming fearfully excited, and his voice seemed to get stronger, rising to a cracked scream. His eyes were glittering unnaturally as he greedily held out his transparent bony old hands to the hole in the wall, his fingers opening and shutting convulsively.

" I can tell you how much money there is in there. I can tell you to a penny. Ha ! ha ! ha ! ha ! There's one hundred and forty-four thousand pounds—all golden sovereigns, golden sovereigns—sovereigns—sov-e-reigns." His voice suddenly became weak again and rattled horribly. He put out his hand and clutched at her gown. " It's all right. It's all—yours—my—girl ; all yours—if—you—if you—don't—— Lots of gold—to—be—yours—if—you—have—no—religion. . . . God——" The word was spat out with his dying breath.

Then the body gave a convulsive twist, and the head fell out over the side of the bed, lolling hideously.

.   .   .   .   .   .

That was the end of the wicked Lord Condicote, and is repeated in awestruck tones to this day by the villagers on his enormous estates. The property and money were so strictly left in tail male that on his death everything had to go away to a distant cousin. But in the bottom of the iron box which he had revealed to his bewildered daughter just before his death was found a will stuck in the toe of an old hunting boot, and dated a few days before his accident.

" I hereby leave and bequeath £144,000, which I have saved out of income, to my only child, Elizabeth, on the condition that she belongs to no special form of Belief or Creed, such as the English Church, the Roman Church, the Greek Church, or any other ' Church,' all of which divisions I abhor and despise. For this reason I have never had her baptised into any Church. Furthermore, my said daughter may leave the money how she likes, so long as my conditions concerning her are conformed with.

" Given on this b—— day (a black frost, so I can't go hunting) January 20th, 1845.

" (*Signed*)   Condicote.

" Witnessed by

" Jabez Rudkin ⎱ Grooms."
" Tom Fowler ⎰

Naturally this extraordinary document came as a tremendous shock to everybody.

Said they, "What a dreadful old man." "Poor child, to be tempted to ungodliness by filthy lucre."

But a saving clause was suddenly found in the person of Mrs. Carey, a younger sister of the late Lady Condicote, and so aunt and natural guardian of the orphaned Elizabeth.

This lady, as a strict evangelical, was convinced that baptism was not necessary to salvation. She looked up the parish register and found that Lord Condicote—true to his word—had never had Elizabeth christened.

"This is wonderful," said Mrs. Carey; "it is surely God's way of working out some special design. The child professes no special form of faith, therefore the money is hers without a doubt, and I will bring her up on those lines which I hold to be right and true."

Elizabeth had been horror-struck at her father's awful death, and her aunt, finding her in a highly nervous and impressionable state, had had no difficulty in getting her to assimilate her particular religious views.

She lost no time or opportunity in impressing upon her niece's mind that the world is fundamentally wicked, and imbuing her with the idea that the playhouse and the ballroom were Satan's favourite abodes, and that the beautifying of the body led to perdition. She took her regularly to Bible readings (attended by some of the highest in the land), and in a short time the girl, who was very quick, knew her " Testament " upside down, and could quote it on every occasion with unerring accuracy.

But even the unbecoming way of doing her hair on which her aunt insisted, and the dowdy yet expensive clothes which she chose for her, couldn't hide her prettiness and her slender but very feminine form. Her dewy pansy eyes looked lovely, even from beneath the most hideous hat, and nothing could dim the brightness of her complexion of pearls and peaches. All these points, added to her position and her fortune, had not escaped the eyes of the Duchess of Camelford, eldest sister of the Duke of Seyntleger. She was much distressed at her brother being— at the age of forty-five—still the most sought-after bachelor in the kingdom. Here was a Duchess to her hand ! Religious, not flighty, pretty ; well-born and with money ! (" It's always useful," she soliloquised, " and even those with £1,000 a day can do with a little more ! ")

She made them meet, and marriage bells were soon ringing

And so it happened that five years from the day of her father's death, Lady Elizabeth Conyers, with much pomp and circumstance, married the Duke of Seyntleger.

No one could have imagined on her wedding day that this serious, beautiful, religious young woman was the same person as the little, wild, heathenish tom-boy who rode astride on her mad old father's horses, and pertly kissed his grooms.

． ． ． ． ．

Meanwhile, the £144,000 of hideous memory was rolling up in the bank. With her father's instinct for hoarding, she let it remain there. "Rainy days may come, and then it will be useful," she thought.

Her children had imbibed a certain amount of their mother's spirit. She had brought them up strictly, amidst distinctly Low Church surroundings. Bible meetings and Bible readings were amongst some of their most frequent pastimes. They were now grown-up, and Stephen would be twenty-one in a few months.

And it was because he knew his mother's feelings and her religious views so well, that he felt glad to-day that she was away.

"Terrible as it must be," he said to himself, "it would be far worse if she were here."

As he came across the great hall towards his father's room he glanced at "Rosemouth's" picture, and a curious feeling of foreboding passed through him. He had always felt superstitious about it ; they all did more or less, and yet none of them had ever mentioned it to the other. Although they loved her she was, in a sort of way, their skeleton in the cupboard.

The Duke sat by the crackling wood fire eagerly scanning the evening paper, and rose to go into dinner as his son entered.

"Well, my boy, I'm glad to see you home again," and he held out his slender, white old hand. "What do they say of it ? What do they say of it ? Did you go to see Granville ? He'd know how anxious I am to hear all the news."

Stephen clasped the extended hand. He thought his father looked like an exquisite piece of porcelain, every line was so fine, so well modelled. He noticed the thin ankles and wrists. How delicate they seemed; yet Stephen knew they were as strong as refined steel.

Despite his sixty-six years he delighted to break in young

horses, and he could easily tire out many of his son's friends through wet turnips in November! His pale grey-blue eyes were still keen and strong, and overhung by thick white eyebrows. His mouth was straight, with compressed lips, and he wore whiskers. These were silver white, and so was his thick and beautiful hair, which had a ripple still running through it, which Stephen had inherited. It was said that no man in England showed so quickly, yet so politely, when he was bored. Yet nobody responded more readily than he to a well-turned phrase, a witty answer, or a pretty face.

"No, Father; I'm afraid I didn't go to the Foreign Office. I hadn't much time in London, you know."

"Four hours, Stephen! Four hours was plenty just for going there and getting the latest news. The whole thing is most extraordinary. So sudden and unexpected. Why! Granville told me himself only a few weeks ago that Europe had never seemed so quiet. Whatever were the French about! It all comes from love of power. Bismarck and that extraordinary fellow, Napoleon, trying to out-do each other at the dirty, old political game. I'm glad we have none of us been politicians, my boy, but only soldiers—soldiers to 'do or die.' I hope you'll be happy in the Coldstream," he said. "Ever since the regiment was raised there's been a Fitz-Urse in it, and I hope there always will be."

Stephen was still at Balliol, where he had done remarkably well. In those days there were only four careers open to gentlemen—the Army, Politics, Diplomacy, and the Church. In the eyes of the Fitz-Urses the first was the only possible one for an honest man, the three latter being too likely to lead into Machiavelian paths.

Dinner over, both men went together to the library. Stephen had been strangely silent, and his father—keenly sensitive to the state of other people's feelings—had purposely done most of the talking. It was true, he liked a good listener, and was quite conscious of his own charm as a conversationalist.

Although much attracted by the spiritual aspect of life, he, nevertheless, was a man of the world and human. He was thus proud of his blood, for it had never flowed in ignoble veins; proud of his family having been honoured by kings because of valiant deeds on fifteenth-century battlefields; proud of their having got to the top like eagles who fly there, and not like reptiles who crawl there. And also, truth to tell—for he was no saintly recluse, indifferent to life, this Duke—he was secretly—perhaps unconsciously—glad of his exclusiveness, and glad that everyone who was anyone schemed and plotted and planned to mate their Maries and Johns with his Stephen and Rosamund.

During the meal, at which uneasy undercurrents made themselves deeply felt by both men, Stephen's mind was pondering his father's remark as to his having had time to go to the Foreign Office.

Of course he had had time, and he now regretted not having made an effort to do so. How natural it was that the old man should have wished to hear inside information on the events which were rocking Europe. Anybody would! The Germans marching on Paris! The Emperor and a brilliant army prisoners! Bismarck dictating to France! Why, of course, it was interesting! Thrilling and extraordinary, beyond words! For who could see the end and its far-reaching consequences? Ruminating within himself, Stephen plainly saw that it was his indifference to the enthralling, absorbing topic which was strange, not his father's interest in it. Intense nervousness overcame him once more, and his lips could hardly frame the words of his thought. He rose and leant against the mantelpiece.

His father looked at him with half-closed eyes.

What was the matter, he wondered.

Debts? Women? Or *a* woman?

He wanted to help him to say the thing which he felt was trembling on his lips. But he knew that silence was the wisest way—the best way. So, getting up, he crossed the room, where he stood with his back to Stephen, seemingly looking for a book.

His son slowly turned his head towards him, a look of unutterable weariness and pathos veiling his eyes. Then stepping impetuously towards his father with outstretched arms—appealingly he said :

" Father — Father — I'm — I've—— Ah, well — Archbishop Manning received me into the Church to-day."

There was a silence. The noise made by the fire and the ticking clock seemed unnaturally loud The Duke turned from the books at last, very slowly.

" Into what Church ? " he asked.

For a full minute Stephen couldn't answer. It was like a two-edged stiletto cutting into his hot tumultous heart.

" But—of course, Father," he stammered. " I mean the Catholic Church."

" Ah ! and *which* Catholic Church ? I have always learned that there were several—Latin, Greek, Armenian, and Syrian. To which particular body have *you* attached yourself ? "

Stephen was nonplussed. He had never studied religions. He knew nothing and cared less about these divisions of the Church of Rome, each recognising the Pope as their head, although possessing different rules as to the celibacy of the clergy, language of the ritual, and the taking of Communion under both kinds.

He had just " become a Catholic " *tout court,* and that was all. His brain was reeling with it, his heart was burning with it, his soul was drowned in it. It was not only Transubstantiation—held by Catholics to be the one great jewel of their Faith—which had conquered his mind, but everything else about it attracted him.

He loved dark churches smelling of stale incense. He loved the monotonous chanting of monks in Latin, a language of which he was a past-master. He loved altars smothered in exotic flowers, and the flickering of hundreds of slender waxen candles. He loved great dim cathedrals through whose carven arches boys' beautiful voices rose and sank in ecstacy and floated up and up and up, to end in a silence pregnant with religious emotion. He loved gorgeous vestments and the magnificent plainness of Holy Week. He loved the joyousness of it and the solemnity of it.

He was curiously attracted by the soft pattering of priests' feet as they mysteriously appeared, and again as mysteriously disappeared into little sentry-like boxes, placed at intervals down the churches. It thrilled him to meditate on the esoteric rite which he was told was being performed behind that wooden shutter. How wonderful it was to think that the man whom he had just seen enter that Box had power to forgive sins—like God—in fact, *was* God for the time being ! Be he fat or thin, bloated or ascetic, clever or stupid, good or bad, kind or cruel, white, yellow, black, or red—he—as a priest—possessed the wondrous unseen God-power, of forgiving men and women their sins !

And thus it was that to be a priest had become the outstanding wish of Stephen's life, and this desire was clinched when once, on reading far into the night, these words of a French priest had imprinted themselves on his mind and heart :

" Every priest, in the exercise of his heavenly function,

represents Jesus Christ, or rather *is* Jesus Christ Himself, who only truly operates what the words of His minister announce—alone binds and unbinds, alone dispenses grace, alone immolates and offers to His Father the victim of propitiation."

The words had gripped him.   *That* was a religion if you like, whose ministers *were* God in the performance of the rites and functions of their Faith

CHAPTER II

TRANSMUTATION

" Lord !   What wilt Thou have me to do ? "—BIBLE.

FOR many nights after this he had lain—sleepless—staring at the
enfolding darkness.   This was the end, not the beginning, of his
gradual change to a different angle of thought in his spiritual life.
It was the result of many long, and sometimes exhausting talks
with Father Carylon—a clever and pleasant Jesuit at Oxford—
and Stephen, partaking more of an æsthetic and artistic temperament than of a profoundly logical and reasoning one, had soon
succumbed to the numerous attractions of the Catholic Faith.

At the Jesuit's invitation, Stephen had often been to Mass
and Benediction at his Church, and it was here one evening that
the feeling had come to him with an overpowering certainty that
he must be a Catholic—and not only a Catholic, but a priest as
well.

To be a Roman Catholic and *not* a priest was—to him—
incomprehensible.

The Catholic priest was, in Stephen's eyes, the greatest being
on earth ;   the holiest, the best.   Possessing God-like powers,
through the hidden potency of the inexplicable rite known as the
" laying on of hands," a priest was, Stephen thought, not only
like God, but, during countless hours of his life, he *was* God.   At
least, this was a claim of the Catholic Church, and, believing in
her, he naturally believed all she taught.

Priests represented Bishops, and Bishops represented the
Pope, who, in all the most important subjects concerning faith
and morals, claimed—through His infallibility—equality with
God.

All this Roman Catholic teaching he drank in eagerly, and he
had even read somewhere that a Pope had said that " during the

Mass, Christ, being the Victim of the priest " (who, so to speak, was His creator at that moment—in view of ths extraordinary rite which he claimed power to consummate), " became for the time being his inferior."

This thought—which to the few Protestant friends to whom he had unburdened his mind at Oxford, was a shocking blasphemy—held Stephen's brain in some mysterious way in almost mesmeric subjugation.

He was thinking thus as he sat in Father Carlyon's church at Oxford, listening to the roll of the " Tantum Ergo " being sung by the whole congregation to the mighty tune of Russia's National Anthem.   Suddenly a tinkling bell sounded.   Clouds of incense floated before his face.   All heads were devoutly bowed as the Host was raised at the altar, encased in a golden monstrance. Stephen alone gazed upwards.

" It's God, it's God, it's God," he whispered.   " How can the priest *bear* it ?   How does he not swoon and die from joy at being so close to his Lord ? " and he very firmly believed in it all.

A few days later he had told Father Carlyon of his intention to join the priesthood, although adding that he was a little worried because he couldn't quite make Roman Catholicism coincide with the Bible, which, of course, as a strictly brought up Low Churchman, he knew exceedingly well.

" Oh, never mind about the Bible," the priest had retorted airily.   " You see, you only have to believe the Church's interpretation of it, so that makes it all quite easy !   You must read the early Fathers ;   they will interest you.   After all, the Bible *un*interpreted is useless as a basis of Faith, and the only *true* interpretation is that made by Holy Mother Church."

So by degrees Stephen assimilated and digested this teaching.

The priest went on to tell the youth of a friend of his—a certain Padre Primavera—who lived near Florence, and he advised him to go there for the vacation.   Stephen was delighted at the prospect, and spent two unutterably happy months away in the hills, under hot blue skies, drinking in longingly, greedily, all that the priest had to tell him of what he called the one, true, Catholic and Apostolic Faith.

Catholicism had seemed so easy out there !   But here—oh ! it was fearful, and to-night, as the boy confronted the Duke, he was literally trembling from head to foot, and his gold curly hair lay damp upon his forehead.

" Father," he said, " I don't really know what you are talking about, but I do know that *I* am a Catholic—a Roman Catholic, if you will—and—besides that, I have made up my mind to become a priest."

The Duke was standing near his son now, but not looking at him.

" You have made two extraordinary statements to-night," he said ; " one that you are a Roman Catholic, and the other that you intend to become a priest. I have much——"

A clock struck at that minute.

" It is late," he said, glancing at his watch. " Ah, well, I will not say anything else now. It's been a tiring day for you, and a sad one for us both."

" Not for me, Father ; not sad for me," said Stephen, his face suddenly lighting up.

" Time alone will shew that," said the old man. " Good night, Stephen," and he went away to his own rooms.

The boy watched his father go, and then turned and stood in the middle of the great hall. His head sank dejectedly upon his breast. Could he withstand and conquer the avalanche he saw descending upon him ?

They had all been so happy together ! They had all adored each other, and had been so proud of each other, and now— what would happen ? What would the future be for him ? All the happy " insouciant " days gone—gone—for ever. He could never talk to any of them with the same absolute freedom. There would always be a feeling of constraint. He felt—and it was like an icy hand upon his heart—that all the spontaneity, the joyousness, the resilience, the natural and childlike gaiety of his home life had gone for ever. He knew that it could never be quite the same again. Against his will the tears welled up, and his quick breathing sounded strangely loud as it echoed hauntingly through the deserted rooms.

The wrench of the affections was terrific, almost surpassing his endurance, and the giving up of so much (for he was sure this would have to be) seemed like a hideous nightmare from which there would be no awakening. He longed for someone to talk with who would understand. Such a few hours ago the ascetic Manning had held both his hands in his, and had poured spiritual balm on to his troubled spirit, and he had been so wonderfully happy. But here—there was no one ! No one who could under- stand ! Stay though, there was one ! Giovanni, the cook ! He was an Italian Catholic, so *of course* would sympathise with Stephen's joy and suffering.

The boy leapt to his feet.

" I must see him," he said to himself, " but where to find him ? I'll get Garland to tell him." He rang the bell and asked the butler to tell Giovanni to go to his room. " Yes—now—at once. I want him."

Garland gasped inwardly. " Giovanni ! What could his lordship want with *Giovanni* of all people ? A furriner—the only furrin servant in the house." There must be something very wrong with Stephen, he thought.

But aloud he only said, " Very good, m'Lord."

Stephen—flushed and perturbed—then let himself out into the cool, fragrant September night, and walked up and down the terrace agitatedly smoking a cigarette. He thrust his hands deep into his pockets, and gazed out over the immense stretch of land rolling away beneath his feet. It all belonged to his father. Ullcombe was planned as a fortress, and reared itself proudly above the flat surrounding country, while the tiny village clung to the base of its immense walls as if demanding protection. Everything was quiet ; redolent of peace and contentment. But just across the Channel guns roared and belched forth death and horror, and men were dying in agonies. Enemies were battering on the gates of Paris. Would *his* soul hold firm against the unseen yet even stronger forces of religion ?

He slowly mounted the narrow stone steps which led to his room.

" Ah, Giovanni—you're here. It's very good of you to come at this hour. I want to talk to you, but first you must be comfortable ! Make the fire burn and then smoke," and he handed him a cigar.

Giovanni—like all his compatriots—loved adventure and loved a drama. He scented both, and was quite prepared to have an enjoyable time. Of course it was something connected with love !

" You're a Catholic, aren't you, Giovanni ? " Stephen jerked out suddenly.

" Eh ? What did mi Lordo say ? Me—Giovanni—a Catholic ? "

Horrible memories of books he had read about the Inquisition rushed to his mind. He looked round wildly !

Here he was in a lonely turret in the middle of the night with an able-bodied young noble (nobles were very powerful in Inquisitorial days), and the walls were covered with guns, rifles, swords, and what not !

" Oh, no, mi Lordo, I not a Catholic—at least, I not a verra gooda one. Why, mi Lordo, I only beena to ze Mass twice in four years, and to ze confess I never go—ze priests in England zey canno understanda me, and, mi Lordo, I do not like ze ' whs-whs-whs' behind ze ' grille ' !   And whata I got to tells in ze confess ? Giovanni he stay at home—he cook for Il Duca and Ella Duchessa, he make ze kitchen famous, he thinka gooda mixtures, he maka gooda sauces, and some time he sing just a leetle ' La bella Napoli ' and ' Santa Lucia,' so he nevva hasa time to do any sins, and " (he was getting wound up now) " he knows ze priests verra wella ! Some verra gooda—but some ' *per bacco !* ' Mi Lordo he been to Italia ? Ha ! ha ! Zey not verra stricta in Italia ! "

This was the last reception to his questions that Stephen, in his wildest flights of imagination, would have dreamt of.

" But, Giovanni—it's dreadfully wicked of you not to go to Mass every Sunday," he said. " It's a mortal sin—you know it is, and its even more wicked never to go to Confession and to Holy Communion. In fact, Giovanni,"—and his voice became very solemn—" I'm sorry to have to mention it, but do you realise that you are no longer in the Church, and that most likely you'll go to hell when you die ? "

Giovanni in his turn was nonplussed. What *could* it all mean ?

Stephen's words had recalled the days when he was being prepared for his first Communion (and, incidentally, his last).

" Oh ! no, mi Lordo, I still in ze Church. I a Catholic. I love ze Madonna. I often ask her to helpa me to make a *beautiful* soufflet. I wear a lota medals. Looka, Mi Lordo," and he took a greasy brown scapular and a dirty silver chain on which hung about sixteen medals all of different saints, from his neck. He looked at them with loving pride.

" Here Santa Maria Madallena," he said, holding up one quite black with ancient dirt. " She verra gooda before she died, and here Santa Simone Stock, he wonderful man, he nevva wash, he do it as a penance for his sins " (Stephen thought perhaps Giovanni also did it as a penance for *his* sins), " and here—— "

But Stephen interrupted the history of the medals by telling Giovanni that he hoped he would make an effort to go to church,

C

and, realising the futility of the conversation, he told the man to
return to bed.

Slowly he went to his bedroom, his ardour just a tiny bit
damped by the man's attitude, for he didn't realise that very few
ordinary mortals would have understood the mood he was in
that night.   In the first fine rapture of his transmutation—his
gradual change to something different—his enthusiasm for his
newly-found bliss was like that of a man born blind and seeing for
the first time the glory of the sun, compared to the longing for a
bandage which consumes the man denuded of his eyelids and tied
to a post in the blazing heat of noonday.

As he lay in bed the pros and cons of the question did undoubtedly rise to clash together in his mind.   His father's attitude had not been ineffective.   But, crying out above every argument which presented itself to his agonised mind, torn this way
and that by conflicting emotions, rose the power of the mysterious
rites and the definite claims of the Catholic priesthood, and this
it was which kept his spirit chained to Rome.   Thinking thus he
fell into a disturbed and tiring sleep.

•   •   •   •   •   •

Delicious September sunlight floated into the room when
Stephen woke late next morning.   He felt old and weary, and the
nerve storm of the preceding night had indeed left its mark upon
him.   At that moment Garland entered.

" Beg pardon, m'Lord, but his Grace told me to tell your Lordship that he and Sir John Arkwright, Lord Claude Knox-Kerr, and
Captain Sykes have gone out shooting.   His Grace said he didn't
know what your Lordship would be doing."

Garland's heart was bursting.   Lord Athelston not out after
the partridges—and such a grand day as it was too !   He couldn't
make it out at all !   Putting several suits for Stephen to choose
from (his old lips were trembling so that he couldn't speak) he
silently left the room.

Stephen sat on the bed.

A hardness, never noticeable before, had suddenly come into
his face.

" So it's begun already," he soliloquized.   " I am of no more
importance than a hall-boy in the house, and he *knows* how I
revel in shooting driven partridges at this time of year, and also
what friends Claude and I are.   And it's all because I'm doing
what my mind tells me is true and what my conscience tells me is

right, and because I am following what my heart loves. I've often heard Father praise the freedom of England, but I suppose it was only in the abstract," and he smiled bitterly.

"After all, freedom is to believe what you think to be true, and do what you believe to be right. Freedom !—freedom !— freedom !" and he clasped his hands between his knees till the knuckles showed through the white taut skin. "Imprison my body a thousand times, but give my mind its freedom ! That at least is my own, and shall not be made the slave of any man. How *dare* Father treat me so, how dare he ? I had no idea that he was so bigoted and narrow-minded ! Fancy a man like him, who has travelled everywhere, met everyone, and read everything ! Oh, it's inconceivable ! Well, I *don't* care ; I suppose he thinks I'll mind giving up all the money and—and—all this. But I don't. What I'm giving it up for is worth it ; it's worth anything, for it's God's truth."

He lifted his eyes and looked out upon all the fair country bathed in golden cobwebbed light. It was entirely beautiful. Involuntarily he knelt at one of the open windows and gazed upon the land of his forebears.

"Oh, Ullcombe, how I love you," he sighed.

With studied politeness his father made conversation to him that night, never alluding to his absence out shooting.

"We got 106½ brace," the Duke said. "Claude shot beautifully. He tells me he thinks he's going to Rome soon *en poste.*"

In cold precision, and as though it came from a different world, his father's voice went on :

"You told me last night that you have become a member of the Roman Church, and that it is your wish to become a priest of that Church. Am I to understand that quite distinctly ? "

"Yes, Father, quite distinctly."

"And you do not think anything will make you change— ever ? "

"No—never."

"Well, Stephen, you know that it is not my custom to preach and I believe we both dislike scenes and ranting. But I wonder how much you really know of the Church which you have joined ? Her inner workings, her ultimate ends ? You know how much I love freedom, and that I consider it one of the chief reasons of England's greatness ? You know that for the last thousand years she has fought for freedom, for it is not only since the Reformation that she has resisted the Papacy—that, of course, you learnt in your studies of history.

> ' But what is Life ?
> 'Tis not to stalk about, and draw fresh air
> From time to time, or gaze upon the sun ;
> 'Tis to be free.   When Liberty has gone
> Life grows insipid, and has lost its relish.'

" Addison wrote well when he wrote these words and, what is more, he voiced the thought of every true Englishman, no matter to what century he belongs.   Well !   You are free, Stephen, free to do what you like with your own soul, though theologians tell us that we may not do what we like with our bodies !   Strange !   For one is mortal and the other immortal !   Still, I maintain that you have every right to do what your brain and your mind tell you is the truth."

Thought Stephen, " How curious, for those are nearly the words I said to myself last night ! '

The Duke went on :

" In this I think Catholics differ fundamentally from all other religions.   An Italian Cardinal told me that one of the essentials of the Romanist's belief is *implicit obedience and complete subjugation of will and thought concerning matters of Faith and Morals.* So that apparently to be a ' good son of Holy Church ' you must forfeit the right of having an opinion on certain subjects.   Believe, and you're in the Church; disbelieve, and you're thrown out and liable to suffer all the Church's punishments—including eternal damnation—for daring to differ from her.

" This law, however, cuts both ways, and, when the Church has had to give way on some of her strictest rules for expediency's sake, logically no ' good Catholic ' should dare to censure her, although they know she is acting against her previously laid down rules !   What will become of people who are forbidden to think ?   Of course one sees that this is part of her spiritual artillery, her marvellous organization for subjugating the human mind !   A kind of militarism of the soul.   Ah, torture my body, but let my mind soar on wings of love and freedom to God.

" Boy, I would like you to have studied *far more deeply* before joining such a Church.   Great and good in many ways she most surely is ; helpful to the weak, and seductive even to certain types of strength.   Expedient very ; making use of the oldest occultism to her advantage ; entirely Eastern in her foundations.   The most highly and subtly organized society ever known.   But divine ?

No, and a thousand times, no! How well and how truly did Newman sing in his earlier days: 'Oh, that thy creed were sound! For thou dost soothe the heart, thou Church of Rome.'

"Did the Son of God dress in fine clothes and seek the friendships of the great ones of the earth? Did He hold a court renowned for its licence, extravagance, and magnificence? Did He plot and scheme for power? No, for He was meek, gentle, humble, and mild. All His actions were prompted by Love. Giving food to the hungry people, curing sickness, raising the dead; miraculous wine at the feast, causing storms to abate, and comforting those who were sad. Only once is His anger recorded, and that in connection with money-makers, power seekers.

"In the Roman Church the holiest and most soaring spirits must toe the line; if they don't God help them, for Rome won't. Even the great Francis of Assisi was not looked upon entirely with favour in the highest quarters. The dialecticians and theologians split hairs and disputed over nice distinctions, but what did he care? With him it was Christ! Nothing but Christ—the beginning and the end, the first and the last.

"He had no system, no views; he combated no opinion, he took no side. Yet of one thing there could be no doubt. Christ had lived, and died, and had risen again. That was the truth. Nothing else mattered. The pearl of great price—here it was— take it or leave it. No dogma—no sacerdotalism—no controversy.

"The pearl of great price—will you have it or will you not? Whether or not there were millions unconsciously and consciously dying for it, sighing for it, crying for it. He bade his followers go forth with neither books nor psalms. The psalms, said Francis, they should have in their minds, and the words and teaching of the Son of God burning in their hearts.

"Why, only one of the five followers of the Saint who first set foot in England was a priest!

"If you want to work for God and give Him your life, why not become a lay preacher? Such men often appear to touch the hearts of their followers better than the clergy. It seems to me that Roman Catholicism is ruled by sort of spiritual lawyers— clever men! But were the followers of Francis of Assisi 'clever'? Was Christ 'clever'? Many did, and still do, call Him a fool, yet He was sinless! 'Cleverness' is the one word which has never been used to express His character, and when St. John wished to say all that could possibly be said of Him to explain His perfection he just simply wrote 'God *is* Love.' He could say no more, he had touched the zenith of the possibilities of human expression."

As he was speaking the Duke's face had assumed a dreamy look, and he seemed almost lost in his thoughts.

To many, perhaps, his words would have been unintelligible. Piffle ! Useless dreams ! Unconstructive idealistic moonshine ! Stephen was taken aback, for his father had never spoken to him in this vein before. He had never preached and never touched a false note. He had always seemed to understand everything, but now he seemed to understand nothing, for he did not understand " religion " as Stephen—in the last few months—had been taught to understand it by the priests of Rome.

The Duke put out both hands to his son, and Stephen's lip trembled as he saw there were tears in the old man's eyes.

" My boy," he said, his voice shaking a little, " this is—in one way—a most terrible blow to me. What a blow I do not expect you, in your present mood, to realize. I am speaking now only from the human point of view. Although I, personally, do not hold with the teachings of the Roman Church, I can understand that such a religion can attract one who is seeking ; but it is your wish to become a priest which is such a deep sorrow to me and such a calamity to our family. Since Stephen's reign we have succeeded each other in the male line from eldest son to eldest son. It is practically unique in Europe."

He brought his fist down on the table to emphasise the words, then, sighing a little, he went on :

" By becoming a priest you will break the chain so firmly welded together during all these past years. Uncle Anthony has no children, whilst I have only you and Rosamund. I see the end, I think I see the end," and he pressed his thumb and forefinger into his eyes.

Stephen detected a slight break in the beautiful musical voice of his father. He was nonplussed, for he had expected vituperation, red faces, and bitter words.

" Oh ! Father, how I hate to grieve you," he said.

There was a longish pause while the father looked deep into the son's face.

" You think I don't understand you ? " he said gently. " You think that I am cold, bigoted, unsympathetic, in fact, almost inhuman," and as he said the words his smile was ineffably sweet and whimsical. " So I will tell you something now that, had circumstances been different, there would have been no reason for me to disclose. Shortly before you were born, I, too, longed to join the Church of Rome ! I did join it ! "

" Father ! So you're one yourself ? So you understand ! How wonderful ! " and Stephen's voice rose on a joyful, exultant note, full of the deep intimate aspect of the brotherhood of a free-masonry ; of two initiates who say with smiling lips and under-standing eyes, " So you're one of us ! "

" So well did I understand," answered the Duke very gravely, " that I went yet further than you, and I turned back."

" *Father !* " The son's voice sank to a whisper of disillusioned and shocked horror.

(Only Catholics can appreciate what others of the Faith feel about one who has left the " Fold."

" For a short time I was happy in the Romanist Faith," the Duke went on, " but it didn't give me what I was daily hoping for, and I—who expected freedom—chafed when I found myself in a cage, though it was of gold resplendent with jewels. No one will ever know what I suffered, for—thinking that I was in har-bour at last—I found to my dismay that there were whirlpools all round me.

" At last, after suffering tortures, and being dragged this way and that by conflicting emotions, not only of the spiritual side, but from other thoughts which made me wonder whether I was morally wrong in being faithless to my new and self-imposed allegiance, I threw off the yoke. When I first told the Italian priest who had received me into the Church of Rome of my inten-tions, he told me that it was a temptation of the devil, and a well-known device of the evil one to make fearful onslaughts upon souls already far advanced in the spiritual life.

" But when he saw that I really meant what I said, he became highy incensed, and told me that if I persevered in my intention I should be damned for ever, for there was no hope, he said, of salvation for one who—having seen the truth—wilfully flings it aside. So, you see, I *know* the road upon which you are travelling !

" I will never speak of this again, for indeed the whole affair has partaken more of a sermon, and preaching at people is my bugbear ! As you know, I have always stood for freedom, and I stand for it still. I have had my say, and will from now onward hold my peace. We are but players in the great game, and those who live will see. Your turning to Rome may lead to higher things yet, for, believe, me, Stephen, *there is something even higher than the Church of Rome.* We are waiting for something to arise from the exhaustion of the old creeds which may yet revivify the world we see languishing around us, *but the dogma of the Roman Pontiffs cannot do it !* Only Christ's teaching, pure and undefiled, can do it ; only implicit obedience to His divine teaching can re-make the world.

" As you know, Stephen, I deplore all bitterness," said his father. " I admire freedom, and I think that we all should be allowed to worship how and where we please. But then it behoves all teachers of religion to ' play the game,' and not to try to get power over men's minds by methods Christ would have disdained. No, I do not wish to see England in the thrall of Rome. I fear I am very blunt, but you must forgive me."

    .   .   .   .   .   .

The Duchess and Rosamund arrived from Scotland early next morning, and, had it not been for Stephen's news, the great excitement was that Rosamund had just become engaged to Lord Traquair, an immensely rich and keen politician, a strong Presbyterian, and possessor of Dunane Castle, said to be haunted by innumerable dead Traquairs.

Immediately upon their arrival the Duke told his wife about their son's recent act.

She was horrified, for her upbringing caused her to have profoundly bitter feelings upon the subject of the Papacy. Her husband never discussed controversial subjects with her, as she couldn't do so quietly, but would get hot and excited, and so, what might otherwise have been interesting, was turned into unpleasant argument.

So few people, he found, could talk about Christ's simple teaching without very soon getting so pink and cross about it all that it was plainly evident that no useful purpose would be achieved in carrying it on. They all seemed to want to read dogma into everything He said.

Persons who uphold their own " religion " at all costs are called devout champions by their own co-worshippers, but are dubbed intolerable bigots by those who do not agree with them ! He often wondered at what point does devotion become fanaticism, and tolerance turn into indifference !

His wife was one of those who, in the realms of religion, had— like most Roman Catholics also—put on blinkers. She refused to see that there could be anything false in her own belief, or anything true in opposing ones. Just as " what Rome says " is the beginning and the end of a Catholic's faith ; " what the Bible says " was the beginning and the end of hers.

" But Stephen can't believe in the Bible any more, then ? " she asked the Duke, horrified. " If it's inspired, isn't it good enough for anyone ? Don't you believe it's inspired, Athel ? And if you do, why do you ? If only you could explain all your reasons clearly to Stephen, I'm certain he'd come back to us, come back to what you and I taught him as a child, kneeling between us night and morning with his dear curly head so close to our faces."

" I look upon the Bible as the foremost book of the world, my dear," he said gently, " and, without doubt, the word of God. Inspired ? Yes. Why do I believe it to be inspired ? Ah, my wife, you mustn't probe too deep. That is perhaps the summit of my faith.

" But, apart from this, I look upon it as containing all the wisdom, the poetry, and the mystery of the world, and unplumbed depths of psychic knowledge. That there are people who put this book aside as boring, obsolete, unnecessary, a fairy tale, seems very strange to me, and only convinces me that our clever modern men are not as clever as they think they are ! For this is indeed a wondrous clever and a most unique book. It took over a thousand years to write, and was contributed to by some of the greatest and deepest of Eastern thinkers ; some of the most wonderful of esoteric mystics. Here one finds the profoundest ideas buried in the most polished gems of literature, and the deepest scientific knowledge encased in a wealth of poetic imagery. Looked upon solely from a historical and psychic standpoint, no thinking person can despise it !

" It is almost impossible for me to explain how immensely and all-important I think the words of the New Testament are.

" After all, if one believes that Christ was God, everything He said was true ; if, on the other hand, He was not God's son, He was the wickedest charlatan, the most criminal whited sepulchre which man's mind can imagine. He has fooled the world.

" But He has *not* fooled the world.

" There are many men to-day, especially those who have lived long in the East, who respectfully affirm that they have constantly seen male persons making the same claim to status and power as did the Saviour of the w orld ; they say that the type is very common. Yet the Bible is packed with the most trenchant and sublime sentences which leave it impossible to doubt of the divinity of Him who uttered them.

" If His affirmations were false, of what good is the Book ?

" Belief in the Book is, I admit, a stupendous though unconscious act of faith, and difficult of performance to some types of intellects.   But what our Catholic friends want to make us believe is even more difficult still ! People who can't believe in the Bible seem to find it quite easy to believe in Catholicism !   This well illustrates the French saying that if there wasn't a God we'd have to invent one ! "

" It's too appalling, Athel," the Duchess said to her husband. " I simply can't believe what you've told me about Stephen.   Is it really, really true ?   To think that such a calamity should have happened in our family.   He is lost to God !   Who knows what those Romans will do to him ?   Oh, I can't bear it !   I think it was very wicked of that old Manning to have taken him over without even consulting you about it ; he must be a dreadful man."

The Duke smiled, patting her hands as though humouring a child.

" No—no, I am serious really," she said rather petulantly. " To think—apart from the awful wickedness of it—that our only son should be a Roman priest, and all our money be used to build churches and pay priests to forgive people's sins, and help funds which are used for having services said for hundreds of years after a wretched person's death so as to get them into heaven at last ! Athel !   I *do* hate it so, and to think that no Fitz-Urse has ever been a Roman before.   It's a terrible degradation to our family," she finished woefully.

" You forget the Reformation, dear," her husband answered gently, " and that I was once a Roman Catholic."

At this she coloured violently.

" Yes, yes, but that doesn't count.   You quickly left it when you saw your mistake, and now you're a good Protestant.   You hate Romanism, don't you ? "

" I hate all ' isms ' ! " he said.   " What we are labelled doesn't really matter, Elizabeth, it's what we *are* that matters."

Then, leading her to a table, he said.

" Look—here is a codicil to my will.   I made it last night.   I couldn't sleep."

" Oh !   Athel darling, how unkind I have been in not sympathising more in your grief in Stephen's horrible conduct.   You must feel it too terribly."

" It's not so much his conversion I mind," said the Duke——

" *Per*version, you mean," put in his wife.

" ——though from a wordly point of view," he went on, "it *is* a tremendous blow. Yet I feel I may not coerce man's unconquerable mind. It would be a great failure in morality were I to do so. But I am distressed that he wishes to become a priest. I distrust priests, and I can't bear to think of the bigoted, hair-splitting, and dishonest training that his brains will have to go through with before he is thought fitted to be given Orders. I wonder if he really has a true vocation, or if this is but a passing phase of ardent spiritual excitement." He spoke the words dreamily.

" But now, about my will. See ! I have left £2,000 a year to Stephen and he ought to be able to get along all right on that, for I don't wish a Fitz-Urse to be beholden to any man. But, as I frankly do not want Catholic clerics to benefit by my money, I am leaving Athelston House and the bulk of my fortune to Rosamund, but only to go to her at your death. Ullcombe is entailed, so that it must go to Stephen, but you will have everything you want ! " and he smiled at her affectionately.

" I shall have nothing if I haven't you," she answered. " You are my king."

.   .   .   .   .   .

Claude Knox-Kerr came to dinner that night. He told them that he was going to Rome the following week to the British Embassy.

" By Jove, Claude, how I envy you," said Stephen, and his eyes became wistful and shining.

" Why not come too ? " Claude answered.

The Duke was looking intently at his son from beneath half-closed lids (a trick of his).

" Yes—why not ? " he said slowly.

The boy's face, which had become pathetically sad during the last few days, lit up radiantly.

" Oh, Father !—I should like it better than anything else in the world."

" A splendid idea," laughed Claude. " Can you be ready next Wednesday ? "

" Yes, of course," Stephen answered happily.

He felt like the pilgrims in the new opera of *Tannhäuser*, which was then the very last word in music, and almost unconsciously the words " To Rome—to Rome," escaped his lips.

His father smiled seriously.

" Yes—' to Rome,' Stephen, and may you be happy there,'' he said.

When Claude had gone his father told him exactly the arrangements he had made about money.

" There, son—I have done all I can for you in view of the opinion which I hold of the Church you have joined. Will you come to prayers now ? It would please your mother.''

Stephen flushed. Since his transference of faith, Anglicanism and everything pertaining to it had become abhorrent to him, for his new-found faith had taught him to believe—amongst other things—that he had lived for the last twenty years in dark ignorance, and that everything which his parents had taught him was untrue. Protestant worship seemed to him now to be quite futile, for he had been taught that they even didn't know how to pray.

" If they only had what *I* have got—if they only knew what *I* know,'' was his constant thought.

Aware that it is against the custom of Catholics to attend the prayers or the services of what they are taught to call heretics, he felt strongly impelled to refuse his father's request, but, moved by his love for him, he at last acquiesced.

" Well—all I can do is to pray for their conversion,'' he soliloquized.

As they knelt together in the tiny stone chapel dating back to the fourteenth century, it pleased Stephen to think that one day he would bring Catholic worship to Ullcombe.

Behind him his mother was sobbing at the thought that idolatry would at some future time be practised again in the chapel, and that scheming Roman priests would come and go as they pleased.

" Retrogression,'' she thought bitterly, and she prayed for her perverted son, as she held him to be.

The Duke looked steadfastly before him. He, too, prayed for his son. He prayed that through all the '' Wander-Jahre '' upon which the boy had just embarked, he might—in whatever religion he travelled—attain to the highest Christian ideal and become indeed a Parsifal : while Rosamund prayed that her George might cut off his beard, not become too pious, and go to the theatre, for she loved dancing and plays, and he had told her that he approved of neither.

Later, as Stephen lay in bed, he realised that this was his last
night in his beloved home as a layman, but, so great was his joy
in the thought of the looming priesthood that he was only a little
tinged with sadness at the entire break he was making with the
past happy days of his youth.

" To Rome—to Rome," sang in his ears till he slept.

CHAPTER III

THE DUKE'S LETTER

" Go thou to Rome, the Paradise.
    At once the grave, the city and the wilderness."
                        —SHELLEY (Adonais).

CARDINAL COSTANZI was seated in a big chair at the window of his library. 'Twas sunset time. The Tiber rolled below, and in the distance the glittering ball of St. Peter's could be seen.

At his elbow was an empty coffee cup, and his narrow, transparent hand caressed a magnificent Persian cat which lay purring contentedly on its master's silken knee.

" Entrate," he called, as a knock sounded on the door.

" A letter for Your Eminence."

" Ah—thank you, Pietro."

The gliding, black-garbed servant put the cup noiselessly on to the silver salver, and withdrew like a shadow.

The Cardinal glanced at the stamps.

" From England," he thought, and, on looking at the postmark, said aloud :

" From Ullcombe ! Aha, what is this ? " and his voice was sad. The letter intrigued him. Slowly he opened the packet and read :

" ULLCOMBE CASTLE,
" *Sept.* 26, 1870.   QUENDRED QUEEN'S.

" DEAR CARDINAL COSTANZI,

" It is now—to be exact—twenty-two years since we met for the last time.

" You no doubt remember that it was at Mr. Geoffrey Widdicombe's house, and that the newly-converted Newman was of the party.

" You were seven years older than I, so that must make

you seventy-two. How the time passes! I am getting to be quite an old man, and the troublous times in which we live do not tend to make me feel younger.

" Thank God, I am wonderfully well, except for my heart, which worries me unaccountably now and then.

" I wonder whether you remember as distinctly as I the nature of our last meeting and our parting? We were discussing my having ' lapsed ' from the Roman Church into which you had received me the year before, and your last words to me were :

" ' Well, Duke, you force me to tell you that you are jeopardizing the future of your eternal soul in the highest possible degree, and it is certain that if you persist in this most terrible and wicked act you will be damned in Hell for ever.'

" Since that day we have never met. Of course I knew that you knew that what you were saying was not true, but that you were merely ' trying it on ' (excuse the expression, which I have picked up from my son), for you had, I remember well, a most remarkable and intimate knowledge of the history of your Church and of the Bible. Yet, on looking back over the years, my dear Cardinal, I can sympathise with your point of view. For it was indeed a case of *in extremis!*

" I was—I own it humbly—quite a big fish for Peter's net ! But I am grateful now that you said those words to me, because they made me begin to think very deeply on religious subjects in a way I would otherwise never have done.

" Much water has run 'twixt the banks of the Tiber since then, and I am sure that in your inmost heart you have come to know that striving not to sin for the love of God is higher than not doing so for the fear of Hell.

" And now, my dear friend—for I like to believe that we are friends—I am going to entrust you with an important secret, and I am sure that my trust will not be misplaced.

" My only son has just told me that he has become a Roman Catholic, and that he wishes most ardently to be a priest. Both these things distress me very much indeed, as you—of all people in the world—can well understand ! I don't believe in the Catholic Faith ; I mistrust it, and all it stands for. Had I not felt this with all my being, I would be inside that Faith to-day. Nevertheless, my greatest endeavour is to be quite fair, so— because personal freedom is my ideal for the individual, and because I am convinced that no sort of human beings ever, or in any circumstances, have the right to constrain others to bend their intellect to theirs—I am leaving my son perfectly free to follow his choice, although I totally and absolutely disagree with every single basic tenet of the Faith in which he so ardently believes.

" I am sending him to Rome, so that he can never say that I obstructed him at this juncture. I am sending him to you, and now, I must tell you my secret. Although I must bear with his change of religion, I cannot agree to his being a priest. Firstly, I don't personally believe that the boy has what he calls a ' vocation,' and secondly, if he doesn't have an heir our family will die out. My son and I are the only Fitz-Urses left in the world. But families cannot go on for ever, and, with a terrible twinge at the heart, I feel that mine has begun to wither. So you see, I am sure, the reason for my great dislike of his joining the Catholic priesthood ? He must not be celibate. He must carry on his race. Yet, on the other hand, I have no right to try to coerce his unconquerable mind as far as his change of religion goes, although I dislike the change more than I can express.

" Next week he is going to Rome with Lord Claude Knox-Kerr, who is a diplomatist.

" Stephen is nearly twenty-one, and I commend him to you. I have told him to present himself to you, which doubtless he will do with alacrity, as he is most anxious to get into the atmosphere his soul loves.

" Matrimony here is difficult for members of your Church, for heretics—as you call us !—do not desire Catholic girls to marry their sons, any more than Catholics desire theirs to marry Protestants ! The few Roman Catholic girls there are, are generally too badly off to go much into society and—as you know—dowerless girls are not generally sought after with avidity as wives for heirs of impoverished estates ! The marriage laws of the Catholic Church have undoubtedly made a great cleavage in English society, and I cannot, of course, agree in the line you have taken up to enforce your plans. But—that is another story.

" The point of my letter is, that he *must* not be encouraged to become a priest. You must help him to marry, and find for him a noble, good, and rich Italian wife. The lady should have money, as the bulk of my fortune cannot now go to him in consequence of his change of religion.

" His so-called ' vocation ' may be nothing but religious exaltation after all, and you will flatter yourself that my family will be vassals of Rome at last.

" Believe me to be, my dear Cardinal,

" Yours sincerely,
" SEYNTLEGER."

Cardinal Costanzi took a little key from his chain, unlocked a drawer in the writing-table near his chair, and slipped the letter in, then, turning the key again, he put it back on his watch-ring.

Pushing the cat gently from his knee, he rose slowly and stood looking out of the window.

He was tall and very thin, almost emaciated, and his eyes—although deeply sunken into his head—looked enormous as they shone out of his ascetic face. They were brilliant, restless eyes which had lost little of the fires of youth. His nose seemed almost to be breaking through the skin, and his long white hair hung in wisps and curled up at the nape of his neck. On his right hand he wore an immense flashing ruby, which rumour said had been given him by a certain famous beauty whom he had known when, long years ago, he had been attached to the Italian Embassy at St. Petersburg. Rumour also said that she was someone's wife, and that Il Principe Guiseppe Costanzi had loved her very much—so much that, as Heine has it in the old song—they both had to die.

Nadine was one day found dead in bed, nearly buried in beautiful flowers, poisoned.

This was the death she had chosen.

Costanzi, overwhelmed with misery, left Petersburg suddenly and for several years disappeared completely from society. Some time afterwards the sermons of a young priest were making a deep stir among the peasantry of Sicily, and his fame soon spread through all Italy.

This was the death he had chosen.

To-day he was one of the most noted prelates in Europe and his name had been freely whispered as the next occupant of Peter's chair. But pomp and power held no attractions for him.

He threw open the window and gazed long and thoughtfully at the rolling river, and then slowly turned his eyes to St. Peter's.

D

Here they rested with a seer's look. Profound, inscrutable ;
with mind deeply conscious that nothing can solve the riddle
of life, with heart torn by the sufferings of humanity, and with
soul poignantly longing for a World-Faith which would transcend
all orthodoxy.

" Oh, mighty Church ! " he said at length aloud ; " what a
lot of sin and sorrow there has to be down here that You may
live ! You have countenanced some of the greatest evils there
have ever been. You are often unjust, cruel, and illogical ; you
meddle—to attain your ends—in the sacred things of married
life. Nevertheless, it is necessary to have a Church and, for
myself, I feel I would be useless outside the Church. Dear me !
what arguments Seyntleger and I had when he told me that he
had changed his mind. How well I remember those words of
mine—inspired by your teaching "—and he pointed to the dome
of Peter's Church, now pressing her rounded cupola softly,
insinuatingly, into the purple sky—" How well I remember them,
and God knows how I have regretted them !

" After I had said them I was overcome with remorse, and
since that time I have worn this." His hand went to his breast,
whence it pulled out a bit of hair shirt. Then, drawing back
his wide, loose sleeve, he looked at his left arm where—just
above the elbow—a cruel steel bracelet bit into the flesh.

He clasped his fragile hands, and with tears gleaming in his
eyes he prayed for a second, aloud.

" Thou whose last action before death was one of forgiveness,
hast Thou forgiven me yet, me and Nadine ?

" Beautiful, witty, fascinating Nadine, how I loved you !
It must be my excuse—that I loved you as no other man ever
loved you. I gave you what I have never given to any woman
before or since—my bodily self, and for the last forty-four years
I have daily, and almost nightly, given you my spiritual self.
Every prayer, every sacrifice, every action, has been offered
to God that your sweet soul might be saved."

Twilight had fallen in the room, and he was not woken from
his dreaming until Pietro entered, bearing some slight refreshment on a tray. But the Cardinal shook his head.

" Not to-night, Pietro," said the old man ; " will you take
it away ? "

" Oh, Eminence," said the servant ruefully, " it is not much !
Maria has only sent an omelette and a little fruit, but we both
beg Your Eminence to eat—just a little ? "

" No, thank you, Pietro," the Cardinal answered gently, " I want nothing to-night."

" Not a little wine, Your Eminence—just a drop ? " the man begged ingratiatingly.

The other smiled as though at the importunity of a child.

" You know that I haven't drunk wine for forty-four years ! " he said. " I need nothing, my faithful Pietro, and I wish to be alone now. God bless you."

The adoring servant kissed his master's ring and disappeared.

When the flat was all quiet and Pietro and Maria had retired to rest, a dim light shone in the Cardinal's little oratory. He never sought his bed that night, and at five o'clock next morning he was saying his customary Mass—just like a simple parish priest—in one of the poorest parts of Rome.

Here he was looked upon as a saint, and the people and children, and the beggars, with their horrible deformities, all flocked round to get his blessing.

.   .   .   .   .

Soon after this he was having tea at the Spanish Ambassador's. They were all very excited about the Germans having entered Paris, and the King of Prussia being proclaimed Emperor at Versailles.

" That disgusting Bismarck ! " ejaculated the Ambassadress, clasping her tiny, fat, useless hands, which were covered with huge marquise rings.

She was short and fat, and she smelt of some peculiar scent, as did the whole room, in which the windows were never opened. She was a kind and entirely brainless old lady.

" Wicked man, I think he must be possessed—don't you, Your Eminence ? He is the enemy of Catholicism."

" Well, certainly the French are in a terrible position, Madame," answered the Cardinal, and ignoring her comments on Bismarck ; " and it is difficult to say how they will be able to pay the enormous indemnity that Germany is asking. But France is a wonderful country, is she not, Pedro ? " the old Cardinal asked, turning to the Ambassador, " and I feel sure she will soon find a way out of her dilemma."

" Of course, of course," squeaked the Ambassador. " France will quickly recoup and things will go on as before there, but to Germany it will make a difference—she will now be an Empire instead of a collection of loosely constructed kingdoms, and I

believe she will make more out of Alsace and Lorraine than France
ever did. It is Germany that will alter, I think. By the way,
we have a new colleague ! A charming young man has arrived
at the English Embassy—Lord Claude Knox-Kerr. He came
to call yesterday and brought a friend with him, Lord Athelston,
was it **not,** Annunciata ? " and he turned to his wife. (Madame
couldn't answer at once as she was getting herself into a terrible
mess over a melon.)

" Yes, yes," said she, when her mouth was sufficiently empty
to be able to speak. " It was Lord Atelston—I sink he is a
Duke's son and he has juste become a Catolique, and he is so
goood, so goood—so devout. I hear he has been cut off by his
father, who is a very bigoted Protestante—like all ze Engleesh
aristocracy—and ze poor young man has no money. Oh ! it
is dreadful, ze bigotry of zose Engleesh, who always talk of
ze Bible, and haf no holy religion. I sink zat ze Protestante
belief is ze masterpiece of ze dévil. Do you not agree, Your
Eminence ? "

The Cardinal smiled quietly to himself as the loquacious
Madame de Cavallhos rattled on. Her remarks amused him,
for he was thinking of an ancestor of hers who had been one of
the most notorious of Grand Inquisitors ! He said :

" I used to know the boy's father years ago. He and I were
friends at one time. I would like to make his son's acquaintance."

" Well, come and dine with us to-morrow night, they will
both be here," said the Ambassador, and he was pleasantly
surprised when the Cardinal accepted, for he knew how seldom
he ever dined out now.

As the Cardinal was leaving, a victoria drove up, in which
two ladies were seated.

" Dear Uncle Guiseppe ! " the youngest one said, " How
delightful to see you."

She had jumped out of the carriage, and was holding his arm
affectionately and looking eagerly into his face.

" Come and talk to Mother. We were at that moment
arranging to go to see you after our visit here."

From the carriage, a tall, languid,and extremely lovely woman
leant towards him. Her enormous dark eyes gazed at everyone
to whom she spoke—whether husband, policeman, Pope, or
lover—with a tragic " Ah ! if you only knew " kind of expression.
Position, money, beauty, and brains combined, had made her
the most talked-of woman in Italy. She was the personification

of seduction and—thoroughly as he disapproved of her—the old Cardinal (who was her husband's uncle) could not help taking pleasure in her society.

At seventeen she had married the Prince di Santa Fiora, who had nothing but his name and his money to recommend him. He was thick and swarthy and looked like a well-dressed waiter. She didn't like him, and for five years no children were born.

Then the relations began to get anxious, and one by one tried to have "sensible talks" with the wayward Princess, hoping to bring her to a more dutiful frame of mind. But it was not until Cardinal Costanzi—who was staying with them at Santa Fiora and had taken her for a long drive in the Appennines —had exerted his unique and marvellous powers of persuasion upon her, that she had at last consented to become a wife indeed.

Maddalena—the brilliant creature who had leapt from the carriage to greet him—was the result—and, alas ! for the line of Santa Fiora—the only result, of his little sermon.

"Go, darling," she cooed to Maddalena, "go and pay Madame de Cavallhos a little visit while we drive round the Pincio. We will not be very long," and the carriage bowled away.

"Dear Uncle Guiseppe," she sadly smiled at him, "what a relief to have you to talk to after having had luncheon at the Steeles ! Sir John is, of course, a dear, but Lady Steele !—I always call her Lady Stale because her jokes are so old—*O Dio Mio*, what a woman !—' *elle est comme une vâche en couche* '— forgive me, my Saint, but it's true ! And I told Maddalena that not even to enable her to see her adored English can I ever take her to their Embassy again."

"Is Maddalena then so fond of the English ? " asked the Cardinal.

"She thinks no one worth talking to but English people ! She knows their history by heart, she devours stories of their great men, and as for Gladstone, he is her ' beau-idéal ' of a politician ! For some unknown reason she adores Freedom.

"She thinks the English are more honest, and tell fewer lies than any other people in Europe, so—I am *au bout*. She won't bother to be nice to the young men of Rome—in fact, she says she would like to *marry* an Englishman."

The Princess looked extra pathetic.

"Did you ever hear of such an ambition ? " she went on. "They are so *stupid !* Santa Fiora is dull enough, although

he does make a scene sometimes—but those stolid English, with
their everlasting famous phlegm! Ah! it's well it's Maddalena
and not I. But, Guiseppe, that child is an angel. Where she
gets it from—unless from you—I cannot imagine. Look at
her father—the most boring man that ever lived, thinking of
nothing but his oxen and his turnips, and getting ' Indulgencies,'
and then look at me; well, whatever I am, I am not an angel,
am I ? " she asked in her pellucid voice.

" She really is a wonderful child, and I am already beginning
to lean upon her; her views on all subjects, except the English,"
she laughed, " are so sound and true. But, of course, she has
learnt much from her talks with you.

" Won't you join us at Santa Fiora next week? We are
going there for the rest of the autumn. Do come! it will make
us all so happy."

As she said the words an idea was suddenly born in the old
man's mind. That Maddalena should marry Stephen Fitz-Urse
was his plan.

" It sounds charming, Bianca," he said, " and I cannot resist
a chance of being with you all at beautiful Santa Fiora during
the golden month of October. May I bring a young Englishman
with me? He is the son of an old friend of mine, and, as you
say Maddalena is so fond of the English, perhaps they would
get on together! "

" What a brilliant idea! " she said. " I have been racking
my brains to find a nice young man to ask, and I could think
of no Englishman who was worth while. What is his name? "

" He is Lord Athelston," said the Cardinal, " the son of the
Duke of Seyntleger whom I met many, many years ago in
England. The Duke is one of the best and most charming of
men. You would not find *him* stupid, Bianca."

" No? Perhaps he would find *me* stupid, which would be
even worse! Well, bring your young man with you—and now
we must go back for my pretty Maddalena. She *is* pretty, isn't
she? "

" Pretty is too slight a word—she is exquisite," said the old
uncle.

As they were driving back to the Cardinal's flat Maddalena
told her mother that Madame de Cavallhos has asked her to
dine with them the next night.

" She said she wondered if you would let me go alone, Mother,
as it was only quite a little dinner and Uncle Guiseppe would

take care of me. She knows how Englishmen bore you, darling, and there are to be two of them to-morrow! She hoped you would let me go ? "

" But of course, my sweet, and you shall wear billowing tulle and a rose behind your ear like the Empress Eugenie, and Cavallhos will want to flirt with you, and *la vieille Nounou* won't even notice, she will be so taken up with enjoying the dinner ! "

" Oh, Mother, you are incorrigible—isn't she, Uncle Guiseppe? I don't think M. de Cavallhos at all attractive—he looks like a blue monkey! I am excited about the Englishmen, though, and I hope they will be fair and tall and—well, look clean ! "

" You see, she is quite *entiché* with the idea of those blue-eyed giants from the North! " said Bianca. " Well, here we are at your flat, and I see the faithful Pietro looking for you out of the window. Au revoir, dear Saint, till next week."

CHAPTER IV

THE HEART OF ROME

" Rome, though her eagle through the world had flown,
Could never make this Island all her own."
—EDMOND WALLER, 1606-1687.

THE drawing-room in the Cavallhos' house was filled with the buzz of conversation, the mingled smell of various scents, and the heavy odour of drooping, exotic flowers, while a son and daughter of the Ambassador—both dark, sultry-looking creatures —moved with an indolent Southern grace among the guests, of whom the chief were Cardinal Costanzi, Lord Athelston, and Claude Knox-Kerr. Dinner was at eight, and now the heavy gilt hands of the old Spanish clock showed nearly a quarter past. The Ambassador was clearly worried. Several times he took out his watch, glanced at it, and returned it impatiently to the pocket of his well-filled white waistcoat.

At last the door opened and the servant announced in a loud and distinct voice—

" Princess Maddalena di Santa Fiora."

Her mother had purposely made her late in starting, so that everyone should be assembled and waiting when she made her appearance.

She half ran into the room, stretching out both shapely arms and apologising for being the last. In one hand she held an enormous white feather fan, and from the other fluttered a filmy lace pocket-handkerchief.

Her small feet, encased in white silk stockings, showed under the masses of flounced white tulle, and her low-heeled black shoes were laced round the ankle with narrow black velvet.

A wide belt of the same confined her slender waist, and her soft, curly, dark brown hair was deftly arranged just above the nape of her neck so as not to mar its faultless line. From behind her left ear a rose peeped. Her face shone like some lovely flower on a swaying, graceful stem. Her dark blue eyes, which looked black at times, and again one wondered if they were not grey, were mysteriously veiled by immensely long, straight lashes. Her short nose was just tip-tilted, and thus showed a glimse of pink from her finely-cut, sensitive nostrils.

Her tender lips lay against each other like dewy rose-leaves, and they were wonderful lips—lips that men would long to kiss.

As she entered, the eyes of Cardinal Costanzi never left Stephen's face, for the astute man of the world had not quite ceased to exist in this very detached and spiritual priest. What he noticed seemed to satisfy him.

Maddalena was taken into dinner by the Ambassador, and Claude Knox-Kerr sat on her right. The Cardinal sat next Madame Cavallhos, and Stephen sat on her other side.

Mme de Cavallhos from the start was so fully engrossed in a heart-felt enjoyment of her *chef's* dishes, which were pagan in their perfection, that the Cardinal had plenty of opportunity to observe, knowing that his hostess would far rather eat than talk.

And this is what he observed :

That M. de Cavallhos was trying to flirt with Maddalena.

That Mlle de Cavallhos was dully jealous of Maddalena.

That Lord Claude was attracted by her, and that young de Cavallhos was slumberously aware of her.

That the eyes of Stephen very often met those of Maddalena, and that Mme de Cavallhos was not thinking of Maddalena !

And, after having noted all these things, the old man sent up a swift prayer that angels might always guard Maddalena.

After dinner he made a point of engaging Stephen in conversation till the girl left, so that neither had done anything but look at each other at their first meeting.

He noted how wistfully Stephen's eyes followed her as she went towards the door, saying that her mother had told her not to stay too late.

"Do you know that I knew your father very well, long ago ?" the Cardinal said in his deep voice—" and he has written to tell me of your visit to the Eternal City. Well, my son, you feel that you have come ' home ' at last ? You must indeed be happy in experiencing all the joys which our great Church

alone can give! You would like, naturally, to visit the Holy
Father ? I can easily arrange a private audience. You speak
French ? Ah! that is well, for you can then have an intimate
talk on the things of the soul, and you will doubtless wish to
tell him of your feelings and plans for the future ? "

The vigilant eyes noticed a look of agitation come over the
boy's face at his last words.

"Yes, yes, Your Eminence," he said. "It is my great wish
to see the Holy Father, and you do not know how wonderful
it is for me to be here in Rome, the centre of Catholicity, and
to feel that everyone loves, reveres, and believes in the sublime
truths that I have just been given the grace to love, revere, and
believe also! It is so different from in England where converts
are looked upon as peculiar people—and so a convert lives in
a sort of arid desert of unsympathetic, cold disapproval. And
then, Eminence," he said, warming to his subject, "as a Catholic
one is prohibited from taking an active part in the Government
of one's country. Naturally, there is no active ill-treatment
like there was in olden days, but sometimes silent, social, and
mental hardships are much more difficult to bear than being
thrown to the lions in the Coliseum ! "

Cardinal Costanzi listened with apparent interest to the
boy's words.

"Oh, cruel spirit of the Inquisition," he thought, " you
are not dead yet ! Clime, time, nor sect—it makes no difference !
Whether by bodily torture, or by cruel, lying stabs of the tongue,
you are still at work, stealthily, like an evil, invisible poison,
trying to make people hate each other for the love of God.
Ah, when will the power of Christ triumph over that of Satan ?
I hope that the soaring spirit of this English youth will not be
disillusioned by the morals and conduct of continental Catholic
society."

Aloud he said, "Indeed! It is sad to hear that. I am
an old man now, and most of my life has been spent in places
where one distinctly heard the hard throb of life. I had so
hoped that before I died I might see a lasting divorce between
Temporal and Spiritual power."

"But Temporal Power is everything, surely, Your Eminence ! "
said Stephen. "I think it was monstrous to fight against the
Pope, and—and it makes me so dreadfully ashamed, so sad,
when I think that my father fought against His Holiness with
Garibaldi. It makes me *burn* to think that a member of my

family should have had anything to do with the wrenching away of Temporal Power from the Papacy."

The Cardinal smiled gently.

"Yes," he said, "it was made into a popular cry at the time, but, to any but the most superficial of observers, it was in reality one of the best things that could have happened to the Papacy!"

Stephen almost gasped—

"Your Eminence!—what can you mean?" But instead of answering the excited youth the Prelate looked at his watch.

"I had no idea it was so late," he said. "The charm of your conversation! I must go home now, as I am an early riser and breakfast at seven. Will you join me at that meal to-morrow? —and we could go together to the 'Ara Coeli' afterwards and perhaps spend a little time in the Forum. These early autumn mornings are very beautiful in Rome."

Stephen accepted with alacrity and delight, but still he didn't quite understand the Cardinal's words about 'Temporal Power.'

. . . . . .

As they sat together the next morning in the Forum, Stephen timidly asked what exactly his Eminence had meant when speaking of the Papacy the previous night.

"Does the question interest you?" said the Cardinal.

"Everything connected with the Pope interests me, and what you said was so different from what my Catholicity had taught me."

"Ah, there you bring me to my point," said Costanzi. "In my view, Catholicity should only teach of God, and of the things of God. It should leave power, ambition, and politics alone. In the eleventh and twelfth centuries the Church had entirely ceased to be a holy institution because of the awful wickedness she perpetrated against heretics to keep her 'Temporal Power.' Take the Huguenot massacre! Was that an act in accordance with the laws laid down in the Sermon on the Mount? And the Inquisition! Yet the Church would justify it by saying that Protestantism would have lain hold of France had she not taken strong action. A typical case of the criticized Jesuit axiom that 'the end justifies the means!'

"Many wise historians say that had it not been for the ambitious inroads of 'Temporal Power' towards England, your beautiful country would never have succumbed to the Reformer.

" Although Luther ended wrongly he began rightly, for there is no doubt that the system of Indulgences was frightfully abused during the fourteenth, fifteenth, and sixteenth centuries, and used as a bribe to make Catholics go forth and kill heretics.

" Poor Luther ! ruined by love of power ! His was a great mind though ; and how ardently he loved our Church at one time ! What beautiful words of his these are when he first greeted the home of the Popes. ' Hail Rome ! Holy City ! Thrice blessed by the blood of martyrs ! ' And again, look at Pius VII., signing the Concordat in order to get back what might be called ' Temporal Power ' in France !

" Now you tell of the unfair treatment of Catholics in England. There you see the same thing at work ! Non-Catholics afraid of the Catholics getting power ! Power ! Satan was hurled from the heavens because he coveted Power, and was afterwards told to be gone from the sight of the Most Holy One, because he presumed to tempt Him with the offer of Power. It is the millstone clinging to religion. No, Stephen, spiritual and temporal things ought to have nothing to say to each other. You cannot touch pitch and not be defiled. The mere words ' State Religion ' has the ring of death in it.

" Oh—it was a great thing, the war of '60. It was the new birth of the Papacy. Never before in her history has she been so much admired by the world as since that time.

" Never before has she been such a spiritual force, and such a real machine for good ; never before has her unseen power been so great, nor has she come so near to the ideals laid down by her Founder, but still——" here his voice sank, and the young man looked at him almost in awe, for he seemed to be in a kind of trance ; his hands were crossed on his knees and his beautiful eyes gazed ardently into space as though they saw something which no one else saw.

Stephen hardly dared to breathe.

" ——still she is, I fear, very far away from following to the last word what he taught," went on the Cardinal. " He who might have held the earth in the hollow of His hand, but would not. He who shunned pomp and grandeur, and spent His days with fishermen and beggars and lepers. He whose whole teaching was the giving *up* of riches, and the giving *out* of Love, and who never once hinted that in order to gain spiritual good it might be wise to amass wealth and power. Yet I fear our Church tries so hard to get both. High and holy as is the great

Catholic Church, it seems to me that . . . there—is still something greater . . . to be achieved . . . before the end of all comes.

"A complete surrendering of wordly aspirations so—that—nothing really—matters—but—God." He stopped talking, and he almost seemed to be in a trance.

There was a long silence during which Stephen remembered that his father had said nearly the same words to him but a short time ago!

He was profoundly moved, and felt in some subtle way that his saintly companion wished to be alone, so he rose gently and moved away to ponder on the Cardinal's words. And as he pondered, Maddalena's face would, with an unaccountable persistency, conjure itself up before him.

For some time he walked with head bent, kicking the stones at his feet, deep in thought. He *must* visit the Pope soon, he *must* make his first Communion, he *must* go to see the head of the English College about his vocation, and yet, in the middle of these thoughts, sweet, dark eyes seemed to look into his.

Hearing steps, he turned and saw the Cardinal coming towards him.

Stephen was in an extremely nervous state, and he was beginning to feel the results of the high pressure at which he had been living ever since he left Oxford to visit Padre Primavera three months ago. Now he was gripped by two terribly conflicting emotions. First, the idea that he was drawn to the priesthood, and now, his dawning love for Maddalena. He needed a friend, and here was one that Heaven seemed to have sent.

"Oh, Your Eminence!" he cried, "I shall never forget this morning, and you do not know how your words have helped me! I feel I must lose no time, and I would be so grateful if you could arrange for me to see the Holy Father. I have not yet made my first Communion!"

"Certainly, my son, I will call on him to-day and everything shall be arranged for a visit to-morrow. Perhaps the Holy Father would administer It to you."

"That would indeed be wonderful," and the boy reddened excitedly. There was a short nervous pause, and then Stephen said :

"Your Eminence, I have not yet had the opportunity to tell you of the greatest object I had in coming here. I—I want

to become a priest." (Maddalena's eyes again looked into his.)
" At least—I'm sure I do, it's such a wonderful life—the highest
in the world, is it not, Your Eminence ? In no other life can
one be so near to God."

Stephen had reached the summit of feelings, brought on by
deep and excited religious emotions of brain and heart.

Here was he, a high-minded, ideal-loving young Englishman,
whose conversion was the talk of all English, and much Continental society. He was now at last in the place of all others
he had wished to be in—the heart of Rome ! His whole being
was in a state of unnatural exaltation, which the Cardinal's
saintly presence and wonderful words had helped much to
stimulate.

He stood in the Forum alone with the highest Prelate in
Rome. Round him were signs of Paganism conquered by Christianity, with Catholicity brooding over all, and to-morrow was
to be the crowning day ! He was to meet Christ's Vice-Regent
on earth in the person of the famous Pio Nono.

He suddenly knelt down and, taking the Cardinal's right
hand in both of his, he pressed it fervently to his lips, while
warm tears fell upon the old man's slender fingers.

Cardinal Costanzi had not devoted forty-four years of his
life to the particular study of souls, and the mentality of men,
for nothing, and he had expected a climax of this sort in Stephen's
case.

He pressed his fragile hand upon the thick, rippling, golden
hair of this modern neophyte, who reminded him so much of
the Apollo in the Capitol.

" Rise, Stephen," he said, " there is only One at whose feet
we must kneel. May He bless you and guide you in all your
ways, and may He show you very distinctly the path He wishes
you to take. Now I must go home, and I'm sure you have
much to do and see. I think the Holy Father will see you
to-morrow, so keep yourself in readiness, and I will let you know
what time to be at my house. Would you like me to go with
you to the Vatican ? "

" Indeed, I would," said the boy.

His whole being was in a whirl. So many different powers
seemed to be fighting within him, and he felt that he needed
support.

.   .   .   .   .

At 3.30 that afternoon a modest brougham drove up quickly

to the door of the Vatican where the Swiss Guard stand, and soon the Pope and the Cardinal were closeted together.

Said the Pope: "You tell me that his father fought against Us? Strange that so many noble English were eager to help Garibaldi! I suppose it was their inborn love of freedom!" and his lips smiled mysteriously. "Island people are by nature freer than others—do you not think so, my friend?

"There is no race quite like the English," the Pope went on. "Compared with other nations they have a higher sense of public morality, and they are naturally the most profoundly religious people in the world. If only we could harness them to Rome! Look to England, my friend—England, with her rich, proud, bigoted aristocrats—*that's* the country that would serve us well if only we could get her! My idea of tightening up the marriage laws is a good one in this connection, is it not? You see, we had to think of something which would ' compel them to come in,' and the lever of the decree *Tametsi* * pressing on to the fulcrum of love will—I confidently hope—ultimately lift the blight of Protestantism from off fair England's face. Love! my dear Cardinal, passion! What will men not do to bestow the one, and to gratify the other?"

"But," gently interposed Cardinal Costanzi, "if, later, the non-Catholic regrets——"

But he was blandly interrupted by the Pope.

"Later," he smiled, "is no affair of ours! What is signed is signed, and we rely on an English gentleman's honour not to break a sacred oath."

"Yet Liguori tells us that oaths may be broken," the Cardinal again interpolated quietly.

"For expediency's sake—yes; when the good of the Church demands it—yes" put in the Pope quickly. "For any oath, be it ever so valid, can be broken or relaxed for those reasons, and we know this must be right for Pius VII. set down that nothing which Liguori wrote was worthy of censure. But, of course, when such important circumstances as these occur, dealing as they do with the eternal welfare of men's souls, it would not be right to absolve from an oath. Ha!" and he smote fist into palm, "how I deplore that we had to prorogue the Vatican Council before finishing those marriage regulations,

---

*Tametsi. The opening word of the Decree of the Council of Trent making marriages between a Catholic and a non-Catholic invalid when not approved of by the Church.

and making them absolutely binding. It's the only way to conquer the country and, in order to get England once more on her knees to Rome, any means would justify the end."

"Yet in so far as I am acquainted with English Law," said Costanzi, "a man is *not* bound by a vow or a promise wrung from him under pressure."

The kind-looking, fat Italian, in whose hands lay power to make or mar the happiness of 400,000,000 human beings, gave an eloquent and Latin shrug under his loose white garment surmounted by the demure little cape.

"English law!" he said scornfully, and lazily curling his lips, he snapped his fingers. "*That*—for English law! We *can* and *will* make our marriage laws so potent and so terrifying that—in the hearts of our children—*our* laws, and not England's laws, shall prevail. *We* are at the wheel of the strongest machinery. *We* can drive the mind. Thank God that my forerunners were such farseeing, statesman-like men. How merciful that—when in 1825 the Prussian Government sought to introduce the law which prevailed in Silesia that the children should be brought up in the religion of the father—they took strong action against it. You will remember, my friend, that Von Spiegel—the Archbishop of Cologne, and the Bishops of Paderborn, Münster, and Treves accepted this order of the Cabinet, and this course led Pius VIII. and Gregory XVI. to declare that a mixed marriage—when it was not understood that the children of either sex should be brought up Catholics—was contrary to 'the natural and the divine law.' Those are the very words, I know them well. Otherwise, it was decreed, the priest could take no part in the celebration. It was an interesting moment in Europe, and of course fraught with much possible future weakness to the Church. You will remember that the recalcitrant German bishops eventually gave in to the Papal Briefs with the exception of the Prince, Bishop of Breslau, who, rather than obey, resigned his See, and became a Prostestant in 1840. The attitude o Germany towards the Papacy has always been extremely interesting, and they are of course—although so strongly Catholic in many ways—one of the last remaining bulwarks of any true importance against the Church. I have often wondered why English statesmen do not seem to realise this more? It's a good thing for us, though, that they don't! Hein?" and the wise, Latin-minded old man gave a fat, contented gurgle, which shook his 'torso' so that it looked like a blancmange.

The Cardinal didn't answer. He could never agree with these kinds of views, and so he had found that silence was his only refuge. That the consciences and minds of simple, honest, ordinary men should be worked upon when in the heat of love or passion, to sign a paper which it had taken generations of manœuvring to complete, repelled all his gentleman's instincts, and despite the fact of his having lived for so many years in an atmosphere of juggling with words, and their myriad possible interpretations, the freemasonry of caste still beat very strongly in him, so that his inborn and inherited idea of honour had somehow managed to survive the workings of the Curia.

"Life is surely difficult enough trying to keep the Ten Commandments," he mused whimsically, "without the Popes inventing more sins ! I can't help feeling sorry for these simple Englishmen, who know nothing, and get taken in by us."

It distressed his honest, gentlemanly mind to think of all the plans which went on in Rome to secure the acquiescence of those untutored young men, in order to make them sign a paper at the bidding of priests whose teaching they held to be false, or else give up the girl they wanted to marry.

He knew enough of England's love of freedom to marvel greatly at the pliancy of so many of her young men. Did this tepid indecision mean a weakening in their Protestancy, a leaning towards Catholicity, or a world-wide indifference towards any sort of spiritual bond whatever ?

"I suppose ' driving the mind ' has become part and parcel of our religion," he went on, "and I, of course, bow to Your Holiness in these matters. I am glad that it is you and not I who have to make the marriage laws, for indeed, Your Holiness, I think it would break my heart."

The eyes of the Pope softened as he looked at his old friend, and the well-known sweet expression came into his face.

"Ah! You! You with your quixotic ideas ! You will never be Pope, my friend ! You have never learned to put the blinkers on ! You are one of the few who have put love of God entirely before dogmatic system—yours is the highest view, but system we *must* have, nothing on earth can be run successfully without it."

Then he looked wistfully at the other.

"Ah, Costanzi, I envy your life ! No fearful responsibilities —no political intrigues—no racial struggles to contend with. No trying to keep powerful potentates ' to heel,' but just a life

E

of prayer and kind deeds; a peacemaker humble and meek,
at the sight of whom all Rome goes on her knees from love.
No one knows better than I how your spirit shuns the Papal
chair. You are no Hildebrand, but rather a Francis. Bless me,
my friend, for I need the help of the people's Saint."

" Your Holiness must not say such things to me," answered
the Cardinal, "and now I want to tell you about Lord
Athelston."

He then recounted the family history of the Seyntlegers, of
their great position and riches, and of the recent reception of
Stephen into the Church by Archbishop Manning, leaving out the
episode in the Duke's early life, and going on to tell of the boy's
wish to be a priest, and of his father's desire that this might, if
possible, be avoided.

The Pope seemed to be interested, and nodded his head when
the Cardinal spoke of the Duke's hope that the family might
continue in the person of Stephen.

" I do not know whether the boy has a vocation, Your
Holiness. I think it may be nothing but a state of intense spiritual
excitement which will pass sooner or later. But it is difficult to
tell."

" A dangerous mood," the Pope ejaculated, still nod-
ding.

" Yes," answered Costanzi, "so perhaps you would speak
to him of his importance to the Catholic lay world, of his position
in England and—and——"

" The carrying on of the line—a wife—children, m'm, m'm—
an Italian, perhaps! Rich—noble—— Yes, yes, my friend, you
can leave it to me." The Pope had finished the other's sentence
for him.

" Yes," sighed Costanzi, "yes, yes." This task was very
uncongenial.

Pius IX. looked at the old Prince-Cardinal with the expression of a loving mother towards her favourite child. He and
the faithful Pietro alone knew of the hair shirt and the steel
bracelet.

" *Il mio Carissimo Santo*, bless me before you go," he said,
and a minute afterwards the door closed gently upon the
undogmatic Cardinal.

" Have I done wrong? Am I playing with this boy's life
to please his father? Is it right to traffic thus in souls?"
thought the old man that night as he lay awake in bed, a prey to

the consciousness that he was an unwilling player in the great game, whose mainspring was in Rome.

. . . . . .

Stephen also couldn't sleep, but for another reason—he was in love. In the last twenty-four hours everything had changed, and what had before seemed so attractive, so beautiful, and so easy, appeared now to be repellent, austere, and difficult, though no less his duty, and, moreover, his fate.

His manhood, which had been almost completely drugged by his perfect faith in the mysteries of Catholicism, and his overpowering wish to be as Christ-like as possible—had been suddenly and violently stirred to its depths. Maddalena's face was always there, and the lovely warm graciousness of her Southern youth obsessed and maddened him. Yet the call of the priesthood was not forgotten, and with a shudder of horror he felt it was the real call.

All night he tossed, wide-eyed and tormented by thoughts and fears. How would the Pope receive him? Would he feel that wondrous God-like atmosphere which he, in his ardent moments, had conjured in his imagination to emanate from such an august and infallible person? Would he advise him to enter a monastery at once or—or . . . ? And here his love for Maddalena rushed over him again, leaving him dominated by one thought, which for the moment excluded all others—that of marriage with her.

. . . . . .

Cardinal Costanzi felt infinitely sorry for the boy as he walked with him the next day through the mazes of splendid rooms which they had to traverse before they reached the Pope's private apartments.

Stephen was trembling, and the dew stood out upon his forehead. Everything was so silent and so vast ; so redolent of past magnificence and ignominy, for he could not at times quite forget what his mother had taught him about the lives of so many of the Popes.

" Of course it was not true, though," he soliloquized, " because no one could at times take on Divinity, and yet at other times be so very wicked."

Very soon he would be face to face with one who had defined Infallibility, and had thus assumed God-like powers.

Shortly afterwards he was ushered into the Pope's presence, and in that second the devastating thoughts, "How could a

fallible company of men bestow infallibility on one of themselves ?
Am I mad ?   Is it all a monstrous lie ? " flew through Stephen's
excited and distracted brain.   But instantaneously the thought
had gone again and the mental curtain descended, thickly enveloping and muffling in its soft, comfortable folds any untoward
or disquieting ideas.

A moment later he was at the Pope's feet eagerly seeking to
kiss them.

To Stephen—in his wonderful, childlike faith, and his real,
honest belief in all in which the priests had instructed him—
this was as near to God and Heaven as could be attained in life.
Higher than everything in Heaven and on earth, with the one
exception of God Himself.

At last he was in the presence of One who was Infallible.   Beyond
all criticism ; subject to no legal forms ; answerable to no one
but the Saviour ; superior to every human being !   At least,
this was what this man claimed !   If it was true, it was *all*
true and absolutely true ; if it was false, it was *all* false, and
damnably false.

Dealing with such stupendous issues there could be no
exceptions ; no " buts," no " ifs," no " perhaps."

Thus Stephen thought as he knelt at the feet of this *genius
loci*, this deity, this wonder-man.   " But of course it's all
true," he whispered—" quite and absolutely true " ; and, while he
knelt, he kissed again and again the hem of the spotless white
cloth garment which hung round this magic monument of Infallibility.   And as he knelt he wondered, " Was he alive ?
Was he a *man* ?   Did he need food and drink and sleep ?   Had
he not taken on *all* the attributes of Godhead when he took
on one of them ? "

But suddenly he was woken from his dreaming by a pleasant,
genial voice addressing him in French.

Two hands clasped his, and raised him from the ground.

" My son, I welcome you to Rome, to the Vatican, and into
the bosom of Holy Mother Church.   I can see what a true son
you have already become !   May God bless you and bring you
ever nearer to His Divine Person through the Sacraments of
His Holy Church !

" And now, dear son, I hope that you will have a happy time
in this wonderful city of ours, and that besides spiritual joys
you may be amused by our society.

" In Cardinal Costanzi you have a friend who can introduce

you to the whole of Italy! I have never known a man with so many relations! He is either uncle or cousin to nearly everybody! How long did you think of remaining here?"

"I have no plans, Your Holiness," answered Stephen shyly. "Everything is so new, so wonderful to me that I feel quite dazed. I have not yet made my first Communion, and I wondered—I had hoped—that perhaps I might have the honour——?"

"Yes, most certainly, my son—I will administer the great Sacrament to you myself. You wish it soon, is it not so?"

So a date a few days hence was arranged.

"Were you thinking of travelling at all?" asked the Pope kindly. "Now that you are here you should make the most of your time, and you should meet some of the young ladies of Rome.

"I am told that in England it is very difficult, for various reasons, for Catholics to make suitable marriages, and naturally you wish to marry one of your own religion? Why, Lord Athelston, we shall all look to you to start a new Catholic family in England! Think what a privilege is yours! The chance given you by grace—to rear up a family in the true Faith! With your name and your position, what an example you could be, and what a great help in bringing other souls into the true fold!

"Here there are many girls of noble families who would be very suitable," and he enumerated some well-known Roman names. That of Santa Fiora was not among them. Somehow, this fact made Stephen's chivalrous spirit lean more than ever towards Maddalena. Why should her family have been left out?

"Yes, your Holiness, I quite see your idea, and I think it would be a great—I had almost said—career—that of bringing up a family in the Catholic religion, but—but I have been thinking very much of becoming a priest."

"A priest!" ejaculated the Pontiff in surprised tones. "Well, my son, of course that is the highest calling of all, but it is a calling which requires much thought and prayer, and which I would advise no one to contemplate without having first had worldly experience. Wait till you are twenty-five. By that time you will be more settled in every way than you are now—and, if I may say so, you will be of more use to the Church also."

Something leaped in Stephen. Something not controlled by

will, or mind, or soul.   It was his heart that leaped.   Here was
a loophole offered him by an Infallible Pope ; the Pope who had
said, " I am Tradition."   And this all helped to make it recon-
cilable with his conscience.   Maddalena's lovely face seemed
very near just then.   Her eyes were smiling, smiling.

The Pope now turned to a box from which he took a little
golden crucifix suspended from a fine chain of gold.

" This," he said, " contains a very small portion of the True
Cross.   It is my gift to you and may God bless you."

He placed the sign of the Cross on Stephen's forehead with
his thumb.

" Be sure and come and see me before you return to England."

Stephen never quite knew how he got out of the room, but
he was happy to find himself once more with Cardinal Costanzi
driving away in his brougham to tea with the Santa Fioras.

Had it been what he had hoped, what he had expected ?
Ah, let us not probe too deeply into the boy's soul. . . .

CHAPTER V

LOVE AND HATE

" There's nothing half so sweet in life as
Love's young dream."
—MOORE.

" He whom passion rules is bent to meet his death."
—SIR PHILIP SYDNEY.

THE day on which the Cardinal and Stephen travelled to Santa
Fiora was wet, and a thick mist enveloped the hills as they
alighted from the train at the little station where a landau was
waiting to meet them. A cart drawn by white oxen stood behind
to carry the luggage. Apparently there was only one other
guest, and he presented himself as M. Lepantchine. Lepantchine
looked about thirty-five, and was rather ugly. He had a square,
strong jaw, surmounted by a heavy face and a clever forehead.
Well over six feet and strongly built, he had immensely wide
shoulders and a short bull neck. Owner of a devilish temper
he could, however, be most attractive if he wished. His
sensual mouth was nearly hidden by a dark moustache through
which his white teeth gleamed. His eyes, though, were his
most striking feature. They were dark grey and very beautiful,
and of a curious sparkle, depth, and fascination. He could
enlarge and contract the pupils at will, which seemed to give
him a kind of mesmeric power, and they changed with incredible
swiftness from sleepiness to vigilance, from tenderness to cruelty.
Grave, penetrating, caressing eyes ; direct, yet remote. Magnetic,
veiled, inscrutable eyes ; yet warm and infinitely compelling. A
mystic's glance was his, yet blended mysteriously with passion
and strength. Eyes that drew you against your will, and made
you do what you would not.
They talked together during the drive up the winding mountain road, but by the time they reached the Castle, Stephen had

taken an unaccountable loathing for Lepantchine, although the man attracted him in a way by his tremendous physical strength and the force of his personality. They drove across a draw-bridge, and there a great, clanging bell was rung and powdered servants in silk stockings and knee-breeches helped them out of the carriage.

A great stone staircase went up straight from the front door and after quite a long walk down a dimly-lit stone passage the three men were ushered into a large smoking-room.

The Prince and Princess and Maddalena came forward to greet their guests. There was no one else.

" You must be cold, all of you, after your long drive, and it's such a wet evening. Come and have some tea," said the Princess in her most limpid voice.

They went towards the gay wood fire ; Lepantchine sitting by Bianca, and Stephen by Maddalena. The Cardinal and the Prince stood talking on the hearth-rug.

" I am going out shooting to-morrow whatever anyone else does," said the latter in a loud voice. " I'll drive to Santa Barbara, and start from there, and I'm finishing up on the swamps near the lake. It's full of snipe. One or two neighbours are coming too."

" And the rest of the party, what are they going to do ? " asked the Cardinal, his look travelling to Maddalena, who seemed to be very successfully entertaining Stephen, who hadn't brought his guns with him to Italy.

" We are coming, too," the Princess answered sweetly. (She knew this would annoy her husband, who hated having women out to luncheon, especially his wife.)

" I have arranged everything except for you, dear Uncle Guiseppe. What do you feel inclined to do ? " she said.

" May I remain at home, Bianca ? I think that at my age it is time to give up the chase of game ! "

" Your Eminence perhaps prefers the chase of human game," said Lepantchine sardonically, who never shot, himself.

Maddalena looked at him, flushing deeply. How she hated this man. What had he come for, she wondered, and why did he look at her mother in such a funny way ?

" He chases nobody," she flared at the Russian. " It is rather we who chase him, is it not, dearest Uncle Guiseppe ? " and she turned to the Cardinal affectionately.

" Very well, then," went on Bianca quietly, although she

was angry at the implied rudeness to their beloved relative, "Maddalena will drive Lord Athelston in her pony-cart and I may go in the phaeton. *You*, Lepantchine—you may do what you like. Nobody really cares in the least." And while she spoke her great soft eyes were fixed upon his.

The colour rose dully in the Russian's cheek. He had travelled all the way from Petersburg at her invitation, and this was how she treated him, and before the others, too !

He was one of the coming men in the Russian Ministry, and had made a name by his strenuous upholding of the autocratic principle.

If his phrase, "chasing human game," applied to anyone there it certainly applied to himself, for he was highly proficient in its devious paths. But of all game, woman was his favourite, and in his successful pursuit of her he had become notorious.

"Simply can't leave them alone," people said, shrugging their shoulders carelessly, "but otherwise he'll make his mark ; he'll be a great man one of these days."

Two years before he and Bianca had met in London, and she had from the first thrown the web of her fascination round his clever brain, as well as round his great strong body, and as yet not one of the delicate meshes had broken.

Bianca was fundamentally attracted by physical strength, possible brutality, and the savageness which nearly always lies at the bottom of most men, no matter how thick the veneer of civilization. A Caliban—a rough lover—was what she liked, not he who scarcely dares to touch the beloved's finger-tips.

And so it was that these two people fatally attracted one another on account of their each possessing to an abnormal degree the power of sex.

Lepantchine's eyes looked mockingly from Gasparro di Santa Fiora to Bianca, and, as they rested on this woman, he made up his mind that she should be his before he left.

"Cold fool," he thought ; "I may as well take her. You don't seem to want her."

$\cdot \qquad \cdot \qquad \cdot \qquad \cdot \qquad \cdot$

As they rose to dress for dinner he came to her side. In his low, vibrating voice he said :

"Princess, forgive me, I only meant it as a joke ! I did not mean to insult the Cardinal."

"It was not the sort of joke we find amusing," she announced coldly, not looking at him.

He was furious. Women didn't treat him like this as a rule. He wasn't accustomed to it. The citadels he attacked generally fell quickly. Bianca di Santa Fiora had filled his mind to the exclusion of any other woman for two years, and now—she talked like this! He was angry in a way which only men of Eastern Europe can be in concerns of passion. He was piqued and furious.

"She shall love me, she shall give in! I will show her how I can melt her assumed iciness."

He muttered these words to himself in his bedroom as he stood before the long glass, admiring his powerful frame. He was used to conquering women, and he knew he could do it.

Dressing quickly, he reached the drawing-room before any of the others. A second later the door opened.

He sniffed the air! It was Bianca. It was his prey. All his pulses began to beat.

She came towards him slowly, her soft pale blue brocade gown shrouded in exquisite filmy lace. Round her—from throat to knees—hung many pearls. In a minute he was at her side, whispering:

"Bianca, forgive me! I had no right to speak as I did."

His deep voice trembled, and his wonderful, compelling eyes looked tenderly down into her lovely upturned face, looked with desire at her red, parted lips.

"It hurt me, Ivan, that you should say such a thing to our beloved Saint. And I was surprised that you should be so rude, for, whatever else you may be, you are never that."

"Ah, forget it, forget it," he said, his voice falling to a whisper.

"Bianca, beloved, say I am forgiven," and he stepped forward till they touched one another. Then, in a second, his strong arms were round her, and he crushed her lips against his, whilst pouring out all his pent-up passion. He kissed her neck, her eyes, her ears, and she did not resist. She liked it. No other man had ever kissed her with such kisses as these. And so it was that Bianca succumbed to the strength of Lepantchine.

.   .   .   .   .   .

Stephen was very happy. At the moment his intense longing for the priesthood had left him—for Maddalena filled his thoughts too much, and the Pope's words to him the week before had

had the effect, desired by his father, of cooling the ardour of his vocation.

He was so burning for the Catholic religion as such, that the words of an infallible priest, surrounded with as much glamour as was Pius IX. in those days, affected him as an oracle in Egyptian times might have done ; and so fresh a convert was he—so emotional and highly strung an one—that infallibility had for him, as for many another good modern Catholic, no end or limit.

In his present high mood anything that the Pope said *must* be right, *must* be true. He therefore grasped eagerly at this loophole of escape from the priesthood offered him a few days ago by the Pope. He was especially glad of it just now when Maddalena's face and person attracted him so irresistibly.

That the semi-divinity of the Vatican had advised him to seek a Roman wife in both senses of the word, was a great salve to his hopelessly vacillating character, for he always sought an anchor. Blindly and distractedly he clutched now at a Pope, now at a woman, seeking always advice, or support, or sympathy.

As they went up to bed he heard Bianca say to her daughter : " Then you will drive Lord Athelston in your pony-trap to-morrow, darling ? " and his heart beat with excited joy at the thought of to-morrow.

The house was a small straggling sort of Castle, some of it dating from the twelfth century. There were plenty of towers, and crooked dark steps at unexpected places. One part belonged entirely to the Prince, and here he had his bedroom, his smoking-room, and a large library which contained a good collection of shooting trophies. Since Maddalena's birth her parents had lived apart, and didn't pretend to feel any affection for each other.

Bianca's rooms were at the other side of the house at the end of a long passage. Here the ground was at a much higher level, so that her sitting-room and bedroom, which communicated, gave on to a small paved rose-garden with a fountain in the middle. Bianca loved these rooms, which she had filled with beautiful things, and here she had often—during the last seventeen years—thought out crucial difficulties of her life, and they had not been few. Many men had loved her, and they had all asked why her youth should be wasted in this unnatural alliance with Gasparro di Santa Fiora ?

Bianca was frivolous and pleasure-loving. She adored the

savour of life, and she couldn't help flirting and drawing men to the very threshold of her favours. Kissing? Oh yes, she had often kissed and had thoroughly enjoyed it, too. But that was all. For, whatever the world thought or said of her, she had never yet fallen below a certain standard, nor given her stupid, selfish husband true cause to revile her.

. . . . . .

The next morning Maddalena was seated in her little pony-trap waiting for Stephen. She was dressed in a short blue linen skirt and a loose red " Garibaldi " shirt. A large leghorn hat flopped over her face.

When Stephen saw her he started in horror.

" What's the matter ? " laughed the girl. " You look as if you'd seen a ghost ! "

" Your dress—like a Garibaldean ! " he ejaculated.

" Yes, of course I am," she laughed, " and it's because I love Italy and freedom. In this dress I feel that I am neither Guelph, Ghibelline, nor Catholic ; only Christian and Italian ! "

Stephen gasped, for he had yet to learn how to understand the type of spirit which can be bred in a country which is ruled by clericalism. He did not realize what a great gift true freedom is to a nation, and he had forgotten what bitter family—as well as racial and political—feuds had raged in the past so that religious toleration, and not priest-craft, should be the character of his native land.

Maddalena smiled at the horror depicted on his face and said :

" Don't you love freedom, Lord Athelston ? "

" Well, it depends what sort of freedom," he answered carefully. " But, anyhow, I hate Garibaldi, don't you ? You ought to as a Catholic, you know ! "

" No, I don't believe I really do, but please don't think too badly of me for that," she added, as the shocked look returned to his face. " I should be very sad if you thought badly of me," and she blushed adorably, he thought.

There was a little pause, and then Stephen—who was very young, and quite unversed in the art of love-making—said shyly :

" Maddalena !—may I call you that ?—how could I think badly of you ? Ever since that evening when I first saw you at the Cavallhos' I have thought you the most delicious girl I have ever met. I wanted to marry you from the first minute I saw you, but then I told myself that you were only a child, and wouldn't be thinking of marriage for years—also, I am not very rich, for, on account of my having become a Catholic, my father hasn't left me much money, and so all the bulk of his fortune—all that he had to offer to my mother—will not be mine to offer the woman I love.   And so, dearest, I felt that I ought to put you out of my mind for that and—and—for other reasons.   But two days after meeting you, Cardinal Costanzi took me to see the Pope, and he spoke to me about marriage, and strongly advised me to marry an Italian.   Then, when your uncle suggested my coming here with him, it really seemed as though it was God's will. From the Vatican, where I had been intensely impressed by the Pope's words to me, we drove straight to tea with you.   And you looked so pretty !   You had on a brown velvet gown, and a little hat of soft brown feathers, and I didn't know which was your hair and which were the feathers !   Somehow, as I sat there talking to you, a great feeling of peace came over me, instead of the nervous unquiet which had filled me lately."

She seemed not to have been listening to the last part of his speech, and, when he stopped speaking, she asked tensely :

" What were the ' other ' reasons you had for thinking you couldn't tell me that—you—loved me ? " and she looked straight into his eyes.

His fair face flushed.   He couldn't tell her all.   He couldn't tell her of the one, great, outstanding thing ; his very real desire to enter the priesthood, nor of the quite extraordinary attraction that state had had for him till he saw her—and had still, if the whole truth were known.

But just at this moment when she was appealing so desperately to his manhood—when he saw embodied in her everything for which a certain part of him yearned—the call to the higher life seemed to be a little blurred, a little less imperative, not so important nor quite so wonderful as it had seemed when he sat in the old Italian priest's garden not two months before.

Nevertheless, the feeling was still there, and, had Maddalena known how deeply its roots were planted in Stephen's sensitive soul, perhaps she would not have consented to marry him.

Would it have been better so ?   Who can tell ?

So Stephen answered :

" The other reasons ?   Oh, I don't know !   I thought perhaps I wasn't a happy enough man to ask you to marry me—life seems rather disgruntled for me just at present. I am happy really, though, only a conversion has its unhappy sides too, and I have hated hurting my father. The wrench has been awful. You see, I admired him so much, and I have always gone to him for advice in everything—and then, suddenly, comes this terrible break with all my happy childhood and youth, and—and—it can never be the same again. I know it can't ; with all the best will in the world they would be super-human if their feelings for me hadn't changed. When religion is changed, feelings are changed. Religion is a terribly strong power."

There was a pause, and a worried frown wriggled itself between the girl's eyes. Somehow she felt that he hadn't told her the real reason after all. Seeing her look, he threw off with an effort the mood which had descended upon them as he had been speaking, and said with his attractive, gay smile :

" Do you know that to-morrow I shall be twenty-one ? I had quite forgotten about my birthday and everything else, since I have known you ! "

He did not tell her of the great doings there would have been at Ullcombe had he not just joined the Church of Rome.

Leaning towards her, he said :

" I wonder if I could ever make you care for me ? Could I, Maddalena ? Could I ? "

He gently lifted the edge of her big shady hat so as to get a glimpse of her averted face.

They had reached the top of the hill, round the edge of which their road wound itself. On their right rose still higher hills, covered with pine-trees, but on the left and in front the ground rolled away, and the great plains stretched before them covered with swaying golden corn.

The sun beat fiercely on the white dusty road, and the still air which was trembling with heat was full of the soft drowsy buzz of tiny insects.

The girl slowly turned her face to his, and looked straight into his eyes with the engaging, unconscious earnestness of a child.

" How lovely it is to hear you speak to me like that ! " she said. " I had never dared think it possible. Do you know that, when I saw you at Mme. de Cavallhos' dinner party, I also thought that *you* were the most wonderful person I had ever seen ? I always imagined I liked Englishmen, although I had hardly met any in my life, but when I saw *you*, I thought you were like a fairy prince ! ''

The pony, feeling rather weary, had stopped of his own accord, and was now browsing happily along the side of the road.

In all the ecstasy of Stephen's recent religious experiences, nothing had been quite like what he felt now. They loved each other, and it all seemed so right and natural ! Heaven and earth were smiling on them, and everything on this wonderful day seemed to conspire to make this their very own special hour throughout eternity.

He lifted her little sun-burnt hands together, with the reins and whip which they held, and kissed them very gently.

" Maddalena, say ' darling ' to me ! '' he said ardently. " Lift up your head, and let me see your face."

She did so, and they looked into each other's eyes. Then Stephen could not resist the delicious trembling which made him long to take her in his arms.

" I love you my precious, beautiful Maddalena," he said, " will you be my wife ? ''

Softly she answered, " Yes, darling, with all my heart I will be your wife," and her words were nearly lost in the meeting of their lips.

" It's too much joy, it's too much joy," she whispered in her pretty English. " Stephen !—Oh ! isn't life glorious ? '' and she impetuously stretched out her arms as though to embrace the world which rolled golden at her feet.

They were now at the base of a roadside Crucifix.

" Shall we sit on the grass together for a little ? '' she went on. " It's so lovely and there's heaps of time, and we'll never have another day quite like this in our lives, shall we, Stephen ? ''

He was longing to kiss her babyish fragrant lips again, but was restrained by a kind of proud awe which was already born in his heart for his future wife. Utterly happy though he was at the moment, he did not exactly like the idea that it was now his right to take this beauteous thing again and again into his arms, and crush her maiden perfume from her. The longing to kiss her, and yet not daring to do so had been, before, an æsthetic joy. But now that she had given him the right he was fearful lest he should misuse it.

He thought of her as a little fair, pink shell which lies upon the sand, and which one holds carefully upon outstretched palm to admire.

He thought of her as a tender, quivering rose-leaf torn from the rose, which needs infinite care, and each morning fresh glistening water to keep it alive.

He thought of her as a man might think of a priceless milk-white pearl, which he carefully locked into a box, for fear of the covetous eyes of other men.

" Come and sit here," she commanded, patting the grass at her side. " I want to tell you something. Listen. Long ago, when I was a child——"

" So long ago ! " he interrupted adoringly.

" Anyhow it seems a long time ago now," said she, smiling sideways at him—" I used to think of the day when I should love someone—not just fall in love as one reads about in books, for that seemed too much like falling into a pond ; one's first idea would be how to get out again ! But real true love—like yours and mine ! " and she slipped her hand into his.

" I liked to imagine what he would say to me, and what I should say to him, and what my gown would be like, and what jewels he would give me, and all those sort of things ! And then, one night, I had a most wonderful dream, and it was this :

" I seemed to be out in a beautiful wood waiting for someone. The sunlight was dancing through the trees, and I was kneeling on the soft moss, and then, suddenly, the man I loved appeared in golden armour. He raised me up and we clasped our hands together at the wrist, and we said these words together to each other :

" ' I love you and, before God, I swear to be true to you, and to cherish you for ever.' Then all the birds burst into the sweetest singing, and their song was our wedding hymn. The golden knight of my dream then put a ring upon my finger. It had been forged from that part of his armour which covered his heart. After that nothing was very clear, but we seemed to go hand in hand, away into the dimness of the forest. . . . Do you think me very silly, Stephen ? "

" Of course I don't," he said. " I think you're the most wonderful girl."

She sighed contentedly.

" Before we drive on I want to ask you something," she said. "*You* are my golden knight ; will you make my dream come true?"

He paused a minute before answering her. These sort of ideas were entirely strange and new to him. He looked at her beautiful face. It was shining with a high, noble enthusiasm ;

such a look as Joan of Arc might have worn as she led her conquering troops. Then he whispered :

"Yes, my darling, I will be the golden knight of your dreams," and he held her face between his hands.

Turning away, she plucked a stray ear of golden wheat from the side of the road, and this she deftly fashioned into a ring which she gave to him. And here, under the vault of Heaven, with the birds singing and the sun shining, in the very true presence of God, did these two—in the words of Maddalena's dream—plight one another their troth. And on the dusty white road he slipped their wedding ring on to her finger.

"Now we belong to each other," the girl said, "let me kiss you, Stephen."

. . . . . .

At the shooting luncheon Gasparro was—as usual—as grumpy as possible. He hated his wife coming out, especially as he knew she didn't enjoy it, but only did it to annoy him. The other guests, however, who well knew his ways, soon fell to talking, and he relapsed into complete silence, with the exception of talking to Maddalena, whom he adored and was intensely proud of.

"Come and sit here, Bambine," he called out to her, "and open the caviare for me."

A special pot of this was always sent out for him. But he never offered it to anyone else, and ate the whole of it himself !

Maddalena devoted herself to him, spreading the caviare on bits of toast, pouring out his wine, and cutting and lighting his cigar, which she put between his lips.

He loved attention but he never got it from anyone but his little daughter, who was the only person who could put him in a good temper.

Maddalena and Stephen drove back a different road, whilst Bianca and Lepantchine took the way by which the young people had come.

"They are desperately in love, those two, *hein ?*" Lepantchine laughed to Bianca as they drove off.

"Yes, I think so—at least, I know he is with her. Who could help it ? I wonder you are not yourself, Ivan ? "

"She is certainly desirable," said the man, "but the uncut cake has no attraction for me."

He thought this rather clever and, to give him his due, he never did pursue girls. Married women, ah ! that was different, if they couldn't take care of themselves, well—*tant pis !*

F

" You know I love you, Bianca, and only you," he said.

" I'd kill you if you dared touch my white Maddalena," said the woman, looking at him swiftly and fiercely.

Usually she was so clinging: gentle, tragic, pathetic that he was almost startled at seeing her thus.

"What a divine woman you are, my Bianca!" he said. " You change like the winds of Heaven—always exciting, always interesting, always fascinating! Do you realize how fascinating you are, I wonder ? "

He took her hands into his, and his deep grey eyes were smiling powerfully very close to her face.

" Thank God you are not afraid to be passionate, my darling," he said. " How I hate those women who seem to be cold. They lead men on, pretending they do not know what they are doing, and all the time they are burning, burning. But they are ashamed of it ! Bah! how I despise them ! "

His voice was one of utter disgust.

" But you—you are different. You are warm, soft, primitive, a true woman. You are not afraid to be natural. Ah, come away with me ! I would give up my life for you. I would live where you wished. I would be your slave. I want you so much. It is impossible to endure it any longer. You must know how I suffer ? "

His words came quickly, and he breathed them hot and low, on to her lips.

" To think that you have never belonged to anyone but Gasparro, and that during all those years he has never loved you ! My God! What a wasted woman you are ! Bianca, I worship you. Nobody will ever love you as I do. Men of Eastern Europe are different from others. You would swoon for joy in my kisses, in my love."

He was passing his half-open lips backwards and forwards caressingly over hers.

" I must come to you to-night. Tell me I may ! "

At that moment they passed the wayside Crucifix, where, a short time before, Stephen and Maddalena had kissed the kiss of pure love. Bianca shivered, and, drawing herself slightly away from her companion, she crossed herself.

Noticing the change, Lepantchine went on very gently:

" You think it would be wrong, my darling ? But why ? I'm sure that you are mistaken ! Such love as ours is beautiful, pure and great. Giving is a wonderful thing, but the giving to each other of lovers is the most wonderful giving of all. The good God could never have meant you—with all your beauty and charm—to merely exist like a nun from the age of twenty-two till the end of your life ! It would be too wicked ! You have always lived in conventual surroundings, and have been taught to suppress all the natural instincts of human beings ! You are told that everything that is primitive is wrong. Perhaps in theory this is wise, but all wisdom is not truth. It is monstrous to think that a woman, like you, should be held by those ridiculous laws. Perhaps it is because I live so near the whisper of the East that I feel like this," he murmured dreamily. " Come away with me. Let us go together from here."

Bianca had shown by her life that she was not weak, and she certainly was not bad. But, since Lapantchine had kissed her the night before, he had gained a strange influence over her, which in the years of their friendship he had not possessed. The daring and power of his love-making had broken down her defences, and she no longer had any will but his.

Softly she murmured : " Ivan, when you talk to me like this I would do anything for you, and if it were not for my little girl I would go away with you. I hate Gasparro ; he bores me to death. He is so stupid and dull. He has never understood me, nor has he tried to do so. You cannot imagine, Ivan, what a fearful life mine has been. I mean being tied to a man like him. I was only seventeen when I married, and my mother thought that a girl ought to know nothing of the mysteries of marriage, except from her husband ! The only thing she told me was that I would sleep in the same bed as Gasparro.

He was twenty-one, and, as he was so slow and dull, he had to be brought up by a priest who lived in the house, so that he never had a normal boy's schooling. All his spare time was spent on the farm talking to peasants about how many little pigs were likely to be born, or the merits of various manures, or the illicit ' amours ' of the villagers. Mixed in with this was much superstitious talk of the ' evil eye,' and the ancient bones of long dead men which periodically ooze an oil which saves one from perdition.

" Well, the man who was the result of this extraordinary upbringing, was the man destined to initiate me into life !

" I shall never forget our marriage day. I think Gasparro had had too much wine to drink, and he so disgusted me that I vowed to myself he should not share my room that night.

" But when we arrived at our destination—the house of a

relation of his— imagine my horror when I found there were no
locks to any of the doors ! I spent the whole of that night roam-
ing about the house with my maid. As soon as it was light we
walked to the station and I went home again. Of course, there
was a tremendous excitement, and in the end—to avoid scandal—
my parents made me go back to him. But I knew more then, and
I insisted upon his keeping to certain conditions. I could have
got my marriage annulled, but to avoid a scandal my life was
sacrificed. Besides this, Gasparro was very rich, and we were
very poor.

" In a kind of way I wanted to have a child, for I often felt
terribly lonely, and, being so young, I didn't know what to do
with myself. I knew nobody in Rome, and when Gasparro
brought me there to his huge and splendid Palazzo, I was too
miserable and lonely for words. Slowly at last I began to make
friends and to learn the ways of the world. There was a Lord
and Lady Gawtrey staying in Rome, who were very nice to me.
She had a picture of her dear little girl, and I think that is what
first made me feel that I should like to have a baby At last
Uncle Guiseppe talked to me about things and then—and then—
Maddalena was born. I worshipped her from the first, and she is
the loveliest, sweetest, best thing that God has ever made. She is
my guardian angel.

" By degrees I began to understand the devious ways of life
and all its tricks. I realised that I could have power if I wished
it, and plenty of all sorts of admiration, and—well—I took it.
Now, Ivan, you know my life."

She raised her liquid, tragic eyes to his. Her lips trembled,
and she put a small white hand upon his knee.

" My poor Bianca," he said, taking it, and pressing it between
his palms. " What a tragedy ! How wicked it is that you have to
suffer so much—but let me console you, beloved, let my love sur-
round you and envelop you. Let me make you forget in its wealth
and warmth all the cold, cruel winter days of these past passion-
less years of your life. You without a lover ! God ! What a
waste ! "

His compelling eyes, his fatal attraction, and his soft, caressing voice had entirely subjugated her. She longed for him to
kiss her again.

Said he : " My perfect Bianca, I know that you love me, but I
want *your* lips to tell me so ! I want *you* to say that you need me.
. . . Just whisper, ' Ivan, I love you, I want you, come to

me ' . . . It would make me so happy, and you know that
I am your slave ! ''

Almost mesmerized, and hardly above her breath, she repeated
his words.

His face was very close to hers, and he whispered back
" Then I may come ? To-night ? At what time ? Tell me ! ''

A helpless look came into Bianca's eyes, but he drew her
irresistibly as the candle the moth.

" Come," she said, and her voice quavered, " come at twelve
o'clock to-night, and I will leave the window leading into the
rose garden open."

Once more Lepantchine drew her lips to his, and her growing
scruples were drowned in the power and rapture of his wonderful
kiss.

Stephen and Maddalena had resolved to keep their secret to
themselves for one day.

" One perfect day, Stephen ! '' cried the girl exultingly,
" when, out of the whole world, it is only known to you and me !
And, Stephen darling, we need not bother about money, because I
know that papa will give me heaps. Not that I mind about it
myself, but I would like you to be rich and to use my money for
Ullcombe. With all my worldly goods I thee endow, my Stephen !
I want to make other people as happy as I am, but I really
don't believe I could do that, for my happiness is beyond all
expression ! ''

And then they both sat hand in hand. Silent. Just happy.

The sun had long since set behind the hills when they came
home, for in their bliss they had loitered by the way. He had
been telling her about his family, and he had tried to picture to her
his relations and his home life. She was a born peacemaker, and
to her mentality it was inconceivable that people should squabble
about religion.

" I know I shall adore your father," she said, " and I think he
has treated you very well, Stephen, considering his views, and
compared to some of the mediæval histories and romances which
I have read about people who changed their religions."

Her ardent convert-lover was, however, rather disappointed
that she did not consider his father's treatment of him unfair
and bigoted. He was surprised that she took it in this way, for
the Cavallhos and others in Rome had been indignant at what thay
had called his father's fanaticism.

" Yet compared to these others what a jewel she is," thought Stephen, " so wise and lovely and good," and as he prayed that night before going to bed, he thanked God for Maddalena, and the call of the priesthood was, at the moment, completely submerged by the lure of the feminine.

In her bedroom Maddalena looked at her little face in the glass as she undressed. Innocently she smiled to see how fair it was.

" It's all for Stephen," she thought, as she leant out of the window and looked at the moon, that silent silver immemorial confidante of lovers. " How Juliet must have longed for Romeo ! " and she was grateful that there was no tragedy connected with her love.

" What a wondrous day it has been," she thought happily, and then she sank her face on to her soft arms, and gave herself up to youthful dreams.

But the more she dreamt the more wakeful she became, and then the thought of her mother crossed her mind.

" Darling mother," she soliloquized, " I feel that I would like to tell just you of my happiness. It is nearly midnight, so the day has been completely Stephen's and mine, but I want *you* to know of my joy before I go to sleep."

She looked at the wisp of straw round her finger and kissed it, then, slipping on soft shoes and a silk wrap, she ran noiselessly through the sleeping house down to her mother's bedroom.

Tapping gently on the door, she opened it before there was an answer, and tiptoed gently across to the beautiful four-post Florentine bed.

" Mother," she said softly, " are you asleep ? It is I, Maddalena. I want to talk to you and to tell you something very important. I am so excited, I cannot go to sleep till I have told you. May I get into your bed ? "

Quickly pulling down the sheets, she sprang in, and cuddled up to her mother like she used to do as a child.

Bianca, of course, was very wide awake indeed, and, when she heard the tapping on the door, she had concluded that it was Lepantchine, who, not being able to find the garden way, had come along the passage instead.

She was speechless with horrified surprise.

Nervously she turned over the awful situation in her mind, seeking for a possible solution. Could she get her daughter out of the room, or could she in any way warn Ivan ?

" Oh, Mother darling," said the girl, slipping her arm through

Bianca's, " I simply must tell you something. What do you think ? Could you guess ? " And at each question she gave her mother's arm an affectionate squeeze.

" Well, it's this—Stephen and I are going to be married, and —and—we are already betrothed to each other, because to-day he put this ring on to my finger in front of the Crucifix on the road to Santa Barbara, and—— "

At that moment Lepantchine stepped quietly into the room.

Two swift, silent strides and Bianca was in his arms, being kissed as only Ivan Lepantchine knew how.

" You devil ! Who are you ? Leave go of Mother ! How dare you touch her ? Beast ! Brute ! I'll scream and scream till everybody wakes and tears you to bits ! " And Maddalena's teeth were deep in Ivan's hands, and her nails were tearing his face.

The man's eyes narrowed dangerously. He was like an animal baulked of his prey.

For two years he had hunted this victim, and now a chit of a girl, springing from the unknown, had cheated him of his over-powering desire. Lifting Bianca high in his arms away from the poor, angry girl, he kissed her again with triumphant cruelty.

" There, you little she-devil ! " he said brutally, " that's all you get for losing your temper."

The girl was now beside herself with despairing rage, and for a minute she saw red. Rushing to the fireplace she took up the poker. Meanwhile, Ivan, seeing the girl's intention, had released Bianca, and was coming towards her in order to wrench the thing from her. But in his hurry he slipped on one of the loose Persian rugs which covered the parquet floor, and fell heavily, hitting his head against the corner of the Buhl writing-table at the bottom of the bed. The poker fell to the ground with a clatter, and the girl's hand was on the bell.

" If you attempt to move I'll wake everyone," she said. Her voice was trembling ; but, to her astonishment, there was no answer, only a groan came from the huge prostrate figure.

Bianca was fluttering about the room like a storm-driven leaf.

" Is he dead ? Dear God ! Is he dead ? " she whispered in awed tones.

And then the two women knelt down to see what had happened to the man.

Lepantchine was unconscious. A stream of blood was oozing from a horrid gash in his face.

" Beast ! " said the girl, getting up, and holding out her hand to her mother. " Beast ! "

" How cold you are, Mother ! Let me find you a thick cloak ; you are shivering." Putting her arm protectingly round the elder woman, she led her into her sitting-room.

The girl then went and looked at Lepantchine again ; there was now a large pool of blood near his head. She bathed his wound with cold water, and put a pillow under his head. Pulling a blanket off the bed, she threw it over him. " Beast," she said again, with loathing disgust. Then she locked the door and closed the shutters, so that, save for one candle, which she left burning on the table, the room was in darkness.

.   .   .   .   .   .

Bianca was excitedly pacing the room as the girl re-entered, and her back was towards her daughter, who stood silently leaning against the door.

Maddalena had come but a few minutes before to tell her adored mother of her and Stephen's innocent, happy love, when, brutally, the secret wisdom which tells the heart what is right and what is wrong in love, had been ravaged from its resting-place and, in one horrible moment, she had witnessed in her mother's bedroom what she felt with all the certainty of her being was wrong. Yet—sickening thought—it was her *mother !* How she wished she had never seen it. She was in love herself, but this . . . !

The more she thought about it all, the more she raged against Lepantchine. How dared he come, the brute, the devil ? A guest in their house, and yet he dared !

Then suddenly she remembered noticing their manner to each other at the picnic—for she was alert then, she had just learnt of things which before she knew nothing about. With an indescribable horror the thought sprang to her mind—" Did Mother expect him ? "

Then she recalled that the door into the garden was open when she came into her mother's room, and that the candles were burning. Those facts seemed significant now in the light of subsequent events, although in ordinary circumstances she would not have particularly noticed them.

Her thoughts flew to Stephen. How tender he had been to her, how careful. He had hardly dared to touch her, but Lepantchine had been so rough, so rude, so violent—and yet her mother was his hostess, and her father's wife !

Her world seemed to be crumbling away beneath her feet. She was overwhelmed—as if by an avalanche—with horror and shame for her mother, and with detestation of Lepantchine. Covering her face with her hands, she moaned :

"Oh, Mother, Mother, how could you ? Tell me you didn't know that he was coming ? Tell me that it was all a mistake, say *something* or I feel I shall go mad."

But there was a silence, and no answer came.

The feeling that this woman had given her birth, and therefore was to be revered and respected, was still the dominant note, but as the strange silence was not broken, something else crept into her heart. Gradually she realised that she was changing. She was no longer criticising her mother as a shocked and disillusioned child, but rather in the light of their common womanhood. Two women faced each other with life stretched out before them—one on its verge and the other at its centre. Each knew the fundamentals of right and wrong as do we all, yet each, humanly, longingly, held out their hands for what they believed to be happiness.

Swiftly Maddalena in her newly-found joy had realised how sad and empty her pretty mother's life must have been in the past, and as swiftly there surged up in her heart—in place of disgust—a heartfelt forgiveness of her behaviour, for gradually, and with almost divine intuition, she had understood.

At last Bianca's soft voice broke the silence.

"Yes. It's all true," she whispered. "I *did* expect him. Darling child, what must you think of me ? How absolutely I have failed as a wife and a mother."

She sank disconsolately upon a sofa, upon which lay great plashes of milky moonlight.

"How forlorn and unhappy she looks," thought Maddalena. "She seems so young now that this has all happened. I feel she is more like my sister than my mother. She must be cared for. Papa must love her more."

For a while silence reigned in the room. No words could cope with the situation, certainly no words of Bianca's.

At that moment Maddalena stepped into the arena of life. Crossing the cold, dim, silent room, she knelt beside the unhappy woman.

"Mother," she whispered, "I feel I know—just now I have come to know—that you haven't been happy with Papa, and, of course, that makes all the difference. Love is so wonderful !

It *makes* life.   I know now, darling, so I can sympathise.   If my Stephen ceased to love me, I think I should die of grief.   Tell me how it all happened.   And don't cry, Mother, don't cry.   Hush hush, my darling."

And so with her child's safeguarding, loyal young arms round her, Bianca told the story.

As the words fell haltingly from her lips, the girl's pity turned to a burning resolve that the bringing together again of her parents should be her loved task and endeavour.

Like all lovers she not only loved one person, but all the world seemed to be caught up in its glamour, and everyone and everything was looked at through the eyes of love.

Suddenly a groan was heard, and then some shuffling.

" He's moving," whispered Bianca, clinging to her child. " What shall I do ?   I can't tell your father, I daren't.   I—I— Oh, God !   Forgive me and help me ! "

" Don't move, Mother, and try to be calm," said Maddalena. " I'll manage it.   You stay here quietly and keep warm."

She lovingly arranged the rug round her mother, and the older woman was glad to let her do her will.

As she opened the door into the next room a voice said : " Who is there ? "

" It is Maddalena di Santa Fiora."

" What has happened ? "

" You came into my mother's room, then you slipped and hurt yourself.   Can you move ? "

" Yes, I think so."

" Get up, then."

Again her hand was on the bell-rope.   With difficulty and very slowly he rose.   The ugly gash was still bleeding and his Slav face looked brutish thus disfigured.   The dark red silk dressing gown with its purple collar and cuffs was foully stained in his blood, and, with his clammy dishevelled hair, dull furious eyes, and white teeth gleaming between sensual, sullen lips, he might have figured in Dante's " Inferno " as the Butcher of the Ages.

Maddalena's slight breasts—which lay, virginal, beneath her soft silk wrap, like folded water-lilies—quickly rose and fell, and from her great, deep, Southern eyes hate blazed.

" Now, M. Lepantchine," she said, " will you listen to my terms ?   Either you come with me at once to my father, and tell him exactly what has happened, or I ring this bell and waken the servants, and get all the farm men to beat you—beat you to

death, perhaps," she added, with an indrawing of her breath.
" Choose quickly, for I loathe talking to you."

Lepantchine was in a dilemma. He felt very weak and queer,
and the girl had the whip-hand.

" The servants! The farm men! No, thank you! The
little spitfire would do it like a shot," he thought. " That fool
Gasparro is the only alternative. He is nothing but a half-baked
boor, and hasn't got the guts of a mouse."

" I'll go and see your father," he said sullenly.

" Very well, come with me."

He was surprised at her words, but not more so than she was
at her own temerity. During the last hour she seemed to have
lived years.

Taking a candle in her hand, she made him grope his way in
front of her. At last they reached her father's bedroom.

" Wake up, please, Father," she said distinctly. " M.
Lepantchine is here, and he wants to speak to you."

Gasparro was snoring loudly, with his head buried under the
bedclothes.

" What a hog he is," thought Ivan.

Gasparro was awake now, and growled :

" What is it—what's happened ? "

" Will you kindly ask your daughter to leave us alone, Prince,
and, if you will permit, I will sit down, as I am not feeling well."

" I won't go away, Papa, so you needn't tell me to," said
Maddalena. Again her hand was on the bell, and her great angry
eyes seemed to be eating into Lepantchine's very soul.

The Prince's dull mind suddenly seemed to scent something
strange, and his heavy face took on an expression of alert cunning.

Getting out of bed, he put on a dressing-gown, brushed his
hair, and walked up and down the room.

" Well, Lepantchine, get on with it, whatever it is," he said.

In smooth, suave tones the Russian spoke :

" Princess di Santa Fiora did me the honour of asking me to
sleep with her. When I entered the room the Princess Maddalena, who was apparently in her mother's bed, tried to attack me
with a poker ; in seeking to defend myself I slipped, and hit my
head against the table. I am not feeling at all well, and I should
be much obliged if I might be allowed to retire to my bedroom ?
I shall naturally leave as soon as possible. It is a pity that my
otherwise pleasant visit should have had such a disastrous
ending."

There was an ominous silence.

" Is that all ? " asked the Prince at last.

" Yes," was Lepantchine's answer.

" No ! no ! no ! "—and Maddalena's voice rang like a clarion through the room. " That is only half the truth. Lepantchine is a liar. Listen to me, Papa, and I will tell you the truth. Mother has told me everything.

" Ever since you met him in London two years ago, he pretended that he loved Mother, but she always said no. She hates him, Papa, and—and—if only you had been always with her—had always loved her, he never would have dared. You know—you both know—that Mother is good, but Lepantchine wants everyone he admires to be as wicked as himself."

Her words were interrupted by a sarcastic grunt from the Russian, who was chafing impatiently.

" Love ! " he laughed sarcastically. " You *child !* You don't know what you are talking about. You know nothing about love."

" Silence, you swine ! " burst from Gasparro at the man's words. " How dare you address my daughter ? How dare you, you lustful brute, mention the word ' love ' to her ? You ought to be gagged and bound on the floor ; you ought to be crawling to me for mercy, instead of insulting my child by speaking to her ! " and he turned to Maddalena and drew her to him.

She looked up innocently and trustfully into her father's face, and said very gently :

" I do know about love, Father, I know about *true* love. I love Lord Athelston, and he loves me, and I am going to be his wife. So you see, I know a great deal about love, but Stephen's love was—was—so different from—*this*," and she turned with a gesture of queenly and supreme disgust towards her mother's would-be lover.

" Oh ! Lepantchine," she said, very slowly and very distinctly, " how I hate you ! "

The words dropped clearly in the silence of the room, like small, smooth stones being dropped at equal intervals into a well. They dropped into the heart of the man who, but for her, would have degraded her mother. And so it was that this fact and her words remained hidden and very deep down in his heart. Never by him to be forgotten ; never to be forgiven.

The supreme idea in Maddalena's mind was that her mother must never be accused, and, her ardent passionate defence of her mother's frailty had unconsciously achieved her desire in a way she had neither guessed nor planned.

Her fervent words, her enchanting youth, her pure, shining eyes, the lilt of her voice when it touched on her love for Stephen, and that she was loved by him, had, with its magic golden key, unlocked the rusty fastnesses of Gasparro's shut-in selfish heart.

The true understanding of love comes to some very late, to others—never.

Till now—he was just forty—love had not yet "entered in." On certain lines he had not developed, and, like Louis XVI., he was the possessor of a wife whose fascinations he, alone of men, could not discern. But as his child's words fell upon his ears, as he looked at her swaying, brave, young figure, and heard the eternal words "I love him" come from her lips, living, burning with truth and happiness, the wondrous door—until now barred to him—swung slowly back, and the garden of his heart was suffused with the glorious, golden, life-giving rays of the knowledge of love.

And, as a closed bud longing for something—it knows not what—opens automatically when touched by the sun's hot rays, so did Gasparro's heart at that moment awaken to the realization that to love Bianca, to live *with* her and *for* her, might mean something very wonderful indeed in their lives.

For some seconds he saw only the vision which Maddalena's words had created, but a groan from Lepantchine brought him back to realities.

Looking again at his enemy, his face became once more suffused with jealous fury. Going to a drawer, he took out two pistols, and began to polish them on the cuffs of his dressing-gown. He quietly looked through them towards the light which was getting stronger every moment.

When Maddalena saw what he was doing she was horrified.

Punishment—revenge—flogging—these things she had hoped for, and fully expected—but death!—no!

She swayed at the thought, and her legs would scarcely support her.

Death! So suddenly! How grim and fearsome! Only a few hours ago they had all been eating and drinking and laughing together. Only a few hours ago she had felt Stephen's lips upon hers on the happy, hot, sunny road to Santa Barbara. But now, through her doing, this erstwhile friend of theirs—this man so strong, so successful, so rich, so alive—would be *dead*.

Her brain reeled. It must be stopped, she thought, but how to do it ? Her father was a renowned shot ; she knew that Lepantchine hadn't a chance. She looked unseeingly from one man to the other, and, half-dazed, she noticed that her father was pushing a pistol into his enemy's hands, and, as though from far away, she heard the words :

"Say your prayers to whatever gods you believe in, you seducer of women, for by the God of heaven, it won't be my fault if you're alive much longer."

He spat the words brutally and insultingly into the other's face.

Since hearing Maddalena's version of the repulsive story, his anger had turned to uncontrollable fury. He was mad with the wild primitive madness of a Sicilian peasant. *He* might treat his wife as he liked ; she was *his*, but *per bacco* no one else might !

"Go to your mother, Maddalena, and wait there till I come," he commanded.

As he spoke the great clanging clock in the stables struck three, and the white mountain mists clung coldly to the house.

In a little time another day would be born, thought Maddalena, and, with the glowing sun would come hope, and much forgetfulness of the horror of the night. The girl looked from the sullen despair of Lepantchine's face to the excited angry expression of revenge on that of her father. For the moment her loathing of the Russian was merged into a disgusted pity. Life was, as she well knew, very sweet. She had not created Lepantchine's life, what right had she to connive—however slightly—at its being taken away from him ?

She doubted that even in such circumstances her father was justified in killing the man. She felt convinced that she must save him somehow, and the knowledge of his sins festering upon his soul obliterated for the moment every other emotion.

"He must not die unshriven," she thought, "and I must get Uncle Guiseppe to come at once, for he will be able to influence Papa."

Quickly she resolved to act on the excuse that Lepantchine must not die without a priest.

"Papa," she said, "you know that none of us should die without doing penance, don't you ? Will you wait a minute— not do anything to him, I mean—while I fetch Uncle Guiseppe ? "

Gasparro's face was swollen with fury, but this request he could not refuse.

" Right. Take these then "—and he put the pistols into her hands. " I daren't trust myself alone with them—and him."

He was trembling violently, and the gleam of battle shone from his eyes ; the gleam of the righteous, natural rage of the betrayed animal against the betrayer. No divorce, no paying-out of money, no legal arrangements would satisfy Gasparro in his present mood ; nothing but death to the betrayer, and that very swiftly.

In a minute the girl's trembling hand knocked on the door of the Cardinal's room, and she was pouring out the story. " Come quickly," she said, " for although I hate Lepantchine, Papa must not be allowed to kill him. You must save his life."

At the door of her father's room she paused, for angry voices could be heard raised one above the other. White-lipped, the girl whispered to the Cardinal, who had followed her with incredible alacrity :

" Thank God, Papa has not strangled him. I even feared he might. Go in, please, Uncle Guiseppe, I shall leave you now. Save him, his body and his soul."

And so Maddalena, God-like, gave Lepantchine his life.

.   .   .   .   .   .

As they say a drowning's man's past appears before him with terrible accuracy, so did that of Cardinal Costanzi as he stood for one second on the threshold before opening the door to a scene which he dreaded. For had he not been guilty of just such an act as had awakened this horror in the innocent heart of Maddalena— an intrigue with the wife of the man of whose hospitality he had partaken ?

" Who am I that I should judge this man ? " he thought. " Little Maddalena thinks I am a saint. Alas ! I am no better than the man she hates, yet, by my priestly status, I am surrounded with a halo to which I have no right."

He turned the handle of the portal of the judgment hall.

Lepantchine had not moved from the chair, and his face looked haggard and jaded in the thin, pale light which was creeping into the room.

Gasparro stood, legs straddled, staring with strained, un-blinking eyes at the distant mountains. The veins stood out at his temples and in his neck, and his jaws moved continuously, as though chewing the cud of thoughts far too bitter for words. His thick, strong, swarthy hands were clasped behind him, and twitched convulsively. Heavy beads of sweat trickled down his dark face, brooding and lowering with passionate hate.

He turned quickly as the door opened and, gripping the Cardinal's arm like a vice, he said thickly:

" Quickly! Shrive the hound, and then go! This is no place for women and priests. He's yours now, but he'll be mine in a minute, and then he shall die the death of the dog that he is."

The Cardinal gently disengaged himself from his infuriated nephew, saying quietly:

" This *is* my place, and I shall stay here. *Your* place is with Bianca. You have always neglected her, and this is the consequence. Go, Gasparro, go to your wife."

With such quiet dignity were the words spoken that the enraged Prince seemed almost mesmerized. He stared at the Cardinal open-mouthed, as though to speak, but the old man raised his white, transparent hand, and pointed to the door.

" Go," he repeated, low and firm.

With a quick look of hatred at his enemy, and another glance at his uncle, whose unflinching eyes looked squarely into his, Gasparro, moved, paused, and then was gone.

.   .   .   .   .   .

Bianca's little jewelled clock pointed to eight as her husband entered her room, flooded with brilliant September sunshine.

Maddalena's eyes feverishly sought those of her father, and her surprise was great when she realized that it was a different man that she looked upon. For Gasparro's soul was awakened at last!

On leaving the Cardinal and Lepantchine together he had gone to finish dressing, and then, with madly throbbing temples and a heart full of murder, he had left the house and let his feet wander where they would. At last he came to the wayside Crucifix on the road to Santa Barbara.

He had walked quickly and hard, and his thoughts had been fierce and hot, but as he breasted the hill his feelings became less stormy, and on reaching the top his angry heart was quieter.

The sun burst out from behind closely-packed lemon-tinted clouds, and as it did so the insufferable agony of the night's happenings seemed to be lifted from him. With a sigh of profound relief he sank to the ground.

" Thank God that I have been saved from killing him," he said aloud, and then, as he lay upon the fair, sweet earth, lovely

Nature's healing hand crept forth to console him. The whole of his and Bianca's past life appeared before him as upon a stage, and the truth of the Cardinal's words dawned upon him in all their true meaning.

"What a cold, arid, senseless life it has been," he thought. "From to-day we shall have a new life."

Thus it was a changed and penitent Gasparro who entered Bianca's room that morning.

Before leaving her parents together Maddalena joined their hands tenderly.

"No one can live without sympathy and love," she said. "Will you give me your re-born love as a wedding present ? "

And standing thus, hand clasping hand, she left them. What happened ? What did they say ? Ah, that is their secret.

.   .   .   .   .   .

As Lepantchine walked away from the castle in the early morning hours following his ill-starred adventures, Cardinal Costanzi stood poised on the drawbridge, as it were, its guardian angel.

The Russian turned and took a last look at the home of Bianca, and then at a corner in the rough white road the place was hidden from his eyes, and passed for ever out of his life.

The talk he had had with the Cardinal had sunk deeply into his being, and he was—in spite of himself and his grossly material outlook—profoundly impressed by the story of the other's own early love-affair which the Cardinal had touched upon.

"We all have our loves, our temptations and our passions," the Cardinal had told him in the gentlest tones. "Some more, some less, and, until we have learnt to ride them heavily-bitted, we are not really of much value to ourselves or to anyone else. I learnt it very young, but you have not yet learnt it at thirty-five.

"Long before that age Christ had laid the foundations of our religion, and died a criminal's death; long before that age Napoleon had conquered nearly the whole of Europe ; long before that age Joan of Arc had saved France, and Pitt was leading England. Yet you, a man—and you *are* a man—are still prowling about, pursuing illicit ' amours,' and seeking to gratify the lowest that is in you. Nearly forty, Lepantchine—you are not yet even the master of yourself."

G

Very sternly, very gravely, the words were spoken, and each one went home.

" You are gifted," went on the Cardinal, " why fritter away your powers on things which require no intelligence ? Why not from now on gather yourself together and concentrate on some work which is good in itself, and worthy of your brains ? All is dust and ashes, everything withers and dies, nothing remains but God. He alone deserves the best that is in us. I wonder what your plans for the future are ? "

" What do you mean ? " Lepantchine asked quickly.

" Well," the Cardinal answered, " from what I know of my nephew Gasparro, he will most certainly ruin the possibilities of any future career for you if he can, and he has a good deal of power in certain quarters. He is, as you know, immensely rich, and officialdom in Italy is, I grieve to say, not less venal than anywhere else. We have saved your body from revenge, but we cannot save your career. In reality, it was Maddalena who saved you."

A purple flush mounted to Lepantchine's face as he heard these words. Such a contingency had never entered his wildest dreams. He ! nearly at the top, and with every door in Europe open to him. He ! a brilliant, successful man of the world, to be beholden to a meddling girl of seventeen. He ! with his pick of the biggest posts that Russia's Foreign Office could bestow, to be in the power of a fool like Gasparro. It was too sickening for words !

" He couldn't ruin me like that ; he couldn't be such a damned cad," he blurted out at last, his voice trembling with anger.

" He could and he would, and he will, and of that I am absolutely certain," said the Cardinal. " *You* are the cad—you tried to seduce his wife—so, humanly speaking, there is no reason why he shouldn't try to ruin you. There are many ways of doing that, but what ruins a woman doesn't usually ruin a man, and you may be sure that he will find something that will hurt you. That he hasn't killed you is all that you can expect of him."

" The fool doesn't care for her, though ! He's only a half-baked boor," said Lepantchine with impotent rage. " What right has he to make a fuss when somebody else wants to take what he shows to the whole world that he doesn't care about ? "

"More right than you have, anyhow, and besides, he *does* care in his own queer way. I know Gasparro," answered the Cardinal. And thus their talk had ended.

They had parted amicably, and Lepantchine was touched on the whole at the priest's treatment of him.

As he walked with long, nervous strides to the station, thousands of wild ideas tumbled through his mind. He perfectly realized now that if Gasparro set to work to ruin him, his future would indeed be a blank; failure and downfall. But, till the Cardinal had suggested it, the idea had never occurred to him. It was a terrible blow. For some moments he walked on, all kinds of thoughts and ideas rushing madly through his brain.

At that moment—while Gasparro was breasting the hill in the opposite direction—the sun burst out from behind close-paced, lemon-tinted clouds, and poured its glorious radiance on to the new day and on to his own new life—for a new life, he realized swiftly, it would have to be. He made a heaving movement as to throw off something that was finished and done with. At the moment that Gasparro determined to go back to his wife, Lepantchine determined on an entirely new life.

"So be it, then," he ejaculated, "I will cast away the past like an old shoe, and I will now start upon my *vita nuova*."

The train carrying the market people to the nearest town crept slowly along, and he was so obsessed with his thoughts that he did not even hear their chattering.

But in and out of his mind there threaded a thought. Persistent it was, and not to be put away.

"That little devil! She baulked me in the end! She's a wonder, though, a rare little beauty; yet I hope to God she'll be made to suffer, for she has made me suffer. That namby-pamby English stripling with his high-brow ideas on religion! What can she see in him? Pfah! He's as cold as a fish! She was made for love, and there's more love in my little finger than in his whole body! No Englishman knows how to love. Their innate Puritanism kills all the natural rapture.

"They have no skill in such matters; they are so clumsy. They are either too stupid or too lazy to work up the situation properly. The English only produce two types of lover—the thief in the orchard, or the bull in the china shop."

When he got to his hotel he was horrified to see the fearful gash across his face.

"It will always leave a mark," the doctor told him.

As he examined his disfigured face in the glass he said to himself: "Maddalena, you lovely wretch! I'd like to wring your neck! I'll be even with you yet, though. You've ruined my life, and I won't forget that!"

PART II

MARRIAGE

CHAPTER VI

" WHOM GOD HATH JOINED TOGETHER . . ."

" Nothing but the Infinite Pity is sufficient for the infinite pains of human life."—JOHN HENRY SHORTHOUSE.

THE marriage of Maddalena and Stephen had taken place in Rome amidst great pomp and ceremony. But, notwithstanding the gorgeous assembly, the lovely music, the booming organ, and the solemn words, " Wilt thou take . . . to have and to hold, in sickness and in health, . . . till death us do part . . ." and the solemn answer—his loud and firm, hers firm and soft, " I will "—" I will "—notwithstanding the grandeur of it, its beauty, dignity and religiosity, it was the marriage service high up in the mountains by the roadside Crucifix on the way to Santa Barbara which, in Maddalena's unworldly, innocent heart, had made her Stephen's for ever.

.   .   .   .   .   .

Maddalena had not told Stephen of the Lepantchine affair, though on all other points her heart and her mind were open to him. For many reasons she wished him to be ignorant of it. She felt that it would cast a slur on her mother, whom she adored, and on their religion, to which her husband was such a new and ardent recruit. He was still walking on air, as it were, with regard to his new faith, and was under the impression—erroneous, to be sure—that no Catholic could be guilty of any serious wrong.

Maddalena did not want that her mother, of all people, should be the cause of any disillusionment to her husband.

She knew that Stephen had instinctively disliked Lepantchine, although one whole day and night only had they been together at Santa Fiora, and during that time they had hardly exchanged ten words. On being told that Lepantchine had been suddenly recalled to Rome, Stephen hadn't given the man another thought.   By a year afterwards he had practically forgotten the Russian's existence.

Cardinal Costanzi's silence on the matter was only rivalled by that of the tomb.   Not even to the Santa Fioras themselves had he breathed a word as to the interview he had had with Lepantchine previous to the man's hurried and dramatic departure from their roof.

Everybody connected with the tragedy seemed to conspire together in a grateful, self-imposed, and tacit silence over the whole unpleasant affair.

Only once was he referred to, when, a few weeks later, the Cardinal drew Gasparro's attention to an announcement in a Roman paper that the brilliant Russian diplomatist had resigned from the Service, and intended to devote himself in the future to the large estates which he possessed in Russia.

" A good thing he did it before I forced him to;" muttered Gasparro, his hands suddenly trembling.   But nothing more than this was ever said, and thus it was that a scandal had been avoided.

.   .   .   .   .   .

And now the great excitement of the Santa Fioras' lives was that their adored Maddalena was expecting a baby.   The Athelstons had taken a house in London, and Gasparro and Bianca were going there in a few days, taking with them Cardinal Costanzi, who was to baptize the infant.

" Won't it be wonderful ? " Gasparro said excitedly, with the naïve pleasure that only a Latin has at a family birth.   " In a few weeks we shall be holding the dear little Bambino in our arms ! "

She laughed at him in gentle raillery, saying he was as excited about it as though he was going to have a baby himself.

And thus these two, still so young themselves, schemed and longed and planned and laughed, and so had, in the end, the happiness in the arrival of their grandchild, which they had missed in the coming of their own child.

.   .   .   .   .   .

Stephen stood at the threshold of his wife's bedroom, agonized with fear and love.

Behind that door his beloved youthful Maddalena lay in the pains of birth.   Bianca stood holding her hot hands in hers.

" Is she in danger ? " asked the mother anxiously.

The doctor looked serious. " She isn't as well as I had hoped, but still, she has a splendid constitution," he answered kindly.

The slow time dragged on. Twenty-six hours of increasing pain had engendered such weakness that Maddalena felt, as in a hideous nightmare, that she would never have the strength to give birth to her child.

For religious motives, common to many of her faith, she refused choloroform, and thus it was in the culmination of great agony that the birth at last took place.

Gasparro stood outside Maddalena's room with Stephen. He was in such a state of nervous excitement that an onlooker would have thought that he, and not the tense and quiet Stephen, was the expectant father.

In one hand he held a diamond *rivière* and in the other a long pearl necklace.

Diamonds if it's a boy, pearls if it's a girl—Santa Maria guard her," he spluttered, and then, taking his rosary from his pocket, he invited his son-in-law to say it with him.

Suddenly the door opened, and a buxom nurse with a brogue looked out.

" It's a girl, m'Lord," she said ; then, on seeing a slight look of disappointment cross both men's faces, she quickly added : " But don't worry, there's another on the way. You go on praying to the Blessed Virgin."

Another twenty minutes passed, and again the rotund one looked forth from the chamber of Life.

" A beautiful boy, glory be to God ! " she laughed, and quickly disappeared again.

Stephen's spirit recoiled at his father-in-law's ebullient effervescence. All the time he was longing to be quietly alone with Maddalena. He hardly seemed to care about the babies. He was intensely anxious about his wife, for the doctor had told him she might be very ill indeed.

At this news the scruples, which Stephen thought he had stifled, peeped out again, and, at that instant, began in this man's life the most exquisite of all tortures—the never-ceasing riding of the soul by religious doubts and fears and a gnawing remorse because he had—as he thought—frustrated God's plan for him in order that he might gratify his human love. Was his wife's illness God's punishment ? he wondered. The thought was an appalling one, and hit him, as it were, straight between the eyes.

.   .   .   .   .   .

Stephen was kneeling by her bed, feeling that he couldn't gaze enough, nor yet ever take his fill of her face. She had so nearly slipped away from him, but, marvellous to tell, she had won a victory over death, and from her eyes her soul, which he loved, was looking out at him, and from her body, which he worshipped, came the sound of gentle, slow breathing.

His whole being was focussed upon her.

" Beloved—do you feel better ? " he whispered, looking yearningly into her face, while he very gently held a hand which lay weakly at her side. How small it looked, and how white !

Like two violets her lids lay wearily over her eyes.

Then he felt a little pressure on his hand, and her voice came very softly :

" Stay with me, Stephen. Send the others away."

" Yes, darling, I will stay. We won't talk, though," he added, as Doctor Edgecumbe put his finger to his lips. " We must be very quiet."

The room was darkened and all was still. For some time he knelt on by her bed, praying with all his strength and all his faith that his darling wife might be spared to him.

And as he prayed, the thought came again irresistibly, like a tidal wave, that this was indeed God's punishment because he had given up a heavenly love for an earthly one, and had exchanged a spiritual, transcendent Lover for a warm, pulsing, living woman.

He was frightened, terrified.

Terrified of God's wrath, and at the same time terrified lest he should lose his Maddalena.

And so in his fear of Almighty vengeance, and a balancing horror at the thought that his wife might die, he made a sort of pact with the Diety Whom he wanted, as it were, to conciliate. He was obsessed with the idea of retribution, and he felt that in some way God would " pay him back," although, to do him justice, his natural and best self told him how unworthy such a thought was. But Stephen was nothing if not the mouthpiece of ideas put into his head by other men.

Thus it was that his curious and limited notion of God's divine omnipotence obsessed him to such a degree that he was led—like the Egyptians of old—to offer propitiation.

The holocaust he chose to lay on the altar of compromise was his wife. Hysterically he promised that, should she be spared, he would henceforth lead a celibate's life, hoping in this way to avert the anger of the most high God, which he felt he deserved for having given up the priesthood.

For even the intense happiness of the first radiant year of their married life had not extinguished the little voice which told him that his love was sinful, and so torn between what was right and wrong for himself was he that he felt should disaster overtake him in any form it would only be Divine Justice working itself out. He was distraught.

The Hound of Heaven indeed did not pursue him, but he himself, the weak, uncertain, shifting man, was the hound by whom he was pursued.

Like many others who are " busy about many things," he mistook the figments of an excited, nervous, religious cannonade for the Divine voice. He was always far too busy in listening to the teaching of men to hear the quiet, consoling voice of Christ.

From now onwards the conviction that his marriage with Maddalena was wrong, never ceased to lay siege to the walls of his soul, and the idea filled his subconsciousness in the same way as a house is haunted by a ghost.

At this moment all the powers of Stephen's soul were endeavouring to tear human love from Stephen's heart. With his feeling as poignant as they were, this added mental agony was well-nigh unendurable.

For three weeks Maddalena's life hung on a thread, but at last the turning point was reached, and she began to get better.

" Sheer determination to live," said the doctor. " If she hadn't given us the whole of her will, we couldn't have pulled her through."

The days of convalescence were very happy ; the twins had ceased to yell, and were becoming quite nice and human ! Their names were Quendred and Stephen Anthony, to be called, of course, Anthony until his father died.

One morning Murphy (the twins' nurse) came into Maddalena's room in a great state of excitement, holding some bits of cardboard in her hand.

" I beg your Ladyship's pardon, but I think it my duty to tell your Ladyship that when Lady Traquair came to see your Ladyship a few days ago, she came in to see the babies, too. They were asleep, and as her ladyship looked at them I heard her say, ' Poor, wretched, little Roman Catholics, it's too wicked—how could Stephen ? ' and then she turned to me and gave me these" (her voice and face expressed utter disgust), and she held out three tracts to Maddalena.

" Protestant tracts, dreadful things ; to think that they should even be in the *room* of the dear innocents, both dedicated to the Blessed Virgin as they are."

" Let me see them, please," said Maddalena.

On one was written : " My little children, let us not love in words, neither in tongue, but in deed and in truth."

On another : " Perfect love casteth out fear," and on the third was : " Blessed are the pure in heart, for they shall see God."

They were printed on shiny blocks of cardboard, and badly decorated with scrolls of gilt and inartistically coloured flowers.

" Have you read them, Murphy ? "

" Most certainly *not*, m'Lady ; I wouldn't pollute my eyes with them Protestant things. Why, they're only fit to be thrown into the fire."

" Well, I would like you to read them to me now," said her mistress, " they are God's words."

The woman did so, flushing.

" Is there anything so particularly *Protestant* in those ideals ? " asked Maddalena.

" No-n-n-n-no," stuttered the nurse rather shamefacedly.

" You can go now," said Maddalena, and as she turned over in her bed to try to rest, she wondered in what place of worship the apostles would be most at home if they re-visited the earth, and the thought made her spirit very weary.

And as she fell asleep, she thought that if those words had been painted on parchment by Fra Angelico, they would be worth thousands at Christie's but, she sighed, the value would be on account of the man-genius who *painted* the words not on account of the divine-man-genius who *said* the words.

CHAPTER VII

DOUBT

" There lives more faith in honest doubt,
Believe me, than in half the creeds."
—TENNYSON.

SINCE the birth of her twins things had changed much in Maddalena's life, and if the old nursery saw is true, she was herself quite a different person from she who—so gaily and innocently—had plighted her troth to her English lover with a ring of golden straw in the golden Italian sunlight.

For she was now twenty-eight, and had thus completed the fourth entire gradual change of the body—and, therefore, presumably of the mind—which is said to take place in us all every seven years.

Her father-in-law was dead, and she was now Duchess of Seyntleger—young, rich, and very lovely. Her husband also had undergone the changes prescribed by nature and, in his case too, these had not left him unaltered.

As the years went gradually by, the idea that he had been faithless to God by marrying Maddalena, became a tormenting phantom which entirely possessed and mastered him, and, although he did indeed love her most profoundly, the other conviction became so powerful and so ever-present that it conquered his mind at last.

Like some slow, creeping disease, it wound its cruel tentacles round his whole being, till neither will nor heart could resist its power.

His soul, long since consumed with love for the office of the priesthood, had no desire to resist, and burned only with an unquenchable longing that the mind and heart and body of Stephen should follow where her exalted finger pointed and hear only her ardent voice—chanting and praising the immortal, eternal, and undying fascination of the life of the celibate, the priest.

And now, as a result, Maddalena found herself the wife of a man who was slowly becoming as a stranger to her ; the wife of a man whose mode of living seemed more and more incomprehensible as time passed, and whose outlook on life was baffling and mysterious.   More and more she heard him praise the clerical outlook on life, and day by day his views seemed to become stricter, colder, and more puritanical.

It filled her with a faint, cold anxiety ; she knew not where she was going or whither he was slipping.   Life was no longer natural.   It was a quicksand, and it terrified her.

One of her great sorrows was that after the birth of Anthony and Quendred no more children had been born.   It was just at this time that she had begun to detect a change in her husband.

Although not holding the key to the secret, the difference in Stephen was so marked as to be impossible to ignore.   And, since then, Maddalena, though seemingly a wife with all its outward aspects of position and responsibility, was indeed a wife no longer. Only Cardinal Costanzi knew what a tragedy her apparently successful marriage had become.

This old man had reached the stage of having been long enough in this world to have outlived the enthusiastic illusions of youth, together with its mad enthusiasms for " causes."   He had now arrived at the stage of finding that his love and pity for the race had increased tenfold, and his admiration of parties and opinions had entirely fallen away from him.

But for nearly two years Maddalena had not seen him, and now he was very ill, and she could no longer tell him her troubles. So she buried them in her heart and bore them—as most of us do —alone.

In order to be near the Jesuits' church in Farm Street, Stephen had bought—with his wife's money—a house in Berkeley Square, and every Sunday one of those priests came to luncheon with the Seyntlegers.

The most frequent visitor was Father Bischoffsheim (an Austrian of Jewish extraction) who, brilliantly clever, had also mastered the art of fascinating the minds of men.

To-day was a Sunday in June, and he had just left the house after his weekly visit, which, however, hadn't passed off quietly, as it usually did.   He and Quendred—Maddalena's ten-year-old daughter—had had a difference of opinion !

At luncheon he had told her she was too young to eat asparagus without its being cut up for her, and had teased her by saying she should be in the nursery with a bib round her neck.

This angered the girl, although answering politely that she was allowed to eat what she liked. He still continued his joking, till at last the attention of the table was drawn to the episode, but even then the baiting did not cease.

Suddenly Quendred's Sicilian blood flamed to her face and, hitting the priest on the arm, she blurted out, " Can't you leave me alone ? " her dark eyes blazing.

But immediately she had done it she looked away, confused. The man turned round and told her in a bantering way that it was a sin to hit a priest, and that he would excommunicate her. He held up his right hand, and began to say some words in Latin.

Now Quendred had been brought up from earliest childhood to revere priests, and to believe everything they said in a religious connection. Priests were persons—she had been taught— to whom had to be given the greatest respect, and to whose opinion everyone bowed, or at least, never openly disputed. She had often heard her Irish " Nanny " say that she would kiss a priest's feet, the view being held by a very large number of those believing the Latin Faith that a priest can do no wrong.

Priests were always given the most important place at her father's table ; priests' words fell upon the ears of the company in expectant and attentive silence ; the approbation of priests was courted, their censure really feared.

And in Quendred's heart this atmosphere had been well and securely established—to such an extent, in fact, that the conviction of their spiritual superiority was so deeply imbued in her being, that it gave them a pre-eminence in other ways out of all proportion with their claims. This, however, when dealing with children's minds, is inevitable, and that is why it is so very important to pause and ponder before filling the minds of our children with matter which, although vastly expedient, is not true.

Childlike, Quendred didn't differentiate between " priest qua priest" and "priest qua man"—this attitude of mind being indeed not unusual in persons of a quite high intellectual development.

The girl's fury at the Jesuit's silly teasing did, however, on this occasion, surpass her inborn obsequious obedience to him as the representative of a dignity she was taught to regard as practically divine. Scarlet in the face, she exclaimed :

" Well, I don't care if you *do* excommunicate me ! "

But as soon as the words had dropped from her lips her high mood forsook her ; the meaning and force of all she had been taught regarding the reverence due to priests returned and over-whelmed her, and, upsetting her chair, she ran round to her mother.

Shy and ashamed, with brimming eyes and trembling lips, she tightly hugged Maddalena's neck. She felt at bay to all the world.

From the other side of the table came her austere father's voice, grave and reproving :

" Quendred, how dare you be so rude to Father Bischoffs-heim ? Don't you know that priests represent God ? Come and apologize at once, and then go up to the schoolroom. I hope I shall never see such an exhibition of temper again."

The girl's natural sense of justice made her at that moment nearly hate her father.

" Oh, Duke," came the suave tones of the Jesuit, " please don't be so hard on her. I am sure she didn't mean to be rude. Come and make friends, Quendred," and, so saying he pushed his chair back from the table, holding out both hands to the girl. Her father's good-looking face was serious and stern—he was frowning slightly, but the Jesuit was smiling—smiling the maddening smile of one who is in the wrong posing as the generous spirit.

On her mother's face alone was sympathy, and the arm which was round her gave her an affectionate squeeze.

At this moment something happened inside Quendred ; one of the chords which held her spiritual anatomy together seemed to snap, and the priest suddenly appeared in the light of an enemy. Appeared as something she didn't understand, something elusive, something she couldn't trust, and she imagined her father—in a way inexplicable to herself—to be on his side—to be his accomplice. Only her mother was her friend.

This strange tumult running through her childish " ego " was, in reality, the unconscious moment of the conception of a nebulous idea which did not attain birth for many years, nor fruition till Quendred was a mother herself. But the first corner on her life's road had been turned, and Quendred received and retained the impression that her mother took her side ; fundamentally agreed with her ; did not condemn her ; was, in fact, her one rock of strength, love, kindness, and sympathy in a world—her little world—of hostility.

Quendred was tall for her ten years, with thick, pale-gold hair and fair skin, but she had her mother's dark, unfathomable eyes—eyes that seemed to understand all the mysteries of the ages, and these were fringed by long, upturned, black lashes. Anthony, on the contrary, was like his father, a true Fitz-Urse; tall and slender, with rippling corn-coloured hair and grey-blue eyes. His disposition, however, was far more that of a Latin than of an Anglo-Saxon, and he had not inherited the puritanical characteristics inherent—though quite unconsciously—in most British men, no matter their religion, status, or temperament.

Latins of all races know by nature how best to enjoy life. They are not always *trying* to enjoy it as we do, they do not need riches—as we think we do—to taste of its savour. They just *do* enjoy it. It's their gift, their inheritance, born in them from thousands of years of hot, blue skies, and hot, golden sun which gives them their ardour and their passion; of oily food which makes them easy-going and good-natured; of the gift of natural, spontaneous song which makes them romantic. But it's the sun, above everything, which gives the Latin his inborn and spontaneous joy in living, and this is what we poor Northerners lack, frozen to the marrow as we are by day after day of sunlessness.

In her bedroom that night Maddalena reflected deeply on her and Stephen's lives, with the result that the future seemed to her eminently unsatisfactory. As she pondered, the riddle became more and more difficult to unravel. *She* had not changed. Her love was stronger and deeper than when she had promised to marry him, and she was far lovelier and more desirable now than then. She was only twenty-nine, and at the height of her beauty.

Several men had wished to be allowed to love her, and had tried to tell her so, but, caring as she did for her husband, their love held no attractions for her. One especially—a shrewd observer of human beings—guessing how things were, had made certain overtures to her. She had been horrified, but it had awakened her to what was thought about her and Stephen. That this man loved her there could be no doubt, and the full meaning of that terrible evening at Santa Fiora suddenly burst upon her in all its force. The loneliness of her pretty mother's life, and her difficulties—like hers in a way, and yet unlike. Her father had only been undeveloped and stupid and selfish, but her husband was something quite different. She wondered impotently how devout

H

one could be without becoming peculiar, and whether it was a necessity to make religion a bugbear in life, in order to be pious ?

But the memory of her mother in Lepantchine's arms ; his heavy breathing, his stealthy entrance through the window to her bedroom, all frightened her to-night, and she longed for Stephen's presence and for his love. Everything seemed so desolate, and she felt very lonely.

" Why was Stephen so changed ? " she asked herself. Was it her fault ? Was it something she did, or was, or looked, or seemed, that in some small way displeased him ? She longed to live the natural life with him again, but she realized that he was always slowly retreating from her. What did it all mean ? She knew there was no woman he cared for, and then, against her will, she was forced to realize that it was religion which had him in her grasp.

Religion ! How far the word had slipped away from the Apostle James's original explanation of it ! Religion ! Religion ! Religion ! with all its tortuous rules, so capably invented by subtle brains to torture and circumvent ordinary men's minds, and which so often takes away God's wonderful simple peace from our souls. For indeed it was religion, masquerading as the spirit of God, which had become between her and her Stephen.

So bitterly did she feel the estrangement that she almost wished it was a woman he loved, a warm, human woman, no matter how cruel. Such an one could only have seduced him with her physical charms, unenduring and evanescent. She could have managed a woman. But what power had she against this frigid, terrible mistress who had enslaved her husband's mind, his senses and his imagination ? What power had she to shatter these torturing scruples, which every day gave birth to new ones, and which were by degrees enveloping his whole being, and bending his erstwhile easy and attractive personality to her cold, stern, and all-compelling will ?

At the idea Maddalena shuddered ; it frightened her.

Surely it wasn't necessary to be like Stephen if one was a devout Catholic ? she thought, and, although brought up so unquestioningly in that Faith herself, doubts as to its perfect truth and entire Godliness sometimes assailed her mind. Since living for nearly twelve years in England she had made friends with many charming, good, spiritual and intellectual Protestants, and the result of their talks had been that she sometimes wondered if she had not been taught a lot of obscure nonsense, and unmeaning moonshine ? Although she had never outwardly swerved in loyalty to the Church of her education, her thoughtful mind could not but be aware that there was much truth in what these friends had said.

Since she had been in England she had seen aspects of life and religion which do not exist in Catholic countries. She had seen people of the same society—who, speaking the same language, honouring the same king, paying the same taxes, fighting for the same country, and obeying the same laws, equal at every other point of life—parted by the marriage laws of the Catholic Church ; parted on the basic rock and reason for all social life and pleasant intercourse. On all other things she saw them mix ; in sport, in business, in philanthropy, in politics, in adultery, in vice, and in virtue ; but in marriage and in prayer alone they are parted ; parted by the illogically expedient, yet adamantine voice from across the mountains.

She wished that she could sometimes talk about things which troubled her with Stephen, but, as Dogma was just as fallible, perplexing and debatable to her, as it was infallible, clear and conclusive to him, she had soon realized how unwise and unpleasant any discussions of this sort would be.

" Tell me why the teaching of the Jesus of the Gospels isn't good enough for Catholics ? " a great friend had said to her lately. " Why do His words need titivating, developing and explaining ? When He uttered them they were so plain ; have not the Latin expounders made them more difficult of comprehension ? Why meddle with Divine words ? Can fallen man improve upon the teaching of the Sinless One ? Why does your Church think it so necessary to mediate when He so distinctly insists that He is the sole Mediator ? What can prelates offer spiritually that is better than what God offers ? "

" They offer Sacraments," Maddalena had said gravely, " and these, with the Mass, are what we Catholics live on."

" Yes," her friend had answered, " I know, but even their number have been changed during the last thousand years, and neither the great Bernard of Clairvaux, nor yet Thomas Aquinas looked upon Baptism as a Sacrament at all, the latter holding that circumcision took away, not only the effects of original sin, but of actual sin as well ; what about the poor little girls, one naturally asks ? But why do you even believe the Pope *is* infallible ? Saint Jerome—and he was far enough back, in all conscience—maintained that the authority of Rome was but the authority of a single bishop. I can never understand how a fallible body of men could have made an infallible pronouncement, as they were supposed to have done at the Vatican Council, and, so little did many others understand it, that most of the best and most erudite Catholic opinion of the day was against it. Because these men could not conscientiously bring their minds to toe the line to the whim of an Italian Pope, your Church lost some of her best, holiest, and cleverest men.

" Infallibility will, however, always be a stumbling block, for no one can say where, exactly, it lies. It seems to me like a will o' the wisp, intangible, elusive ; rather like Sir Richard Boyle's bird ! Apparently a Pope may convoke a particular Synod and, in unison with it, define an Infallible doctrine, or it seems that he may call a General Council to make a decision on Faith and Morals, which is Infallible ; or again, I am told, the Church dispersed all over the world may make an Infallible rule ! I would like to know whether the Pope can make an Infallible decision absolutely on his own, so to speak, without consulting Cardinals, or Synods, or Bishops dispersed through the world ? "

But Maddalena didn't know. Such thoughts had never come her way in her Italian home, where all such things were taken for granted.

" Our priests study all those technical questions," she had answered, with a puzzled look in her lovely eyes, " and we just believe broadly what they tell us ; it's so much easier and nicer."

" That wouldn't do for me," her friend had answered. " If I thought anything was worth believing in, to the infinite extent all Roman Catholics believe in their religion, I'd never be satisfied till I was the master of it, and all its intricacies and subtleties ! "

" But Catholics aren't *allowed* to think," Maddalena had answered.

" Yes, I know," her friend had laughed. " When people are interested enough in religious matters to seek to drink at the spring themselves, and, in consequence, can no longer hold the same views as they were taught in childhood, they are called ' heretics ' ! What a stigma is attached to those simple little words ' I choose ' ! "

" What a lot you seem to know about our religion ! " Maddalena had said on this occasion. " Why don't you join it ? You'd make a splendid Catholic ! "

" You *sweet !* What a typical remark," her friend had answered. " We always want to make everyone else do what we like doing ourselves ! If we are drunkards, everyone else must be drunkards ; if we are Swedish exercise maniacs, all our friends must at once twist and turn their limbs for ten minutes every morning !

" No, I could never join your Church, because I am born with an ingrained tendency to doubt, and a disposition to accept all received opinions with the greatest reserve. Always I have been listening to what Tennyson calls ' the two voices,' and sometimes many more ! I have not got the dogmatic temperament. Newman said that no English people have. It has to be drilled in them, he always maintained."

Maddalena hadn't answered, but the woman's words had sunk into her heart, and, secretly, views that she had always held to be of unassailable integrity, assumed in her mind a different angle.

And now, in the disillusionment of her married life, Maddalena wondered how much her religion of laws and rules could comfort her ?

" Of course, Faith is everything," she muttered. " I keep on saying ' I believe in God,' and yet I don't suppose I really believe properly at all. If He is Almighty He could help me in my trouble. I *must* get my Stephen back. I must, and I will. I love him, I want him. I am his, why can't he be mine ? My darling, my husband, and once my truest lover. That he loves me still I know, and anyone daring to say different, lies. I'm his wife, and who should know if I don't know ? "

Her room was dark, and she stood in her white nightgown looking out on to the shimmering leaves of the trees in the Square. It was a beautiful, warm, dark blue night, and a slim moon hung over Lansdowne House.

A dull weight lay upon her heart, for there she had the fluttering feeling, the nervousness of the unknown, which wakes us up at night when our minds are laden with worry or sorrow. And again her mind flew back to that terrible night at Santa Fiora ; that liquid night in Italy ; that night of her betrothal to Stephen, when all the world seemed hers and when, half drunk with happiness, she had leant across the window sash of her little virginal bedroom, thinking unspeakable thoughts ; lovely, rapturous thoughts. What a wonderful day it had been, and then—what a terrible, sickening night. A night in which she had leapt with a fearful suddenness from innocence to knowledge, from the sunlit heights of her childhood to the depths of the realization of evil. But even that horror had not overpowered her so much as the feeling which possessed her to-night ; the feeling that her Stephen was changed ! What would eventually happen, she wondered ? Things couldn't go on as at present. Could their love ever become less and dwindle to passive philosophical indifference ? Could such a horrible thing happen ? And—as though pressing away some loathsome animal—she pressed her hands forward through the unresisting air.

Turning from the window her eyes fell upon the white marble statue of the Saviour—the same which stands above Paris on the lurid heights of Montmartre. It was lit up by the ruby lamp which gleamed through the darkness, and which shone upon the outstretched, everlasting Arms.

" Come unto Me all ye that are heavy laden, and I will give you rest," it seemed to say to her.

Sinking on to her knees, she murmured, with profound feeling, " I do come. Give me back my Stephen's love. Make him remember those words again that he was not ashamed to vow to me before You on our wedding day.

" Did he not proudly say that he worshipped me with his body—in Your name ; that he wedded me with a ring of gold— in Your name ; that he endowed me with all his worldly goods in Your name ? Did he not promise to comfort and cherish me, and forsake all other for me ? *Make* him keep those promises ; *make* him see that any other call is wrong, and is breaking his marriage vows."

And so she prayed with an ardent tempestuous prayer— fiercely. Then, getting quietly into bed, she prepared herself calmly for rest.

In some indescribable way a feeling of safety and consolation had come to her.

.   .   .   .   .   .

After a little while she heard a noise ; sitting up, she listened breathlessly. Then a soft tap came on the door, and Stephen's voice said :

" Maddalena, are you asleep ? May I come in ? "

She thrilled ! It was like a lover coming and yet—how marvellous—it was her husband !

"Come in," she answered very low.

Gently he tiptoed across the room, and knelt down beside her bed on the soft carpet.

"Darling—may I? Do you mind my coming? But somehow—a few minutes ago—I felt impelled to come and explain something to you, something that I think it is right that I should tell you."

"Do you want to stay, Stephen?" she asked tremulously.

"If you will let me."

In a second she was in his arms.

Then, with her lashes flickering against his face, he told her of the pent-up agony that he had suffered during the past years, on account of the desire of his adolescence to have been a priest. Of how wicked he had come to think his life with her was, firstly, because of his having married her while he felt he had a vocation, and secondly, on account of the solemn pact he had made with God on the night of the birth of the twins.

He told her of his promise that if she was spared to him he would in future lead a life of renunciation; a celibate's life.

The proverbial feather could have knocked Maddalena down at that moment. She was so surprised at the unexpectedness of this sudden confession, she was so aghast at what the confession had revealed.

So now at last she knew! She knew that it was *fear* which ruled his soul, and, indeed, his whole being. Was this fear, she wondered, the result of superstition, or religion, or love? But no matter, for whatever it was the result of, it had produced misery; a broken married life, a wretched tortured man, and a sad, disillusioned woman.

"But, darling," she whispered, "did you not think of me? Surely you knew how I adored you? That you were the beginning and end of my happiness? You knew we were one? You were the prince of my heart. Did you think it fair to make such a promise? Had you forgotten your marriage vows to me?"

"My marriage vows!" he said, astonished. "Why, I never thought I was breaking them! From that point of view I suppose it *was* wrong. I never thought of it like that! But you were so dreadfully ill, and I nearly mad with grief. I had to do something, and I felt that sacrifice would appeal to God, and perhaps induce Him to answer my prayer. And then—

when you got well, I was in the most terrible dilemma, no one knows how I have suffered all these years."

"Why do you believe that God loves sacrifice so much, Stephen ?" she asked him.   "He says He will have mercy and not sacrifice."

"That was the form my prayer took in my agony," her husband replied, "and I felt bound in honour to keep it.   But to-night a strange power seemed to take hold of me, and forced me to come to you.   Even now I don't know whether it is right or wrong."

As he spoke a look of fear and worry came into the face of the weak, vacillating Duke.   "But," he went on, "anyhow, I've come, and oh, darling, I'm so happy."

The terrible strain was over, and for the time being he seemed to be at rest.   But was the change real ?   Was it lasting ? Even Stephen himself didn't know, so how should you or I ?

Between these two there was, for a time, a deep silence.   The clock ticked gently, the bell of a belated hansom tinkled in the distance, and the "clop-clop" of the horses' feet on the wood pavement got louder, and became softer again.

Maddalena lay very still, thinking deeply.

"So now I know," she said to herself.   "He wanted to be a priest before he knew me, and so it was against his will that he loved me.   In reality then, I suppose I represent something evil in his life ?   I'm a lure, a temptress ; I'm the forbidden fruit whose witchery enticed him from the priesthood, and therefore, *he* thinks, from God !   Yet to me it was all so perfect, and so right.   I danced into it, unfettered, triumphant.   How little did I think that the man whom I believed to love me as I loved him was coming with me unwillingly to the altar ?   How could I know that at the bottom of him, his whole being cried out and revolted against my power over him ?   How could I have imagined that he—although perhaps unconsciously—resented the spell I had cast over him, and that he was, on our wedding day, a constrained prisoner in my heart where no one but he had ever reigned nor ever would reign ?

"He *did* love me, though," she thought fiercely.   "I know he did.   He worshipped and adored me, and it's religion that has torn him from my side.   I—I could almost hate religion !"

Suddenly Stephen held her closer, and his kisses banished for the moment her bitter musings.   Again and again he told her how much he loved her, of how much he had wanted her all these years, and of how well-nigh unendurable the separation had been.

Although deeply wounded and unutterably saddened at what he had just told her, Maddalena, nevertheless, felt intense happiness at their re-union.

Just now she felt that nothing else really mattered. Stephen loved her still—loved her as he had done on the road to Santa Barbara.

" You don't know how lonely I've been all these years, my darling," she whispered, " and how much I have longed that all might come right again between us."

And so after ten long years Maddalena once more fell asleep in the crook of his arm, and her soft breathing beat gently against his heart.

CHAPTER VIII

THE UNSEEN LURE

" To love you is pleasant enough,
  And oh ! 'tis delicious to hate you."
                              —THOMAS MOORE.

A FEW days later their new-found happiness was broken into by a telegram from Rome saying that Cardinal Costanzi was dying, and Maddalena at once started off so as to be near him at the last. She took Quendred with her.

Stephen—wonderfully happy at their joyous re-union—was feeling especially lonely without Maddalena, and so, after a solitary dinner in Berkeley Square, he walked through the mellow summer evening to Farm Street church, where the last sermon of a series for men only was being delivered by a renowned preacher.

As he entered the building the thick, unpleasant odour of humanity, mixed with stale incense, which assailed his nostrils, almost made him recoil, but the note of a pulsing and attractive voice held his attention forcibly enough to compel him to enter the already overcrowded church.

From the excited pitch of the preacher's tone and the tense quiet which brooded over the congregation, Stephen knew that the sermon was drawing to its close.

From where he stood leaning against a pillar he could well see the figure which swayed backwards and forwards in the pulpit.

He was a tall man and of a big-built frame, yet emaciated to an extraordinary degree. His head was that of a thinker, but not a dreamer ; an organizer, not a shatterer. He was an affirmation, not a negation.

A generator of impulses, a creature of " verve," action,

vim, and ardour ; a live wire, healthy, strong and determined, seemingly profoundly believing every word he spoke.

There was no unsubstantiality, no vacillation about this man, and as Stephen listened he became in some curious way caught up most powerfully in the atmosphere the priest had created, and he was held there, thrilled and absorbed.

The voice was saying :

" Give not the power of thy soul to a woman, lest she enter upon thy strength, and thou be confounded. For many have perished by the beauty of a woman, and hereby lust is enkindled as a fire.

" Thus, my dear brethren, did Solomon of old warn all men against the sex, and he very plainly shows us that the foibles of women must never be allowed to get the better of us—must never be allowed to enter upon our strength and confound us.

" Life is one long fight with self, and self is carnal. Women are undoubtedly God's greatest and most wonderful achievement—with their alluring physical attributes, their soft voices, and their dancing feet ! Yet, just because they are His greatest work, they are Satan's most deadly weapon.

" No one and nothing was ever better devised to ruin and debilitate man than woman. She deprives him of his strength, she blunts his edge, she weakens his will power—in a word—she unmans him.

" Although she has been and will ever be, the spur to many of his finest deeds, she can be, has been, and always will be, the drag on his best self, the effeminizer of his greatest impulses, and the destroyer of the wall he has been trained to build round himself to keep immune from her attacks

" She is always attacking, my friends—always. Let there be no mistake about that ! If not in one way, then in another. Even your wives—with the secure legal and Christian position they hold as such in our modern civilization—even *they* can be a form of temptation in so far that they can work upon a man's mentality—just because he is their husband—to make him do something which perhaps his inmost self, his best and truest self, tells him is wrong."

" And so woman remains ever the temptress, as she was planned to be by the Creator in the Garden of Eden. The temptress who lures us, the avalanche which destroys us, the tigress who tears at our hearts, the turtle-dove who softly calls to us. Our sun who burns us up, our moon whose cool curves

she has stolen, our laughing syren, our tender love whose voice
whispers to us like the gentle swaying of the tree-tops. Ice
which freezes us, a drug which stupifies us, and the great everlasting fire by whose ardent burning the world is kept going.

" For, believe me, my friends, that woman is fire and man
is tow. Beware lest your tow—always inflammable—be ignited
by the wrong person, or for the wrong motive. That you may
preserve intact your strength against all such temptations, is
a blessing I wish you all. In the name of the Father, and of
the Son, and of the Holy Ghost. Amen."

The preacher vaguely drew the Sign of the Cross in the air
over the heads of the dark-garbed throng, and then slowly and
pensively descended from his castle ; coward's castle, as pulpits
have been somewhat aptly named.

Preceded by the cleanly-scrubbed little boy in scarlet cassock
and amazingly starched and pleated surplice, holding a book
sedately in front of his nose, he walked quietly back to the altar
through the packed congregation.

Kneeling in a quiet corner, Stephen sank his head into his
hands. What he had just heard hurt terribly, and it revolted
him too—he who had just re-married, so to speak, his wonderful
wife.

But the words of the preacher wouldn't be silenced, and
again they returned to his mind, making him wonder feebly at
first, and then more definitely, whether last night's happiness
had been sinful or not ?

The sermon, he mused, seemed to have been invented for
him, and for him alone ; surely to no other man in the church
could it have appealed with just such particular bitterness as
it did to him ? And, thinking thus, he knelt on until the church
was silent and deserted, and only the red lamp shone softly,
flickering rosily through the growing gloom.

Much despondency had entered Stephen's heart again. Once
more, as usual, he was vacillating and wondering. He blew
hot and cold ; he knew not what to be about.

He loved Maddalena so dearly at the bottom of his heart,
and the recent renewal of that love had made him calm and
happy, but what had this priest just said ? Was she really the
temptress luring him from the high things ? Was she the one
whom he must push away if he wanted to follow the highest
and the best of his inspirations ?

Thus tortured in mind and body he arose and, as was his

habit, sought again advice and support, unable as usual to make up his mind himself as to his course of action. Going to the sacristy he asked whether he could speak with Father Ignatius.

"I am he," said a deep, low voice from within the church, and from out of the dimness came forth the tall figure of the preacher.

"Can I help you in any way, my son?" he asked kindly.

"Yes, Father," Stephen answered nervously, "I want to speak to you. I live quite near here. Could you come back with me for a few minutes to my house?"

"Surely, my son," answered the gracious, gentle voice.

As Stephen bent to unlock the door, the light of the street lamp fell obliquely on to his face. Waves of teasing remembrance came to the priest, and for a minute he felt convinced that he had seen this man before. The remembrance was disturbing, but would not be located.

"Come to the library," said Stephen, "it is the only room fit to sit in now. My wife has just gone to Rome, and everything is put away."

Intrigued, the priest followed the stranger silently, wondering in whose house he had suddenly found himself. Stephen flicked an electric bulb and, as the light flooded the room, it revealed to the Jesuit's astonished gaze a large picture of a woman with a little girl hanging over her shoulder. The picture hung opposite to him on the wall as he entered the room.

"Bianca! By all that's wonderful!" his mind flashed, with a swift return to past emotions of passion. Just so had she been when he had loved her. And then—as the vision on the road to Santa Barbara faded, and the memory of his ruined career returned to him forcibly—"Princess di Santa Fiora, by all that's damnable!" he thought, with set jaw.

.   .   .   .   .   .

It was with a very definite purpose that Lepantchine—after the affair at Santa Fiora—had sold his estates in Russia.

He dropped the world out of pique, knowing full well that had he not done so it would have dropped him, for Cardinal Costanzi was right when he had said that if Gasparro didn't kill Lepantchine, he would certainly ruin him. Till his *débacle* his career and his love-affairs had been the two ruling masters of his life, and into them he had thrown his overpowerng energy.

But now all this was changed. He had made up his mind to eschew the world and, as was his custom in all he undertook, he did so as completely and unreservedly as he had hitherto pursued and enjoyed it. The priesthood and all it meant had become the dominant note in his life. With its full force his will threw off all that was worldly, and took on—with a keenness and a passion in no way inferior to his former zest for success and love of the fleshpots—the pursuance of the ascetic outlook ; the detached, cold view of life of the trained celibate.

At least, this was what he appeared to be to the world, but underneath all this affectation of austerity and aloofness there burned a passionate jealousy of earthly happiness, and a deep-seated hatred of the innocent Maddalena, wholly incompatible with his priestly vocation.

So fanatically had he undertaken his new career that it might almost be said that he loved the suppression of love and passion with passion. Women and their lure became to him as a red rag to a bull ; the incarnation of all that was evil ; the eternal temptress ; the seducers of men ; the burning flame that lit only to destroy ; the untiring pursuer of man and their ultimate wrecker.

To elude and circumvent was now in his eyes commendable ; to overcome her he thought praiseworthy.

So imbued did he at last become with the certainty that it was his rôle to be a scourge in this respect, that he came to regard himself as the mouthpiece of the Most High in warning men against the danger of women, and innoculating them, so to speak, with a mental germ which would safeguard them against the perverse advances and the tigerish instincts of the female race as a whole, and of individual women in particular. He was the enemy of all women in the abstract, but particularly was he the enemy of Maddalena Seyntleger, the radiant, ardent girl who had saved her mother's virtue, and ruined his career.

But, strange as it may seem, this fact was so deeply buried in his inmost self-consciousness that he was practically unconscious that this emotion was indeed the spur to the whole of his life as a priest.

So burning was his rhetoric in this cause, so striking his delivery, and in such a lofty way did he phrase his arguments, that it was not long before his fame as an orator and almost indeed as a " holy man " spread throughout Europe.

As was fitting, London very soon secured the services of

this eminent ecclesiastic, and a set of sermons, " For Men Only,'' was arranged to be given by him at Farm Street.

Under the non-committal name of Father Ignatius, S. J., Lepantchine—unknown to and unsuspected by any of those persons concerned in the tragedy of Santa Fiora, or indeed to anybody else—took London by storm. His forcible and trenchant sayings, his peculiarities of style, the aptness of his imagery, together with an undeniably attractive personality, soon made him one of the most widely discussed figures of the day. When he preached the church was crowded, and men of all creeds and of all stations in life flocked to hear him.

Statesmen rubbed shoulders with crossing-sweepers ; Bishops with free-thinking journalists ; while princes, bookies, publicans, and missionaries, all sat cheek by jowl under the pulpit, whence flowed a stormy castigation of human frailties not surpassed since the days of Savonarola.

No subject was left untouched in the sermons, and the most stagnant minds went home whipped up by the lash of his tongue.

Much controversy was raised by his attacks, and the papers were full of letters, both signed and unsigned, protesting against, or agreeing with, his very pronounced views on women.

Where was her vindicator ? the papers asked. Would one arise ? Did she need one ? What in reality was she at the bottom, with all her trappings torn off ? A mother ? A temptress ? A wife ? An angel in disguise ? A snake ? Man's better part ? A virgin by choice ? or—always and ever—a rake at heart ?

.   .   .   .   .   .

There are many sides to romance, and romance in some form or other is the spur to the actions of the majority of extraordinary men.

Not only is love romance, but hate is also, and power, and wealth, and business, and philanthropy, and revenge. If certain men once dream a dream that seems to them worth dreaming, they will never cease to act until that dream has become a reality, and Lepantchine was such a man.

Since he had stood on the drawbridge of Santa Fiora watching the sun transfuse the mists of morning which clung round the Castle of the shattered dreams of his materialism, another dream than love or than hate had taken possession of his being, and that dream was revenge.

Now Lepantchine, as long as he had life in him, had to act. He was positive, not negative. If his powers were thwarted in one way, they must find an outlet in another.

If Lepantchine cannot live on in the reproduction of his species, or in a wordly career of social and official successes, he must live on in other ways, and it was thus that he realized most fully that love is not the only expression of romance.

In the strangest way and entirely unsought by him, fate—if there be such a thing—had cast him on to the doorstep of the only woman who had ever frustrated his desires. To his mentality this was an extremely pleasant and dramatic development in the game of life.

Obeying Stephen's slight gesture he sank into a comfortable arm-chair near the open window, through which was wafted a gentle moonlit air, bearing upon its breast those London sounds which come so softly into such sheltered spots as these, and drug the senses so efficiently as to almost make their owners oblivious to the fact that the great city has other aspects than that of rich ease, beauty, peace and seclusion.

Thus quietly, silently—and with no suspicion on Stephen's part that anything but Godliness was emanating from his priestly companion—was the second act rung up in the romance of revenge which obsessed Lepantchine's life.

Completely master of himself, Father Ignatius sat at the window while Stephen—a prey to his nerves, his sense of duty to God, and his newly-awakened passion for his wife—feverishly paced the thick carpet, stopping now and then to touch some small object lying about the room, or to pass his hand over his hair, now darkly golden.

Said the priest : " You are worried, my son ; you need advice, help ? I can see that for some reason you are deeply moved. Can I be the instrument of my Divine Master in giving you any kind of solace ? "

The low voice—the wonderful voice which in the old days had made him, against her better self, the master of Bianca—had lost neither power nor sweetness. Above all things, the voice of Lepantchine was the voice of the wooer.

Immediately Stephen was charmed ; the flood-gates of his being were unlocked ; and the pent-up torrents of torturing scruples together with the pull of human love, cascaded from brain and heart.

Out of the tumultous flow in inchoate words endeavouring

quickly to relate ten years of agonizing doubt and fear, love and revulsion, spiritual longings and material ones, the experienced priest gathered that here indeed was a case to his hand.

Stephen poured forth his whole history—from the ardent Oxford days, when he learnt to love the Church of Rome, and to long to give up the world for the priesthood, till the present moment. He told how, in spite of all this, he had suddenly loved Maddalena, and of how she had—to use his own words—drawn him from spiritual things to wordly and fleshly joys.

This was the way his curious and fanatical mind looked upon his union with his wife.

So interested and lost was he in the narration of his woes and emotions, that he didn't notice the curious change which came over the priest's face as he listened to this tragic story. A story of bitterness pushing away love ; of sacrifice shuddering at gratification ; of natural, normal, affectionate life being turned into something evil and repulsive by the introspection of a neurotic, religious idealist.

The Jesuit pressed the tips of his thick white fingers together, and, as he listened to the story of this strange, egoistical weakling, his eyes narrowed, and a sphinx-like look of cold satisfaction momentarily passed over his face, but only momentarily. Then quickly again one saw the priest, the so-called healer of souls ; the Jesuit—for obvious reasons—the charmer of men.

Delightedly he recognized that here was a spirit over which he could cast the spell of his power ! That such a soul was lodged in the body of the husband of the beautiful " chit of a girl " who had robbed him of the realization of his dearest passion was infinitely gratifying to a certain part of his character, although indeed he had, to do him justice, become deeply imbued with the conviction that the priesthood is the highest call of all, and must in no circumstances be made subservient to any other, however strongly one was bound to it by legal ties. He had passed the stage when, like a dog worrying a bone, sex was a thing he could neither enjoy nor forego.

While Stephen spoke, he had nodded his head at intervals, and when the young man had finished, he let a few seconds of complete silence fill the troubled, electric air. Then he rose and laid his hand upon the Duke's shoulder.

His touch penetrated Stephen's being to its foundations. It was magnetic. It seemed to press a chord which responded to, and was completely in tune with, the great symphony of his

I

adolescence—his change of religion with its apparently natural sequel—his overwhelming desire for a celibate priesthood claiming the transcendent power of Transubstantiation.

His body, quivering nervously at the priest's mesmeric touch, slowly succumbed to the inherent power of the other, and, by degrees, a great trust in this power was to develop in his unquiet soul.

Support was what he most needed, for he could never decide for himself, and support seemed to his distressed spirit exactly what this man could give him.

" Your nerves are upset," said the priest gently, " and I don't wonder ! Seldom have I heard such a tragic story. Nevertheless, I feel that the call to the priesthood is the one which you must *not* ignore. Things are hard for you, and it looks well-nigh impossible to come to some *modus vivendi*. But I must seriously warn you that you will be doing wrong if you live with your wife any more as her husband. . . . *That* part of your life must end if you wish to please God. Whether you enter the priesthood or not is another matter, and would of course require deep consideration."

" But I vowed I would be true to my wife," said Stephen. " I vowed that I would have and hold her, for better, for worse, for richer, for poorer, in sickness and in health, to love and to cherish till death us do part, according to God's holy ordinance, and thereto I plighted her my troth. The idea of being false to this vow bothers me just as much as the feeling that I have been false to the priesthood. How *can* you tell me that it would please God for me to break my vow made according to His holy ordinance ? "

" There are some vows which it is right to break," said the priest slowly but, seeing a look of incredulous horror on the Duke's face, he changed his tactics.

" Ah, well," said he suavely, " that, of course, is a highly technical matter, and all you want to know now is how to arrange your future life as much on the right lines as possible. Is not that so ? . . . Your wife—ahem !—is she of a very ardent nature ? "

Stephen's English blood rushed to his face. Had anyone else said the words he would have shown him the door but, taught by the Church of his adoption to look upon priests as little gods, he suffered the question with a submissive equanimity of a doormat quality, only to be found in the most devout of his Faith.

"She loves me," he said hesitatingly and rather shyly, "with all her being. She is not English. I think I mean everything in the world to her—everything. Yes, indeed—she loves me very much."

"Would it be—er—great suffering to her . . . if . . . if—er—you were to live the life of a celibate?" the Jesuit asked in a voice of intense sympathy which, however, he was far from feeling.

Stephen turned his back on the priestly questioner, the Inquisitor of his soul.

To the man who had been living—self-imposed—just such an existence as was now being advised and who had, but twenty-four hours earlier, convinced himself that it was not wrong to leave it and to return once more to the woman he loved, the words of his companion were bitter in the highest degree. And yet, he cogitated, it is a priest who speaks thus to me—a clever, experienced Jesuit, whose advice I may not lightly ignore.

Frowning nervously and with twitching, sensitive lips, the weak, pious, good-looking Duke tried to answer the question he would have found intolerably obnoxious had it been put to him by any other than a priest of his own Faith.

"Yes," he answered softly, though extremely distinctly, "I think it would cause her very great suffering."

At the answer there glowed for a minute behind the veiled inscrutable eyes of Father Ignatius, the sensual eyes of Lepantchine.

For such a feast as this he had often longed when, in moments of impotent fury, he had raged against the power of Maddalena, who had been the cause of his wordly downfall, yet never in his wildest dreams of revenge had he imagined such a perfect situation as this. Before him stood the man she loved so deeply and so passionately! With a terrible feeling of animal gratification he realized that at last the tables were turned and it was now in his power to tear from her that which she loved so dearly and needed so profoundly, just as she had torn his great desire from him eleven years ago.

"Cold young fool!" he thought, as Maddalena's husband still gazed at the moon. "I always knew you weren't worthy to touch the fingers of that glowing Italian girl, even before you had so purely bestowed maternity upon her. But now I'm told she's one of Europe's beauties, and here you are asking me if you should give her up! Cold young fool! Well, you've asked

for it—you who've not got the moral or mental guts to think
for yourself—and so you shall have it ; full measure, pressed
down and brimming over. She shall have it too, that beautiful
chit of a girl who, rising from nowhere, baulked me of my one
desire, and ruined my career. Revenge is sweet—it's very, very
sweet."

    .   .   .   .   .   .

Silence fell again ; this was an encounter where silences were
more potent than words, for the matter with which they dealt
was almost beyond being adequately grasped, and dealt with
by words.

Like a scheming spider sitting in the middle of its web,
complacently biding its time till the foolish fly walks into its
parlour, Father Ignatius contemplated in silent, aloof interest
the effect of his speech on the soul of the Duke of Seyntleger.
When the interval had reached what he felt to be its proper
psychological length, he said slowly and forcefully :

" I gather, then, that your wife will feel very deeply the
separation which I feel bound—after hearing your story—to
tell you it is your duty as a Catholic to make and to keep.

" From what you tell me of your feelings for one another it
will doubtless be hard, but you must remember how intensely
pleasing to our Divine Master sacrifice is."

Half crushed, yet filled with the spirit which led the martyrs
of old to suffer the most appalling of tortures for what they
thought was the truth, Stephen turned to the great Jesuit.

Under the gaze of Lepantchine's compelling eyes, his soul
was vanquished much as Bianca's good sense had been vanquished
on the road to Santa Barbara by those same eyes, but with
a difference. Bianca had given way against her will to what she
knew was wrong ; Stephen was being forced to give up, largely
against his will, what he knew it was right to love, for a call
which so dominated one side of his character as to have completely decontrolled his power of unbiased and true judgment.

When discussed by Father Ignatius, the case, so baffling
and tormenting to him, seemed right, and sounded grand and
splendid to his mutable mentality ; so clearly put, he felt convinced that there could be no other view. Just so had Bianca
felt when he had persuaded *her* to give way to his will.

Holding out both his strong, virile hands, the priest took
Stephen's limp ones in his, saying :

" And you'll be brave, my son ?   Yes !   I know you will !
You're an English Catholic—the best Catholics in the world !
You never think for yourselves, and that, of course, is the perfect
spirit.   What the Church desires is utter and unquestioning
obedience to Her commands, and that is what the Englishman
gives whole-heartedly.   And all honour to him, for he will be
blessed—if not in this world—then in the next.   To obey blindly,
implicity ; that, of course, is the perfection of our most holy
religion.

" Good-bye.   Keep the Faith.   Fight the good fight.   Finish
the course.   If ever you need my advice do not hesitate to ask
for it.   Things may get more difficult.   I give retreats at my
headquarters in the Bavarian mountains—an ideal spot wherein
to feel the temperature of the soul !   When you need me, come !
I am your friend !   I understand.—Don't forget me.   Good-bye ! "

.   .   .   .   .   .

But as he walked back across the square he laughed to
himself, or rather he emitted a hard, mirthless chortle.

" Young idiot !   Why can't he plan out his own life himself !
Why the deuce doesn't he make up his mind and stick to it ?
I always knew he wasn't worthy to touch that girl ; God—nothing
on earth would make *me* leave her if she were my wife—not even
Lepantchine turned priest !   Cold, scrupulous young fool !
He's got what he deserves, anyhow."

CHAPTER IX

THE SHADOW OF THE DEAD HAND

" The Shadow—cloaked from head to foot
Who keeps the keys of all the creeds."
—TENNYSON.

PIETRO opened the door to Maddalena and Quendred as they ran up the stone steps to his flat.

" He is not dead ?   Tell me he is not dead ! " the former asked breathlessly.

" No, Duchessa, but he cannot live long," said the old servant.   " He is so weak, it is terrible to see him struggling for his breath.   He has denied himself all comforts.   He has had practically nothing to eat, and he won't let me get anything for him."   The faithful Pietro rubbed tears from his eyes with the back of his hand as he let them into the house of his beloved dying Cardinal.

" I sent the telegram because he was always asking for you mi'Lady.   He was always saying, ' I want my little Maddalena— I want to explain—I want her to forgive me,' and so, mi'Lady, I had to send for you, so that my Master should have peace before he dies."   He then took them both to the Cardinal.

The room in which the old man lay had nothing but bare boards for a floor, furniture of the simplest description, and no curtains or blinds to keep out the heat of the noonday glare, or the cold of winter nights.   His bed was of the roughest wood, and was composed of planks covered with a straw-filled mattress. The pillow was lumpy, and the sheets, betwixt which lay the emaciated Cardinal, were coarse and thick.

He smiled as they entered the room.

" I am so glad that you are here, Maddalena, and dear little Quendred too ! " he said, speaking with difficulty.   " But I am sorry the others haven't come, for now I shall not see them. I . . . shall be . . . gone to-night."

Maddalena took his transparent hand in hers and kissed it.

" No, no," she murmured.

He laid his hand upon Quendred's head, and looked at her with an infinite yearning love—such a look perhaps as Jesus of Nazareth had for the children of the Jews.

" To do kind actions," he went on softly, " and to keep oneself unspotted from the world, *that* is the beginning and end of all religion ! Had we poor, so-called Christians only stuck to that ideal, more than half the wars and miseries and bitterness of history would never have happened, indeed, there would hardly be any history to learn !

" Although you may not understand my words now, little Quendred, don't forget them on your journey through life. Christ has always to bear the blame though, for man's blind, insensate bigotry, and the insane results of our mad craze for place and power. My poor, gentle, beloved Christ ! I wonder what you really think of the world ! Child, my great wish for you is that you may most truly perceive the deep, hidden things of God, for it is because so many of us have failed to perceive that love of Him is transcendent, and must conquer in the end if His words mean anything at all, that we have let ourselves be deluded by dogmas and creeds, and have allowed ourselves to be terrorised at the point of spiritual bayonets with man-made laws for the sake of human expediency. . . . Man-made religions must, perforce, become idolatrous. But when you have taken hold of Jesus Christ and have grappled with Him —in the way a pianist grapples with his scales, an actor with his part, or a mathematician with his Euclid—then you will know Him, and only then will you come to enjoy Him as the pianist, the actor, and the mathematician have come to enjoy the fruit of their work, fruit they have given their sinews to possess.

" Then, and only then, will the garment of your Faith, little Quendred, be of such surpassing whiteness so as to dazzle the eyes of every understanding, and when the soul has put on such a gown it becomes invisible and inaccessible to the Evil One and needs indeed no other props. You can then resist Satan, being steadfast in Faith. Faith such as I wish for *you*, is the Devil's strongest and most cunning foe !

" Over the shining, white garment of Faith put on the green coat of Hope. Hope will fill your soul with such energy and resolution, such longings for eternal things, that, in comparison, wordly affairs will lose much value.

"And lastly, you shall don the crimson cloak of Love. This splendid robe will so enhance the beauty of your Soul that it will protect it from all sin for, where there is a true Love of God, there is no room for self-love or self-indulgence. Do not let anything lead you away from the simple teaching of Christ, Quendred.

"In inventing dogmas and creeds and heresies and religions men have tried to do better than the Founder of Christianity. What He taught was too simple and straightforward for their great, scheming, artificial minds to ' descend ' to ! . . .

"With avidity we swallow man-made religions. . . . but we will have none of Christ's Christianity. Since I have become an old man I have often wondered whether . . . indeed, creeds are not millstones round the neck of truth ? "

A film gathered over his eyes for a minute, and he paused after such a long effort. He sighed with relief as though something he had long wanted to say had, at the eleventh hour, been said.

He seemed now to be nothing but spirit ; it seemed as though it was no longer a human being who spoke to them, but some star from another sphere that had, for the moment, come to give the earth a message.

Then he said very softly :

"God bless you, Maddalena and Quendred . . . dear children ! May He be with you in all your ways . . . and may you find the Kingdom of God ! It is not far to seek," and he smiled wonderfully. "It is within you ! "

His voice failed, and his head turned weakly on the pillow. Quendred's eyes looked enormous, and were full of sad, excited wonder.

"No one has ever talked to me like this before," said she to her mother. "I feel just as though I have been listening to God talking ! Uncle Guiseppe's voice sounds like a deep, silver bell ever so far off, and when he puts his hand upon my head I have a kind of funny feeling that I want to shiver, although I am so hot ; and since I have been in his room I feel quite light—as though I could just fly like a bird ; Mother, it's so wonderful ! "

Her mother, thinking the child was being too deeply excited by this strange experience, gave her over to the care of Pietro and his wife, and then returned to the Cardinal.

"Maddalena," he said gently, "I have something to say to you before I die. . . . Did—Stephen ever—tell you that—he wished—to enter—the priesthood? It may—or—may not have—been—a real—call. . . . In his state it was . . . very hard to tell."

Maddalena nodded her head.

"I knew something about it," she said.

With difficulty he took a little key from a chain round his neck.

"Will you—open that drawer? In it—you will—find a letter. Do not—read it—now, but it will—explain—many things. We all—his father, the Pope and I—may have been mistaken ; these things of the—soul are so—difficult. Is it not —best perhaps to—leave them—alone ? "

He lay quietly for a little while—his thin lips moving slightly. . . . Then he spoke again.

" For the last ten years," he said, " I have thought ceaselessly —of you, for you had hinted to me—that all was not well between you—and Stephen, and yet you had no idea—what the cause of it—could be ? I was so upset that you—were worried. I wanted to tell you—something, and yet again I thought it would be better in many ways—not to tell you, and so then the years passed—and you, my dear, good little niece—*you* had to suffer— the consequences of the thoughtless, selfish, and foolish acts of three men who all had—more or—less, I suppose—persuaded themselves that they were doing right. Again we—were all hoodwinked by that disastrous idea that—the end justifies —the means——"

He fell back quite exhausted, and, as he uttered the last words, a smile that was almost bitter in its self-condemnation hovered like a wraith over his pale, compressed lips.

The woman kneeling by the bedside gazed at him with wide uncomprehending eyes. She couldn't understand his speech ; he was referring to things about which she knew nothing. She thought that Stephen's confession to her in Berkeley Square had been the whole explanation, and yet now she was on the verge of hearing something else—or was the old man wandering ?

She took his hand and held it in hers.

" There is nothing to forgive, dearest Uncle Guiseppe," she whispered in his ear ; " you have always been my best and truest friend."

" There is," he gasped. " Unwittingly I—they—we all—

did you a great injury, but I—can't tell you—I—don't—dare.
Read the letter. Then you'll understand. I did what Stephen's
father asked me to do, but now I know what a mistake it all
was."

She saw he was failing every second, and all this talking
had been more of a strain than he could bear.

"I forgive you," she said in a loud, distinct tone. At
the words a smile of unutterable sweetness, peace, and gratitude
lit up his transparent face, and, although she knew not what
she had forgiven, she was glad that she had done what he wanted.

Suddenly the Cardinal held up both emaciated arms as though
greeting someone. His eyes shone, his lips smiled.

"My Lord and my God!" he sighed, and then his Soul
slipped away.

　　　·　　　·　　　·　　　·　　　·　　　·

After the funeral the Seyntlegers with their children went
to spend a month at Santa Fiora.

One day Stephen and Maddalena walked up the road to
Santa Barbara and, stopping at the wayside Crucifix, they sat
on the hot grass, and gazed at the billowing fields at their feet,
already golden with the promise of harvest. It was the first
time they had been there since they had become engaged eleven
years ago.

In Maddalena's pocket lay the letter which the Cardinal
had given her—unopened. She was uncertain what to do with
it, although she knew that she would never open it herself.
Something told her that it would bring yet more ideals crashing
down about her head. But, of course, she thought, Stephen
must be told about it.

Still overjoyed at the happiness which had been theirs in
London such a few days ago, Maddalena was almost like an
engaged girl once more. She was intensely happy that they
were lovers again, and the sadness that she felt at the Cardinal's
death seemed to be less poignant in this precious spot, hallowed
with such delicious memories for her.

Slipping her arm through Stephen's she whispered :

"Do you remember that other time when we sat here?
That wonderful day when you told me that you loved me! I
was not forward then—I was a shy maid, though idiotically in
love. But now I am a forward hussy, and I tell you shamelessly
that I love you as no woman has ever before loved any man.

Are you glad? Does it please you? Are you proud that your pretty wife is so crazy about you—for I am pretty, Stephen, am I not? Look at me, and tell me that I am beautiful."

She glanced at his face—his so-loved face, and, in that millionth part of a second, all the fine rapture of love's re-birth fled screaming, terrified, from her happy heart.

For the look she saw was cold, stern, and preoccupied; it was the old, tortured, haunted look of the hunted animal which she knew so well, for it had lurked in his eyes for years. It had disappeared as though by magic in that unforgettable night in Berkeley Square, but now she saw, to her horror, that it was in possession again, and she knew that a stone wall stood once more between him and her.

"What can have happened to him during these days," she wondered. "What has made him go back to the old unhappiness which I had hoped we had bridged for ever?"

Stephen seemed as though surrounded by a prickly hedge. He was unapproachable. Apparently completely indifferent, he sat smoking a cigarette, and moodily poking the earth with his foot.

"Yes, Maddalena, I remember," was all he said.

She started to her feet.

"Stephen!" she cried, "what has happened? A few days ago we were happy—radiant; we were lovers. Aren't you happy now?"

"Are you?" he replied nervously and coldly, with averted face.

And thus was the poison given, the shaft sent to a vital spot.

With one short, swift blow all her love, her ardour, her resilience was struck at, and life seemed once again to be dull, hopeless, and dead.

She recoiled from him as though he had struck her, and she could not find words to answer, for she had nothing sensible in heart or mind she wished to transmit.

"I don't know," she faltered dully. "I thought in London that I was. I thought we both were. But now—I just can't understand you. Do you regret our marriage?"

He flushed.

"No, of course I don't. How can you ask such a foolish question! I've got the best wife in the world, why should I regret it?" And then there was a deadly silence.

.   .   .   .   .   .

When he spoke again he had changed the *venue* of their conversation and he didn't return to it again for many years.

"I went to see the Pope after Uncle Guiseppe's funeral," he said, "and he has promised to hear the twins' First Confessions before we return to England. I think he was rather surprised that it hadn't been made sooner, and, of course, I couldn't tell him that it was on account of your wishes that it had been put off till so late. Most children make it at seven."

"Seven years old seems so very young to begin to make their minds dwell upon the introspection of sin," said Maddalena. "I do hate introspections, although I fully appreciate the value of making them learn as young as possible the difference between right and wrong. But sin! They don't know what sin is, thank God! Sin is something utterly evil, loathesome, and hideous!—willingly done with the intention of hurting our Saviour. Ten is surely quite young enough"? And she thought of Lepantchine's wicked, lustful eyes, and then compared them to Anthony's large blue ones; and of Quendred's soft dark ones looking innocently into hers as, every evening, she kissed them good night.

And then her mind flew right away, and she was hardly conscious that Stephen was speaking. It distressed her to feel how all his ideas were beginning to bore her, and yet they were the ideas of the man of her heart, the man of her choice, the father of her children.

In a flash her mind went back over the years to the day of *her* First Confession.

On this occasion she was seven years old, and her mother and her governess had been explaining it to her for some time, and now that the day had come she was trembling with nervousness. How well and distinctly she remembered it all!

Her mother had taken her to the chapel and left her there alone, saying that Father Thomas, a Franciscan who was staying with them for the occasion, would soon come. She was so frightened that she could hardly kneel still, and every now and then she looked furtively behind her at the tall, dark confessional, which seemed enormous and out of all proportion to her excited imagination.

"I can't go in there," she whispered, half crying, to herself, and an uncomfortable lump came into her throat. "I can't, I can't! I'm sure there's a bear in there." (Till she was years older she had lurking fears that bears would pounce out upon her from behind doors in lonely parts of the house, but she had never told anyone of these fears.)

The silence of the church was broken by tiny, frightened sobs, and meanwhile she tried to remember the little list of sins which her governess had told her to say. Nervously she counted them on her fingers for fear she would forget one—for if she missed one out it would be a sin, too. Then she went over the formula, her knees shivering :

"When I go into the Confessional I must say—' I confess to Almighty God, to Blessed Mary, ever Virgin, to Blessed Michael the Archangel, to Blessed John the Baptist, to the Holy Apostles, Peter and Paul, and to all the Saints, that I have sinned exceedingly in thought, word, and deed ' " (how could a child of seven have sinned *exceedingly* in thought, word and deed ?) thought Maddalena—" ' through my fault, through my fault, through my most grievous fault.' " (Here she had to beat her breast three times.) " ' Therefore, I beseech Thee, Blessed Mary, ever Virgin, Blessed Michael the Archangel, Blessed John the Baptist, the Holy Apostles, Peter and Paul, and all the Saints, to pray to the Lord our God for me.' "

And then, she supposed tearfully, she would begin somehow like this :

" Please, Father, I disobeyed Signorina Melzi; and I wouldn't eat my pudding when Papa told me to at luncheon and . . . oh, yes ! . . . I was very rude to Maria, and told her she had enormous feet and a moustache ; and I—I——" But at that moment the door of the Church opened rather noisily, and the tall, brown-robed, sandalled figure of Father Thomas came in.

Maddalena remembered how violently she had started at that moment, and how suddenly she had become so abjectly terrified that a domestic tragedy occurred, so that, when the priest came and took her gently by the hand, there was a tiny pool to be seen on the blue tiled floor.

More nervous than ever he led her toward the Confessional, but as he did so she had pulled away from him.

" What is it, my dear little child ? " he asked kindly.

" I can't, oh, I can't go . . . in th—th—there . . ." she answered, beginning to cry.

" Poor little one," he said, " well, we will not go in there. Come and sit down with me, and we can have a talk together."

He was very nice and very gentle, and after a few minutes talking he said—" There, my little one, you have made your

First Confession ! Now I will give you absolution.'' Putting up his hand, he made the sign of the Cross over her, all the time saying some words in Latin. Then he told her everything was finished.

But Maddalena had never forgotten that day, and, as quite a young girl, she had made up her mind that no children of hers should ever run the chance of being made so miserable for the sake of confessing things which were not sins.

For a moment she felt inclined to tell all this to Stephen, but then she thought that he would misunderstand her even more than he did at present, and so she left it.

Stephen's brows were contracted as he looked out across the hot, peaceful landscape, all exactly the same as it had been eleven years ago when he had succumbed—wrongly, as he was now convinced by Father Ignatius—to his love for Maddalena di Santa Fiora.

Outwardly all the same, but the hearts and the minds of these two were not the same.

Although the talk Stephen had had a week before with Father Ignatius had made a great impression upon him, it had also perturbed him in no small degree, because, believing so profoundly in the permanence of the marriage tie, and the power—in married life—of the sacrament of marriage to keep one happy and content, he could not understand why the Jesuit had made so very much of the call to the priesthood, while practically ignoring the marriage vows.

On the other hand, the priest's personality was so strong, and his power over Stephen so peculiar, that it had even succeeded in making him uncomfortable and self-conscious when alone with his wife! Intimate conversation had suddenly become impossible, and so, looking at his watch, he rose, absently remarking that it was time to go home.

The invisible wall which she had hoped she had battered down for ever a week ago had risen again, and she could almost see the frustrated hands of his vocation grappling triumphantly with his heart once more.

She resolved never to drive along the road to Santa Barbara again. She felt, too, that the moment in which to show him the letter had passed for ever. And so the packet lay unopened in her pocket. It was a fateful packet, she sensed, and somehow the thought of reading it frightened her. It was like a dead hand hovering round her heart.

PART III

TRANSITION

CHAPTER X

THE MIND OF QUENDRED

" . . . But what am I ?
An infant crying in the night :
An infant crying for the light :
And with no language but a cry."
—TENNYSON.

SEVEN years had passed since Cardinal Costanzi's death, and Stephen was more than ever haunted, fascinated, and held by the conviction that he had a vocation, and that it was his duty to throw up everything else and follow it.

This feeling had eaten into his being, and had there made a wound as deep and as unhealable as that which gnawed at the vitals of Amfortas.

Since the talk he had had with the great Jesuit preacher seven years ago in London, Stephen's scruples had become well-nigh unbearable. Entirely obsessed by the thought that his life with his wife was sinful because he was being unfaithful to God's highest call, the idea had got on his nerves to such an extent as to be almost what his doctors called " mental."

Now he looked sad and dejected, and there was a nervous tension in his eyes which reminded his wife of some wild but imprisoned animal. She was disconsolate, and she only wished now to do what was the best for him, even though it broke the cup of life for her.

The twins were seventeen, and Anthony was beginning to be rather difficult. On account of the religious question, his father wouldn't send him to either of the Universities, and so he was to go straight to Sandhurst, and thence into the Blues.

In consequence of Maddalena's enforced alienation from her husband, Quendred and she had drawn very close together. They were inseparable friends. Maddalena had been able to

K

give herself up entirely to the personal supervision of her child's education, because Stephen never went into Society, never stayed in other people's houses, and only went to London for the opening of Parliament, or a religious ceremony.

The central idea of Quendred's life was her mother's opinion. She thought her the loveliest person in the world and the cleverest. She cared for no one's praise but hers, and if her mother was pleased all was well.

With her thick, honey-coloured hair and dark, velvety eyes, Quendred had become a striking beauty. Her mind was very alert, and unusually developed for her age. She loved the history of romance, valour, chivalry, and the stories of the great northern Sagas. Learning was never "lessons" to her, and she soon out-stripped the Miss Jones, the Fräuleins, and the Mademoiselles, who had tried to mould her seeking young mind to their conventionally "finished" ones.

"You're not 'finished,' you dear darling," Quendred had said to her mother, "and that's why you're so wonderful."

Maddalena hoped that she would always be able to live up to her daughter's estimate of her. She realised how much capacity the girl had for " going far," and she was determined never to hinder her, and, if possible, always to support her. Now, at seventeen, Quendred was begging her mother to take her abroad till she came out.

" Most girls go with governesses, don't they ? " she had said coaxingly to her mother, " but I want to go with you."

" But what about Father, darling ? " Maddalena had said.

" Couldn't he and Anthony both come out to us at Christmas ? " said Quendred. " And I'm sure that Father won't mind us leaving him alone at Ullcombe ! He hardly ever talks to us at meals now, and we don't see him much at any other time of the day."

The Duke's life was now spent chiefly in entertaining bishops, paying nuns' over-drafts, building churches, going on pilgrimages, financing Jesuits, and flying off to Rome to see the Pope to discuss a campaign—on foot in the Vatican—as to the best and quickest means of converting England. His was a feverish, creed-ridden life, and he was more interested in the flattery of clerics —who hoped thereby to gain more financial favours at his hands —than in seeking to enter into the hearts of his children. In consequence, it wasn't surprising that Quendred hadn't much sympathy with her father.

" What an absurd idea this is, wanting to go to Dresden,"
he had said to his wife. " Surely Quendred can be educated quite
well at home ? Convents, of course, are the right places for
girls. Anyhow, I can't afford to send her gallivanting all over
Europe. Where is the money to come from ? That's what I
ask—where is the money to come from ? "

" Well, you seem to have plenty to give to the Church,
Stephen ! " Maddalena couldn't help the so obvious *riposte*.

Immediately her husband looked stern.

" Don't you know that it is an ordinance of God that we should
all give a tenth of what we possess to the Church ? " he said very
gravely indeed.

" Yes, I know," she answered. " But I should think you
give about seventy-five per cent of what you possess, and that
not only once in a lifetime, as I read the words to mean, but every
year."

" You pain me, Maddalena. You almost shock me," he said.
" You ought to enter joyfully with me into all these schemes for
helping on the Church in England."

" I'm afraid I'm more interested in helping on my children
and making them happy than in doing the same for priests,"
Maddalena said ; and Stephen, sighing deeply, remarked as he
went towards the door :

" I fear you don't really love our Holy Church as a true and
devout Catholic should. I must, however, say that I do not see
my way at present to sending Quendred abroad."

" ' At present ' is the only time that's any use, Stephen," his
wife said. " But it doesn't matter. You needn't bother about
it, for, of course, I can manage, and we'll go there together for
about nine months. You and Anthony must come out and see
us there, and do remember that the twins aren't children any
more, and that you must wake from your religious reveries to
do your duty by them."

.   .   .   .   .   .

Quendred's most treasured possession was a Stradivarius
which her grandfather had given her, and, as the months went by,
her playing—under the tuition of the first violin at the opera—
improved out of all recognition. The great man was delighted
with her.

" Dat is gut, dat is gut ! " he had said. " You have the
proper bowing, *Gott sei dank*. You keep the elbow down, and

there is no break. You make her sing—sing, and "—here he
tapped the left side of his coat excitedly—" you haf de heart
perhaps too much for your own happiness, *aber geiger zu spielen,
es könnte wundervol sein—colossal.*"

And then he told her that hearing good music was part of
her education, and so she began, under his guidance, to go to all
the concerts and operas which the Athens of the Elbe provided.

The first opera she heard was " Siegfried." It was a disappointment to her ; it seemed nothing but a conglomeration of meaningless and disconnected sounds with a kind of tune appearing—like
a meteor—now and then—and just when you thought you understood something, it all melted away and you were left more involved
than ever !

But as she heard more and more she learned to love this great
trilogy, the deep human meaning of which her mother explained
to her so well ; how, so long as the gold of the Rhine remained
safe on its rock at the bottom of the green, swirling river, the world
was happy, but as soon as the spirit of avarice awoke and—
forswearing love—grabbed the alluring thing to put it to its own
evil uses, disaster and misery came crashing into men's lives, and
only sorrow seemed to follow those who touched the ill-gotten
gold.

How she loved the long, drawn-out note which, ushering in the
Prelude to " Rhinegold," turns into a ripple, and slowly becomes
a great wave of sound beating through the orchestra ! How she
loved to watch the first violins, and see their steady strong bows
all going upwards and downwards together ! They seemed so
confident, so jubilant ! For it was they who were making the
glorious music which held men and women spellbound from all
corners of the earth.

What great musicians they were ! What a love of romance and
beauty must lie buried in their souls, she thought.

On Sundays she and her mother used to go to Mass at the
Hofkirche, a fine building with a beautiful copper roof gleaming
green in the sunlight, facing the Opera House, and standing
opposite to the exquisite picture gallery built by the famous
Frederic Augustus, reputed father of three hundred children.
But inside ! Never was there a less prayerful church, nor an uglier !
Everything was repellent and cold, and Quendred literally couldn't
pray there.   It was then that she first began to realise the subtle
power of atmosphere.

The places of worship which she knew best were Farm Street,

the Chapel at Ullcombe, which her father had altered when he came into it, and the village church at Santa Fiora. These were all dim, and the sun's rays only entered by piercing richly-tinted glass. They smelled strongly of incense, and seemed to have some faint, soothing, secret, and inexplicable attribute which shed balm upon the spirit of all who entered in.

In these churches an unseen, but strongly-felt something, forced one to speak in whispers and walk softly ; to kneel at length with head bent, often to become oblivious to everything but God ; to give oneself up for the moment to a delicious feeling of utter divorce from the world—hearing the pattering of the feet of men, their gruff voices calling ; hearing the sudden shrill scream of a child ; hearing the clattering passing of a cart ; but to feel far from it all. To feel that in here was sanctuary, in here was safety, in here was peace, in here was a great loneness from the world, but a great oneness with God ; in here the things of Mammon *seemed* not to matter, in fact, for the moment, did not matter. This was what she liked to feel, and this was what she thought she felt because she believed in the True Presence of God in Roman Catholic churches, and therefore this sensation had always been of the greatest solace to her. Although her father's intense religiosity worried her frightfully, the strong feeling—result of her education—that Jesus Christ was *really* and *truly* in these places, comforted and reassured her wondering soul for much that was otherwise hard to dovetail into place.

Her father always talked of religion, and yet he never made their home happier for it. He had succeeded in turning " Almighty God " into a bugbear when they were small.

By a too constant use of certain phrases and words, they, be they ever so noble, lose the fine savour of their inner meaning.

The strict atmosphere brought into Ullcombe by Stephen's conversion had been fanning the tiny flame of revolt which the incident of Father Bischoffsheim had left in Quendred's being many years before at luncheon in Berkeley Square, although she didn't realise it.

.   .   .   .   .   .

On entering the church in Dresden she felt a chill descend on her. It was all cold, unattractive, ugly. There was no beautiful stone-work, no graceful aisles, no stained glass, no smell of incense, no decorated side-altars as at Farm Street, or no tawdry rococo gold ornaments and old brocade hangings as at Santa

Fiora, all of which had been offered by the faithful as a proof of love.   There were no banners, no statues, no profusion of flowers ; even the sanctuary lamp flickered coldly, white and meaningless, instead of burning a deep, glowing ruby, as it did in most other churches—a sign of the undying ardent love of The One !

The girl was dismayed.   She knelt to pray, but she found that she couldn't.   There was no atmosphere, no mystery, no hint of unseen powers.

What had happened ?   Was this a Catholic Church ?   Was Jesus Christ really here ?   If so, why didn't she *feel* Him ?

And then this thought came to her : if He is in all our Churches, then He must be *here*, no matter coloured windows, incensed air, glowing sanctuary lamps, stations of the Cross, baldechinos, reredos, sweet-smelling flowers, jewelled monstrance, mosaic walls, rich hangings, valuable vestments, or gold candlesticks !   Mysterious, dim, awe-inspiring, soul-soothing atmosphere there was none ; therefore she felt nothing.   What did it all mean ?   What if the feeling that God was really present on Catholic altars was imagination after all !   Imagination buoyed up and fostered by those beauteous and sensuous outward surroundings !   Perhaps !   Perhaps everything was imagination. How was she to know ?   She tried to put the hideous thought away.

The months flew by with engaging rapidity.   She loved her life ; it was full of interest.   Added to her study of the violin, which she worked at for several hours a day, she was learning Latin and German.   At her special request—a strange one, her teachers thought, in such a young girl—she went through a stiff course on the History of Religion.

Many things began to trouble her mind, and she at last wondered dimly whether all that she had been taught as a child could possibly be true ?

By degrees she came to see very clearly that, from earliest childhood, she—we—they—all of us—in all ranks and departments of life, are most cunningly raised on fear.   From the very earliest beginning youth is threatened—" If you don't do this I'll put you in the corner " ; " If you don't do that I'll cut you off with a shilling " ; " If you don't obey Us you will go to hell."

That's the system.   Threats.   Threats of a supperless bed, a dark room, a whipping, no half-holiday, no pocket-money and the bogey-man.   Then, as youth advanced to manhood, these childish swords of Damocles assumed the more important names of " Father," " the headmaster," " the colonel," " the boss," " the policeman," " the priest," " the magistrate," " the mistress," and—for Roman Catholics—" hell-fire," " excommunication," " damnation." It is called education.

Various systems, both lay and clerical—jealous of keeping, and desirous of acquiring power over the human being—have found it to be a vastly expedient weapon, and humanity is to a large extent so drenched in its old clinging, grasping force that it cannot shake itself free of its dire domination.

Very early then did Quendred learn to understand all this. Deep down at the bottom of her she realized that when we are frightened *enough*, we are easy to rule.

And because Quendred was casting out fear she was becoming difficult to rule.

Fear.

Slowly and gradually it dawned upon her developing conscious-ness of facts, that Fear was a power largely used in the govern-ments of both body and soul.

Fear.

Yes, it was, no doubt, a very great power not to be ignored as of no value in the game of life.

It was—she now realized—of an outstanding, yet enormously subtle, value.

.   .   .   .   .   .

It was Christmas Eve, and the Seyntlegers were at Midnight Mass in the Royal Church. As Quendred knelt through the long service listening to the superb music, her mind was filled with tumultuous thoughts. Their seats were upstairs in a side gallery, and from here she looked down at the mass of tightly-packed beings below. All nationalities, representing all creeds, were there ; sinners, saints, criminals, fools, wise men, and ordi-nary folk ! And what were they there for ? Some because they believed, some because they didn't believe, some to hear the music, some out of curiosity, some because it was exciting to go to a service in the middle of the night, some to see the Royal Family in their gold cages overlooking the High Altar, some to honour God, and some to amuse themselves ! More than ever that night Quendred felt unable to pray.

Although the church was decked in " gala," it still lacked the warm, enfolding atmosphere for which her being longed. In-stead of being cold, undecorated, and empty, it was hot, decorated.

and full. Nevertheless, it was merely a great spectacle to her.

Some time before, the son of a Saxon prince had proposed to her, and his father had, to her astonishment, made excessive love to her at a State ball.

Prince Neiphausen was said to be the best-looking man in the army. He certainly looked quite splendid in his gorgeous white uniform, and she had been rather flattered when he singled her out that night for his very marked admiration. But everything had been spoilt by his love-making.

In church to-night she raised her eyes from the mass of people below, and her glance fell upon him kneeling in seats corresponding to hers, on the opposite side of the church.

His shining silver helmet lay on the velvet cushion over which he leant, head bowed, hands clasped—typical of a devout Catholic, a good soldier, a faithful subject, and a great gentleman. Then her thoughts flew to the far-away room in the castle, where the music of a Strauss waltz could only be faintly heard in the distance. She remembered how those praying arms had held her, crushed her, hurt her; how that reverently bowed head had pressed on to her cool young shoulders, and how those fervently-moving lips had bruised hers until the blood had come, and had poured out words of passion ; words that she never knew men said to women, words indeed that she had never even heard.

And thus it was that Quendred's door into life had been opened.

She looked at him again. His head was still bent, he seemed indeed immersed in prayer. How strange it was, she thought. that one can be a good practising Christian or Catholic, and yet be able to do and say such things ! It was the first shock to her ideals.

The choir was singing Gounod's " Messe Solonelle," and it had just reached the " Sanctus," the exquisite and heavenly strains of which brought her back to thoughts of the Mass. All bent their heads in preparation for the Elevation of the Host. As the magnificently arrayed priest lifted his arms and held between his fingers and thumbs the shining white disc, Quendred lifted her head and looked at It.

Could It be God, she wondered with almost feverish anxiety. Could It ? Oh, could It ? How much she longed for a sign—no matter how small—that this was indeed the Body of Christ. She believed that her faith and love could make it so, if she were far enough advanced in the spiritual life, but whether the whispering of words over it by any sort of a priest could make it so, was another question, and one that caused her mind to agonize. If the little white circle would only flutter into the priest's hands just to show her that it had life! And with all her heart she prayed, like the disciples of old, "Increase my faith."

The head of the man who loved her had also not been bent during the extra solemn portion of the Mass, but for a different reason. Thoughts of faith never worried him! To him the Catholic religion was true, and that was an end of it. He didn't know why, but it just *was!* He never thought about it. His eyes were riveted on Quendred, his thoughts were not with God. Slightly thrusting forward his chin, he formed his lips into a kiss. "How I wish you were mine," he muttered.

His wife—a kind, gentle person, whose figure had suffered from bearing him many children—imagined that he was praying.

The Prince and his wife found themselves next to the Seynt-legers as they were all waiting for their carriages when Mass was over.

Quendred was standing nonchalantly with her arms behind her. The eyes of Maddalena saw everything, but were more especially alert when Prince Neiphausen came on the scene. She covered Quendred's hands with one of hers. In a moment he had edged himself to the girl's other side and, amidst the flutter and excitement of the people leaving the church, Maddalena caught his eager whisper: "*Ach Du! wie lieb und schön Du bist, meine prachtvolle, Lady Kendred.*" At the same time his strong hand grasped the Duchess's, thinking it was her daughter's.

The girl moved quickly down a step, and her mother slipped into her place next to the Prince. He was certainly a magnificent specimen of a man, tall and powerfully built, with a wonderful head and shoulders, and ways which countless women had found irresistible. But Maddalena, glancing at him, shuddered, for she involuntarily thought of Lepantchine's huge form holding her mother in his arms, while she sprang at him, biting wildly at his hands. Her blood was coursing madly now with anger, and she longed to do the same to this man.

She looked him full in the face.

"If you don't leave my child alone, I'll tell the Queen," she said swiftly and low, her eyes flashing.

Now the Queen was renowned for her piety, and her Court was one of the strictest in Europe. Had this become known, the Prince's future at Court would have been doomed, for all his interests lay in those circles, and he was one of the richest of Saxon magnates. Also he was very anxious that his son should marry Quendred, for it was known that she would have half of her Italian grandfather's immense fortune. Their rank and religion were the same. What could have been more suitable ? So, bowing towards her, he said in his faultless English, " As you wish, Duchess."

. . . . . .

It was the last night before Stephen and Anthony were going back to England, and the Neiphausens were giving a big ball. Quendred had told her mother that their son, Count Borvin, had asked her to marry him, but she had said nothing about the old Prince's behaviour. However, she felt from her mother's treatment of her lately that she knew something, so that was enough. Maddalena had been so tender and loving.

Sometimes she would talk to her daughter of her own life and tell her little things—difficulties, and pitfalls—and of how to beware of them, but all in such a human and understanding way that Quendred felt she could have told her mother anything, for she was sure that she would have always understood.

Her mother was never shocked, she never preached, and never discussed her daughter with other people. Quendred knew she would never fail her, she knew she could trust her implicitly, and she was learning to know that absolute trust is the only true basis of lasting love.

" I would like to tell your father about Borvin's proposal, darling," Maddalena said one day. " I think he should know."

" Very well, Mother, do so if you wish, but I don't suppose it'll interest him ! It doesn't even interest me. He thinks of literally nothing but soldiering, and I'm sure that he bellows orders in his sleep ! "

And so Stephen was told.

" But why won't she marry him ? " he said. " He seems a nice young man, quiet and sensible, and a Catholic. I think it would be very suitable. It will be difficult for her to marry well in England, and I absolutely refuse to give my consent to any but a Catholic marriage. Why don't you encourage it, Maddalena ? "

" But she doesn't love him. She doesn't want to marry him in the least," said his wife.

" What does she know of love ? " he replied. " She's only

a child! And besides, a lot of nonsense is talked about love. The great thing is that it should be suitable, and have the elements of success and durability about it. This case complies with all my ideas of a good and sensible marriage. I wish that you would advise her to marry him." He spoke querulously.

"I couldn't, Stephen," answered Maddalena. "From my standpoint of life, it would be too wrong a thing to do. But why don't you, if you wish it? You're her father just as much as I'm her mother. Why should all the responsibility fall on me? Besides, I wish you would talk to her sometimes—really talk about things that matter—not merely asking her if she likes her violin lessons, or if she is going to make the *novena* for the feast of the Immaculate Conception, or telling her that you don't like her hat just when she is all dressed up, and is rather pleased with her appearance! Stephen, dear, perhaps you don't quite realize how all such tiny things tend to alienate her from you."

She was standing near the chair in which he was sitting, and she gently stroked the strong waves in his thick hair now turned from gold to brown. She thought he was the most beautiful man she had ever seen, and she wondered if he at all realized how the separation which he willed made her suffer.

Ah! how splendidly they had loved each other up there on the road to Santa Barbara! Would her little Quendred ever have such a joyful, wondrous betrothal? Would she ever feel as Maddalena had felt as she leaned out from the window of her little virginal bedroom in the Italian mountains? And, if by chance such happiness *were* in store for her, would it end like this?

Stephen had remained silent at her questionings, and now she looked into his face. How thin it was, she thought. His eyes were closed and there was infinite pain in the furrows between them. Even in his youth he had always had a serious earnest look, and now this look had turned to one of almost habitual mournfulness; only very rarely was his face lit by the old buoyant, radiant smile, which had first captured the heart of lovely, noble little Maddalena di Santa Fiora, as she almost ran into the drawing-room at Madame de Cavallhos', lace handkerchief fluttering, white tulle gown shimmering; the embodiment of youth, beauty, desirableness, and grace—the embodiment of all which he had made up his mind to eschew for ever for the love of God!

And for eighteen years the thought that he had been faithless to what he held to be the greatest call of all, had been eating into his soul like a canker. It had been a terrible struggle, for he had loved her tremendously. Really, in his heart, he still loved her—still (to his horror)—and, against the advice of Father Ignatius, he felt her *allure*.

But the soul of him yearned for God and for God only, and his brain, which his religion taught him contained the three powers of his soul, always told him that he was leading a sinful life, always urged him to break with it, always whispered that the priesthood needed him ; always hammered into his heart that the first love had been the altar of the Most High, always confronted him with his weakness at having returned to his wife just before the death of Cardinal Costanzi, and thus having added to his sin by the breaking of the serious vow which he had made on the night the twins were born. He felt that he had given up the spirit for the flesh, austerity for ease, and God for Mammon.

And now the fateful word was always ringing in his mind Faithless ! Faithless ! Faithless !

Mocking—bitter—taunting—cruel—ceaseless ; it smote remorselessly into the very essence of his being. Waking or sleeping, the thought of the wrong which he had done never left him. Faithless ! Faithless ! Faithless !

As Maddalena stood by him, so tender, so loving, and still —in his inmost heart—so infinitely dear, the feeling that she, his perfect wife, was the temptation of his life, swept over him with renewed force. He had pretended things for so long, and in the ordeal his nerves had gone to pieces. He veered this way and that, like a ship without a rudder. Pushing her away almost brutally, he rose. He could hide it no longer, this tiny scruple, which by its constant presence had transformed itself into a sinister and frowning mountain of misery. It had ruined his life, and it was *her* fault ! He had tried for years to hide it from her, but to-night he had come to the end of his endurance and his anguish was unbearable. And so at last he blurted out the unvarnished truth and told her so, told her with terrible bitterness that he looked upon her as the Eve of his life.

" Can't you forgive me, Stephen ? " she said sadly. " It wasn't done purposely. I knew nothing about you that night when I met you first at the Cavallhos', and I loved you at once. How could I know what was going on in your heart and mind, except that I thought from the way you looked at me that you cared too ? It all seemed such a golden dream in those youthful, happy days—and now—it has melted all away—just like a golden dream ! Stephen ! It's torture to me to see you so tortured. . . . How can I help you ? Do believe that I would do anything in my power to give peace to your mind again."

"You can't give it back to me, although it was you who took it from me," he said roughly. "Don't talk such nonsense. I wanted to be a priest, and you *made* me love you. There's nothing more to be said or done. It's all hopeless—hopeless."

"Do you still wish with all your heart to be a priest ? " she asked in steady, even tones.

He turned his eyes upon her.

"Yes, I do," he said. "Ever since I was at Oxford where I read some words showing the power of the priesthood, I have longed most ardently to be a priest ! Maddalena ! I don't believe you realize the magnitude of it all ! I believe comparatively few people do. To be a priest ! Why ! It's almost like being like God Himself ! In fact, at times priests *are* God ! "

He strode towards her and gripped her arm. He looked wild, and in his eyes gleamed the light of fanaticism.

"Poor Stephen," thought his wife, " poor, beautiful, religious Stephen."

Holding her firmly, he went on talking excitedly, hot, eager words pouring from his lips.

"There's nothing like it in the world ! Nothing ! Imagine having the power of changing a paltry piece of meaningless wafer into the God who made Heaven and Earth ! The God who can shatter kingdoms and build them again ! The God who can make the fern unfold its fronds, and who can cause the ground to burst open and swallow cities ! It's the most stupendous thing ever devised ; of course it is, for God devised it ! Think of a priest each morning of his life, transforming that little, brittle, white thing into God's very Body and Blood, Bones and Flesh, Hair and Nails, Limbs and Features ! . . . I wonder how they imagine Him when they hold Him there—the Lord of Creation—between their fingers and thumbs ! Do they think of Him as a Baby whimpering on His Mother's knee, or as the beautiful Boy profoundly expounding the Scriptures in the Temple ; as the angry, radiant Man casting out the buyers and sellers from His Father's house ; as the sorrowful,

weary, heavy-laden One weeping over Jerusalem, or as the
crumpled, tortured Body slowly, painfully breathing out Its
sacred life upon the Cross to save the World? I wonder!
I wonder how *I* should imagine Him!"

He ceased speaking, and Maddalena noticed how his lips
were moving, muttering. It was a habit which had slowly been
growing upon him during the last few years. She supposed
him to be praying, and how queer he looked! "Is he mad?"
she half wondered, terrified even of her own thought. Poor
man—how she pitied him. Gently disengaging his hands
from herself, she half led him into his bedroom, where, by his
bed, was a beautiful gold crucifix, studded with precious stones,
while countless rosaries and books of devotion lay upon the
table.

"Let us pray together that God may comfort you, and show
us both what is best to do," she said.

She knelt down, and he rather reluctantly did so, too.

Suddenly he pulled the Crucifix out of its velvet case, and,
flinging it on to the floor, he said angrily:

"It wasn't like that—all gold and diamonds and rubies—
it was hard, common, vile wood, with great ugly, rusty nails
tearing His tender hands and feet apart. Wasn't it, Maddalena,
wasn't it?"

"Yes, dearest," she replied tremulously, for she really was
frightened now.

She felt his hand—it was burning. He must be unwell, she
thought, and suggested not going to the Niephausens that night,
because he was ill.

"Most certainly not. I am quite well," he answered, "but
I did get upset just now. I always do inwardly, when I think
of my missed vocation, and to-day, for the first time in my life,
I have let out what I really feel! It's awful, nobody knows
how terribly I suffer keeping it all pent up. Thank you for
being so patient with me, dear. I hope you realize how grateful
I am," he said, as he rose to his feet again.

The paroxysm was passed, and for the moment he seemed
well, and said he wished to be left alone.

.   .   .   .   .   .

That evening at the Niephausens' Stephen had been told
to take one of the Princesses to supper. Suddenly the faithful
eyes of his wife—which had scarcely left his face since they had

arrived—saw him put both hands to his head in a strange and groping manner. In a flash she was at his side, and, with the help of Quendred and the deeply enamoured Borvin, he was taken to his carriage and so home.

The next morning it became known that he was seriously ill. The doctor said it was brain fever.

CHAPTER XI

THE PSYCHOLOGICAL WIZARD

" What the light of your mind—which is the direct inspiration of the Almighty—pronounces incredible, that, in God's name, leave uncredited ; at your peril do not try believing that."—CARLYLE.

AFTER many weeks of critical illness, the Duke was convalescent, and a sigh of relief went up from the overwrought " villa."

The snows were long since over and gone, and spring came leaping through the land. It was about nine months since Maddalena and Quendred had been in Dresden.

" Do let's go away from here, Mother," the girl said one day, as her father lay on the balcony overlooking the exquisitely laid-out " Grosse Garten," for which Dresden was famous. " I have learnt a lot since I have been here—a lot of things in many ways ; and I can play the violin well enough to please myself and you, darling, can't I ? And that's all I care about. Beautiful Mother, let's go away from here, away—away ! You understand ! You know ? " and she held Maddalena's face between her hands, drawing them gently down till the slender fingers met below her chin.

" Who is talking in there ? " came a weak, querulous voice through the open window. " You know how much I dislike hearing conversations going on in undertones ! I suppose you whisper so as not to disturb me, but it does disturb me very much indeed. I wish that you wouldn't do it ! "

They both went out to him—a pair that a king might have been proud to own as wife and daughter.

" Dear Father, I'm so sorry," said Quendred, " it was all my fault. I was just telling Mother that I would like to go away. Do forgive me for worrying you," and she stroked his thin, white hand which lay so languidly on the arm of his *chaise longue*.

To his wife it was a great pleasure that Quendred had become affectionate to her father since his illness.

" Do you want to leave this place ? " he said eagerly. " I am glad, for I do also. I cannot bear the Protestant atmosphere. I long to be in a country where the church-bells are always ringing, and the people full of simple, child-like faith. Here it is so cold, so ugly ; one can tell that it is not a real Catholic country. When shall we go, Maddalena ? " he asked, turning to her.

For the first time since his convalescence he seemed to take an interest in things.

Her immediate suggestion of the Austrian Tyrol was acclaimed with pleasure by both father and daughter ; and so it was that a week later they wended their way to the mountains where nestled a village of great antiquity and which, incidentally, was the home of one of the greatest psychological doctors in Europe. Of this, however, no one knew but Maddalena. She was still very anxious about Stephen's well-being, and she wondered whether any of the doctors who had seen him understood his case properly ? She had heard wonders about the Tyrolese Dr. Offenbach, and was enchanted that an opportunity had so simply presented itself for taking her husband there without any fuss.

.   .   .   .   .   .

It was a radiant May afternoon when the train conveying the Seyntlegers breasted the Brenner Pass, and then gaily slipped down and down into the widening valley which eventually led to the plains of Italy.

" How divine ! How divine ! " thought Quendred, as she stood at the open window of the corridor, breathing in the pure, fir-laden air. " How I hope it will make Father well again. Poor Mother, it is so dreadful for her—his being like this."

She turned and looked in at the invalid carriage, where he lay propped up with cushions, the " Imitation of Christ " lying open on his knees.

He looked so sad and worn and thin !

" I wonder why he is like that ? I wonder if all girls' fathers are made so unhappy by ' religion ' ? I wonder if ' religion '—at least, what we *call* ' religion '—has turned out to be something

L

quite different from what Christ ever intended that it should be ? " . . . But her cogitations were interrupted by the train stopping in a village of steep, red-roofed houses, the top windows of which looked like long, side-glancing eyes. High mountains, carrying fir forests on their backs, and capped by glistening snow, stood around, roughly cutting into the deep, dark blue sky, while alongside the railway dashed a wild, foaming river, emerald green and icy cold from being fed with mountain snows. In the distance cow-bells tinkled on different notes, and the Angelus—it was just six o'clock—rang from a score of churches scattered through the village, and from numberless chapels all over the hillside.

They were at their destination at last.

At last—to Stephen's infinite mental relief—they were landed safe in the heart of a real Catholic country.

.   .   .   .   .   .

" Well, Duchess," said Dr. Offenbach, " I have a most thoroughly entire examination of the Duke made, and I think with care, and very great desire on his part, I can him to his bodily health restore. But he to me respond must. That is essential—essential."

The old doctor stood before Maddalena and looked straight at her with his pale, piercing blue eyes, overhung by untidy long white eyebrows. In making his patients do the strangest things, he obtained most marvellous cures !

Here might be seen American millionaires suffering from megalomania caused by the overwhelming burden of an immense fortune—walking bare-footed at six o'clock in the morning in the glistening dew, having first been douched out of a pipe with snow-water. And again, a Russian Grand Duke, who had perennial cold feet, would be told off to cut up wood, and walk up the mountains in sandals for six hours a day, with only a drink of sour milk at bedtime ! Then a Polish Countess, dying of consumption would, by his command, lie on her balcony day and night, covered with compresses made of whey ; and an anæmic heir to a throne would have to strip and take a sun-bath, lying on prickly pine-needles which exuded hot life into him.

To add to the sorry band had come the ailing English Duke.

" And so you really think that my husband will get quite well ? " asked Maddalena in answer to the old man's words.

"Ah, no—quite well, I did *not* say. I cannot tell yet. I have not his case sufficiently studied. His body I think I can cure, but he must dream, every night he must dream, and he must his dreams to me relate."

"But why, Dr. Offenbach? " Maddalena asked, very much surprised. "What can his dreams have to do with your curing him? "

"Ah, that is my invention, my idea! " said the old man. "It is this. Most illnesses have got to do with the digestion —that is really the stohmmack—or the nervous system. Nearly all complaints can generally to one of these two things traced be. In the case of the digestion, it is dat these organs do not the work properly do, and so in time uric gasses are formed, and they the whole body poison do. *So ists!* This requires very careful diet, and something to make the blood to move. Here in my *Anstahlt* all dat is well understood. Dat is why I give the cold *guss;* dat is good, it makes the blood circulate. It is common sense, common sense! In bad cases of uric acid I give the dry diet. Dat is one soft boiled egg, some toast, and a few dates for breakfast—no drink," and he waved his podgy hand to and fro emphatically. "A very little meat and vegetable once a day and no drink. In the afternoon you may have tea or coffee, what you like, but the coffee must be made out of special beans which I recommend. At dinner a little fish and fruit—no drink. In a few weeks the worst patients do a great relief find.

"Now as to the nervous system. This is more difficult, for in every case they vary do, so much—*ach colossal ists!* I must study each individual with much thought, and this takes a long time. I cannot a case undertake unless the patient will put himself in my hands entirely for three months. During this time he will a special diet make, and each day some gentle exercise take."

"Yes, I quite understand," said the Duchess. "We can easily stay for three months, but what about the dreams? Do explain that to me. It sounds so extraordinary."

"Yes, yes, I will tell you that also, but I must explain everything to you, so that you will quite understand what my cure is before I begin to treat the case of the *Herr Herzog*. Now as to the dreams." He sat down on the uncomfortable sofa, covered with a woollen material of glowing, ill-assorted colours, and crossing his short, fat legs and joining the tips of his fingers and thumbs together, he began to explain to Maddalena his famous " cure."

" You know, of course, that we all of us within our being have a mysterious unknown knowledge which has been our subconscious self called ? Now, *Herzogin*, I am not going to read you a treatise on the subject, but I will just say that it is in itself a vast study of the most enormous interest, and has a bearing very direct upon the vicissitudes of man's life, his welfare and happiness, both in mind and body. For the last forty years I have given up much of my time to learning all that I could of this phenomena.

" It was Socrates who said that ' A doctor is a curer of the mind,' and this indeed most marvellously true is. Now in my experience I have found that sometimes a little episode, a sentence, a book, an action, a thing of apparently no importance will be found—in middle life—to have unconsciously the whole life and mentality and temperament of that person tinged and changed. This often has a great effect on their health, and yet there is nothing organically wrong whatsoever. This is what makes such a case so difficult to deal with. It is so elusive, so subtle, and it is here, *Herzogin*, that my theory of the dreams comes in."

Maddalena—who was much interested, was listening intently and silently—nodded her head.

" When a person to me comes and says : ' I am ill, I don't know what the matter with me is—cure me '—I say to them : ' Neither do I know what the matter with you is, but I am going to *find out* ' ; and I tell them to try and remember their dreams, and each morning when I to them come to relate them to me. Many tell me that they never dream. I merely answer : ' But you *will* dream, and if you do dream, tell me what they are.' Thus you see I suggest to them that they dream—and—in a few days—they *do* dream, and soon I can make a good idea of their past lives."

" But it's confession ! " said Maddalena.

" Nothing else," said the doctor.

" Of course you are a Catholic ? " queried she.

" No, no," he said thoughtfully, his lips slightly pursed, and his head on one side. " No—I have no dogmatic beliefs."

" Then please do not let my husband know, for I am afraid he would take a dislike to you, and that would prevent your being able to cure him properly, wouldn't it ? "

" Ach so ! He is like that, is he ? " and the old man gently stroked his beard, twirling the ends of it slowly backwards and forwards. " H'm ! Those cases are more difficult. An English milord came here some years ago to be cured of an internal growth. It was very hopeful. I could him quite well have made, but he asked me whether I believed in the Dirty-nine Articles. I said dat I had never heard of dem. He was surprised, and said dat everyone in England knew of dem. I said perhaps it was something very Engleesh, like Yorkshire Pudding, dat I had never tasted. He looked angry then, and he asked me if I was a Protestant. I told him—as I haf joost told you, *Herzogin*—dat I had no dogmatic beliefs. He then said dat he could not put himself under my care, dat I was not a Christian, and he left the next day. Soon after he sent me those papers, texts, I dink you in Engleesh call them, and on one of them vas written—' Do unto others as you would be done by.' Later, I heard dat he had died of this tumor. If he had let me carry out this great Christian precept, he most likely would not have then dead been." He shrugged his shoulders dramatically. *Aber, es war so !*

" You said just now that my cure was confession. Well, so it is. Confession is a tremendous mental relief. When people are unhappy and depressed, they feel they want to tell it to someone else, do they not ? At least, that is the best, the natural thing to do, and generally it to them relief gives. There are some, of course, who very reserved are. They hug their sorrow, their fear, their burden, their sin, their meanness, or whatever form of suffering it may be ; they cannot tell it, they cannot speak of it, they cannot confess ; and, by degrees, it works on their mind and their nervous system like a growth upon a person's body. It assumes huge dimensions, it becomes intolerable, and a nervous breakdown often the result is. It is the cancer of the mind, and one of the greatest of these cancers is religion—not Christ's, but man's.

" By my system—after several weeks of suggestion to dream, the patient will do so, and will nearly always dream about what is—consciously or unconsciously—causing their mental or physical condition ; for the result can be physical too. You will stay here ten weeks, three months, will you ? And I feel sure I can do much for der *Herzog*, but I will tell you what I have gathered of his mental condition after I his dreams have heard."

Maddalena and the old man became great friends and, during

his spare moments, which however were very rare, he would come in and talk on psychological matters, in which they were both interested.

Sometimes Quendred would be there, too, and not a word that was ever said was lost to her eager mind.

On this his first visit to the Duke, Dr. Offenbach's vigilant eye had not missed noticing the objects of devotion with which the room was littered; rosaries, statues, prayer-books, and medals.

His whole nervous system was still much shattered, and he had by no means entirely recovered from the *débâcle* of the Neiphausens' ball.

But as the days passed, and he faithfully kept to the " cure " —the hardships of which were eased by the companionship of his wife and daughter, and by the beautiful scenery and weather which the place afforded—he really seemed to be gaining strength, and the harassed, worried look became less.

As the summer wore on he was able to make expeditions, and one day they settled to go to St. Ulrich, a delightful village high up in the Dolomites, where the peasants carved objects of devotion.

" I want to get a Crucifix—a real one," he had told Maddalena, for he had given the priceless gold one to the Bishop of Dresden as a parting gift.

After a long, steep drive through dense pine forests, with the hot sun glinting between the massive boughs, they came at length to the village where they spent the night. It was a lovely evening and some peasants " yodelling " outside their inn added to the charm of it all.

Andreas Vogel appeared to be the genius of the place, and so to his cottage they went the next day. He was alone and working, deeply intent upon the figure of a Madonna holding the divine Child in her arms. The whole work showed intense feeling, and they felt at once that they had come to the right man.

Andreas was a fine type of Tyrolean peasant, sturdy and sunburnt, his strong, pillar-like throat showing brown where his shirt was open in front. His hair was dark and curling, and his eyes were the soft, dreamy brown ones of an artist. As they approached he looked up and greeted them with a radiant smile, showing white, even teeth.

Quendred, as the best linguist, began to explain that they

wanted him to carve them a figure of the crucified Saviour, but that how the face had to be something very special ; how it must not only be a face of suffering, but that in the face hope must be shown, and love and sympathy, and a deep yearning for humanity and a wistful understanding for them.

" Can you do this for us, at least, for my father ? " she asked in her charming way.

Stephen had left their little carriage, and was sitting on a felled tree in the sunshiny yard, which was strewn with bits of wood of all sizes and descriptions.

Andreas turned his slow, mild eyes from the joyous loveliness of Quendred to the piteous face of the man.

" Is that your father ? " he asked gently. " Then I will carve his face for the nobility and suffering of Jesus, and I will put in the hope myself, the hope that we must all have, *gnädiges Fräulein*, if we are real children of *der Heiland*. He is ill, your *Herr Vater ?* But he will become well in our beautiful mountains ! Will the *gnädiger Herr* choose a piece of rough wood, any he likes, and I will carve the figure straight out of it ? "

Quendred told her father what the man had said, and together they searched till they found a bit that Stephen liked. This he handed to Andreas with that rare smile so seldom now seen on his face.

Andreas gazed earnestly at him, and then, as they were preparing to depart, he—following the custom of the mountain people—kissed their hands.

As he took Quendred's in his he said : *Grüss Gott! Küss die Hand, du schönes süsses Kind.*

She was enchanted !

How different was his graceful, courteous compliment out here in the endless pine woods, to Prince Neiphausen's objectionable admiration in the lonely, dark room of the old Castle !

Two months of Stephen's cure had passed, and, although the doctor was pleased enough with the improvement, he knew in himself that Stephen wasn't happy, and never would be so till a very great change was effected in his life.

By this time he had, through his system of dreams, thoroughly probed to the depths of Stephen's character and mentality. Maddalena had purposely told him nothing. He had never had such a case before, and his heart went out in pity to them both. It was near the day of the Assumption, and Stephen wished to go to Confession and Holy Communion on this great feast of the Church. So it was arranged that a priest should bring him the Blessed Sacrament, and Maddalena and Quendred had asked to be allowed to receive it with him.

All was arranged ; suddenly the tinkling of the little bell heralding the priest's arrival was heard, and Maddalena, looking at Stephen, saw the wild, fanatical look leap into his eyes once more, and his lips began muttering and mumbling. His pale, fine hands were pressed together, and the blue veins looked as though they would burst.

The tears rushed to her eyes.

" What will be the end of it all ? " she thought. As the thin Host melted away into nothing upon her tongue, she prayed with all her strength that God would enlighten her and him and the doctor, so that they would be shown how to act for the best in this enigma which had taken such a hold on their lives.

As the priest placed the wafer in Stephen's mouth, Quendred looked at them both.

The giver of the Sacrament was a fat, bloated, sensual-looking man in a dirty, stained *soutane*, which, owing to the protuberance of his figure, was several inches shorter in the front than at the back. His coarse, purple lips muttered the words of consecration indistinctly and hurriedly. He seemed anxious to be gone. His nails were bitten to the quick, and his fat, not over-clean fingers, looked as if they would crush to atoms the frail Host—the Body and Blood of the Saviour as Catholics *believe*—which they held so clumsily.

The receiver of the Sacrament knelt erect, his slim form —clad in loose-fitting tweeds—was perfectly motionless. The brown wave of his hair was brushed off his high, white forehead, his eyes were reverently closed, and his finely-cut, refined lips were moving inaudibly. His ascetic face seemed quivering with intense spiritual emotion.

Maddalena swallowed the remaining particles of her Host with a slight effort, wondering at the same time whether, with the melting of the wafer, God disappeared also from inhabiting her body ?

The little bell began again to tinkle, and the dirty priest, bearing in his soft white hands what Catholics believe to be the creator of Life, wended his way back to his breakfast.

" If either of those two men have any occult or unseen power," thought Quendred, " it is most certainly not that dreadful man. If God Himself were to come down and choose a priest to officiate at His altar, I'm sure he would have chosen Father, rather than him! Whatever Father's peculiarities may be, I know that his faith is faultless: it is like a child's, innocent and real and warm. If *Faith* can effect the change, then he could do it. Father looks like one's idea of a priest anyhow. I simply can't believe that that person who has just left the room has any apostolic power whatsoever. Somehow I feel that he is evil; if he is, how can he *do* good? How can he handle the Most High? How can he transubstantiate?

"I have been taught that one little venial sin is so loathsome, putrid, and disgusting in the eyes of God, that could we see our souls we would faint with horror and repulsion at the sight. Then how can a man possess this awesome power if his soul is so revolting to God that He turns away from him and cannot bear to look on him? For I suppose no priest is sinless? I wish I could understand all the strangeness of the Catholic creed!"

.　　.　　.　　.　　.　　.

One day, when the three months were nearly over, a knock came on Maddalena's door.

"Come in," she called, and Dr. Offenbach entered.

"*Herzogin*," he said, "I have come to speak to you about your husband," and he moved to his usual seat in the window niche, overlooking the rushing snow-river, and assumed his favourite position—legs crossed and finger-tips pressed together.

"You perhaps remember," he said slowly, "that when you here first came I told you that I thought I could the *Herzog* cure? Well, I have done so! He is now physically a strong man—in his body. He is well. He can his food eat with appetite; he can up the mountains walk for many hours. His sleep is good, and he weighs twenty-one pounds more now than the day when I the first examination made. He is no more so pallid; now in his cheeks there is a good colour. Oh! yes, your husband is much better—in his body."

There was a slight pause, and Maddalena said:

"Then what is the matter with him? Is it his mind? Tell me! I'm not afraid! I want to know the truth. In fact, I half guess. I know a lot about my husband, Dr. Offenbach," said she tensely.

"Ah, I am glad to hear dat, for I shall be spared the pain of explanations. You realize then that the *Herzog* desires and wishes only one thing in the world, and that is to be a priest ? "

Maddalena bowed her head, as if to an inevitable blow which, nevertheless, she had vainly thought she might escape.

" *Herzogin,* you must let him go, or in a few years he will be a madman ! " He kept his eyes fixed upon the river ; they were brimming with tears.

CHAPTER XII

"ON THE MOUNTAIN-TOPS IS REST . . ."

" The noblest spirit is most strongly attracted by the love of glory."
—CICERO.

A FEW days before leaving the Tyrol for Santa Fiora where
—ever since their marriage—the Seyntlegers and their children
had spent the months of August and September—Stephen went
to pay a short visit to the Prinz-Bishop of the district.

He was to be away for two days, so his wife and daughter
took this opportunity to make an expedition to the top of Schneeköpfchen, the highest negotiable mountain in the neighbourhood,
and which boasted a little hut for travellers on its summit.

To their great joy no one else appeared to have chosen that
day to make the ascent. Everything was sparkling in the fresh
morning air, and they were entranced by the fairy-like beauty
of their walk. Wild, rocky, lovely ravines, down which dashed
foaming water where the sun never penetrated, would suddenly
lead to a soft, mossy glade full of sunshine and shadow, and bil-
berries and ferns ; these would gradually cease, and they would
emerge into an open space upon which the sun beat mercilessly,
and in a little time there would be no trees to afford them any
shade.

Here and there were dotted tiny white churches, whose
scarlet roofs gave a splash of welcome colour to the endless
green, and whose bells would ring out the remembrance of God
upon the clear, wondrous air, air that was like ethereal wine.

Now and then they came to small villages, hardly villages
indeed, only a few huts huddled together, which the animals
seemed to share with the aged-looking young women and pale-
faced, quaintly-attired children, whose poor little figures were
tightly squeezed into hot cloth frocks reaching to their feet.

Any natural expansion was looked upon by these strange mountain folk as impure, and therefore an offence against religion. Their hair was smeared with some sort of grease, and was tightly wound round their little heads, so that from about the age of four they all looked like tiny stunted women.

Maddalena and Quendred were much amused by their running after them and kissing their hands, calling out, *Grüss Gott—Küss die Hand* without ceasing till a few *kreutzer* found their way into their hot, dirty little palms. They would then scurry away, and gleefully count the money out to each other under the shade of a huge Spanish chestnut, with which trees the mountain-sides were covered.

In the villages might be found a tiny inn where climbers could rest and be sustained by new-laid eggs, excellent coffee with creamy milk foaming over the thick cup, home-made bread and butter, enormous yellow pears, crimson apples, and juicy mountain strawberries. In such a little house they rested till the greatest heat of the day had passed, and then in the coolness of the afternoon they renewed their way. The scene became one of reckless beauty as the earth turned away from the sun. Soon the sky changed to a wild mass of purple and tawny clouds—the world seemed to be on fire. They had just come out of the darkling woods where the trees were casting ghost-like shadows on their rough path. Quendred touched her mother's arm as they sat together on the burnt-up springy grass.

"Where is *Brünhilde*, Mother?" laughed the girl. "Look at that great jagged rock! Can't you imagine *Seigfried* leaping from one ledge to another; up, up, through the scorching flames, undaunted, till he finds the lovely maid behind the walls of fire, hidden from prying eyes, and then—suddenly—he was frightened!"

"Does love really make one frightened?" She stole her arm through her mother's, and her eyes gazed down upon the mountains, mysteriously veiled by the evening mists. Their hands were clasped; there was a long pause.

Since the episode in Dresden something had begun to stir in her, as the leaves of the forest trees are stirred with a gentle, strange movement before the great storm comes. And her woman's heart had whispered to her that what she expected had to do with love. Of course it would be love! What else could it be? *Love* was the great mysterious thing which every real woman in the flush of her youth secretly longs for, ponders over, dwells upon, and wonders in which of its myriad guises it will come to her? And then suddenly something *had* come; but instead of the flame of knightly adoration of some radiant youth of which she had dreamt, the passion of an old married man had fallen like a disfiguring blight upon the tender petals of her dawning womanhood.

Hand clasped in hand, alone upon those silent mountain-tops, mother and daughter sat together, and at last Maddalena said:

"When two people love each other with real love—buoyant, brave, and trusting; eager, warm, and unselfconscious—it brings the most marvellous happiness, darling," she said, while a dreamy look filled her eyes. She looked at the girl's face, delicately outlined against the purple and gold sunset. She felt that at this moment her child had reached one of life's turn-styles. How thankful she was that she and no other was there to help her over it.

She did not want her Quendred to have a tarnished idea of love, and she feared rather that the Neiphausen episode might have already blundered in where angels fear to tread. So she welcomed this opportunity to present her view in a simple way, as against the distorted one on which she felt certain he had anyhow tried to instil into the girl's mind. Girls are often vain and inquisitive, and so, not unnaturally, are flattered at first when such men as these single them out for their attentions, and so, by degrees, they are led on by the charm of feeling, by excitement, and by the longing to know hitherto unknown things, to lengths that they could never have imagined possible.

Of course, it's all a great secret, and that's what makes it so fascinating; and it's all done so gradually, so pleasantly, that they do not realize that they are no longer shocked at things which shocked them a short time ago, and that sometimes things are said at which they blush when they are alone. Of course they never tell their mothers! "Mother wouldn't understand," is what they generally think, but perhaps in a moment of ecstatic trust they will tell a beloved friend, who, of course—they believe—is a monument of discretion! And so the mothers get left out of their lives just at the moment when they are so urgently needed. Where does the fault lie? It is hard to say. And on these things Maddalena had many a time pondered.

"What is your idea of love, darling?" she now asked Quendred.

"Oh, Mother, what a difficult question! I won't say that I

have never thought about it, though, because I have, often and
often! And I think that my idea of love is—well—just *giving*.
I feel that some day I shall suddenly see someone, and that an
overwhelming feeling will rush through me, and then that I shall
only wish to be with that person, that I would willingly suffer
pain for him, that nothing would matter as long as he smiled,
and that I should long very much indeed for him to take me in
his arms and—well, nearly eat me, Mother, like one feels when
one has a soft, lovely baby in one's arms! You know one always
feels as though one would like to eat them for love, doesn't one?
You're not shocked, Mother, are you? Oh, please don't be!
because you know perhaps I do think funny things sometimes.
Perhaps I oughtn't to think them?"

"I love to hear what you think," said her mother. "You
know how much everything about you interests me. Tell me
everything—don't be afraid. I shall understand. Even if I
have not thought the things myself, which is quite likely—for we
are all different—even so I can sympathize, my darling."

And so up there in the loneliness of the mountains, with
cool night falling upon them, and bright stars appearing one by
one out of the dark, dense blueness of the sky, Quendred told her
mother the wonderings about love which had come to her since
the affair at the Dresden ball. And Maddalena, after letting her
talk her fill, explained to the girl the great life-giving mystery,
the knowledge of which should come to every man and woman in
the right way, and not be looked upon as a shameful secret, or
something horrible which was—in its essence—wrong. She
explained to her how it was this kind of view of life which spoilt
life, rubbed off all its bloom, and made it sordid and ugly.

"Yes," she went on, "you are quite right, loving *is* giving.
Those who love each other, give themselves with joy to each
other. Coarse, ugly jokes are made about—what is in reality—
the most wonderful thing in the world, but in the possibility of
the heights to which it can attain, only a God could have invented
this union, Quendred. In it we should look not only for a physical
satisfaction, but an intellectual and a moral one as well; our
husband should be our lover, our friend, our mate, our partisan,
and we should grow so close to him that when the autumn days
of life descend upon us—for they do descend, darling—we shall
know with a happy, peaceful heart that he to whom we gave ourselves in marriage with such a happy, ardent abandonment, still
cares more than anyone else in the world what sort of lace we wear

on our petticoat ! Do not be afraid or shocked of what marriage involves, for it is ideal and beautiful if a man and a woman truly love each other ; but man has so often pulled it down and besmirched it in the mud of his earthiness, that a totally wrong impression about the whole matter gains an entrance into the hearts of some girls and boys. That it is a distinctly physical action is true, but whether it becomes an animal satisfaction, completely divorced from an intellectual one, depends entirely upon ourselves."

While she had been speaking Maddalena had held her child's hand in hers, and neither hand had ever flinched.

.   .   .   .   .   .

It suddenly became chilly. They rose, and as they walked slowly upwards, arm linked in arm, Quendred said :

"For quite a long time I have seemed to have one idea in my head—an idea that I have never breathed to anyone, for it really is so silly that I am quite ashamed to speak of it, but somehow I can always tell you everything."

"What is it ? " asked her mother.

"Well—it's—it's that I have a tremendous wish to have a son—a son who will be in some way very great indeed—a man who will leave a mark on the world—a man whose name will never be forgotten."

"I don't see anything to be ashamed of in that ! "

"No, but that's not all, Mother ! You see, I feel that I can't just fall in love with *anybody*, as all those girls in Dresden did. I feel I must love someone very special, and in a special kind of way. I—I feel that I must choose with great care the man whom I wish to be the father of my child, and of course I must love him. I felt that Borvin was the last person on earth who was like that, and it really made me feel sorry for Father the other day when he told me what a pity it was that I had refused him, as it was so suitable ! Oh, Mother, how can I tell even *you* these thoughts of mine ? "

Since the birth of her children Maddalena's greatest wish had been that they should really love her ; love her in such a way that, had she not been their mother, they would have been irresistibly drawn to her.

The sentimental view of motherhood had never appealed to her. That her children ought to be consumed with eternal gratitude because she and her husband had conferred the gift of life upon them, was repugnant to her free and intensely natural personality. " We didn't do it to please God," she said, manfully confessing the truth to herself; " we did it entirely to please ourselves."

To her, the fact of physical motherhood was nothing. Given certain hygienic qualities, anything living can accomplish it. She wanted only to be the psychological, warm-hearted, profoundly human mother. Not the mother who looked upon the child as her perquisite, her chattel, her puppet to pull this way and that at her slightest whim, or to force into a mould of thought and type because of her own ideas as to what was correct, or true, or proper. But rather she wished to be the mother whose love had in it far more of the qualities of an ideal friendship than the virtues usually associated—somewhat coldly—with parenthood.

" What is this life worth," she thought, " if it is not to help each other ? And if this was true of friendship, and a test of it, how much more true it was of the mother's attitude to the child ? "

Yet mothers are mostly not like this. Many of them have, from the earliest age, given over their girls almost completely to the care of nurses, who, as they grow older, pass from stage to stage of governesses, and are seldom with their mother for more than a couple of hours in the day at most. Such a mother takes little or no responsibility on herself as to any part of her daughter's growth and development, yet is bitterly disappointed if the girl is indifferent to her when she grows up.

Then there is the sternly dutiful mother—who is always pursuing duty, whose whole idea of the management of her children is " my duty," and who thus assumes in the mind of her child the character of accuser far more than that of pleader.

Some women really see in themselves—in the capacity of " mother "—the reflection of the Godhead, and, in consequence, assume a rôle of perfection through which they, in some kind of terrible way, acquire an autocratic sway over their unmarried daughters.

They seem to love power over these unfortunate, defenceless creatures. They cling to it, press it, and insist upon it, and so sometimes become almost like an octopus in the way they live upon and assimilate the youth and virility of their children.

So Maddalena hoped always to be Quendred's best friend ; she hoped that she might never come to the end of her development, shut up, as it were, like an iron box, and thus leave her child to wander through the Elysian fields alone. She must see to it that Quendred should know the book of life, without beginning at the most sordid page first as she had done.

.   .   .   .   .   .

Soon Maddalena went into the hut to prepare for bed, but Quendred could not drag herself away from the overwhelming and unique beauty of the night. Walking slowly away from the hut, she soon found herself in a strange little fairy-like space, closely surrounded by rocks. Climbing to the top of one of them, she felt almost like a god looking down upon the sleeping earth. It was a moving and a most stupendous scene. Below her the passionate world lay sleeping, and all around was silence.

Silence ! Silence ! Still and sweet—sweet and soft.

Silence !—such a silence ! It seemed to speak, it was so silent.

Suddenly raising her hands unclasped to Heaven, she cried —a trumpet blast amid those everlasting, sleeping hills—

" Oh, God, give me some day a son who will be great ! "

.   .   .   .   .   .

Quendred was awakened early by light coming through the chinks in the loosely constructed little room. She rose, and, dressing quickly, went and sat outside to await the great sight of sunrise. As yet the sky was but of early grey and she felt chilly, so to get warm she collected sticks and made a fire and fetched water from a tiny, trickling stream near by to boil it for their breakfast. Soon cheery flames were crackling, and the blue smoke went clouding upwards. And now the sky was slowly changing to a transparent daffodil hue.

Quendred called her mother, and, while she was dressing, went out again to make the tea and to lay out an appetizing little meal with a few provisions which they had brought with them. She then fetched the rugs and cushions on which she had slept, so that when her mother joined her everything was ready.

Here, while they ate their breakfast of hard-boiled eggs and bread and butter, they beheld the sun burst forth, from the shades of night, in beauteous scarlet glory upon the newly-awakened world. And at his advent, life—which had been sleeping—woke to work. The leaves began to move gently, animals appeared and shyly ran away again ; in the distance the lowing of cattle could be heard, and later, the voices of men would

M

float up to them from the distant little homesteads. They sat very quietly, enthralled by its grandeur.

Up there, though, it was none too warm, and so, packing up their things, they soon made ready to descend.

"Dear little hut—good-bye," said Quendred. "In all human probability I shall never see you again," and she kissed her hand to it as a turn in the path finally hid it from view. As they went down, the air grew deliciously warm and fragrant, and they seated themselves upon the soft moss, to read and enjoy the long day which they had before them. Maddalena had long wanted to tell Quendred all about her father, and she felt this was the moment for doing so. She told her.

"And so, Mother, will he really leave you and go to be a priest ?" asked the girl, whose eyes had grown wide with surprise as her mother pursued the strange story. What struck her most was that her father should wish to leave her mother ! She couldn't understand it.

"But, Mother dearest, I thought that the Catholic Church forbade people to leave each other, besides—I thought that only wicked people ever wanted to part ? But you and Father ! It's dreadful. Oh, Mother, what shall we do ? What a fearful disgrace to us all ! "

"You mustn't say it's a disgrace, Quenny dear, because, of course, being a priest is a very high calling—really the highest calling in the world."

"But still," said the girl, " the marriage says so distinctly, ' for better, for worse—till death us do part.' I remember it well, because I read the words over to myself the day after Borvin asked me to marry him, and I felt I just couldn't ! Will the Church let him leave you ? They can't if they really mean what they say, can they ? "

"The Church can do anything she likes, darling, if she sees fit," answered her mother. " You see, it's not for us to give an opinion. In matters upon which the Church has laid down certain serious rules—apart even from when she speaks ' ex cathedra ' —Catholics may have no opinion of their own. One of the fundamental ideas of our religion is discipline ; implicit and unquestioning obedience to the rules of Holy Church—just like an army ; obey your Commanding Officer or you get shot—obey the Church or you go to hell ; that is really what the basic teaching is. Everything has been thought out for us. We have only got to obey without thinking."

" But, Mother, it's impossible not to think," answered Quendred. " Besides, one's whole bringing-up was one long litany of ' think.' *Think* before you speak—*think* of what you're doing— *think* of what I told you—*think* of what you're learning—*think* of what you saw. Then if one does think seriously one is told not to ! I suppose the truth is that if one thinks their ' think ' it is all right, but if one thinks one's own ' think ' it is all wrong ! "

Her mother smiled. " Private judgment is not encouraged you see, dear, in our religion," she said, " for we are all part of a huge wonderful machine whose electric spark is in Rome. Uncle Guiseppe always told me that the idea which was started in the Middle Ages that men, on becoming priests, should lose their citizenship, was founded for this very reason, so that they should only be citizens of the Church—work only for it, and be held by ties neither of blood nor of patriotism. The Church demands the entire service of priests—body, mind, heart, and soul, and to her alone is their allegiance due."

Between them there fell a long silence—and the girl, feeling her mother wanted to be alone, sauntered away, leaving Maddalena by herself in that great loneliness to combat her grief ; to linger over and caress the past before she laid it in its shroud of memory ; to brace herself for the future which seemed to be so bristling with difficulties and the wagging of tongues.

" How strange it is," Maddalena thought, as she lay on the mountain-side, " that I should have had such a blaze of happiness at first. How I worshipped every look in his eye, every turn of his beautiful head. How gloriously proud I was of being the one whom he had chosen. That first year ! What halcyon days they were ! It was all like treading on air till the children were born and then—when I thought that our bliss was most jubilantly crowned—our castle seemed to crumble to pieces ! So gradually though, so imperceptibly, that sometimes I thought it must be my imagination. But my darling *had* changed—I, in my heart of hearts, knew it. I tried to think it was not true. I prayed that all might come right again, and that we could be lovers once more. And yet, with all his growing coldness to me, and with all the hardening of his little ways towards me, I could sometimes detect a fleeting wistfulness in his eyes as I found them lingering on me, when he thought I was unconscious of his look. Then he would redden and move away, and make an irrelevant remark, and for days would avoid me in a furtive kind of way. And so I felt, and somehow I still feel—although there is this tremendous power dragging him away from me to the priesthood—that down at the bottom of his being he loves me still and, what is more, will always love me. I know now that he thinks I led him away from his vocation, and so, in blaming himself for his weakness, he cannot help blaming me also.

"Poor Stephen, poor darling! But—will you be happy if you go? I wonder! I pray that you may be, but it is not willingly that I let you go."

She stretched her hands out upon the hot earth as she lay prone, as though beaten to the ground with sorrow. All of us must pass through our hours of *Sturm und Drang*, and she was now passing through hers, as Stephen had been through his that night twenty years before, with ' Rosemouth,' radiant and soulless, smiling upon him in the great hall at Ullcombe.

And as she lay there—for those few hours so far from the world of business, and plans, and cheque-books, and lawyers, and agents, and religiosity, and newspapers, and correspondence, and callers, and politeness, and servants, and bills, and the one hundred and one little bothers that go to make up life—she wondered how she was going to cope with it all, and how it would end.

In a little time Quendred returned, and as they sat together she asked her mother what would happen about Anthony's coming-of-age, and their future lives?

"It will seem so funny—living at Ullcombe without Father! And who will be the master?" she asked.

There was no answer, and she turned to her mother, whose silence she then saw, to her dismay, was caused by tears. Her mother crying? This was a thing that she had never seen before.

"Oh, my darling," she cried, "forgive me for being so thoughtless and cruel. In my great surprise at what you have just told me I didn't think of what you must be feeling. Poor, pretty Mother," and she hugged her. "How can Father leave you? How can he *want* to leave you? Why! everyone in Dresden, and here too, thinks that you are the most lovely person they've ever seen. Do stop crying, Mother—do stop! Let me bathe your eyes for you," and she ran off to a tiny stream near by, bringing back her handkerchief soaking wet from its icy water, with which she bathed her mother's eyes.

"Quenny, dear, I am so sorry that I have let you see me like this," her mother smiled through her tears. "I had always

hoped that I should be able to bear it quite alone ; but I wonder
if you can realize how much I have loved your father, and how
much I love him still ?   When I gave my heart to him years ago
at Santa Fiora I never thought about children—as you told me
last night *you* do ; I just only wanted him, nothing else."

And then she told her child the story of their betrothal by
the roadside Crucifix on the road to Santa Barbara.

"I have always kept the little ring of golden straw with
which he wedded me up there in the mountains "—she smiled
sadly—" although it needed no ring of gold or public promises
to bind me to him for ever !   But, alas ! I have come to see that
it was but a ring of straw after all."

.   .   .   .   .   .

The next day, when Stephen returned from his visit to the
Prinz-Bishop, he was in a very silent mood.   His physical
health was perfect once more, and he looked younger than the
day the depressed little cortège had arrived from Dresden.
The bishop was a middle-aged, good-looking man of the
world, and belonged to one of the highest families in
Hungary.   Before he had become a priest he had been one of the
best-known dancers in Europe.   He still went to London every
year, where he made a brilliant figure at social functions in his
scarlet robes, and was a much sought-after guest at the most
chic houses in London.   He found it rather difficult to enter into
Stephen's mentality, and advised him to go and stay with his
brother in Hungary, where he would get some first-rate shooting.

"He has a son just about the right age for your daughter,
of whose beauty and charm even my sequestered celibate ears
have heard ! Why, Duke, you ought to be engaged upon taking
her into society and finding her a suitable husband, instead
of morbidly regretting the past of your own life ! You were
young once and had your chance, your free-will—and—well,
from what you tell me, according to your present ideas—you made
a mistake which, with the passing of the years, has grown to be a
sin in your view and seriously obsesses your life.   But what's
to be done ?   I see no way out of it ; you must shake it off.
Don't let it get hold of you.   Isn't there some work which you
could take up actively, and so help your mind not to dwell on this
idea of yours ? "

"I'm going to be a priest, though, my Lord," said Stephen.
"I believe it can be done, although no priest has ever definitely

told me so.   But there are precedents for it, and I can't bear my
present life any longer.   It's torture—torture."

" Yes, yes, of course it can be done," replied the Churchman in soothing tones, " but still, it's a funny thing to want to
do."

" Funny ! "   Stephen broke in excitedly.   " Why funny ?
How can you—a priest of God—use the word *funny* with regard
to *me ?* I want to be a *priest,* don't you understand ?   I want
to be able to change the bread and wine into the Body and Blood
of Our Lord.   I want to have all those wonderful powers which
Christ gave to His apostles before He died.   I want to live as
near to God as possible—I want to be able to perform daily at Mass
the miracle of the world."   His eyes were shining again with the
old fanatical look.

" How can *you* a priest, " he went on—" *you* who possess
this wonderful, glorious power—how can you say it is *funny*
of me to wish to enter the priesthood ? "

Both men were upset : the bishop at his inability to understand or comfort Stephen, and Stephen because the attitude of
the worldly-wise cleric pained and worried him.

Luncheon was announced, and they sat down to a meal of
foie-gras, freshwater trout, roe-deer, mountain strawberries,
rare hock, and enormous peaches, finishing up with Viennese
coffee and Tokay, that wonderful sunlike liqueur of which
the bishop had inherited a hundred dozen bottles from his
grandfather.

Stephen—all the time they were eating—was longing to discuss the things of God, the doings of the Saints, and the rules of
the Catholic Church, whereas his genial and pleasant host insisted upon talking about his *chef's* attainments, or his many
friends in London, very few of whom in reality Stephen knew at
all, as his keeping so entirely out of *le monde ou l'on s'amuse*
had cut him off from much that was delightful in England.

The bishop seemed surprised at this.

" But I love London," quoth he.   " I think it is the most
agreeable town in the world.   Why do you see few people ?
Does it not seem a pity ?   And for your children too !   Your
daughter must marry—eh ?   You are not going to turn her into
a nun, I hope ? "

" No, I suppose she will marry some day," replied Stephen,
moodily, " but for English Catholics matrimony is a difficult
business.   You foreigners—living in countries where pratically

all aristocracy is Catholic—do not, I think, understand our position. ' Mixed ' marriages are greatly deprecated by the Church, and if I were Pope I'd stop them altogether, so deeply do I disapprove of them."

" But surely, Duke, you can convert the young men ? From what I noticed in England they didn't strike me as being very religious ! Just a fine-looking lot of perfectly charming fellows living chiefly for sport, while they let the middle-class people do the governing. That is what your beautiful England seemed to me, and here it is very much the same."

" *Convert* them ! " said Stephen. " Why, my Lord, you cannot realize the wall that there is between Catholics and Protestants in England, although to a superficial eye it may not be apparent. And conversions are very rare ; I mean important ones. Mine, together with that of two or three other peers, have been the first ones of any social significance which have taken place for years, and it has nearly entirely cut me off from any pleasant intercourse with my relations, who are all very great Protestants."

" But surely those charming Englishmen, in whose delightful houses I have spent many enchanting days, and who appeared so easy-going and even thoughtless, about religious matters— surely *they* could be easily got to sign the paper which is all that the Church requires in the cases of ' mixed ' marriages ? " said the bishop. " I remember talking to a Protestant once in England on this subject, and he told me that although he would never become a Catholic himself, he wouldn't at all object to his children being brought up as such, for he said our Church seemed to be the only people who had something definite to teach about religion."

" Yes, I know that is constantly being done, but not amongst our set, not amongst aristos (I can speak like this to you, my Lord, because you will understand, belonging as you do to a nation which thinks more of these things than any other in the world, I suppose). No, as a whole, the great families of England have set their faces against Catholicism. They do not encourage their sons to meet Catholic girls of their own rank, no matter how pretty they are."

" The prettier and the more attractive they are, the less they wish them to meet, naturally," interjected the bishop with a knowing smile.

" And," continued Stephen, " there is practically no peer or eldest son of a peer who has signed that paper to marry a Catholic girl. I am now speaking of the great old families. The new lords hardly count, of course," and a look of his dead father flushed over his face.

The words found an echo in the heart of the handsome priest, whose exalted family boasted no less than one hundred and thirty-two quarterings!

"A few have done it, but really very few, and some of them did it with the full intention of not carrying it out," Stephen went on. "Conversions come chiefly from the clergy, University dons, schoolmasters, writers, actors, and artists, and also a certain number of younger sons and daughters of good families, who, as a rule, do not object to signing, and the younger children are of no importance, of course. But the heads of the families seldom do it. You see what I mean, my Lord?"

"Yes—yes, I see," said the other, drumming his well-manicured fingers upon the beautiful damask cloth, in which was woven the Royal Crown, which his name entitled him to use. "England wants to keep out Rome! She fears Rome! Even from the earliest days, though—Catholic days, I mean—she has resented papal authority, hasn't she? From your description social life in England must be a great difficulty for Catholics, isn't it? Yet, after all, marriage is the end of all social intercourse! I really had no idea it was like that!"

"No, I don't suppose you had. Few foreigners would understand it," said Stephen.

"But surely many Protestant girls marry Catholics?" queried the Bishop.

"Yes," said Stephen. "But you see there is not quite the same difficulty there. It's the man, after all, who carries on the name, and it is more natural for a woman not to object to merging herself in her husband's family than it is for him—as the head—not to wish his family's religion changed by a marriage."

"That seems rather unfair, though," laughed the other. "The naughty Protestant damsels are poaching on Catholic preserves, eh? What happens to the poor little Catholics? They go into convents, I suppose, as numberless Austrian girls do, for there are not enough men to go round!"

"Yes, either that, or they marry nobodies," said Stephen. But a second later his face lit up, and he said vehemently: "Even so, I'd rather that; I'd rather *anything* almost than that my daughter married a Protestant. It is a false religion

—it is the religion of the devil. Never, never, could I allow it."

The Bishop sighed.

" Ah, well," he said, " you'd better come and live in Austria, where we have no difficulties of that sort, as everybody is of the same religion, and the matter is seldom discussed. In England it seems you are kind of martyrs for the Faith ! "

" Yes, that's the beauty of it," replied Stephen fervently. " One only realizes how glorious one's religion is when one has to suffer for it."

" It seems a lot of unnecessary suffering, though, for the fact of being English ! " said the Bishop. " For in Austria, Hungary, Italy, Belgium, Spain, France, and Bavaria there would be no difficulties such as you describe, and your house is one with which even our greatest families could mate, I should think."

He said this in such a natural way that Stephen was rather amused, but couldn't refrain from saying, " In spite of everything, though, I'd rather be an English Catholic than anything else, and I'm glad that we don't go in for making all the fuss about sixteen quarterings as you do on the Continent, and so we can marry whom we like."

" Quite so, quite so," said the Bishop suavely. " Well, I only hope that your son will marry whom he likes ! There must be very many little English *fraüleins* who would be only too delighted to become Lady Athelston ; and as for your daughter —well, you must find her a good Catholic husband ; one of those University dons you told me about, for instance."

This made Stephen angry.

" She'll marry whoever she likes, I should think," he said quickly, " and she's already refused Neiphausen's son."

The Prinz-Bishop was very much surprised ; for this bit of news had not yet come to his ears, as such news generally did, through his enormous number of relatives dispersed through Europe.

" The Neiphausens are great people," he said, stroking his chin. " The son is one of the plums of Europe. A pity ! Couldn't it have been arranged ? Had it been one of our girls it would have taken place."

" You do not know Quendred ! No one can ' arrange ' her," said Stephen, momentarily rather proud of the daughter of whom in reality he entirely disapproved. " May I see the chapel before I leave ? " he asked, and was shown into a little pink and white marble room with a gold-domed roof.

The altar was delicately carved in rose-quartz and behind it hung dark blue velvet curtains. A solid silver candelabra hung before it, containing the familiar ruby light of all Catholic churches. Both men knelt. Stephen, with head devoutly bowed, was at once lost in prayer, and became oblivious to everything but his Divine Maker hidden there in the Tabernacle under the form of a wafer.

The bishop looked at him. " Poor fellow," he thought, " poor fellow; but anyhow, I have pricked him a bit, and it may make him see that his domestic ties do come before any dreams of another life, be they ever so holy or exalted. I really must tell Johann to put some fresh roses into that bowl before Our Lady's statue."

And so they parted : Stephen to his unsatisfactory, impossible life—uncomforted ; and the Prinz-Bishop to prepare for to-morrow's journey to Hungary, where he was going to shoot partridges with his brother—his yearly holiday.

" A hopeless case—a hopeless case," he soliloquized, as he looked down the barrels of his guns after he had bidden his unhappy guest farewell.

.   .   .   .   .   .

That night Stephen and Maddalena had a long talk. She was anxious to know how he had fared with the bishop, although he showed no interest in hers and Quendred's mountain trip.

That he wasn't much impressed by the sanctity of his late host, she could plainly see, although he said he had sensible matter-of-fact views.

Walking nervously up and down her bedroom, with the noise of the gushing snow river coming in through the open windows, and wearily passing the back of his hand across his forehead, he said :

" This existence of ours can't go on, Maddalena, can it ? We have talked it over before, always hoping to find some way by which things could be arranged. However, since my con-versations with Dr. Offenbach I have thought about it all even more seriously, if possible, than ever before, and in consequence I have been corresponding with Father Bischoffsheim, and he, with Offenbach, agrees that a final decision must be made *now*, You know how ill I've been, and I feel that the same might hap-pen again if this awful tension goes on. It's cruel to expect me to live as I have been doing for the last years any longer. I can't, it's killing me, and I feel I might go mad if I go on with it any more."

For a moment his wife lost her self-control.

" And what about me ? Is *my* life, *my* happiness, of no account ? Are *you* the only person whose feelings are important ? Leaving out the human aspect of our lives, how can you reconcile it with your conscience and your religion to—— "

Stephen held up his hand.

" Please don't bring in religion in that way, Maddalena, it is the most important thing in the world, and everything else is only secondary to it. I believe—though I am at present not quite sure—that the Church *does* allow a man to leave his wife in order to enter the priesthood."

" The Church ! the Church ! the Church ! " she broke in bitterly ; " you have almost made me hate that word, ' the Church.' I deny that ' the Church ' has the right to allow a woman's life to be ruined. The love in our lives I will not touch upon, although God knows that we have loved each other, and I —I love you still. . . . But how can you reconcile the breaking of your vows with any sense of duty to our children and to our position in the world ? I can't understand you, and your utter selfishness is beyond my comprehension."

She stepped out on to the balcony to let the cool night mountain air play upon her face. Wringing her hands together she murmured, " This Church, this everlasting Church," and the mountains seemed to echo in a mysterious whisper the word— " Church." From behind her and simultaneously came Stephen's voice uttering automatically the cold, bloodless formulæ ; words that Jesus never said, words that almost made her scream :

" No one may question the Church's decision, she represents God—in fact, *is* God, so nothing she teaches can be either wrong or false."

" That is the secret of its power," thought the distracted woman. " It teaches this so continuously, so persistently, that even against one's will one is forced to believe it, for—from the Catholic point of view—it savours of terrible blasphemy not to believe it."

In a little while she turned back into the room, her anger gone. Going up to her husband, she put both hands upon his shoulders.

" But the Church has parted us, Stephen ; would *Christ* have parted us ? "

" I am a sword," quoted her husband sternly, and then she knew that she must fight no more for her love, her rights, her children and their future, but bow her head to the axe.

" You had something special to tell me, I think," she said, withdrawing from his side, and standing again at the windows.

" Yes, I had," he said, relieved at this last attitude. " It's this. Some time ago I met a wonderful Jesuit—the one who has preached so much in London. He gives Retreats for men somewhere in Bavaria, and he told me that if ever I wanted advice and sympathy I was to go to him. He and I had a long talk once," and at the words his cheeks flushed dully, for he thought he had been happy before this famous " talk," and he wouldn't for the world like his wife to know what the priest had said. He didn't want her to know of the effect the Jesuit's words had had upon him.

" He is said to be a kind of second Ignatius Loyola," he finished rather lamely.

" Good gracious ! " said his wife.

Supremely indifferent to her opinion of that Saint, he went on : " I feel such trust in him, and Father Bischoffsheim advises me so strongly to go to one of his Retreats that I have arranged to do so. I shall then make up my mind quite definitely. I shall go entirely on his advice, for I have seldom—I might say never—been in contact with such a holy man."

" Priests, always priests," sighed Maddalena.

" I have settled to go next week," went on Stephen, ignoring her interruption. " It only lasts four days, so I shan't be away long. I will go with you to Santa Fiora, though, for a couple of days, as I want particularly to see Anthony and your father before taking this final step.'

" Yes," said Maddalena.

" Good-night, dear," he said kindly, as he kissed her forehead.

When he had gone, she drew a chair on to the balcony. One by one the lights from the neighbouring houses had disappeared, and a deep silence fell, broken only by the wild rush of the river just below.

Last night she had slept on the very top of one of the great mountains at which she was gazing so earnestly now, trying to fathom deep serious things which baffled her faith, but not her intellect.

Up there for those few hours the importance of things which worried her so much down here had suddenly dwindled. Were those their rightful proportions, or were these ? Did all these strict Church laws *really* matter, or did they only *seem* to matter ?

And then into her sick and weary brain slipped a heaven-sent medicine, cool and refreshing like a draught of icy, sparkling, pure water is to the parched tongue of the sun-baked, fevered explorer of the desert. A strange, soft voice seemed to be speaking to her—" Nothing matters but God—nothing matters but God," it repeated quietly and calmly, and then, as though to still the last torturing doubt, it added very gently and with a magical potency of supreme and profound conviction :

" And this Church is not God, nor does it represent ME."

CHAPTER XIII

THE HEART OF QUENDRED

" He knows behind all creeds the spirit that was One."—ANDREW LANG.

ON arriving at Santa Fiora they were told that Anthony had
gone to Rome.

" He found it so dull here, poor boy, so we let him go," cooed
Bianca, " but he promised to be back to-night.   A train arrives
at 10.30, so I said we'd all wait up for him."

" I certainly won't," said the culprit's father.   " It's disgraceful of him to behave like this.   I've come here on purpose
to see him.   I really wish you had persuaded him to stay."

He spoke petulantly, and glanced angrily at his mother-in-
law.   They didn't care for each other.

The retort, " Well, I don't suppose he'll mind whether he
sees you or not, from what he tells me," sprang to her lips, but,
for the sake of peace, she repressed it.

Anthony didn't return, however, and a cloud fell upon them
all.

Maddalena went to Bianca's room when the carriage came
back empty from the station, and they talked far into the night.

" Tell me what you think of Anthony ?   Has he been nice
here ? " asked his anxious mother.   " I'm afraid he's rather wild,
and I'm so distressed about it, as I had hoped he would have
been like his grandfather and Stephen were when they were
young ; and of course Hugh Traquair is always being held up
to me as a pattern of a young man by my mother-in-law."

" I think Anthony is a dear boy," said Bianca.   " He is so
good-looking, and amusing, and gay ; we're never dull when
he is in the house.   And as for his being a little wild—well, all
young men are that, aren't they ? "

" I know it's the fashion for them to be, but Stephen never
was," said Maddalena.

"And look at him now," broke in her mother, shrugging her shoulders.

"I did so hope that he would never drop below a certain standard of behaviour. I had wanted him to be a true Knight of the Grail," went on Maddalena, ignoring her mother's interruption.

"You are too anxious, dear," said Bianca. "You worry too much about such things. All young men have their *amitiés* and their *amours* before they marry—it's only natural—but after marriage *bien entendu* all that changes, and they settle down to a *belle vie de famille*. It will always be like this, you cannot change it."

"But that is just where I don't agree, Mother," said the daughter. "I can't see why, because a thing has always been, that it should always go on being. Of course there will always be sin. But I feel so convinced that by education men can be made different. I know it's true, for I have seen it ; and I think it very often is the result of having a wonderful father. People talk so much about the mother's influence, of how men's mothers make the world, and of children praying at their mother's knee, but I think that the reason why wonderful sons are rare is because wonderful fathers are rare. Good mothers are necessary, of course, but good fathers are just as necessary. By good fathers I don't mean religious bores who cast a dreary gloom over everything, any more than I mean that when I speak of a good mother. I think a father should be his son's standard of perfection."

Bianca didn't agree with these views, which were too unlike anything which she had ever been accustomed to, so she merely answered :

"Anthony will turn out all right, you'll see. Perhaps even a better man in the end for a little ' wild oats.' You mustn't be too strict ! And now, tell me about Stephen. I can see you are worried about him, and so you would naturally get more upset than's necessary about Anthony. Leave him alone and he'll come home, and bring his tail behind him ! "

Maddalena laughed at her ever-youthful mother's efforts to comfort her.

And so Maddalena told her everything, and of how Stephen was going to a Retreat in Bavaria next week, and that was why he was particularly annoyed with Anthony for not having come back.

" You see, I think he wanted to make final arrangements here, and to get Father to help him to make his will," she said.

" Whose idea is the Retreat ? " asked Bianca.

" Apparently he is being much influenced by that Father Ignatius," answered Maddalena, " whose sermons made such a commotion in London two years ago. I didn't know Stephen knew him till the other day, it came out by chance in conversation."

" Who is this priest ? " asked the Princess. " He has been everywhere, except to Rome, it appears. He seems to be a marvellous linguist. Apparently he only preaches to men though, and no one knows anything about him, except that he is a Jesuit."

" That's enough, I should think," mused Maddalena.

" You seem bitter when you speak of Jesuits ! Have you changed since you lived in that cold, wicked, Protestant England, where no one can be saved ? " said Bianca.

" Mother ! You really don't believe that no Protestants can be saved, do you ? " said the daughter.

" Of course I do, darling, the Creed says so. It says distinctly that anybody who does not hold the Catholic Faith shall be damned. Surely that's clear enough ! *All* Catholics must believe it, darling, and I *hope* you do."

" But I can't, Mother, I simply can't, and when my English Protestant friends ask me if we really and truly *do* believe that they can't be saved, I always say that of course we *don't !* I always try to make the best of my Faith to those outside it, and I tell them that it is only their woeful ignorance of our Church which makes them think things of her which none of us in reality believes. And yet when I read the Service of the Form for the reception into our Church of a non-Catholic I am dumbfounded, for there I see the words printed, ' I (N.N.) having before my eyes the Holy Gospels, which I touch with my hand, and knowing that no one can be saved without that Faith which the Holy, Catholic, Apostolic, Roman Church holds, believes, and teaches ; against which I grieve that I have greatly erred . . .' and so it goes on. So what is one to believe as to the Church's point of view ? I'm not surprised they think we think they can't be saved ! Our Lord's words, on the contrary, say so clearly that if we believe in *Him* we shall not see death for ever."

" Did God say those words ? How do you know, Maddalena ? " asked her mother.

" Well, they come in the Bible."

" Oh, Madre de Dio ! You don't read the Bible, do you, my

child ?   Whatever can have happened to you since you have lived in England ?   Have you lost your faith ?   Fancy reading the Bible ! "

She paused a moment and then said sadly :

" It may be a retribution to you for reading that Protestant book that Stephen should want to leave you and go to be a monk !   I daresay you've worried him into it, Maddalena, by having such strange, irreligious ideas.   Dear, dear, it's all so different from what we thought and hoped long ago, when Stephen came here first."

" Yes, I know," her daughter replied, " but I believe that it was always his wish to become a priest—from the very beginning of his conversion.   He says he has always thought it the most beautiful thing in the world."

" Did he ?   Why did he marry, then ? " asked Bianca.

Maddalena paused a little before answering.   " I think—I believe—that he almost fell in love with me against his will ; in fact, he has practically told me so, Mother dear," and she smiled piteously.

" But he pursued you, and when you were there he never took his eyes off you.   What nonsense !   Men can't be turned from a really great vocation so easily.   It wasn't even propinquity.   It happened in a minute.   Uncle Guiseppe told me that he literally saw it happening the famous night you met at the poor old Cavallhos' house."

" But don't you remember how often Uncle Guiseppe brought him with him to see us ?   Now that I look back to it, I think that he rather urged it on," said Maddalena, and then a light suddenly broke over her face.   The remembrance of the letter the Cardinal had given her on his death-bed came to her.   It was still unread, and then a sudden thought seemed to strike her.

" I wonder !   Oh, I wonder if—— " and she paused.

" What do you wonder ? "

" I wonder if Uncle Guiseppe made him marry me ? " and Maddalena's eyes narrowed as though she were cringing away from the swing of a lash.

" You're getting morbid, my child," said Bianca, assuming a gaiety she didn't feel.   She couldn't bear to see the storm clouds gathering round her beloved Maddalena, and, being rather superstitious, like all Sicilians, she managed to purloin Maddalena's Bible from her bedroom, and throw it into the fire.

N

Meanwhile Anthony hadn't wasted his time in Rome, and had ended it by getting a violent concussion through riding in some races on the Campagna. This was the reason for his not having arrived to meet his parents.

The whole establishment was in an uproar of excitement on account of his illness, and his mother and grandmother rushed to Rome to nurse him.

Stephen went to his Retreat, and Quendred was left with her grandfather, who allowed her to do everything she liked.

With Stephen out of the house a sense of calmness and peacefulness descended and took possession. How delightful and restful it was not to have to talk when she didn't feel inclined to—to have her meals when she liked, and to go for long walks in the mountains, which were looking specially beautiful now in the golden harvest and the burnished lights of early autumn.

One day she found herself on the road to Santa Barbara, and, being tired, she sat down to rest and eat her sandwiches at the little wayside Crucifix. Suddenly she heard someone singing. It was a man's voice, full and sweet, and it was English and not Italian in which the singer sang.

"Strange," she thought. "An Englishman in this wild, out-of-the-way place. Who can it be?"

At that moment a man appeared round the bend in the white dusty road—a tall figure walking merrily with swinging gait. On seeing the girl, he stopped his song, and over his dark clean-shaven face came the most attractive smile she had ever seen.

He went towards her at once, saying courteously in bad Italian: "I beg your pardon, but would you allow me to eat my sandwiches here also? This Crucifix was the object of my walk, as the people at the inn at Santa Barbara told me that from here can be seen the finest view of the country for miles round. I hope I shall have your permission?"

She almost laughed, for he spoke with such an obviously English accent, and yet, curiously, not quite English. She was a little puzzled, and became anxious to know his exact nationality.

"Please sit wherever you like, the place doesn't belong to me," she answered in her fluent Italian.

Thanking her, he went a little away and sat down. There was silence for a time, and then she thought how ridiculous it was.

"He looks rather nice," she thought. "I think I'll talk to him."

" Are you staying near here ? " she asked conversationally in Italian.

He answered that he was making a walking tour through Italy. They conversed for a short time, but she saw that it was really difficult for him.

At last she laughed saying, " Why don't you speak English ? You'd get on much better."

A look of intense surprise crossed his face. " But you—would you understand me if I spoke in English ? "

" Oh! yes, I know it as well as Italian," she answered smiling.

" You don't look like an Italian, somehow," he said.

" Nor you exactly like an Englishman," she returned.

" Well, perhaps I'm not English," he answered, whilst he began to untie his little parcel of sandwiches.

She looked at him scrutinizingly from under her enormous straw hat, and rather liked what she saw ; a clever, Dantesque type of face, with thoughtful brows and deep-set, flashing eyes.

" I hope you do not mind my talking to you in this un-ceremonious way, signorina, but it seems natural that we should do so, meeting as we have in this out-of-the-way place. It is very beautiful. Do you know it well, or are you—like I am—but a wayfarer here ? "

" No, I'm not a wayfarer," she answered. " This country is like a second home to me. I live here for several months every year."

" May I ask, then, where your real home is ? "

" I live in England," she said.

" Ah ! England is a wonderful country, and the English the finest people in the world. I have never been there yet, though I hope to be able to manage it soon. Every year I go for a trip. Some day perhaps it will be England."

" Don't you live there, then ? " queried the girl.

" No," he said. " Could you guess where I live, I wonder ? "

" Well, you look rather French, but I'm sure you're not that. No, I can't imagine where you come from. You speak English so well. Tell me."

" Well," he smiled, " I come from Canada. My family have lived in the West for three generations."

" How interesting," said Quendred, " I have always longed to go to Canada. It must be a glorious country. Its wildness appeals to me, and its great wide spaces ! Europe must seem tiny to you after living out there, doesn't it ? "

He smiled at her, delighted at her enthusiasm. It was a quality which he liked. As she talked, he looked at her more closely, and he realized how lovely she was, how, in fact, he had never seen such a lovely girl before. And sitting there on the road to Santa Barbara, by that wayside Crucifix, he told himself that she was the most beautiful, the most lovable woman whom he had ever seen, and that whoever she was—or wasn't—he would surely make her his wife.

"Yes, everything seems rather cramped here," he answered. "Europe is like a perfectly finished picture, whereas we are only just beginning to work on Canada, and there's plenty to do there."

"What a wonderful work—to make a country!" mused Quendred. "As you say, Europe is finished; but isn't it a glorious place all the same, with its huddled old towns reeking of history, its galleries full of pictures which kings have stolen from each other as they made history, and every bit of land stained with heroes' blood, given freely without counting the cost for their kings? That is what the new world lacks—history, tradition, romance! Don't you feel that when you come to Europe?"

"Yes, I do," he answered. "Yet you know Canada has a great charm of its own—especially the far west. As you said just now, its great endless spaces, its strong, enormous rivers, its forests so unknown, so full of mystery. No past, I own, belongs to Canada, but a very great and important future is hers. She may out-last the parent who gave her birth."

"You don't really believe that?" queried the girl.

"*Chi lo sa?*—stranger things have happened," the Canadian answered. "But I do think that old Europe's innings are about finished, don't you, signorina?" And with these words he rose. Quendred was quite sorry, for she rather liked the stranger.

He came towards her, hat in hand.

"*A riverderci!*" he said. "Some day, somewhere, I shall see you again. Will you allow me to give you my card?" Then, taking her proffered hand," he said: "No, I will not say good-bye."

He walked slowly away in the direction from which he had appeared, and in a few minutes he turned the corner on the hot, dusty road, and disappeared from the girl's sight.

She looked at the card: on it was written:

Simon de Villancourt,
Vancouver,
B.C.

and in the left-hand corner was given an address in Ottawa.

"What a funny little episode ! I wonder if I ever *shall* see him again ? " she thought, as she wandered home in the lengthening shadows.

To the man who retraced his steps towards the vine-clad inn at Santa Barbara the world was a different place from what it had been in the morning. A woman had appeared in his life, and no woman had ever had a place there before. He was thirty, and yet this was true. He had never yet loved anyone. He liked women, and their society attracted him, but beyond ordinary social intercourse his record was a clean sheet.

"Who would be a beautiful girl with fair hair whom I saw on the road of the Crucifix ? " he asked of the maid who waited on him at his frugal supper that night. "I don't quite think she was an Italian."

"Oh, that was the grand-daughter of the Principe di Santa Fiora, who lives at the Castello on the other side of the hill. She *is* beautiful and *Inglesi,*" the girl said.

"Really ? " answered the man, feigning a nonchalance which he didn't feel. "You don't happen to know her name ? "

"I can never remember her name, signor, it is so funny, but Signora Landini will know, she always knows everything."

"It really doesn't matter," said de Villancourt, getting up and lighting a cigarette. *Buona notte,* and he strolled out into the soft, languorous twilight.

He had met his fate and he knew it. Love was hammering at the door of his heart and would not be denied. He had always hoped that it would come some day, as he felt he had much to give ; and now, at last, it was here, and there was no mistaking its voice.

As he walked through the fields far into the summer night much wonderment about her filled his mind. That he and she would marry eventually was already an established fact in his life. Living without her would be impossible. Her personality and her beauty enthralled, held, and enveloped him. He walked on air. Life was glorious ; the world—an oyster—lay at his feet, already slightly opened. What more would it not hold for him with this exquisite girl as his wife ?

Next morning Signora Landini herself brought him his breakfast of aromatic coffee and fresh rolls. Of course the little maid had told her of the conversation she had had with M. de Villancourt on the previous night, and their ardent Southern

natures were tingling with excitement at the thought of a romance.
Their only fear was that the quiet gentleman who said he was a
Canadian would be *troppo fredo* for the lovely *Principessa Inglese*,
as she was called by the people for miles around.

" Has the Signor been to see the Castello di Santa Fiora ? "
she asked him cunningly, as she placed the appetizing little meal
in front of him.　　I think the Signor said he would be going away
to Rome next week, and it would be a pity not to see the Castello.
It is very old and picturesque."

Her beady eyes did not fail to notice that a flush crept
under his dark skin at her question, and of course he knew what
she was up to.

He looked at her, and they both laughed.

" Well," said he, " I will make no secret of it, and I would
very much like to go to see what there is to be seen at the Castello
di Santa Fiora.　It's a pretty name, is it not, signora ? "

" *Si si, signor*, a pretty name and many pretty things to be
seen there, if you know where to look ! " she retorted.

And, without waiting to put him to the discomfort of asking
any questions, she reeled off the history of the family, whole
and entire, leaving no episode unrevealed ; so that when, that
afternoon, de Villancourt found himself walking down the
rugged little road which led to the Castle, he almost felt uncomfortable at all he knew about the family whose home he
was about to invade.

" I don't think I'll like the Princess," he thought, " and
most likely the Prince is narrow-minded and badly-read.　I
can't make out what she means about the Duke—it sounds as
though he were a bit mad.　The Duchess I'm sure I shall get
on with, but the eldest son doesn't sound much in my line.
Quendred !　What a quaint, attractive name !　Quendred !
Mine !—some day ! "

He was now walking towards the house, and at a turn in the
drive he met a fat, good-natured looking man with greyish hair.

" The Prince," he thought ; then, taking off his hat with an
air which was his by nature, he courteously asked if this was the
Castello Santa Fiora, and that if so was it permitted for strangers
to see it ?　The Prince looked curiously at the striking, well-
grown stranger, whose manner had not been lost on him, and liked
him at once.

" The fellow knows how to take off his hat, at any rate, which
is more than do most young men to-day," he thought.

" The Castle is not shown," he answered.

" Ah, what a disappointment ! " said the other. " I had so hoped to be able to see the Carlo Dolci picture, which I believe hangs in your private chapel."

" Not a Carlo Dolci," answered the Prince, looking very pleased, " it's a Veronese. Had you heard of it ? We are very proud of it, although it is not much known."

Villancourt, who had invented the picture on the spur of the moment, and who cared nothing about what the Castle held except Quendred, looked not in the least abashed. His Canadian training had taught him to use his wits.

" Veronese ! Yes, of course ! How stupid of me ! I believe it's a beauty. I wonder whether I might be allowed, signor . . ." and he hesitated questioningly, " just to get a glimpse of it before I go back to Santa Barbara, where I am staying for a few weeks ? "

" I am Prince di Santa Fiora," said the old man, " and I shall be very pleased for you to see the picture as you seem to take so much interest in it. I'll call my grand-daughter and tell her to show it you, and perhaps you will have some refreshment before you go back. It is a long walk. May I know your name ? "

Villancourt handed him his card.

" Ah, you are French ? I know the Duc de Tréfontaines, whose family name is Villancourt."

" Well, of French descent, Prince. My family have been settled in Canada for some time though, and I have never yet been to France. Every year I make a pilgrimage to Europe, and next year I intend to wend my way to the home of my ancestors, which is in Touraine and, I am told, very beautiful. It belongs to the man you say you know. He is a distant cousin of mine."

They had reached the house, and the old man called Quendred, who appeared from behind a heavy leather door.

" Here is a stranger, darling, who wants to see the Veronese in the chapel. Will you show it to him and offer him some tea before he goes, as he has a long walk back to Santa Barbara ? I must go and see the new litter of pigs. You will excuse me ? Good-bye."

So the two were left looking at each other.

" I wondered whether I should see you again," said the girl, smiling and holding out her hand to him.

" And I *knew* that I would see you again," he answered gravely, taking it and holding it for a second longer than is customary.

"What a warm, honest, monopolizing sort of hand-shake he gives," thought the girl, slowly withdrawing hers from his, and for the first time in her experience with men she felt shy.

"So you have come to see the picture ? " she said, a minute later. "How did you know about it ? "

"I didn't know about it," he laughed. "I made it up. I felt certain there must be some good Italian masters here."

"How wicked of you ! It was a bare-faced untruth then ? "

"Yes, I'm afraid it was, but I wanted to see you again, you see, and it was the only thing I could think of to get into the house ! Are you really very angry with me ? Won't you forgive me ? "

"I suppose I must—but I do hate lies," said the girl, walking in front of him towards the chapel.

"Yes, so do I, but all's fair in—in war, you know," he ended lamely.

"I don't see the point, and I don't see why people should ever not be straightforward," said Quendred.

"What a darling she is," thought the man, and he loved her still more.

They looked at the picture, which he duly admired, and then strolled out into the sunlit garden. Talking of many things they soon discovered they had a mutual love of music.

"One of the great things which I miss in Canada," he said, "is the opportunity of hearing good music."

"Why not live in Europe, then ? " she asked.

"I can't," he answered, "all my interests are out West. I have to make money, you see, and it's nearly impossible to make it over here ; not in the way it can be made in Canada, anyway. Besides, there's nothing to bring me to Europe really—to live I mean. I'm not a rich man, and it's no use living here unless you are rich. Life must be hardly worth living. I have some distant relations in France, and they are dying out by degrees, I believe. The head of my family—to give him all his names," said the man, laughing a little, "is Duc de Tréfontaines, Marquis de Chevernoix, and Sieur de Villancourt, and he is to be found somewhere in the Gotha, so you may know I am not an impostor ! "

"What beautiful names," said Quendred. "Tell me some more about these relations of yours ; they sound rather interesting."

"They are very distant, though," Villancourt answered. "You see, we were originally Huguenots, and during the wars of the sixteenth century the Tréfontaines of the day became Catholic when Condé died, but did not follow him again when he returned to the religion of his childhood.   My ancestor—brother to this Tréfontaines—always remained a Huguenot and escaped to England, where his descendants lived till about one hundred years ago, when they migrated to Canada.   Apparently, all that remains of the family is the present Duke, a very rich man I am told, who has two sons of about ten and twelve, and myself. So now you know all there is to know about me !   You ought to come out to Canada for a trip.   It's all so vast, and seems to call you with a mysterious, alluring voice.   It certainly has a something that Europe lacks, although it lacks much which Europe possesses.   Europe seems to be so impregnated with the actions and the thoughts of thousands of years that one feels one is unconsciously being influenced.   But out there it is all so new.   We are making its history, and there are no unseen powers trying to throw their tentacles about us, to pull us and push us where we wouldn't go.   It's all free out there.   No traditions, no history, no conventions ; more natural, more primitive, wilder ; less held and swayed by the old thoughts, old fashions, and old ways.

There was a little pause.   Then Quendred murmured :

" Primitive and free : what a glorious combination !   What a nation you ought to be ! "

He looked at her quickly, interested.

" Does that appeal to you ? " he asked.

" Yes," she said.   " Freedom appeals to me above everything in the world—all sorts of freedom, but more especially freedom of the mind.   The older I grow, the more I love it."

" Yet you are not so very old, are you ? "   He smiled. (His smile was so maddeningly sweet.)

" I'll be twenty-one quite soon.   I don't call that very young," said Quendred.

" Don't you ?   I wish I were as young as that, anyhow.   I'd still have all my ideals, I'd still be enthusiastic, whereas now . . ."

" Whereas now . . . ? " she prompted.

He looked at her and then laughed.

" Well—they're difficult to keep very bright out in the West, you know.   You can't make money if you're too idealistic."

" How old *are* you ? " she asked suddenly.

" I'm thirty."

" Yes—you seem to have a kind of seriousness that I didn't expect.   I thought you were younger when I saw you first."

" Perhaps that comes from living so much alone as I did for many years on the prairies," said Simon. " It was a frightfully lonely life, and it made one think. When I come to towns, and see people always living huddled together, talking a great deal, or constantly pursuing amusement, I often wonder what they think and when they think."

" They don't," said the girl. " They never think. Very few people ever do. They're either too occupied, too lazy, too callous, or too frightened."

" Too frightened," he repeated, looking at her with a swift, penetrating glance. " Yes. *You* have thought, anyhow, whatever others have done, or you couldn't say that, and twenty-one is young to have begun to think out abstract things for oneself ! How did you manage to start so soon ? " and he turned his deepset brilliant eyes full on to her face.

" I can't remember when I didn't think," she answered slowly, and not flinching under his direct gaze. " It began years ago when Father Bischoffsheim used to come to luncheon. I listened to him and my father talking about religion."

" Who was Father Bischoffsheim ? "

" A Jesuit friend of my father's in London."

" Is your father a Catholic, then ? " asked de Villancourt, in a surprised voice.

" Yes, why do you look so surprised ? "

" Well, so few English seem to be. All I know about you is that your name is Quendred. Signora Landini at my inn told me that."

So she laughingly enlightened him as to her parents' name.

" Are *you* a Catholic, then ? " said he.

" Of course," she replied.

" Why, of course ? "

" Because my parents are."

" But that need not always follow, need it ? " he asked, smiling.

" But, of course," the girl answered.

" Yes—yes," said he, " stupid of me. I was thinking all the time that your parents' was a ' mixed marriage.' "

" But even then the children are brought up in the Catholic religion," Quendred said quietly.

" Not necessarily," he answered. " Isn't it the general rule for boys to take after their father's and girls after their mother's religion ? And in certain cases the marriage can take place in a Catholic church without any promises being signed by the non-Catholic person."

"Oh—surely you are mistaken, Mr. de Villancourt! That I certainly know to be impossible."

"How do you know that it's impossible?" said he. "Impossible! *Le mot n'existe pas*, as the great Corsican said."

"Well, it is," she said, "at least I'm sure that's what the Church teaches. She says such a marriage would be a mortal sin——"

"The Church! Mortal sin!" he interrupted quickly, rapping a foot on the gravel as though suddenly irritated. "What is the Church, and who says that 'Mortal Sin' is 'Mortal Sin'? Do you believe all that, Lady Quendred?"

A worried look troubled her lovely eyes.

"Yes, I do in a way, and yet in a way I don't," she said. "Still, we must have a Church, mustn't we? After all, Jesus Christ came to found His Church and to preach It, didn't He? So we must belong to It if we wish to be His."

"The Christian Church—yes, certainly," Villancourt said. "*It* was primitive, simple (yet not easy), unsubtle, God-like, straightforward; disdaining—nay, refusing—pomp and circumstance. How unlike the modern Church, which divides us all up and labels us! A man only *is* what he believes with his mind, what he loves with his heart, what he does with his body."

"But I've always been brought up to believe that what the Church teaches is absolutely and irrefutably true," Quendred said staunchly.

"Brought up to believe!" repeated the man. "But supposing that later you were to find out that what you had been taught as truth was falsehood? What would you do then?"

There was an electric pause, and Quendred stood gazing helplessly into his face. But suddenly he changed and said rather coolly, and perhaps, too, a little shyly:

"Lady Quendred, I must go, and I must apologize for the length of my visit. I have stayed too long and said too much. I may have wounded your most cherished beliefs. I had no right to speak as I have done, knowing you as slightly as I do. But my feelings—always strong on the subject of the freedom of thought, man's glorious birthright—ran away with me, and for the moment I had forgotten myself. Please forgive me, and forget what I have said."

His voice no longer quivered with warmth and feeling, but

was impersonal, almost cold. He bent down to her with his charming, wonderful smile, which had so attracted her at their first meeting twenty-four hours before.

But with cheeks aflame and glowing eyes, she rose and faced him, her slender body erect and eager.

" Freedom," she breathed, " man's glorious birthright ! How well you put it ! Indeed, I am not hurt or angry. Everything you say is exactly what I feel, yet I have been taught that such thoughts were wicked, and should be put away as a temptation of the devil. Shall I always have to beat impotent wings against my cage ? "

Something deeper than interest and admiration crept into his eyes as he looked at her standing bravely in front of him.

"Of course not," he answered, tightly clasping his hands behind him, lest he should take her into his arms. " Of course not. It rests with you to grasp your freedom, but, like all other things worth having, it needs a fight."

She looked down, very grave, and made no answer.

" Good-bye, Lady Quendred," he said. " Try not to forget me too quickly. I shall never forget you. If I go to England may I let you know ? "

Again she made no answer, for she wasn't certain whether to see this man again or not.

" I don't know. I must think. Good-bye," she said at length. But she put both her hands into his when he left her at the gate. As she watched him slowly disappearing in the autumn haze up the winding mountain road towards Santa Barbara, another mountain scene clouded her vision and the words which she had spoken to her mother on the top of *Schneeköpfchen*, away in the Tyrolese fastnesses, floated through her mind. " If God ever gives me a son it is such a man as that whom I would choose to be his father."

The next morning a little note lay at Simon's plate at the breakfast table.

" Let me know when you come to England.—Q. F."

PART IV

THE PULL OF LOVE

CHAPTER XIV

" . . . LET NO MAN PUT ASUNDER "

" As the stars are distant from the earth, and as fires differ from the sea, so does the expedient differ from the right."—LUCANUS.

IT was dark when Stephen's *droschke* drew up in front of the famous Jesuit house in Bavaria.

The heavily iron-studded door gave on to a narrow, cobbled street, and in it was fixed a small, sliding panel behind a narrow iron grille. He rang the bell several times, and listened vaguely as its reverberations clanged in the distance.

At last a shuffling of feet was heard, and then the panel was pulled aside. A mouth appeared at the aperture, and a voice asked, " Who is there ? "

" The Duke of Seyntleger," answered Stephen, whereupon a loud noise of rattling keys was heard, and by the faint light of the lantern which the Brother held the great door was laboriously opened, and the Duke entered the Jesuit portals.

" I will take you to your cell at once," said the man, " and to-morrow morning after breakfast, which is at seven o'clock, Father Ignatius will preach his opening sermon in the chapel. I will come and show you the way."

By this time they had reached the tiny room allotted to the Duke for the next three days. On a table in the centre of the room was bread, cheese, and beer.

The lay-brother motioned him in, saying, " Father Ignatius told me to put this here for you in case you should be hungry. Good night," and in a moment Stephen was alone.

It was a lovely early autumn evening, and the moon was so bright that he could almost read by it.

The little cell was clean, and the bed turned down, over which hung a Crucifix. A candle and matches stood near.

Sweet-smelling night air poured through the open window from the garden, where the great trees stood like silent sentinels. It was very peaceful, and Stephen well understood the feelings which prompted Charles V. to leave his grandeur and his empire, and withdraw to a mountain monastery.

" He was about my age, too," mused the man, as he prepared himself to rest.

The following morning, after a silent breakfast taken in the company of perhaps a score of other men whose names—by mutual agreement—were not divulged at these Retreats, Stephen and the rest made their way to the chapel.

Dark and austere it was, with much plain stonework and little decoration.

At the altar rails stood the tall, commanding figure of Father Ignatius. His eyes were closed, and, as the men settled themselves in their places, he pressed a small Crucifix to his breast.

His attitude and whole appearance struck Stephen as being the embodiment of worldly detachment.

In a low voice he began to speak, and then as he slowly made his points his voice gathered force.

Soon his audience raised their heads and fixed their eyes on this dynamic person. Before long, all distractions had been banished from their minds by the interesting way in which he treated his subject, and, as usual to him, he soon had them in the thrall of his overpowering personality.

Mostly he kept his eyes shut, but, when particularly wishing to emphasize a point, he would step forward and open them widely, gazing upon his hearers in a manner so magnetic and so odylic, as to make them wonder if he were blessed archangel or satanic sorcerer.

At these moments Stephen always felt strangely uneasy, and vague memories flitted fitfully through his mind.

The two days passed very quickly, as is always the way when every hour is definitely arranged for, and Stephen's unquiet, wondering spirit found a certain peace in the Retreat.

At breakfast on the third day a note was handed to him from the Jesuit, who asked him to go and see him that evening after the last sermon, before he retired for the night.

During the past days Stephen had been more than ever impressed by the sanctity of the preacher, and by his great knowledge of the world and of human affairs.

" And so, Duke, you are leaving us once more to plunge into

the world? Now, of course, I know who you are, a pleasure which was denied me at our first strange, yet dramatic, meeting! How goes the world with you? Have you arranged your life to your contentment, or are you still sitting on the fence?" And he led the way to some horse-hair seated chairs. "Are you fairly settled, or does the priesthood call you still?"

"It calls me still, and I am most unsettled," said Stephen. "I have just recovered from a serious illness which has left me convinced that I must—now and at once—fulfil the vocation which I have pushed aside."

"The call—as I know from my own experience—is extremely strong," said the priest, "and cannot be ignored. It can even overcome the call of the world and the flesh."

Well he knew that the flesh had never called this chaste man, as it had called him, nor had the fascinations of the world ever cast their spells over Stephen as they had over Lepantchine.

"Yes, that is true," said Stephen painfully, "but you see, Father, I *did* ignore it, and that is what is gnawing at my heart —that is what is killing me—that is what is driving me mad. My conversion was based upon the overwhelming desire for the priesthood because—and solely because—of the power they possess of turning bread and wine into the real Body and Blood of our Saviour," and as he said the words his lips trembled, and his eyes glittered with the old fanatical light. "But I married instead, and I have never—" he hesitated—" well, hardly ever, ceased to regret my action and bewail my weakness."

The Jesuit's unblinking eyes were fixed on Stephen, and his pupils were contracting and dilating in the most mesmeric fashion.

"Love is very sweet," he said slowly and evenly, "and its toils are very strong. There is nothing so evil as women, yet there is nothing so maddening and so irresistible. Women can be she-devils, and these ones deserve to be made to suffer. I knew one once like this, and any man who loved her would have found it hard to leave her. But if a woman comes between a man and his God, that woman—even though she be his wife— must be cast aside as a lure of the evil one, for the Divine call must be responded to above everything else, and at all costs."

As he spoke visions of Santa Fiora flashed spasmodically in and out of Stephen's consciousness, and from that his mind travelled easily to his wedding-day in the great Roman church, and he heard the words, "For richer, for poorer, for better, for

O

worse, till death do us part. . . . Whom God hath joined together
let no man put asunder." At this point his mind wobbled a
little, and he said :

"Do you maintain that there can be no doubt that it is
right for a man to part from his wife if he truly wishes to be a
priest ? "

" Absolutely none," answered the Jesuit ; " the Church most
definitely allows it."

Stephen sighed with relief as his mind readjusted itself
again, and he clung contentedly to the word " Church " as a
drowning man clings to a raft.

Father Ignatius had walked towards an enormous bookshelf,
from which he took a book, " The Catholic Dictionary."

" Besides," he said, " it is a distinct command in the Bible,
is it not, to leave father and mother and wife, if need be, for
God's sake ? "

Deftly turning over the closely-filled pages of very small
type, he stopped under the heading " Irregularity," which word
was defined as " Canonical Impediment." Reading to himself,
the Jesuit passed his finger down the lines—" m.m —m.m——"

" Here ! " he exclaimed to Seyntleger, who was dreaming
again, " this is what affects you. Look, read this."

The Duke looked, and read :

> (5) Ex Defecta Libertatis.
>   Excludes slaves and generally those under the power of
>   others, also court officials occupying public positions. These
>   rules still subsist, and married persons are only excluded at
>   least from Holy Orders until they obtain their wife's consent,
>   and she, if young, enters a convent.

The room was dark and they read by a candle. Silently
Stephen pored over the words in the unequal light, while the
priest watched him closely ; then, drawing himself up, he sighed
deeply. Was it with relief or regret ? The Jesuit wasn't
certain.

" But what about the Duchess ? " he said. " I know she
will *consent*, because she knows how unhappy I am, but she can't
possibly go to be a nun ? "

" Oh, that is easily arranged," answered Father Ignatius.
" As long as she fully agrees, and you live in different countries,
the Church is satisfied."

" Well," said the Duke, " there is no doubt that t is

permitted, and that my action will be—in the eyes of the Church
—legal and valid. What the world thinks, of course, doesn't
matter."

" Not in the least," answered the priest, and his mouth shut
like a trap. " The Church's ultimatum on faith and morals
overrides all other definitions and rules. It always was so in
Catholic days, and we hope it will be so again. That, of course,
is what we are working for—to bring the whole world under the
sway of Rome. A universal religion ! How beautiful and how
powerful."

As he spoke the last word his eyes narrowed, and for a moment
the guileless soul of the Englishman was repulsed.

" Beautiful, yes," he said, " but powerful—why ? It is that
aspect which sometimes troubles me when I think about it."

" Don't think, my son, don't think," said Father Ignatius
professionally, metaphorically patting Stephen's soul as a
doctor pats a man's shoulder ; " it's a great mistake and leads
to endless worries. As I was just saying, if once Rome could
regain her pre-Reformation power, what wonderful work could be
done for God ! " (He saw that this was the food for Stephen.)
" Much good work is already being achieved on these lines, and
the marriage laws—most important laws—are going to be considerably tightened up if ever the Holy Father is able to re-open
the Vatican Council."

" Are they ? I *am* glad to hear that," said Stephen eagerly.
" In what way ? "

" In Rome it is hoped," went on the other, " that the *Ne
Temere* decree may soon be promulgated all over the world,
and very especially in England. That will, of course, give the
Church complete power over marriages, which is as it should
be."

" Certainly," asquiesced Stephen.

" We have great hopes of England, you see," said the priest,
" because so many thinking young people are beginning to see
the futility of Anglicanism, and therefore they either believe
nothing, or they turn easily towards Rome. In fact, it's becoming rather the fashion to be a Catholic now in England !
Naturally, the Holy Father wouldn't enforce the decree unless
advised to do so by the highest clerical advice in the land, but
the reports from England are so reassuring, that I believe Rome
will quite soon feel justified in making the decree operative by
placing England once more under the Council of Trent. And

now, Duke, since you have had a little taste of priestly life, do you like it ? Will you not find it too difficult after your worldly life of ease ? Beware lest you enter rashly in, and then find that you cannot continue ! Are you strong ? It needs a strong constitution to go through with it, you know, and generally men of your age are not so well adapted to a radical change of life as younger ones. I know that from my experience—I didn't enter religious life until I was thirty-five, which is rare for a Jesuit."

"Yes," mused Stephen, but his thoughts were far away. He was never much interested in anything except himself. He said :

"So you think that I ought without doubt to leave my wife and children ? You think it right ? It is to know this quite definitely, it is to know your true opinion, that I have come here."

"Yes, Duke, undoubtedly I think so," said the Jesuit, "and the sooner the better. No woman's power should be allowed to interfere in such high matters, as I told you in London. *You must leave your wife*. Since talking with you I fully realize that is your only course. I wonder what Order you will join—for it will, of course, be an Order ? The Benedictines, I suppose ? "

"No," said Stephen, "I do not want contact with the world any more. I do not want riches, power, education, travel. I only want God. To forget, and to be forgotten. Humanly speaking, I'm a failure ; perhaps my God can comfort me. I shall join the Trappists somewhere in Italy."

There was a little pause, and then the priest said slowly : "Yet what of your wife, Duke ? What of the Duchess ? Does she love you still ? "

Seyntleger reddened and swallowed painfully, closing his eyes as if to shut out something which hurt.

"Yes, she does," he said. "She loves me as she has always loved me, with high idealism and with pure passion. Ah, Maddalena, how am I treating you ? How often have I had to be brutal to you against my will, lest you should draw me to yourself again ? Yet I believed I was doing right, for you had put it all so clearly in your sermon, Father, and you had told me so plainly what my duty was that night in Berkeley Square. But still—it has been terribly hard. Night after night—at your bidding as a priest of God's most Holy Church—I have fought with my love for my wife as though it were a deadly adulterous beast."

Slowly he paced the austere little room, saying the words in dream-like tones as though he were alone.

From a corner the priest watched him, with his hand pressed to his dark, shaven chin—watched him as a spider watches a fly.

With a sudden involuntary shiver, Stephen threw back his head, and passed his hands wearily before his face, as if trying to ward off an inexorable destiny. Then his greyly-golden head dropped—beaten—on to his breast.

"Thank you, Father," he said after a minute. "Thank you for your great kindness to me, and your patience. Good night and good-bye, I leave very early in the morning."

"Good night, Duke, and good-bye. May God bless you," and the priest held open the door as the other passed quickly out into the long, dim, stone passage, at the end of which was situated the chapel. Through the ever-open door could be seen, gleaming, the eternal, ruby light, sign, in the minds of Catholics, that Jesus is there.

As Stephen's tall, slight form disappeared all became once more profoundly silent. Father Ignatius stood for many minutes with his strange eyes fixed upon the light.

"Revenge is sweet," he whispered, "and Maddalena has suffered, is suffering, and will suffer yet more. Still, I have helped him to follow the great ' call.' " Then, turning into his room once more, he drew his breviary from his pocket and fell upon his knees before a large Crucifix with muttering lips, for each word of a priest's office must be articulated.

CHAPTER XV

MADDALENA'S " AMARI ALIQUID "

" Measureless Liar, thou hast made my heart too great for what contains it."—SHAKESPEARE (Coriolanus)

SINCE Stephen's return from the Retreat everyone noticed a marked difference in his behaviour—his whole being. Even Anthony spoke to Quendred about it. " He's so rude to Mother," the boy had said, " he absolutely ignores her except when it's literally impossible not to."

Their twenty-first birthday was drawing near, and after its celebration their father had told them that he had definitely arranged to retire to the monastery of Trappists in Italy. Warm, golden Italy ! Italy, where he had first known the beauty and understood the truth of the Catholic religion ! Italy, where he had met his only love and wooed her with ardent emotion, while deep, deep down in the backwoods of his consciousness a tiny voice had kept on whispering : " Faithless—weak. False to God—false to yourself." All the undying memories of his spiritual and physical life were bound up in Italy.

And now, after all the years which had been so terrible, he was going to give to God what he felt he ought to have given to Him twenty-three years ago. The thought which had once seemed difficult now seemed nothing at all. Not only was he not sorry to go, he longed to go. Longed to throw off the shackles of the world ; longed to be free of responsibilities and cares ; longed to be away from the tumult and turmoil of the paraphernalia of life ; longed to lay his head on the peaceful bosom of Christ, and so to ease at last the awful gnawing pain at his heart caused by the thought that he had failed to come to his Master when He had called.

" And yet," he would sometimes say to himself, " both Cardinal Costanzi and the Pope clearly advised me to wait and to throw myself into Society and worldly things ! Strange !

I wonder why they did it ? I should have thought that they
would have been glad to have welcomed me into the Church as a
priest. I should like to know why they did it, but that can now
never be known."

.   .   .   .   .

Late one night Maddalena had noticed a light under his
study door. Though knowing how much he hated being disturbed, she nevertheless ventured in. He was surrounded by
fluttering papers, and a thick cheque-book lay open on the table.

" Anthony's bills," he sighed wearily, without looking up.
" The last I shall pay for him. Moreover, when he's twenty-
one he'll be his own master. Only one month more and then—
freedom ! " He clasped his hands behind his head and yawned.

His wife stood at the back of his chair, and put both arms
round his neck.

" Oh, Stephen, my darling ! " she said. " I wonder whether
you realize how it hurts me that you should want to leave me ?
You are forty-four—I am not yet forty, and yet you are cutting
me adrift in the middle of our lives and leaving me—to what ?
I cannot imagine what my life will be ! Married, and yet not
married ! A wife, yet not a wife ! . . . And so it has all ended !
Our great, sweet love—up there on the road to Santa Barbara,
I remember every word you said ! It *was* sweet, Stephen,
wasn't it ? " And she bent her warm lips to the nape of his
neck.

" Sweet ! " he almost shrieked, getting up and pushing her
from him. " Sweet ! Why, it was the most baleful day in my
life. The day that I gave up God for the fascinations of the
flesh and the world ! Sweet ! Pfah ! " and a look of utter
disgust crossed his quivering face.

Never had he treated her quite like this before, and she
finally realized how completely he had gone from her since his
return from the Retreat.

But, notwithstanding all this, something kept on telling her
that he still loved her, that his true self loved her, and that the
way he had acted towards her since the memorable night in
Berkeley Square was the result of some outside influence, some
alien power, which was not the true Stephen. Yet—what is
the true Stephen, she had often wondered ? My lover or my
tormentor ?

Since the Retreat he was always speaking of Father Ignatius;

the wonderful Jesuit who had so helped him out of his Slough of Despond by showing him the utter worthlessness of all human vanity ; and in some curious indefinite way she had come to fear Father Ignatius, and to look upon this man's influence as a cruel and sinister power which she could not overcome, and which was stronger than herself, or anything else in Stephen's life.

Now, at his words, something in her died—died quite quietly, without pain, without hate, without rancour, and a kind of numbness seemed to envelop her like a cloak. Her eyes, which had been frightened and defiant a moment before, were now gentle and tender, and a wistful look shone from them, like that of a tame gazelle wounded to death by the hand it loved.

Later, prompted by she knew not what, she laid the letter which Cardinal Costanzi had given her at his death, on the writing-table in her husband's bedroom. It had never been opened. The Duke fingered it several times, and then put it among a few papers he was taking to the monastery with him.

"I will read it there when I have time and leisure," he murmured, as he turned on his pillow to sleep.

.   .   .   .   .   .

At last the birthday came, and Ullcombe was—for a week—given over to festivities. The guests included the Santa Fioras and Stephen's mother, now a wonderful-looking old lady, with silvery hair piled on her head like Marie Antoinette. The pansy eyes of her youth were still dark and brilliant, although rather deeply sunken into her delicately ivory-tinted face. A diamond cross glittered demurely amongst her soft black satin and lace, and she always used a pair of gold and tortoiseshell lorgnettes, which made her eyes look like a great soft owl's.

Stephen's sister, Rosamund Traquair, and her two good-looking sons, Hugh and Mark, were there also, both of whom were —against their consciences, however—allured by Quendred. Strictly brought up in the Evangelical mentality, they had been taught to believe that dancing, card-playing, and drinking were wrong. But in all the devious ways of sport they excelled, and Quendred was very devoted to these two sturdy Puritan cousins of hers, who boxed, and rode, and swam, and ran, and played polo so well. Another guest was an Italian cousin of the Santa Fioras', Count della Meglia, an undergraduate at Balliol, and a very gay person, who played the piano, and danced, and sang like a professional.

Hugh suffered agonies of jealousy when he saw him dancing with Quendred, and after dinner would stand and watch them from beneath the picture of " Rosemouth "—hands deep in trouser pockets, strong white teeth moodily chewing the cud. A well-built, graceful figure, with wide, sloping shoulders and slender hips ; sturdily defiant, the living embodiment of British Tractarianism versus Latin Ultramontanism !

" If he can dance, I can box," thought he, and longed to be at della Meglia's throat. " What Quendred sees in him beats me," and his eyes followed their bodies, perfectly swaying to the lure of a valse. " Wretched chap—he only comes up to her shoulder ! " But he made up his mind to learn how to dance.

Amongst the others were two school-fellows of Anthony's : John Poynder, son of a rich Liverpool cotton-spinner, and Denis Connor, a gay, charming, and witty youth, who owned acres of useless land in the West of Ireland, penniless and debonair. The only brother of five wild, pretty sisters, his great ambition was to find them husbands.

Anthony was his best friend. No small schemer was Denis.

" Patricia, his eldest sister, was in London. He'd so *love* her to see Ullcombe ; she hardly knew England at all. *Would* the Duke ? *Would* the Duchess ? He'd think it so awfully kind . . ." Naturally, a telegram was sent, and Miss Patricia arrived next day, having made up her mind to scalp the heir of Ullcombe As I said, she arrived the next day, and with her a small and modest trunk. In the trunk reposed one evening gown made in Wexford, a couple of plain silk shirts, an old tweed coat and skirt, a black satin skirt, a lace blouse, and a riding habit. But it *was* a habit ! Made by London's greatest tailor, and paid for by money made by Denis on an outsider who had just won the Grand National ! He had been " put on " to the horse by the parish priest at Ballyhoysh, his home in Ireland.

No doubt it was an extravagance, but it was worth it. She looked as though she had been poured into it. Another folly had been a perfect pair of doe-skin breeches. How she loved stroking their nice brown softness ! Thus equipped she felt ready to conquer the world.

" Put me on a horse, and, well . . ." she shrugged her slender square young shoulders, laughing roguishly.

Looking in the glass before she went down to dinner on the night of her arrival, she summed herself up as follows :

" Crisp, wavy, Titian hair, most vilely untidy. (Must try

and do it better while I'm here.)   Dark blue eyes put in with a
dirty finger (quite all right).   Turned-up, freckly nose."   (She
put out her tongue at it.)   " Mouth too large, but saved from
being quite disastrous by small, white teeth.   Shape like a boy ;
and last, but not least, good legs and feet."

Added to this she was also possessed of the gift of fascinating
" little ways."   But of this she was quite unconscious.   Now
when " little ways " and blue, side-glancing eyes attack with
determination the citadel of youthful man's heart, the siege will
not last long !

" I wish that I didn't get so red in the face after meals in
hot rooms," she sighed audibly, as she took a last glance at herself
in a *cheval* mirror.

She thought that her dress looked rather nice, not perceiving
that the material was too cheap, and the *décoletage* unfashionable.

" A fault on the right side," thought the Dowager Duchess of
Seyntleger, looking at her during dinner with intense disapproval.
The only thing which she noticed about the girl was that her
arms were too fat above the elbow and red, and that she talked
with a brogue.

As Patricia entered the drawing-room where most of the
others were already assembled, she realized with a blaze of shy
discomfort how hideous her dress was.   Everybody seemed to
be so rare and exquisite in their trailing and shimmering garments.   All was gleaming arms and shoulders, and beautifully
poised small heads, with not a hair astray.

Patricia felt a hobbledehoy.

She almost hated all these perfect people, so absolutely at
their ease and in their element.

During dinner she sat between John Poynder and Mark
Traquair, Rosamund's second son.   Mark and Patricia didn't
get on.   She thought him heavy and dull, and he thought her
rather—well, not quite out of the top drawer.   He didn't like
the way she yawned.   " I know I'm dull," he soliloquized, " but
it's no excuse for yawning like *that*."

After dinner there was a dance, to which all the county were
invited.   Everybody thoroughly enjoyed themselves, except
Lord and Lady Traquair—who retired early—and their two sons.

Anthony looked upon these two cousins as " awful asses."

He danced twice with Patricia, and she must have made the
most of her time, because before they parted he had promised
at her request to have a riding paper-chase the next day.   Hugh

Traquair was delighted at the news. At last he would have a look-in after having had to forgo the pleasures of dancing and acting, to which his religious upbringing had advised him to have nothing to say. But when it came to sport, few of his acquaintances could equal him.

When Patricia retired that night she prayed that Anthony would propose to her, for after their last dance he had said : " Well, Miss Patricia, the paper-chase was your idea ; so I think you'd better have the arranging of it, and I'll go with you and show you the way."

Everyone who was at all young took part in it ; and everyone thoroughly enjoyed themselves except Count della Meglia, whose horse bolted with him and left him a shaken mass on a heap of stones by the roadside !

All Hugh Traquair's feelings of animosity vanished when he saw the poor fellow lying there unconscious, with many of his beautiful white teeth—teeth which Hugh had detested the night before—broken. He was not even jealous when Quendred undid his collar and bathed his head with a handkerchief she had wetted in the ditch. As he had concussion and was quite unconscious they would have to carry him home. The rest of the chase had gone on, so Hugh and Quendred were left to take care of him. With the help of some men whom they found in a field near by, they lifted him on to a gate, and making him as comfortable as possible with coats they started their four-mile walk back.

Quendred thought how good-looking Hugh was, so tall and fair, with ruddy neck and sparkling blue eyes. He took such long, manly strides, and his old tweed coat and cord breeches fitted him so well. She liked walking with him. He was just right for the occasion, and fitted in beautifully with the surroundings. He was as right here as he would have been out of his element in a London ball-room, or at a Foreign Office party.

As for Hugh, he was walking on air ; for, notwithstanding the—to him—awful fact that Quendred was a Catholic, he thought her the most wonderful of girls. But her religion positively hurt him. He only knew two other Catholics, and they were Austrians, which, of course, was different. One expected foreigners to be Catholics. But Quendred !

They had walked in silence while these thoughts were revolving in his brain. Quendred, knowing his moods, had made no effort to talk, but at last she asked him if they would see him in London during the season ?

"You're going into the Coldstream, aren't you?" she said. "You'll like it awfully, I should think. Anthony does, although, of course, he's only been in a few months."

"I wonder whether I *shall* like it?" answered Hugh, his blue eyes suddenly looking serious. "It would be awful if I didn't get on, wouldn't it?"

"But why shouldn't you get on?"

"Well," he said hesitatingly. "Well, you see, my religious beliefs may be a stumbling-block. It's no use pretending that I don't realize that Father and Mother have brought us up differently from most men, and I'm sure it'll make some things difficult. I sometimes am afraid they'll think me such an awful fool, and ignore me, and that would be rather hard to bear, wouldn't it?"

"Yes, but you're such a topper, Hugh! You are so sporting, and everything in that way that you do you do so well—they couldn't despise you!"

"I don't know," he returned rather sadly. "But it makes one feel odd compared to them—if one doesn't drink, and play cards, and go racing, and do theatres, and—and—well, all the things that the others do." As he said this his ruddy neck got scarlet.

Quendred could have cried with compassion for this young giant striding along beside her. He had such an innocent, puzzled look in his eyes sometimes.

"Well, I'm sure you'll get on all right, Hugh dear," she said, "and if you can just put up with it for a bit, they'll all get to love you, I'm certain. Come and see us in London whenever you like, and write to me when you're depressed. Promise!" and she held out her charmingly gloved hand to him.

He took it, and held it in his as they swung along the road together.

"Thanks awfully, Quendred. You don't know what that will be to me—to feel that you are my friend. I shall never speak to anyone again as I have spoken to you. Quendred dear, you mean such an awful lot to me. Did you know?" he said. There was a pathetic tenseness about his whole bearing—a desire to give out, yet a very strong wish to withhold. The atmosphere surrounding him had vibrated with it.

. . . .

That night things seemed different.

They danced in the great hall just the same, but the gay, irrepressible della Meglia lay ill in bed, and Quendred wouldn't dance. Hugh was delighted at this, and he followed her about like a faithful dog all the evening.

Meanwhile Patricia was getting on capitally, and had succeeded with her Celtic wiles and " little ways," her superb riding and flirting eyes, to make very considerable advances on Anthony's susceptible heart.

" I say, you are a little ripper," he was murmuring to her in a secluded corner that evening. " I've never seen anyone make Tarquin go as he went for you to-day ; you must come and have some huntin' here next winter—will you ? " and he bent towards her, trying to take her hand.

But she withdrew it demurely and rose, saying she was " dancing this one."

" Oh, don't go, Miss Patricia !—we've hardly been here a minute," he pleaded.

" I hate cutting people's dances," she threw back over her shoulder, " but I've got one to spare after supper if you have," and she had gone.

Anthony went out on to the terrace.

" What a topper she is," he thought as he mopped his rather hot forehead. " And so awfully natural and easy to get on with. I must ask Mother to get her here again in the winter. She'll liven us up. It'll be a pretty queer situation for us all when Father goes off to his monastery ! What an extraordinary chap he is, *wantin'* to go. That's what I can't make out. After all, he's quite young still, considerin'. What he wants to be a monk for beats me. He's got everythin' a man can want."

He walked to the parapet and then turned to look at the huge, glorious shadowy pile which was his home. How mysteriously, yet how strongly, this place linked him with England's history. Back, back into the days of the sturdy bowmen, and then he thought of the beautiful Quendred, Queen of Mercia, whose home it had once been long ago.

" I wonder what those words on the picture of " Rosemouth " mean ? " he thought to himself, as he blew clouds of smoke out on to the still night air. " I had hardly ever noticed them before till Patricia asked me about them to-night." (He started at catching himself thinking of her as "Patricia.") " They are rather odd, though, and made me feel quite queer for a minute when I read them. I wonder who invented them ? "

He repeated the words in a low voice, and as he did so an unaccountable shiver ran through him :

> " If Rosemouth hang in the Castle Hall
> No evil shall Fitz-Urse befall ;
> If Rosemouth fall or movèd be,
> Fitz-Urse, Fitz-Urse shall surely die."

" Does it mean that one particular Fitz-Urse shall die, or that we'll all die ? It can't mean extermination of my race," but, as he thought this, he laughed nervously, for it suddenly struck him that he was indeed the only man of their family left. His grandfather's brothers had had no sons, and his father had only one sister—Rosamund Traquair. " I am the only one," he said to himself, rather scared at the sudden realization of the fact. " Well, of course I'll marry, besides, what *could* happen ? There are never any wars nowadays to kill people off.—How awful a war would be, though—but of course it's unthinkable ! "

He walked back slowly towards the house, still feeling rather upset at the result of his train of thought, and musing as he went :

" Naturally, I'll marry some day. I wonder what Patricia thought of those words ? I remember now she didn't say anything. Irish people are awfully superstitious, of course. Banshees and horrors of that sort. Perhaps she thinks *we* have a Banshee."

Already (unconsciously) the thought of marriage and Patricia were vaguely linked together in his mind.

As he went into the house he met her coming out with John Poynder.

" Come and have some supper ? " he asked her.

" I've just had some, thank you, Lord Athelston," she said, in her best " purry-puss " voice. " Mr. Poynder and I are going to look at the moon," and she rippled out a pellucid little laugh.

" Oh—I say, that's too bad, and I haven't had any yet ! Do come and have some more ! Jack, you go and look at the moon by yourself, old chap, that's all you're fit for ! " he laughed good-humouredly. They were the best of friends.

So Patricia, with a pouting *moue*, accompanied Anthony back to the dining-room. He thought her very irresistible at that moment.

" Well, what were you thinking about out there all alone ? " she asked. " Your wicked past ? "

" Not my past, but my future," answered he. " I'm in an awfully funny position. Did you know that my father is going to a monastery in a few weeks ? "

" Well, I've heard something about it," she said. " It reminds me of the woman who founded a convent. She was married, and one day her husband came and told her that he could stand married life no longer, and that he had settled to go to a monastery, which he accordingly did. She had to go and be a nun, although much against her will, as I believe there is some rule in the Catholic religion which says that if a woman's husband becomes a priest she has to go to a convent ! Rather rough luck on the poor brute, isn't it ? "

" Awful," answered the man. " I say, my mother won't have to be a nun, will she ? "

" I know nothing about it really," Patricia answered, " but I *do* know that after this particular man had been in his monastery for a year he found he didn't like it a bit, and so he went to his former wife's convent and battered on the door and told her she had to come back to him—that he had changed his mind. Her answer was that she had also changed hers, and that nothing would induce her to leave her convent for any man ! So there he was left, neither fish, flesh, nor fowl."

" What an extraordinary story ! " said Anthony. " I had never dreamt of such a possibility ! H'm—by Jove !——" and he pushed up his incipient moustache with the thumb and forefinger of his left hand. " Might put one awfully badly in the cart, mightn't it ? " There was a little pause, and then he went on :

" My father's leavin' everythin' to me on condition I make a suitable marriage. That is, everythin' except the house in Berkeley Square, which, of course, belongs to my mother."

" Oh ! " said Patricia innocently. She was noticing that under the influence of wine he was becoming extra talkative and communicative. She let him talk. She was a good listener.

" Father showed me his will the other day," went on Anthony, " that's how I know. He's fearfully keen on our marryin' Catholics, and has practically left us nothin' if we don't. In fact, the will says that if either of his children marry non-Catholics he will never see them again, and they are to have £150 a year and nothin' more. The rest of the money would—at my mother's death—go to charities. Rather extraordinary, isn't it ? I can't see anythin' so very terrible in marryin' a Protestant, can you ? "

But at this the Irish Catholicism in Patricia was fired at once, and for the first time since she had been in the house she spoke seriously.

" Yes, I do see what he means," she answered. " I think it's a great mistake to marry a Protestant. It's a false religion— a bigoted, cruel religion, which consists chiefly in ringing bells on Sunday, and giving all the best jobs to their own people."

" You say that because you're Irish," he laughed. " Denis has often talked to me about Ireland. He's mad about Home Rule and ' down with the Sassenach ' kind of idea, isn't he ? "

" Quite right too," she flared up, and then from her lips poured a truly Celtic flow of invective—moving, audacious, clever, pathetic, true up to a point, but impossible and unconvincing.

He looked at her for the first time with deep admiration.

The expression on her face had quite changed. She no longer looked frivolous and flirtatious ; she was desperately in earnest.

"England has behaved monstrously to Ireland, and all because she's Catholic. Protestants are terrified of Catholics getting any power. They talk such a fat lot about England being Freedom's champion, and yet devil a bit of it they give to poor Ireland. It's all eye-wash they wag their tongues about in that House of Commons of yours, where, when they talk about Freedom in connection with Ireland, they seem to use Samson's most famous weapon—and as for English newspapers ! Well, you don't know what truth *is* in this country ! Personally, I never read anything but the *Freeman's Journal* when I want to know anything about politics. Anyhow, it is true to its name, and *is* a free man's paper." Her eyes were blazing blue darts, and her face was scarlet.

He loved looking at her, and had never realized before how really awfully pretty she was.

"I didn't know you were so patriotic, Miss Patricia ! Is everybody in Ireland like you ? "

" Every *true* Irish person is," she answered, " that is— except the rich Protestants—Cromwell's lords—and, of course, they are not truly Irish."

" I know nothin' about it, really," said Anthony. " You must tell me more some time."

" That's just typical of the whole English attitude ! That's just where I fault you," she flung out excitedly. " You

pretend you understand it, you give out your opinions, you try
to rule us, and you know absolutely nothing about us the whole
time, and, what's more, you care less."

" Oh, well, don't be too hard on me ! I am just one of the
people who don't understand and don't pretend to ! Our two
countries can't be divorced, and they can't live together. So
what's to be done ? "

" They could be separated."

" Not on a sound financial basis, I'm told," he laughed.
" Well, let's drop politics, and come and have another dance."

As they crossed the great hall he stopped her in front of
Rosemouth's picture, and read the words aloud to her.

" Aren't they queer ? " he said. " What do you think they
mean ? Do you believe in these sorts of forebodings and
sayings ? "

" Yes, I'm afraid I do," she answered in a low voice. " But
don't let's talk about it. I—. I hate to think that anything might
happen to you, Lord Athelston—it's awful—dreadful ! " She
gave a little shudder. " I hate the picture, too," she went on,
giving it a vicious little pat. " Horrible woman ! "

Looking behind it, she noticed how firmly it was attached to
the wall.

" Nothing but an earthquake could make that fall down,
though," and she laughed with a return to her usual gaiety.

As they danced together he held her very close. He thrilled
her, and she was excited and expectant. They danced beautifully together, and she was intoxicated by everything. The
splendid house, the comfort, the ease, the perfect servants. It
not only seemed, but it *was* a different world from her harum-
scarum home in Ireland, where they scratched along with two
maids and a " bhoy," aged about seventy. And to think that if
all went well she might be the mistress of it !

He bent his head to hers, saying softly : " Would you *really*
care if anythin' happened to me, little Patricia ? "

" Yes, dreadfully," she whispered ; and she meant it.

.   .   .   .   .   .

Hugh and Quendred were alone in Olaf's turret, where he had
begged the girl to go with him.

Hugh was in an unhappy state of mind, for he was in love
with Quendred, but he knew enough of his upbringing and hers
to know how impossible such a marriage would be, even if

P

Quendred cared for him, which he was certain she didn't. Nevertheless, he had made up his mind to try his luck before leaving Ullcombe.

" I want to tell you something, Quendred," he said, fingering his tie—" and I hope you won't mind ? "

" I never mind what people say, if it's what they truly think. Go on, old Hugh, I'm longing to hear."

" Well," he said very shyly. " I do wish so much that you weren't a Catholic."

" Is that all ? But why should I mind your saying that ? "

" Oh, I'm so glad you don't, as I should hate to have hurt your feelings ; but, you know, I simply can't understand how you can believe all they tell you."

" You don't really know very much about it, do you ? At least, you only know what you've been told—you have not studied it yourself," said Quendred.

" No, perhaps I haven't, but I know that you don't believe that you're saved by faith, and that you do believe in the awful doctrine of Purgatory. You go more by the Athanasian Creed than by the Bible, and yet you don't agree that the Creed functions in the case of Protestants, because your Church insists that ' Catholic ' in this connection means only ' Roman.' Your Church insists on *her* readings of the Bible and the Creeds, doesn't she ? And that's exactly where I come up against her, for I think that she is wilfully obstructing the possibilities of a true and world-wide Christianity. Thousands of us could join in a common faith if it wasn't for Rome's laws."

" It seems to me," said Quendred, " that we can read the Bible to mean anything we like, and that is why it was so clever of my Church to invent the idea of making the acceptance of her interpretation a condition of Communion with her ! I wonder whether we shall all be labelled in Heaven, Hugh ? I wonder whether the Athanasian Creed amuses God ? There He sits up in His Heaven, serene, all-knowing, and omnipotent ; watching His millions of children running this way and that like futile ants, so busy in pitting the Creeds against each other, so eager —in their finite limitations—to assume the attributes of Divinity, so burning with zeal to exterminate all those who don't agree with themselves ! I can quite imagine Him saying—' So *that's* what the Roman Catholics teach that *I* think, is it ? Yet who shall know the mind of the Lord and who shall be His Councillor ? ' Oh, Hugh, I often think how God must smile ! "

Much surprised by her sentiments, he said :

" You aren't nearly as strict as my mother told me you were, Quendred ! "

" Aren't I ? " she laughed. " Poor Aunt Rosamund ! I suppose she's just as convinced that all Catholic girls are the ' Scarlet Woman,' as Father is certain that no Protestants can be saved, and that it was once the fashion to believe that Napoleon was the ' Beast ' of the Scriptures."

" But—don't you really believe in Romanism, then, Quendred ? " he asked hopefully.

" Never try to pin me down to a Creed, Hugh," she said. " I only want to be known by my fruit. But if you want to have a passage of arms with a real, proper Catholic, you'd better talk to Patricia Connor ! She'd willingly go to the stake for her religion."

" Well, so would I—for God—willingly," answered Hugh.

" Yes—God's different," Quendred said dryly. " I suppose you realize that she's going to marry Anthony ? "

" She's not ! " gasped her cousin. " Whatever makes you think that ? "

" Well, anyone could see it."

" I didn't."

" No, *you* never see *anything*, you dear old bat," laughed the girl.

" Except you," he said slowly, looking at her with dog-like devotion. " Nothing or nobody is worth thinking about when you're there, Quendred. Can't you, couldn't you care for me ? If you aren't such a strict Romanist perhaps you wouldn't mind marrying a Protestant as much as I feared you would."

He came close to her, and knelt on one knee at her side, taking her hands in his, and holding them to his lips.

" Quendred, darling," he pleaded, " will you ? "

But as he said the words a vision rose before her. She heard a deep musical voice singing happily, and she saw the white dusty road to Santa Barbara bathed in golden September haze. In this vision a man stood near her, above her, looking with earnest, clever eyes deeply into her face. From his lips came words which put perfectly clearly what her brain had been juggling with and groping for almost since her childhood. This man held her and dominated her.

" Simon," she thought. " Simon, I must see you again ; I need you ! "

And in a flash she knew that, whatever else happened to her in life, she would marry Simon de Villancourt. But her vision was disturbed by again feeling Hugh's lips upon her hands, and his tense, low voice once more asking her to be his wife.

"Hugh dear, I can't," she said softly, "and yet I love you for all you have said to me to-night. Religion shall have nothing to do with my choice of a husband—it's the *man* I shall marry, not his religion. But perhaps I shall never marry at all."

"Of course you will," he answered sadly. "Everyone's in love with you. If you don't marry, you'll be the most wasted woman in the world."

"You and I are going to be the best of friends," she said, leading the way back to the dancers. And Hugh had to be content with that.

. . . . . .

The next day at breakfast Anthony announced that he was driving over to Quendred Queen's, and stopping to luncheon at his father's old friends', the Knox-Kerrs', on his way home.

"Who'll come with me?" he asked in a gay voice, and, without waiting for an answer, he said, "I think you'd better, Miss Patricia, and if the young horses I'm driving jib or bolt you'll know what to do! Will you come?"

"I'd love to, and may I drive?"

"Certainly, and then it'll be on your head if I'm killed."

The words were scarcely spoken before he regretted them, and he saw by the change on her face that she shared his feelings.

"But this is too ridiculous," he thought to himself. "I mustn't let those doggerel lines get hold of me like this. It's idiotic; I'll become quite morbid."

But when they started Patricia firmly refused to drive, saying—

"I've never had an accident in my life, but somehow your saying that at breakfast has quite shaken my nerve."

They both felt in some indefinable way that their knowledge of each other's tiny, secret fear was a bond between them known only to themselves.

On the way home Anthony said to Patricia:

"Lord Claude made such a curious remark after luncheon when we went to the smoking-room. I was talking about my ather joining an Order and going away for good in a week's time, and he said, 'Of course, he's wanted to be a priest ever nnce his conversion—I was always very much surprised at his marriage.' Then he went on to tell me how well he knew my father as a young man in Rome years ago, and of how my father had told him on their journey out (for they had travelled together) how he longed to be a priest, and that his sole reason for going to Rome was to see the Pope and tell him of his great desire. Lord Claude said he could think of nothing else, and that the idea apparently obsessed him, and that marriage never entered his head even. Then suddenly, after only having been in Italy a few weeks, Rome heard of his engagement to my mother. It's a funny story, isn't it ? "

"Yes—extraordinary," mused the girl.

Since she had come to Ullcombe she seemed to have stepped into a different world, and her old, wild, higgledy-piggledy, anyhow kind of life was already somehow a thing of the past. Yet, behind all the glamour and apparent peace and happiness in this new world, she felt that a mysterious something lurked, an unknown phantom, which no one had ever seen or consciously thought of, but which would one day appear, and then something would happen—something tragic, something blighting. All she felt was so vague, though, and she could explain nothing accurately or sensibly even to herself.

"It's dreadfully sad, Lord Athelston, to think that your father must have been very unhappy during some part of his life. How beautiful he is ! I have never seen such a beautiful face on any man, and yet it's such a sad face, and there's such a hopeless look in his eyes sometimes. I hope he'll be happier when he goes to his monastery. What will you do when he's gone ? Don't think me indiscreet, *please*, but it's such a unique situation, and I am so interested in you all, although I've known you such a few days."

"Well, you've cheered us up tremendously," he said. "We'll miss you awfully ; at least, *I* will, anyhow. Must you really go to-morrow ? "

She looked up wistfully, charmingly. Their eyes met and held each other—when they reached the house they were engaged.

So when, before all the guests departed, Anthony announced his engagement, Hugh, at least, was not surprised.

It was not received, however, with the enthusiasm that Patricia would have liked. Although they were all very nice, quite friendly, and most considerate of her as the *fiancée* of Ullcome's future master, she was conscious that they weren't really pleased, and that there was no delicious natural spontaneity in their behaviour to her, faultless and charming though it was.

She had overheard the old Duchess remark to Princess Santa Fiora that, " although the alliance is not one which we would have chosen, her religion is satisfactory to my son, who will not hear of anything but a Catholic marriage."

This filled her proud heart with an anger against Anthony's relations, and fixed a gulf between them which widened as time went on.

Stephen, on the other hand, was *really* pleased when his wife told him of it. She complained that Anthony might have married anybody, and that, after all, she was an unknown Irish girl, whom none of them had ever heard of till a week ago.

" What would your father have thought of it, Stephen ? " she asked.

" I know, I know," he answered petulantly, " but he's in Heaven now, I hope, and so realizes how little worldly things count, and that the only thing that really *does* matter is whether people are Catholics or not. And now, dear, I can go in peace. Anthony married to a nice Catholic girl will live here. You have got all you want. Besides this estate—which I am making over to Anthony at his marriage so as to escape death duties—I have only unentailed property to the extent of £2,000 a year, as you know. £20,000 of this I have left to the Jesuits to build a church at a new school they are starting."

" But Stephen," said his wife, aghast, " if you haven't enough to leave to your children, you surely haven't enough to bequeath to priests ? "

" You forget, dear," he said reprovingly, " that in leaving money to priests one is in reality leaving it to God, or anyhow to what represents God's interests on earth. It is very bitter to me to see all the Fitz-Urse money left to the Traquairs. They will, of course, use some of it to uphold Protestantism, so I am in duty bound forced to leave as much as I can to my beloved Church. Without your money, dearest, I don't know how we could have managed."

' Surely the Ullcombe estate—being in the splendid condition your father left it—was really enough for us to live on without bothering so much about the unentailed property," she remarked quixotically, " and you know that it was the greatest joy in life for me to feel that my money could make things easier and pleasanter for you," she said. " You promised to endow me with all your worldly goods, why shouldn't I equally endow you with mine ?   Surely this is one of the proofs of love ? "

While she had been speaking, her husband had edged towards the door.

" Yes, yes," he answered nervously, and quickly slipped out of the room.

" I mustn't talk about love," he thought, as he hurried back to his library.   " Father Ignatius wouldn't advise it."

.   .   .   .   .   .

A week later Stephen had said his last good-byes to his children and relations, and Maddalena went with him to London. He had arranged to stay there one night, as Father Ignatius had come to England to give some retreats, and he wished to see him before going away for good.   The Jesuit and the Duke spent an hour together the next morning, walking up and down in the Park opposite Stanhope Gate.

The next afternoon Maddalena saw him off at Charing Cross. The train disappeared in the distance, and Maddalena walked across the shrieking, noisy station—alone.   As she drove back to her empty house, a vision of the road to Santa Barbara rose before her—the golden haze in the distance ; the air quivering hot ; her boy-lover's arms around her once more, and she, trembling with happiness as he held her to his heart.

A lump rose in her throat.

" My God, how I have loved him ! " she thought.

Bending forward, she told the footman to stop at the Jesuit's church in Farm Street.   Benediction was just finishing.   The dim church was full of inclining figures, chiefly women.

From the altar came a soft blaze of subdued light.   Fumes of incense hung upon the air, which was full of the smell of exotic flowers and women's perfumes.   A sexless voice was singing hauntingly, *Tantum Ergo Sacramentum*, " Down in adoration falling."

The words fell like balm upon her bruised and aching soul— and great comfort came to her as she knelt in this church, where he and she had knelt together for nearly twenty-three years.

The service was now over, and the officiating priest left the altar.   He passed so close to Maddalena that the vestment he wore knocked her prayer-book out of her hands, and, looking up, she saw the face of Lepantchine.   Neither years, nor emacia- tion, neither shaven lip, grey hairs, nor unsightly scar could make that face unrecognizable to her. Hardly looking at her, however, and immersed in the thoughts of God, this woman—thickly veiled—meant nothing to him.

Maddalena went painfully to her carriage. When she reached home a note lay on the table in the hall for her.

" Dearest," (it ran)
            " Leaving you has been a far more terrible wrench than I ever could have imagined. Dear woman, dear wife, dear mother of our children, there is nothing in my heart for you but love and admiration, but this awful pain at the knowledge of my falseness to God's call has been too much for me to bear, for all the time I felt it was wrong to love you, and then when Father Ignatius—that wonderful man—showed me so plainly that in God's cause I must leave you, I could no longer ignore it. So great and strong in spiritual matters do I feel him to be that I am certain that he—of all our friends—could help you most just now, for he so thoroughly *understands*. I have asked him to call on you to-night to comfort you. It will comfort me, too, my dearest, to think—when I am putting the narrow strip of cold, grey sea between you and me—that this holy man will be at your side to bear you up.

" May God bless you, wife of my heart. All my prayers will be for you.

                              " Your devoted
                                    " Stephen."

She crushed the note in her hand and told the servant who stood near her that Father Ignatius would in all probability call after tea. " He won't be here long," she told the man, " so be ready to show him out the moment I ring the bell."

Upstairs she paced the drawing-room, fumbled nervously with the tea-things, spasmodically drank some tea, and paced the room again. Then, ringing the bell, she told the servant to take it away. " I must be calm," she kept repeating to herself. " Oh, Stephen, what have you done to me ? " She went to her bedroom, where she changed her clothes, held cold water to her eyes, and re-arranged her hair so that she was perfectly composed when her maid, knocking at the door, told her that Father Ignatius was in the drawing-room.

Lepantchine was dressed in the usual unattractive and sombre outdoor clothes of a cleric.

His shoulders were slightly bent, as though from much study, and his now iron-grey hair was brushed straight back, showing his finely-developed forehead. His erstwhile sensual mouth—from which his white teeth had been wont to gleam—had dwindled to a fine, narrow, bloodless line—so often indicative in later life of disillusionment and bitter disappointment, or of the ascetic mode of thought.

Because of the thinness of his face his jaw was more bony and protruding than ever, and it was a great, emaciated hawk of a man whom Maddalena found pacing her drawing-room.

"But his eyes haven't changed," thought the woman, as, standing with her back to the door, she looked steadily into his face. Those wonderful eyes of Lepantchine's—soft, wide, mesmeric; gentle as a gazelle's, seemingly nothing but palpitating pupils, and then suddenly narrowing; compelling, sinister, cruel; remote—yet intimate; eyes which made you do what you would not.

For a moment neither of them spoke, and as though by tacit understanding their hands did not touch.

Twenty-four years had passed since they had last met.

He expected more surprise on her part, and the words :

" So you knew who I was ? " were forced from him.

" I saw you in Farm Street just now," she answered quietly. " Ah ! "

Maddalena, dressed in softest grey crêpe-de-chine, with rows of pearls hanging from her firm round throat, pearls dropping from her ears, and bracelets of pearls clasped with sapphires round her lovely arms, looked very beautiful, very seductive. Her thick, soft, brown wavy hair was gathered in a simple knot just above the nape of her neck, as when he had seen her last, and her figure—long-legged, slender, and flat-backed, with rounded hips and Southern bust—showed a woman in the flower of life.

" How *could* he have left her ? " ran through Lepantchine's mind. " How could he have left such a woman as this ? "

.   .   .   .   .   .

" What have you come here for ? " Maddalena demanded coldly. " Is it in the best of taste ? "

" The Duke begged me to do so," the man answered. " He wanted me to explain to you why he so definitely made up his mind at last to be a priest. It *is*, after all, the greatest call, and the call of the lure of woman, wife, and children, is as nothing compared to it.   Only he who has heard the voice knows how sweet it is," he continued unctuously ; but heavily veiled as his feelings were, Maddalena wondered if she detected a little bitterness ?

" Please spare me your heroics," she replied.   " Say what you have to say and then go, or I'll ring the bell—— "

" —and wake up all the servants and have me flogged—eh, Duchess ?   You were very wild in those days, but life and its disappointments, and its complexities, have toned you down—as it does to us all.   It is, of course, only a school, a preparation for the greater, fuller life that is to come, that is prepared by a just God for all who are true children of Holy Church."

At the last two words Maddalena shuddered, then, pulling herself together, she spoke coldly :

" I think I see things more clearly now, and there is not much to be said between you and me, Lepantchine.   I see that in your priestly capacity you did not brush aside the opportunity which Fate offered you to come between my husband and myself, and that—in full possession of the facts—you willingly stooped to do me harm ; in fact—I see it all so plainly now—it was an act of revenge.   You could have stopped my husband leaving me but, in order to revenge yourself upon me, you worked upon him to go."

The priest held up his hand deprecatingly, and in a soft voice of reproof replied :

" Ssh !   Such words are not seemly.   Revenge ?   What had I to do with revenge ?   Through you—although unwittingly— I have been able to receive the greatest blessing possible to a man—that of daily offering the Holy Sacrifice of the Mass ; naturally I could not deter another from participating in the same inexplicable, mysterious felicity—when God's finger seemed to be pointing so strongly, so determinately that way for him. You are distressed, and naturally so, in the circumstances, but I must beg of you to compose yourself, and not to forget that I am a priest of God.   But there—I understand.   It is difficult, it is hard, it is perhaps even cruel ; but in the eyes of the Church it is right, and you remember the words of our Saviour—that a man must leave father. mother. wife. and children for His sake, if need be."

As he spoke his eyes had narrowed, and his pupils became suddenly as pin-pricks, and as pin-pricks they seemed to be running into her heart, and keeping it there, a struggling, unwilling captive as it might be a butterfly. Thus for some seconds he held her with his eyes, and then, slowly opening them again, his wide, tender, warm look enfolded her in a kind of magical, mesmeric grip, and a weakness never experienced by her before crept over her.

"Poor little Mother!" she thought. "In a priest this compelling power is dangerous enough, but in a lover! Poor darling! I'm so glad I was tender to you. Perhaps at that moment I was rather arrogant in the possession of a love which was pure, splendid, and knight-like, and—as I thought—eternal. But your life, beginning so darkly, has ended in such a happy, contented *camaraderie*, while mine, which I thought so glorious and was so proud of, has ended—thus."

Aloud she said : "I cannot regard you as a priest, Lepant-chine ; to me you will always be what I saw that night in my mother's bedroom, when you brought all my ideals crashing down about me."

"Cannot you forgive, Duchess?"

"Yes, I have forgiven you, as I hope I shall be forgiven ; but I can never forget—— "

"Yet true forgiveness includes forgetting," he interrupted her softly, his wonderful eyes throwing themselves over her once more, and holding her.

She moved as though to get away from the power emanating from him, and went towards the bell.

"—that you as a man," she went on, ignoring his words, "cast the first shadow on my girlhood, and that you as a priest—and all that priests stand for—have practically ruined the rest of my life."

"You shouldn't speak like that," said he, "for priests represent the Church, and the Church represents—no, *is*—God. Be careful lest—in your present mood, and no doubt unwittingly —you blaspheme. Ah! If only you could resign yourself to God's most Holy Will, what a very great happiness you would find in placing this sacrifice at His feet."

"Lepantchine," she said—" priest or no priest, you nauseate me—and I will now ask my servants to show you out." She spoke coldly and deliberately. She pushed the bell, and immediately her commands were fulfilled.

"How could he have left her?" he thought to himself, as he slowly walked across the darkening square. "How could he have left her, and money, and position, and power, and the sweet, sweet, throbbing life of a man with such a wife, for the cold passion of the priesthood ? But, like many of us, he'll be disillusioned with the life, and then he'll regret his Maddalena, and then I'll have had my revenge."

He stepped into the church, flicking holy water on to his forehead, and sank into a kneeling posture on the floor. One or two frequenters of the church noticed him.

" What a holy man, so humble, so simple," they thought, and that night he preached a magnificent sermon to a packed congregation of men on the disillusions of human and material love, and of the best way of keeping one's passions in check. At the same time Stephen sat in a third-class carriage travelling to Florence, to poverty, to renunciation, to chastity, to obedience, to the priesthood, and therefore—as he was most profoundly convinced—to God, in the most personal way possible this side of the grave. In his hand he held his rosary, and his lips moved feverishly.

Yet often he thought of Maddalena, and the thought brought to him a terrific recoil of the senses—as a horse, when suddenly jagged at the mouth by a cruel bit, is pulled up on to his haunches.

But he had said good-bye. He had kissed her, and said good-bye. Good-bye ! There was no other word to say but this.

CHAPTER XVI

MY " LOVE " OR MY " CHURCH " ?

" Shall I ask the brave soldier who fights by my side
  In the cause of mankind, if our creeds agree ?
Shall I give up the friend I have valued and tried,
  If he kneel not before the same altar as me ? "
                                        —MOORE.

SIMON DE VILLANCOURT, finding that it was impossible to exist
any longer without seeing Quendred, had written to tell her of
his intention of being in London on a certain date.

" I'll ask Mother to invite him here," mused the girl. " I
know she'll like him, because they've both got the same kind
of mind."

" And where did you meet this man ? " Maddalena asked
her, smiling.

" On the road to Santa Barbara near the wayside Crucifix.
We talked a little—— "

" But, my darling—— ! "

" Oh, there's nothing to worry about, Mother. I know who
he is, because the next day he called, and Grandpapa saw him and
liked him, and he told me all about his relations, who are French
people. Grandpapa knew them."

" I suppose it's all right then," laughed her mother. " And
do you really like him, Quenny ? Do you really want me to ask
him here, because between the lines of that letter of his I can
see he's fond of you, and it's no use—— "

" Yes, Mother, I do like him very much, but I don't know
him well, and I want to know him better," said the girl.

So it was settled, and a week later Simon arrived at Ullcombe,
where all was in a state of confusion on account of Anthony's
approaching marriage ; but Quendred and he were able to be much
alone, and no one interfered with them. Every day they went
for long walks and rides together, and every day it became clearer

to both that love had opened the door of their hearts, and entered in.

And then the day came when—riding through the bluebell-carpeted woods—he asked her if she would be his wife.

"You have so wound yourself round my heart," he said, "that I cannot pull you out. If I did so my heart would come too, and I should die, for who can live without a heart? Will you marry me, Quendred? Will you?"

"You know I will," she answered, smiling seriously into his face, while her slender hand slipped happily into his big one.

"My Quendred," he whispered, "mine for ever."

.　　　.　　　.　　　.　　　.　　　.

In her mother's room that evening she told her great news.

"My darling," Maddalena said as she kissed her, "if you are really happy and you really love him, I am content. And I know that you love each other, for I have been watching."

They sat together, crying and laughing in turns, as women often do when talking of such things.

"Do you like him, Mother, and don't you think he is frightfully good-looking? Tell me, tell me!" and she took hold of her mother's arms, putting her face quite near to hers.

"I like him extremely, and I think he's one of the best-looking and nicest men I've ever met! There—are you pleased?"

"Pleased? I'm mad with joy! One of the greatest prayers of my life has been answered. It was that you should thoroughly approve of, and like, the man I would marry. It's too wonderful. Oh! Mother darling, I am so frightfully happy," and she hugged her again and again.

.　　　.　　　.　　　.　　　.　　　.

That night Maddalena lay awake. Many misgivings crossed her mind, for—Simon de Villancourt was a Protestant and, she had noticed, a devout and a strict one. He read his Bible too, it seemed, for her Italian maid had told her so with a frightened expression. She imagined he was not rich, and there would be no money forthcoming for Quendred if she married a Protestant, for neither her own father nor Stephen would tolerate it. Yet her one idea and hope had always been not to blight the " first fine careless rapture " of Quendred's love when that wondrous and fragile thing came to her, and in this she had most certainly succeeded for the moment, for Quendred was lying in bed—her cheeks flushed at the remembrance of his look, her heart throbbing with joy at the thought of their speedy union.

"He loves me, I love him, and Mother is pleased." She could have sung with Pippa in her burst of exaltation—" God's in His Heaven, all's well with the world."

But her mother knew that the subject would have to be broached before anything definite was settled, and, till things were arranged, they could not be publicly engaged. She did not want to blur her daughter's happiness, yet was it kind to put off a discussion which was, in the circumstances, inevitable ? What was best to do she wondered ? She was worried by this ever-lasting question of religion, which raised barriers at every point of life.

"I had better ask Father Chinnock," she thought, as sleep at last came to her troubled spirit. "Priests understand all about these difficulties, I suppose."

So the next day she told their private chaplain of it.

"You won't allow it, of course ? " he said at once.

"Why not ? " asked the Duchess.

"It's strictly forbidden by Holy Church."

"I know, but there is such a thing as a permit from Rome, isn't there ? " she answered.

"'M—yes ; but Rome isn't so keen on giving it, you know, and nowadays there must be very strong reasons."

"Isn't love a strong enough reason ? " the Duchess said.

The priest looked at her, surprised.

"Lady Quendred is very young," he said. "This is only a girlish infatuation, most likely. She can be made to forget him ; at her age these things are merely passing emotions. She had better forget him ; it will be happier for her. What does she want to marry a Protestant for ? There are plenty of Catholic men for her to choose from, surely ? "

"Are there ? " said Maddalena aloud, and then to herself, " how little priests know about the society they try to control ! "

"But I suppose there'll be no difficulty in getting the permit when he has signed the paper, will there, Father Chinnock ? " she asked.

"Well, I don't know," the priest answered provokingly. "I rather think there will. You see, it's distinctly against the laws of the Church to countenance ' mixed marriages.' All the bishops are getting very strong on the subject now, and many of them won't allow such a marriage to take place at the High

Altars of their churches, even if the prescribed paper *is* signed."

"In fact," said Maddalena, "they endeavour to make it as much of a hole and corner affair as they possibly can. Personally, I think all that sort of thing disgraceful, and it's extremely insulting to those taking part in the ceremony that their marriage day is turned into such a hurried affair with no music or singing. I shall have to tell my daughter what you say, Father Chinnock, and I foresee scenes. She has a strong personality, and very pronounced views of her own upon such matters, and I do not visualize her obeying the Church without a very hard struggle."

"But surely you will support the Church's view, Duchess ? " said the Chaplain, who was both irritated and surprised at her words and her attitude. "You are born and bred a Catholic, and you come of one of the most Catholic nations in the world."

"That may be so," answered Maddalena calmly, "but I am also born a woman with a tremendous understanding of and sympathy for lovers, and I have evolved—no matter what I was taught—into a mother whose heart beats a thousand times more ardently that her beloved child should be happy, than that the Catholic Church should win."

    .   .   .   .   .   .

It was nearing the time of Simon's departure, and Maddalena —still only longing for the complete peace and happiness of the lovers—had put off the disagreeable discussion. At last, however, she made the necessary effort, and asked Quendred whether she had talked about religious questions to Simon.

"What questions, Mother ? "

"Well, he is a Protestant, isn't he ? " Maddalena answered. "Has he said he will sign the paper that has to be signed before a marriage can take place between a Catholic and a non-Catholic ? "

"Oh, we've never talked about it ! I'm afraid I never thought about it," she laughed gaily. "Besides, Mother, he's not a Protestant, you know."

"Well, what is he ? A Huguenot, as his name implies ? "

"H'm, well—I don't think he's anything really. I don't believe that he has got a religion—I mean what *we* are taught to call religion. At least, I've never heard him say that he belongs to any creed. I know "— this rather shyly—"I know he hates being labelled anything, and he says that it is what we *are* that counts, not what we are called.

" I hope you don't mind hearing this, but I know, as a matter of fact, that Simon *has* no fixed religion in the way we—in the way Catholics have.   He says that he doesn't agree that person a has got to ' belong to a Church ' in order to be a Chri∻tian.   Are you shocked ? "

" No.   You know this sort of thing doesn't shock me," said her mother, " and although I get joy and consolation from being a Catholic, I would never take it upon myself to say that it is the only religion which God likes, or that it is the only one by which we can be saved.   It seems to me that the great object of life is union with God after death, and I could never believe that only one road leads to that union.   But if your Simon has no fixed credal beliefs, as you say, I don't suppose he would make any difficulty about signing that paper ?   In case you haven't seen it, here is a copy.   You had better show it to him when he comes back."

MARRIAGE FORM TO BE FILLED IN BY A CATHOLIC AND A NON-CATHOLIC WHO WISH TO MARRY EACH OTHER

I

Man's name.
Domicile.
Religion.
Place and date of Baptism.

Woman's name.
Domicile.
Religion.
Place and date of Baptism.
Canonical reasons (to be stated fully).

II

PROMISES TO BE SIGNED BEFORE APPLICATION

(To be signed by the Catholic party)

I, the undersigned, do hereby solemnly promise and engage that all the children of both sexes who may be born of my marriage shall be baptised in the Catholic Church and shall be carefully brought up in the knowledge and practice of the Catholic religion ; and I also promise that (according to the instructions of the Holy See) my marriage in the Catholic Church shall not be preceded nor followed by any other religious ceremony.

Signature ....

(To be signed by the non-Catholic party)

I, the undersigned, do hereby solemnly promise and engage that I will not interfere with the religious belief of.............my future wife

Q

(or husband) nor with her (or his) full and perfect liberty to fulfil all her (or his) duties as a Catholic ; and that I will allow all the children, of both sexes, who may be born of our marriage to be baptised in the Catholic Church and to be carefully brought up in the knowledge and the practice of the Catholic Religion.

Signature ....

N.B.—The third promise concerning the conversion of the non-Catholic party, which would be sought after to the best of one's ability, ought to be made by the Catholic party at least by word of mouth. Moreover, if the parties have already co-habited, it must here be declared if there has been any offspring of the union, and, in so far as the answer is in the affirmative, whether it has been baptised and educated in the Catholic Religion ?

Quendred took the document to the window to read. It was a terrible revelation to her, and it shattered with a heavy, unjust, and cruel hand all the glorious dreams of free, untrammelled love of a happily engaged girl.

Like croaking birds of ill-omen, the little black letters seemed to dance a jig of delight at her misery.

And the words and the phrasing ! How coarse and material they appeared to her, when her heart was so full of the best and the highest love for Simon.

Her lips quivered ; her face flushed. The thought of his burning words about freedom—every one of which he meant and believed with all his manhood and strength—came to her, as her eyes gazed—glassily dazed—at the paper which trembled in her hand.

She turned, helpless and crushed, to Maddalena.

Joyous, brilliant Quendred—on the threshold of love and fulfilment ; Quendred—who never said an unkind word, and who wouldn't have hurt a fly—was beaten to the ground.

" He will never sign *that*, Mother. It's no good, I know he won't," and she left the room.

" My poor darling," her mother said, above her breath.

.   .   .   .   .   .

Through the country, soused with heavy spring rains, Quendred was trudging manfully. Anything, anything, to disperse the awful, cruel, miserable hopelessness which had fallen on to her soul since she had seen that fatal paper.

" I know he won't sign it, I know he won't," she was saying. " And the Catholic Church won't marry me, and we shall have to part from each other. I can't—I can't. I love him far too much. Why should the Church be so cruel ? Why does she want to

ruin people's lives ?   Who said she was to do so ?   Who gave her
the power ?   Power !   Yes—it's love of power which makes her
do it.   ' Compel them to come in ' is her motto.   It doesn't
matter how ;   anyhow will do !   The end justifies the means."

And then in a flash all that she had thought and read since
that long-ago day in Berkeley Square, when Father Bischoffsheim
had pretended to excommunicate her, came back to her, and she
realized that she was caught and held ;   that she was not free ;
that she was imprisoned in a net ;   Peter's net, perhaps, but not
the golden net of Love woven by Christ.

" I *will* be free ! " she cried.   " I will be *free!* " and the echo,
returning to her from the bank on the other side of the lake where
she was standing, wailed mournfully " free."

 . . . . . .

That night she showed Simon the paper.   At first he laughed,
although he had heard the thing talked about.

" It's not true, darling," he said, " it's a joke.   Such things
are of no avail in our sensible, broad-minded, fair, modern days.
They're only doing it to frighten you ;   it's only a silly ' try-on.' "
And he thought of wild places in Canada where the only law is the
law of the gun.

" But it's *not* a joke, Simon, it's deadly earnest.   They—the
Church—I don't know who—but ' they ' want to separate us
because you're not a Catholic, and this is the way they'll do
it.   You will sign it, won't you, dearest ?   Say you will ? "
and she slid her hands up his coat till they were clasped round
his neck.

He was holding the fateful scrap of paper, not six inches
square, which he suddenly realized might shatter their new-
found and marvellous happiness.   His eyes looked angry, and
there was a bitter frown between his brows.

" It's damnable !   Those damnable priests ! " he muttered.
And it was as Quendred knew—he absolutely refused to sign it.

A sudden glimmer of hope came to her perplexed and
miserable mind.

" Will you speak to Father Chinnock about it ? " she asked
him.   " He is quite kind, and fairly broad-minded, and I'm sure
he would explain it to you, and then perhaps you could sign ?
He'll tell you about the Catholic religion ;   it's not really so bad
as you think it, perhaps ! "

" It couldn't be much worse than I think it, darling," had

been his answer ; " but I'll go to please you.   I'll do anything
to please you."

"Then sign this paper," she said, leaping at the words.
" And, after all, perhaps we'll never have any children. Why
ruin our happiness for such an uncertainty ? "

He looked at her sadly. Did she imagine it, or were there
tears glistening in his eyes ?

" Beloved, I will not sign that paper,"he said, " even for you,
whom I love better than my own flesh. I will never sign it.
If you cannot marry me without it being signed, then I cannot
marry you. My only little darling, how I loathe myself for
saying such words to you—you whom I worship—you without
whom I shall have no more real happiness. But I cannot do it,
dear. I cannot. It is not according to God's word. He never
decreed it. It is a man-made law to proselytize for the Church
of Rome. Besides, this is a new invention of theirs.

" Forgive me, darling, I don't want to hurt your feelings, but
to me the whole thing is absolutely damnable ! The Roman
Catholic Church says she speaks God's mind on matters concerning faith and morals. She claims that her teaching never
changes, and that she cannot make a mistake ; and she stuffs
this teaching down her credulous children's throats from baby-
hood upwards, like geese are stuffed to make foie-gras. I maintain
that she *can* and *does* make mistakes—and that it is the duty of
non-Catholics to maintain their rights against her, and definitely
to insist on her not meddling with the marriages of British subjects, which is, of course, her most prolific and useful investment,
and from which she gets the best and the quickest returns. You
must marry me in my own Church, darling, if they won't marry
you in your own."

" But I *couldn't*, Simon ! I couldn't be married in a Protestant church," she said. " They'd excommunicate me and send me
to Hell when I die if I did. I'm much too terrified. Do you
believe they can send me to Hell ? All the priests tell me they
can," and tears shone in her large, dark eyes.

" Of *course* they can't ! " Simon said angrily. " Why, can't
you see that it's all done to frighten you into submission, and the
whole system is based on threats and fears ! I really can't
understand how any thoughtful, intelligent person can believe
it—really believe it, down at the bottom of their hearts, I mean.
Don't let fear frighten you, but rather you frighten fear."

" But I've been told that the Church cannot teach falsely,

because she is the true voice of God," Quendred said, " and to dislodge this feeling from my mind would be as impossible as it would be to make me believe that my mother leads a life of vice. Oh, Simon ! how lucky you are not to have been brought up a Catholic ! "

.   .   .   .   .   .

The next day he went—as she had asked him—to see Father Chinnock. As the priest rose he put down his breviary, from which he had been reading his prescribed prayers.

Simon spoke quickly and in a business-like tone. Clerical interference bored him.

" What a nuisance they are with all their rules ! " he was thinking.

" I hope that I shall be able to help you," said the priest kindly. " Have you ever thought of joining our Holy Church ? "

" No."

" Ah—well, I daresay that will come later. Marriage works wonders ! Love ! Eh ? " and he laughed knowingly as, rubbing his hands together, he searched in a drawer for something.

" Here," he said presently, " this is just a little declaration which we ask all non-Catholics to—— "

" Yes, I know, I've seen it. I won't sign it though," Simon said abruptly.

" My dear sir, you surely can't be serious ! Perhaps you haven't read it properly ? Besides, the marriage can't possibly take place if this isn't signed," and he tapped it significantly as it lay upon the table.

" Very well, there's nothing more to be said," the other man answered, preparing to go.

The priest was rather surprised.

" But surely, M. de Villancourt, you love Lady Quendred ? You wouldn't *not* marry her for such a paltry reason ? See ! All we ask is that the mother (who, after all, is the natural guide of her children) should teach them her religion—the beautiful, holy, Catholic religion. What more could any man wish for his children than to see them standing at their mother's knee, imbibing God's holy truth ? I should have thought a man of your type was much too intellectual and broadminded to be so bigoted ! "

" Yes," laughed Simon dryly. " You call *us* bigoted if we stick out against *your* Church's law's, but you call your own people ardent and faithful if they stick out against *us*."

The priest smiled mirthlessly.

" But I think you *ought* to be a Catholic if you are going to marry Lady Quendred," he said. " Hers is a great family, and your position, your personality, and your brain would be a useful power in the Church. I believe you'd make a splendid Catholic, M. de Villancourt."

Simon smiled sceptically. " You think so ? I don't. I have only two wishes : one is to be a good Christian, and the other is to marry my lady. With all due respect to you and to your Church, I swear I'll achieve it, and without signing that—that paper."

" Well, if you force Lady Quendred to marry you anywhere but in a Catholic church you will be acting the part of Satan, and deeply imperilling her salvation. Is this then a sign that you *love* her ? " The priest spoke scornfully.

" What you say is not true, and, what is more, you know it," said Simon very distinctly, looking at him with stern, unflinching eyes. " I shall marry her, and I shall not sign that paper. I am leaving to-morrow, and so I shall not have the pleasure of discussing the matter with you again. You must forgive me for having trespassed upon your time, but I did it at Lady Quendred's express wish. Good-bye," he said stiffly, without offering his hand.

Simon told Quendred of the result of his talk with Father Chinnock, and once again begged of her to marry him in an Anglican Church.

She felt now that a final decision had to be made. She realized that she must now sift very carefully the chaff from the wheat in her faith, and find out exactly what she *did*, and what she did *not*, believe. Did she really believe that she would be damned if she were excommunicated ? The Church told her (through the mouths of her priests) that this would be so if she married a non-Catholic anywhere but in a Catholic church. The Church wouldn't marry them unless the paper were signed, and he wouldn't sign the paper ! A dilemma !

They loved each other—they would never marry anyone else—and they fully intended to marry each other—what was to be done ? It was like beating her head against a stone wall. She was in a vicious circle, and couldn't get out of it. It was— either way—a great test. Would her religion, or her lover, prevail over her heart ?

She felt that, much as she adored Simon, she would give him up if she really and truly believed with her whole mind and being—steadfastly, as her father believed—that what the Church taught was true ; really, really true.   Yet, on the other hand, she couldn't see how it could be *wrong* to marry a man like Simon, who was good, honourable, clean-living, clean-minded, an idealist, and her beloved lover.   The unfortunate girl was tormented by doubts, tortured by her love on the one hand, and her fear of the Church on the other.

Her father had written from his monastery in Italy that it was his special wish that she should have a talk with Cardinal Ripon, who was a friend of his.

Maddalena it was who told Quendred of her father's desire, to which she had instantly acquiesced.

" I hate making him sad, poor darling," said Quendred, " and I'd do anything to please you both, but why is the Church so cruel ?   I've done nothing harmful to her !   I don't want to ruin other people's lives—I'm not wanting to commit a crime— all I want to do is to marry the man I love, and to be left in peace.   Why can't it be allowed ?   The Church gives me neither peace nor comfort, Mother, why should I remain within the fold if she starves me ? "

Maddalena had no answer ready, but she squeezed her hand saying that perhaps Cardinal Ripon might give a special per- mission for her marriage to take place, and that meanwhile she must cheer up and hope for the best, and, as Anthony's wedding was next week, she could go and see the Cardinal when they went to London for that ceremony.

.   .   .   .   .

The famous Prelate looked very handsome and magnificent in his red and purple robes, and struck Quendred as being rather theatrical when she called on him two days later.

She had expected to feel nervous, but when she saw his bold, clever eyes looking at her from out of his high-coloured face she merely felt supremely indifferent.

Apparently he knew nothing of the reason for her visit, and while she told him her story he sat very still with the tips of his shapely white hands meeting.   He kept his eyes fixed on one spot on the floor, and pursed his lips.   Every now and then he crossed and uncrossed his legs, which made his silk garments rustle.   When she had finished he looked up, and said :

" Ah, yes—and you think he will not sign the paper ? "

" I know he won't," Quendred said.

" Well then, my dear child, the only thing for you to do is—to give him up." As he said the last four words, he parted and joined his hands together again, at the same time shrugging his shoulders as though the case were final and the subject could be dismissed. " You know the Church's teaching on this point, I presume, Lady Quendred ? "

" Yes," she answered, " but I wondered whether you could do anything for me ? Couldn't you get me a special permission from Rome ? It seems so hard, Your Eminence, that my religion won't allow me to marry him ! If he were morally bad—divorced, a drunkard, a lunatic, a criminal—anything you like —I would understand the Church forbidding it. At any rate, there'd be some sense, some reason for her action—— "

" Tschut, tschut, child ; tschut, tschut ! " breathed the bishop.

" I'm not a child, my Lord," the girl flashed quickly. " I'm a woman, and I want to talk about the things that matter. I am not a child. I've thought, and read, and experienced, and suffered. I want to learn ; I want to understand *why* I must believe—under pain of going to Hell—all the things which the Catholic religion has taught me ? I am perfectly willing to believe if you can prove to me—prove to my thinking brain—that what you teach is true, that it is not largely evasion of truth for the sake of expediency."

The Cardinal looked pained.

" Tschut ! " he said again. " Tschut ! You shouldn't *think ;* you're sure to get out of your depth if you do. Let *us* do the thinking for you, and you just take it on trust. You'll find it much less trouble, you know, far more comfortable. You ought to be amusing yourself, not *thinking !* " and he smiled a sour little smile.

" But why should I take on trust the most important things in the world ? " said the girl, returning to the fray. " I take plenty of other things on trust—temporary things. I trust my cabby won't let his horse fall down. I trust my cook not to poison the soup. I trust my doctor not to give me an overdose, and so on ; but when it comes to eternal things, things which by non-belief in them can damn me, and by belief in them can save me, then surely I ought to think ? If they are as important as you say, then they must be worth studying and trying to comprehend ? No one would think I was much of a Shakespearian scholar if I only knew the text books, and a few quotations from Hamlet, would they ? "

" But you seem to forget the Church's authority and Papal Infallibility, my child," put in the Cardinal, in a noticeably controlled tone. " Once we have an infallible guide on matters concerning faith and morals, there can be no doubt of the truth, no grounds for discussion on the basic subjects."

" It's just Papal Authority that I *do* doubt," said Quendred, who—though she felt that she was annoying the Cardinal, and that it would be more tactful and less trouble to stop arguing—could not stop just then, for she wanted so desperately to get at the truth, or some of the truth, at any rate. " Granted that I do believe in infallibility, *why* do I ? Who made the Pope infallible ? "

He closed his eyes and paused a moment before answering. When he did so it was in a resigned kind of voice, as though giving in to an importunate child.

" You don't seem to realize that the faithful have always believed in Papal Infallibility, although it was not proclaimed an article of Catholic belief until Garibaldi's treachery to Holy Mother Church."

" Please don't defame Garibaldi's memory to me, Your Eminence," she said. " I see now that he had vision and prescience. He saw that a gradual sinking into complete nothingness and moral stupor can be the only future for a country composed of people whose minds are not allowed to think about the most important things in the world. My ancestors come of a country who have produced some very great thinkers, Your Eminence, as you know as well as I, and one of the truest things they ever uttered was, *Le clericalisme, viola l'enemi.* I see it now very clearly, although I had never realized it before I stumbled into it through my present dilemma."

The Cardinal—though no woman had ever spoken to him like this before—was very patient, and said :

" As I said just now, Lady Quendred, you ought to be dancing, not studying. You'd be much happier."

" —and much less trouble, wouldn't I ? " she answered. " Yes, I believe you'd like to see us all dancing, rather than reading and thinking, if it leads to questioning the truth of what you teach ! "

" Well, it is useless to argue Lady Quendred," said the Cardinal. " What the Church has said, she has said. You are either *in* her, or *out* of her.   What we want to-day is another Hildebrand.   *He* was a man, he got his way."

"A strong peasant who, *because* he was a peasant, gloated in stamping upon an emperor's neck !   Well, whatever happens, I shall never go to Canossa."   Thus Quendred.

As she said the words she got rather red, for it flashed across her mind that perhaps she ought not to be talking to a Cardinal in this strain.

"Of course, I don't want to be rude," she said to herself, "but, after all, he's only a man, and just as human as I am."

At her last sentence the Cardinal rose, looking at her sharply, quizzically.   He wasn't accustomed to be spoken to thus by chits of girls, nor, for that matter, by anyone at all.

"Yet it is Canossa or nothing," he said.   "If you will not go to Canossa—out you go !" and he made a significant gesture with both his hands, as though pushing away some rubbish.

"But now, about this paper," he said officially.   "We have got to see that it is signed before applying to Rome for a permit. What kind of man he is has nothing to do with it.   If he loves you so much, surely he won't go on refusing !   Men generally give in to anything when they're in love."

This had often been said to Quendred lately.   It was a cruel taunt and she felt it deeply.   What if it had been the other way about and that she was the Protestant who wanted her Catholic lover to give in to her bringing up their children in her Faith ?

"Why don't you convert him, Lady Quendred ?" the Cardinal went on.   "That is one of the greatest uses such charming ladies as you can put your powers to.   Charm your lovers into the Church ; *you* attack the heart, *we* attack the mind.   Perhaps you don't realize how powerful ladies can be in getting new recruits for our Holy Mother Church !"

Quendred recoiled.

"Outward forms repel him, Your Eminence," she said coldly.   "To him Christ is the only Mediator between his soul and God, so you see the Church and her priests would have no significance for him," and at that moment her faith in the Church of her education as the inspired mouthpiece of the Most High, died.

"The Popes," she thought, "will have to find something more terrifying, and more in tune with our times than the *vieux-jeu* of excommunication with which to frighten modern

women. I wonder how much anybody *really* believes in such
un-Christ-like nonsense ? ''

She turned to the Cardinal, who stood looking out of the
window.

" Your Eminence—— "

" Yes, my daughter ? "

He came towards her with a slightly triumphant smile, for
he felt certain that during this little pause she had made up her
mind to give in.

" I have been praying that you might have grace to win
through," he said, holding out both his hands. He had rather
an attractive voice, and could intensify it when necessary.

" I won't give him up," said she. Her eyes shone with love,
and her cheeks were flushed with excitement and nervousness,

The man within the priest was touched. For a fleeting second
he desired to take her in his arms. She was a lovely woman
he a full-blooded man.

" Poor, pretty creature," he thought as a man. " Obstinate,
tiresome woman," he thought as a priest. " I'll frighten her,
and see if that has any effect, but I doubt it, for she has spirit."

" Well, of course, if you persist in your wicked behaviour," he
said crossly, " and are married to this man in a non-Catholic
church, you will in all probability go to Hell when you die, for
you are doing it with your eyes open. It is a serious matter,
and you do it willingly ; therefore, it is a mortal sin, which is—
according to the teaching of Holy Mother Church—punishable by
eternal torment."

Was it the girl's imagination, or did he almost smack his lips
as he said the last words ?

" Can't you give me permission to marry him in a Catholic
church without the paper being signed ? " she asked.

" No, Lady Quendred, no ; I fear such a thing would be
impossible. Quite outside my province. It would have to
go to Rome, and even then I doubt extremely of your wish being
acceded to."

" Good-bye, then," she said from the door.

" Good-bye, Lady Quendred."

.   .   .   .   .   .

That evening Simon came to see her, and she told him of the
result of her meeting with the Cardinal.

" I don't mind about myself, Simon," she said, " for I really

don't believe in the Church's claim and powers any more, but I
don't want to grieve my mother, and I know how terribly upset
she would be if we were to marry in a Protestant church, although
perhaps you can't understand this ? "

" Indeed I can, my darling," he said, and, seeing her so
unnerved and distraught at the whole affair, his strength was
suddenly weakened, and he said :

" Look here, I don't want to seem a bigoted brute to you all.
I'll sign a paper—not the one issued by Rome—but a wording of
my own. Sweetheart, I simply can't *bear* to see you like this—
to hurt you so."

He drew a sheet of paper towards him, and on it he wrote the
words :

" I, Simon de Villancourt, do hereby promise that I will allow my future
wife, Quendred Fitz-Urse, to bring up any children who may be born of
our marriage as she likes, and that they may be baptised and confirmed in
the Roman Catholic Church.

(*Signed*) " SIMON DE VILLANCOURT."

He took her in his arms.

" There, darling, will they let me marry you now, do you
think ? These weeks of separation have been awful, and when
I thought that it might be for ever I felt I could not bear it."

Their lips clung together. They were so happy.

.   .   .   .   .   .

Quendred never doubted that what he had just written would
suit the Church, and so, with a joyful heart, she despatched it
that night to the Cardinal, only to receive it back again with a
little note saying how sorry he was, but he had to tell her that
nothing but a signature of the printed form would suit Rome.

Simon was furious. Tearing up the paper he had written
himself, he swore that he would never go half-way to meet them
again.

And so all was darkness this time, and Quendred felt as if her
mind would collapse. She couldn't bear all these conflicting
emotions, and she felt herself becoming terribly over-wrought.

And at last the awful thought—put into her mind by others
—that he didn't love her because he wouldn't give in to her, began
to take possession of her.

The evening before Anthony's wedding, Simon came to see
her in Berkeley Square. It was to be their last meeting. After

it, he had promised the Duchess not to see Quendred nor write to her for a year.

When he came into the room she hardly spoke, and stood by the window fiddling with the blind-cord.

"Quendred," he said softly, "what's the matter? Won't you speak to me? Are you angry with me?"

"No, not angry, Simon."

"Well then, what is it? Why so cold? Darling, speak to me. Tell me."

"Simon, I don't—I can't—I feel that you don't really love me. You are making me so dreadfully unhappy, and yet everything lies in your power to change it, and make us happy as we were last week. Was it last week or last year? It seems such ages ago."

"Beloved! How can you say such words to me," he said. "I not love you, when you know that you are my heart's desire and my only happiness? Who has been putting such wicked lies into your head? Come to me. Turn to me. Show me your sweet face. I not love you?" And there was a swift indrawing of his breath as he held out his arms to her.

When she turned at last he saw there were tears in her eyes.

"They've made you cry with their lies," he said. "They're trying to break your spirit, and no weapon is too small or mean to use if they can do it in the end. Your sweet, brave, brown eyes are full of tears," and as he gathered her tenderly to him, the knowledge and profound conviction of his love for her fell over her like a cloak. But she was worn out, and he marvelled to see this lovely, radiant, fearless girl all crumpled up by the mental thumbscrews which the Church was applying.

"Say that you believe I love you best of all, now, and for ever, and that whoever says to the contrary is a damned liar, Amen," said Simon.

He so seldom spoke like this, that through her tears—as he held her close to his heart—she could not help but smile.

.   .   .   .   .   .

The church was crowded, and, as Patricia walked up the aisle on Denis' arm, all heads were craned to get a glimpse of the unknown little Irish girl who had captured such a plum.

John Poynder was Anthony's best man, and Hugh Traquair and della Meglia—glaring at each other when they weren't gazing at Quendred—helped to show the guests into their seats.

Father Bischoffsheim preached the nuptial oration, and told them of the innumerable blessings and the innumerable duties of marriage—that marriage was not a joke to be lightly undertaken, but a serious duty ; that marriage was not always easy, but that the best way of helping things to go smoothly was to marry one of their own Faith. That marriage was instituted for the pro-creation of children, and how happy was the home when the nursery was full of babies.

After dilating considerably on this delicate subject, he wished them all God's blessing. The register was then signed, the Wedding March pealed forth, and the people began to ooze out of church.

Lord and Lady Athelston drove away in a yellow and blue barouche, with outriders and postillions, much to the enchantment of the populace ; and after a huge reception, at which tons of food were eaten by the servants, and beautiful presents were guarded by detectives disguised as guests, the newly-wedded pair departed—amidst showers of rice and the smiles of relations—for Paris and Venice.

CHAPTER XVII

SIMON SPEAKS UP

" Rebellion to tyrants is obedience to God."—Anon.

It was mid-winter, and Ottawa lay sparkling and glittering like a diamond in the sun.   Thick, deep snow shrouded her, and the waterfalls on the river hung in mid-air—gigantic lumps of billowing ice.   On this glorious Canadian day a crisp tang filled the breeze, and soft dry snowflakes fluttered gently to the earth.

A family party who had been sleighing all the morning was now eating hungrily of luncheon at Government House.

Lord Traquair sat at one end of the table.   He was being a very successful Governor-General, and was already intensely popular from Newfoundland to Vancouver Island.   He always said the right thing, and never forgot a face or a name : a royal gift.

" Who'd like to come with me to-night to the Senate ? " he was saying.   " There will be some good speeches, I think, and it may be an interesting evening.   Canada's relations with England, and the subject of Federation and Freedom will be discussed. "

" May I go ?   I'd love to ! "   It was Quendred who spoke.

" Certainly, pretty niece ; I'd be proud to have you sitting with me."

To-night Quendred's and Simon's year of waiting was over, and she would soon know whether time, and loneliness, and distance from her, had broken down his religious convictions, or killed his love, or made it even stronger ?

Quendred sat with her uncle in the gallery, dressed in masses of softest blue tulle, with a wreath of dark red roses pressed low on her heavy gold hair.   All eyes were upon her.

Her radiant, brilliant glance fell on to the packed throng below, and she suddenly felt a little tremor of pride that England should have won this great young country to her side to help and support her in the race of nations.

The speeches had begun. One after another old men and young stood, and spoke, and sat again.

Suddenly a voice fell upon her ear, and it was Simon's voice ! Instantaneously a scene was conjured to her vision. She heard a voice singing, a gay, mellow voice—and it was the same voice! The same voice that had wooed and won her in England a year ago, and that had vowed that no human power should separate them.

She listened to it so intensely, and so excitedly, that she forgot to breathe, and a great sigh escaped her—" 'tis a goose running over your grave," say some, and others say " 'tis a drop of blood from your heart."

Eagerly she peered down among the crowd of Senators, and there he stood—tall, erect, good-looking, and well dressed ; brimming over with intelligence, life, and enthusiasm. A real person ! A live wire ! The man she loved !

And this is what she heard him say :

" Federal government is one of the oldest ideas in the world, and in the passing of the centuries it has been proved to be good. Even the Greeks about 300 B.C. used it in their tribal system, and it was only dissolved at their treaty with Rome. The word itself is derived from *foedus*, a treaty, and so, naturally, it becomes a kind of system of ' give and take.' We are one of our great Mother England's children. She has given us our freedom, because she trusts us, and we, in return, give her our corn and bread with which to feed her children ; when she wishes it we will give her our men to fight for her." (Cheers.) " Men who will willingly give their blood and their lives for the gift of freedom which she has, with such noble prodigality, bestowed upon Canada." (Cheers) " For freedom is the greatest thing which a man, a nation, or a world can possess. Out of the house of bondage were the people of old freed by Moses ; out of the clutches of the Old Law was a weeping people freed by Christ ; from the yoke of the infidel did all the Christian heroes of mediæval times seek to free men. The whole history of the world is one prolonged wail, one great struggle, one heroic effort for freedom ! Freedom from sorrow, freedom from care, freedom from poverty and disease, freedom from the power of others—from evil and sin : freedom of body and freedom of mind ! This yearning threads its way like a tiny, gleaming ray of light through the centuries, sometimes there, sometimes gone, as the light in a cottage window appears and disappears to a traveller lost in the gloom of a forest.

" Freedom has a twin sister, and her name is Peace. Indeed,

they might be called Siamese twins, so closely are they bound together, and one cannot live without the other.

"Freedom on the spiritual plane is also very important. In the fourth century even the pagan Themistius besought Christians that they should bear with one another, saying: ' The religious beliefs of individuals are a field where the authority of a government cannot be effective, compliance can only lead to hypocritical professions. Every faith should be allowed freedom ! ' And what are those words of Milton ? ' Give me the liberty to know, to utter, and to argue freely, according to conscience, above all other liberties ! ' These are great words indeed !

"But one could give numerous instances, and quote numberless men, who have uttered inspired words on this engrossing subject. It is this great longing—unconsciously working in men—which has been the stimulus and the motive power of all human effort throughout the ages. And this marvellous gift, gentlemen, this priceless blessing, England has given to Canada."

Amidst a hum of applause, as he sat down, he turned and looked at Quendred.

Her heart beat fast ; she glowed and became cold.

"He knew, he knew," a voice within her was singing. " He had seen me ! It was to *me*, for *me*, that he said those words. He hasn't forgotten me as they said he would ! He loves me still, and they said he didn't because he wouldn't sign. Will he do as I ask him now, or will it still be a miserable, heart-breaking *impasse?* I can't go through with it again. I won't give him up at their command ; I'm only doing it to please Mother, because I don't believe in it any more myself now. I'll run away with him if the priests go on tormenting me so."

During the last year much small worry had been caused to Quendred by receiving notes from her father to the effect that he was praying for her, and that he hoped she would have strength to resist Simon's love, or else bring him successfully into the Church as a convert, and of how much she would be blessed if she could achieve this crowning action of a Catholic's life.

"Love ? " she queried—" does all this pressure and terror and bitterness mean love ? I have read that love is something which never tireth, which spurs one to do great things, and is not detained by things of earth. Love, which desires liberty and freedom. Love, than which nothing is sweeter, higher, or nobler. Love, which flies and will not be held ; is happy and gives all, asking no

R

return. Love, which watcheth, and, when sleeping, slumbers
not. Such love can do all things, whereas he who loveth not,
faints and lies down. Such love is like a lively flame or torch
all on fire : it mounts upwards and securely passes through
all opposition. Whoso loveth knoweth the cry of this voice."

And Quendred indeed knew the cry ! So well did she know
it, that she was sure that the united flame of her and Simon's
love would mount upward, and securely pass through all
opposition.

    •   •   •   •   •   •

Simon went the next day to see Maddalena. He hated annoying her, for he had the greatest admiration and affection for her,
yet he felt that it was impossible for polite evasions to go on for
ever.

"But I *cannot* give in, Duchess," he said gently, as they
drove together over the deep snow in a sleigh. "*Please* don't
make me feel such a rude and ungallant brute. Can't you see
that *I, too*, believe in certain things *just as firmly* as you do, and
that it is not pig-headedness on my part any more than it is—if
I may be allowed to say so—on yours, or, rather, on the Church's.
Don't you realize how strongly I maintain and uphold the view
that Rome's distinctive doctrines are erroneous, and that her
unprimitive and unscriptural claims are absolutely visionary and
impossible ? However, because these are my views, I shall never
agree that I am debarred from marrying the woman of my heart
until and unless I promise that my children shall be brought up
in a Faith about which I feel as I do. So, dear Duchess, I tell
you straight that I'm going to fight for my Quendred with all
my strength, and you bet your sweet life—as we Canadians say
—I'll win her in spite of the rules of the Roman Catholic Church."

He had never spoken in this vein before, and Maddalena was
rather taken by surprise.

"Please do not let any disagreeables come between you and
me," he said quickly, seeing her look. "We like each other ; we
are friends, and in everything else we agree. Is there anything
I can do ? Shall I go to Rome ? Surely people can get
Papal Dispensations ? Tell me what to do ? I'll do anything,
anything, to marry Quendred, and to please you."

"Then sign."

"That, never ! "

There was a silence, and nothing was to be heard save the

jangling of the bells as the runners glided silently over the snow. At that moment Maddalena knew that the lovers would win, and that if the Church wouldn't compromise they would ignore her. She found herself wondering tensely, " Does Quendred believe all the Church teaches, I wonder ? " And then a feeling of great loneliness crept over her, for she felt in some indefinable way that Quendred did not believe any more ; that she would wait no longer, and that whatever happened or whatever the Church said she would go with her man.

Two days later Quendred and her mother sailed for England. It seemed that Simon had booked his passage on the same boat.

" But I can't have you running about after Quendred if you aren't engaged to her, you know," Maddalena said ; " her father wouldn't like it."

" I must go to England, Duchess," he answered smiling. " I've been offered to stand for one of the big industrial seats at the next bye-election. It's a great honour and may lead to more important things. I was pleased about it for Quendred's sake, too, for we could then live in England."

Maddalena couldn't help smiling.

" Love laughs at locksmiths—— " she said.

" —whatever the Churches may say," he finished. " Oh, do let's be happy for a moment, and forget the tiresome Church," he added boyishly.

Quendred sometimes compared Simon to Samson, and now she really hoped that he wouldn't give in.

" If he does," she thought, " it will be like the cutting of Samson's hair : he will be shorn of all his strength ; he will be a nonentity—nothing.

.   .   .   .   .   .

When they arrived in England they heard that Patricia had just had a son. This was a tremendous bit of news, and was also a great relief to Patricia ; for, deep down in her being, she had a secret fear of the words on Rosemouth's picture, and they often rang in her mind, although she spoke of it to no one. So the birth of her baby boy and heir set her mind at rest considerably, for she felt that anyhow the line was more secure. He was called Patrick, although Patricia's in-laws didn't like it. " It's so unlucky," they said, " to have anything but a Stephen or an Anthony."

.   .   .   .   .   .

Suddenly there came the news of the serious illness of the Prince di Santa Fiora, and Maddalena, Quendred, and Anthony went in all haste to see him. For some weeks he lingered, but in the early days of a beautiful May death came for him.

A great sadness fell upon them all, for he had been an adoring and indulgent grandfather, and Quendred had been particularly spoiled by him.

The bulk of his enormous fortune was left to his widow and Maddalena, and £20,000 apiece was placed in trust for Quendred and Anthony on the understanding that neither of them became a Protestant or married one.

While they were in Italy the Duke wrote from his monastery saying that he wanted Quendred to go and see Father Primavera —the priest who had converted him—who still lived near Florence. He was now a very old man, and quite a saint, so the people said.

Heartily sick of these endless séances with clerics, Quendred, nevertheless, felt it a filial duty once more to obey her father's wish.

"But this is the last time, Mother," she said. "If they don't give in I'll marry Simon in a Protestant Church. "Don't ask me to do it again, for I shall not obey you any more."

Never before had the girl spoken to either of her parents like this, but she was *au bout*, and all her nerves were on edge.

.   .   .   .   .   .

It was a glorious spring day as she drove out from Florence to visit the priest.

The rickety little carriage slowly pulled up before a vine-clad cottage in the midst of a radiant garden, and in the doorway appeared an old, white-haired man, who greeted her with charming gentleness. He led her into a room kept cool by green shutters and offered her a meal of eggs, wine, and fruit, fresh white bread, butter, and black coffee.

"And now, my child," he said in his soft Italian, as they sat together in his garden, " I hear you have a great trouble. Your dear father writes to me a sad history, and has asked me to explain things to you.

"I hope I may be able to help you. I do feel for you, my child. Perhaps we may be able to arrange something."

"I'm afraid I'm very hopeless, Father," she answered. " You see, it's been going on for so long now, and I see no possible outlet unless I settle to defy the Church and marry in a Registrar's Office."

"Ah, no!—you will never do that. I know it! You would not get the blessing of the Church, would you?"

"I don't think I mind whether I get the Church's blessing or not," she answered pettishly, "and I'm tired of being played with and tortured, like a cat with a mouse. But you know my story, I suppose, Father Primavera, and I have come here just to know if I can be married in the Church, or not?"

"Yes, I know everything," he said quietly, "and I'm going to tell you that I will marry you to this man. Are you pleased? Are you happy?" And he looked into her face with the kindest, gentlest, tenderest look.

"Just such a look as our Lord might have had," she thought.

"But how *marvellous*," she said, surprised beyond measure. "They have always told me it can't be done."

"It *can* be done, and *I* will do it," said the old man. "Have no fear. I will marry you, and *he need not sign that paper*, and all will be well. Your mother has written to me and told me what a good Christian man he is, and of how his past life has been faithful to his future wife. If we all could live up to Christianity like this, there would be no need for sharply-defined creeds."

Quendred was speechless.

For nearly two years her mind had been tortured by threats of Hell, and all kinds of horrors—eternal and otherwise. Now suddenly—the veil was lifted, light was poured in, and all the sadness and hopelessness of it was vanished. And because Simon's life and religion complied in spirit with the highest ideals of the Roman Catholic Church—ideals which she could generally only enforce through fear of the confessional and eternal punishment —he had won through!

If—as is taught—all priests represent the Church, then Simon had won a victory over her! What an extraordinary thing! How proud and happy she felt, and all the world seemed to be dancing and singing for joy. A great and intolerable weight was suddenly lifted from her heart, and she felt as light as a feather floating in sunlit air.

She took the priest's worn old hands in hers.

"How can I thank you, dear Father Primavera?" she said. "How can I ever thank you half enough? This has just made all the difference in my life. But I don't understand yet how you can do it ! My being and my mind are still so saturated with the idea of the Church's enormous power over the lives of her children. Her enormous, cruel power ; and yet you—you are so kind to me ! " She sighed wistfully and gratefully. " I have been so weary and so sad ; I have been made to hate people so bitterly whom it was natural for me to love, and I have been forced sometimes to long for a thousand tongues that I might preach against the wicked claims of the Catholic Church. I— Quendred—whose nature it is to love peace and unity and happiness. But *you* make me feel quite different ! You are so kind and gentle to me," and from Quendred's proud eyes a few hot tears fell on to the withered hands of the priest.

He smiled a slow, wise smile !

" It is not for nothing that I have lived here alone amongst the peasants and with Nature for forty years," he said. " During that time I have thought and prayed very much for light. People who live alone understand life and God's great fundamental truths differently from those who always mingle with men, and I think perhaps one gets nearer to divine things, to the Divine One Himself, when one lives apart. It is very sweet, such a life—being so near to Him."

But when her father heard the news, his only comment was that he wished that—instead of being as lenient as she was on the subject of " mixed marriages "—the Church was much stricter.

" I wish *I* were the Pope," he thought, as he wrote a short note to advise the bank to send Quendred £3,000, which represented all he intended her now to have, because of her marriage with a non-Catholic, and the manner in which it was done.

.   .   .   .   .   .

Six weeks later Simon de Villancourt and Quendred Fitz-Urse were married very quietly in the whitewashed rococo little church of Father Primavera, so garishly decorated with tinsel flowers and plaster angels ; and the only blot on their perfect happiness was Quendred's sadness at parting from her mother.

Their honeymoon consisted of slow delicious travelling through Italy, France, and Spain.

When in France they stayed with Simon's kinsman, the Duc de Tréfontaines, who lived in a castle on the Loire. The family consisted of the Duke, his wife, and two little boys—the latter the only lives which stood between Simon and all that his kinsman was, and possessed.

PART V
SACROSANCT

CHAPTER XVIII

BITTER-SWEET

" Great floods have flown,
    From simple sources, and great seas have dried
    When miracles have by the greatest been denied."
                                        —SHAKESPEARE.

THE Boer War now fell upon England, and no one had realized that those Dutch farmers could fight as they did. Would it ever come to an end ?

Denis Connor, Hugh Traquair, and Anthony all went out, and when the news of Denis' death came Patricia's hitherto happy life seemed to enter into the land of shadows. It lingered on and on, and then suddenly a telegram came for Patricia. Through hot, blinding tears she read that Anthony was seriously wounded.

In four weeks she was at his bedside in Capetown, to find that he was blind, and that his left leg had been taken off at the thigh on account of blood poisoning.

Long, long weeks, lengthening to months, did she nurse him ; and at last one spring day she brought her maimed and aged husband back to his home.

As they passed through the hall " Rosemouth " seemed to laugh, Patricia thought. She loathed the picture now ; nothing seemed to console her, and she hardly noticed the children. Her whole life was given to Anthony.

He, on the contrary, was in reality a happier man than he had ever been hitherto, and took to carpentering and all kinds of work which in the old days he never would have thought of doing.

His boy was the centre and joy of his existence, and father and son were hardly ever apart.

No other sons were born, and Patrick became the idol of his parents and was allowed to do anything he liked.

Love, Birth, Hate, and Death were busy with this family as with other families, and, during the Boer War, the Dowager Duchess of Seyntleger had died. She had always been a kind, though somewhat aloof, relation, for the change of the religion of the Fitz-Urses had been an intense grief to her, although she had discussed the matter as little as possible. And so it was with great surprise Quendred found that her grandmother had left her—in her will—all her queer old great-grandfather's money which he had hoarded up in the wall, so many years ago.

The money had been well invested, and, as the Duchess had never used it, the capital had rolled up, and Quendred now found herself possessed of about £8,000 a year.

A sealed letter addressed to her from her grandmother had been found with the will.

Here it is :

"Quendred, in my youth I was narrow and bigoted, but your sainted Grandfather taught me much ; his sweet gentle wisdom always pointed to the path of toleration, and made me understand that many paths can, and do, lead to God.

"You, I know, have had much to suffer in these last years, and I often prayed for you, but I said nothing. Perhaps you thought me unsympathetic ?

"I was not ; I felt for you so much, dear child, but—I left you to wrestle with it, and fight it out for yourself.

"In the great crisis of one's life no one but oneself can do the thing, no matter how many good friends one may have. This *is life*, and the sooner we learn how to be self-reliant the happier we will be.

"I know that your father made a will in accordance with his conscience, which left you a mere pittance, so that you have been forced to live entirely on your husband's money. I do not like that this should be the case, and so I now leave and bequeath to you the sum of £200,000, which was left me by my father.

"Use it well for God's honour and the poor, and should He bless you with a son it is my wish that this money should pass to him at your death.

"That he may be like his wonderful great-Grandfather in spirituality and breadth of outlook, is the last wish and prayer of your devoted Grandmother.

"ELIZABETH SEYNTLEGER."

Since her marriage Quendred had only been receiving £37 a quarter in accordance with her father's will. She had had no idea how odd it would be to find herself in these circumstances, after having never known what it was to want for anything from her earliest remembrance. As Simon was also not well off, they had to live very differently from what she had been accustomed, and so this fortune was a most welcome surprise.

Soon after this a great joy came to the Villancourts in the birth of a son. The event took place at Maddalena's house in Berkeley Square.

Quendred had been rather dreading it in a way, as her father had been agitating again about the baptism of the expected baby; not to her, but to her mother; and her mother—who had always been so dear and sympathetic with the whole of Quendred's life—had been forced, much against her will, to speak to her on the subject.

Stephen, of course, wanted the child baptized in the Catholic Church, thinking that perhaps now that Simon had got what he wanted, and was living happily with Quendred, he would give in when the moment came. This he pressed in his letter to his wife.

" But "—as Simon said to Maddalena—" the whole point of my *having* resisted the pressure of Rome was that the children should *not* be baptized into that Church ! Now the testing time has come, why should I give in ?

" Dear Duchess, do not let us have any more words about it," he said to his mother-in-law. " My impression was that all was settled when Padre Primavera married us, and that he did it on the complete understanding that there *should* be no further question about it ; in fact, I have a letter from him saying that once we were married I would have complete freedom on the religious up-bringing of the children.

" You have always been so kind to me," he went on affectionately, " that I particularly dislike discussing a matter which can but be distasteful to you and to me. Cannot we let it drop ? After all, we were married by a priest who knew all the circumstances ; is it logical, or in any way proper, for Catholic lay people to keep up the question ?

" It seems to me—from the Catholic point of view—that by the clerical action all judgment in the matter has been taken out of their hands ; for if they look upon the actions of priests —when acting with their priestly powers—to be above question reproach, and criticism, then logically they ought to leave the matter alone and not have any ideas of their own. Am I wrong ? "

" I see your point, Simon," said his mother-in-law rather sadly, " but naturally you can't expect me to agree with all you say. I was bred and born a Catholic, and I shall never be anything else, but I certainly allow that all human beings have a right to judge for themselves, and I trust my Quendred is not acting against her true conscience (for I differentiate between a true and a false one, and I firmly believe in the natural con-science as against the trained and acquired one). You see, I am really in a dilemma. I adore Quendred and I want her to be happy. I like you, and I wanted you both to be able to marry each other ; yet, on the other hand, I want to please my hus-band so far away from us all in his monastery ; and I believe that the Church—my Church—must be obeyed. Why do you hate my Church so much, Simon ? She is the mother of all Churches, and her wonderful history ought to appeal to a man of your intellectual powers. How I wish I could make you all happy ! "

" You are a very wonderful woman, and your faith in your Church is indeed touching," Simon said feelingly, " but, you see, you have never been ' up against ' her, have you ? Quen-dred says that no one knows how cruel she can be till one chances to have to break a lance with her ! "

So the child was baptized into the English Church, and was given the names of Christian Anthony Simon.

" My little darling," whispered Quendred, as she held him to her, " you for whom I have longed so much ; what will you be, I wonder ? "

And she gazed adoringly into his funny little face, all crinkled with crying, and held his two cold, ever-moving, tiny hands in one of hers.

" Will you be great ? Will you be good ? Will you help men ? Will you do a work in the world ? No one will ever know how much prayer has been offered up for you, even long before my marriage ! For years I have loved to imagine what my son would be like if I ever had one, and now one has come to me !

" Out of the unknown, out of God's hand, you have been given to me ! "

And the years rolled on.

.   .   .   .   .   .

A difficult time had now come for Quendred ; the moment had

arrived when some religious training had to be given to her son.

Simon held no credal or dogmatic belief ; she, on the other hand, had been born in them, reared in them, and steeped in them. She had been hampered and fettered by them, and had suffered deeply on account of them, and so, from the bitter knowledge of her own experience, she had no wish to start the obstructing system all over again with this fresh young life which she had brought into the world.

Yet what alternative was there ? In all forms of Christianity there seemed to be some sort of organized plan or system—all disagreeing, yet all claiming the Bible as their common inspiration ; which rock, in splitting them all, had itself remained intact.

So Quendred was quite resolved to teach her child nothing which she herself didn't ardently believe to be perfectly true.

" Where shall I find the truth about Christ and His teaching ? " she had once asked Simon in desperation, and he had answered, " If it's not in the Bible it's nowhere."

" You have set yourself a difficult task," said some of her friends, and others remarked, " How foolish, how wicked ! "

Nearly all sensible people said :

" But after all, you *must* teach your child something ; there *must* be some coherent basis in its religious education, poor little thing. It *must* belong to *some* Church ; it is not perhaps important *which*, as long as it belongs to *a* Church . . ." and so forth and so on.

Quendred saw their point, but it was a point from which she was determined to get away. She thought :

" I want him to have a deep and wide vision ; I want him to be permeated with Love, not Fear.

" I want him to shake off dogmas and creeds, as a prisoner shakes off his fetters when he wants to escape, and run from confinement.

" I want him to understand the things of God through the Spirit, not through the Law.

" I want him to abstain from sin for love of God and not from fear of Hell, or priestly threats, or social ostracism, or prisons, or death.

" The greatest saints at their greatest moments acted freely, because of their free communion with God. When they performed supernatural deeds, such as healing the sick, and the many other amazing things which are recorded of wonderful souls, their power was not theirs because they conformed to

Rome or to *Canterbury*, or that they *non-conformed*, but surely it was theirs because of a boundless love caused by a boundless faith, and thus, and thus alone, they were able to do what the Son of God had promised. He said—'These things shall ye do—and greater things than these shall ye do—if ye believe in Me'; not, 'if ye are anglo-Catholics, or Protestants, or Roman Catholics.'' And it was on such thoughts that she fed the soul of her son, and also on the one of Knighthood. She read him stories of heroes who didn't know what fear meant, and of knights who never lied. She told him about the glorious Bayard, and he had asked her what exactly was meant by *Sans peur, et sans reproche?*

Quendred paused a minute, for she hardly knew how to explain it so that he would understand.

"The words mean 'without fear, and without reproach,'" she said at last. "You see, he was never frightened at anything. Not of dogs, nor of getting on a horse; nor of things hurting him— like having a tooth pulled out; nor of what people said or perhaps told him they would do to him if he didn't do what they told him, or what they liked. We call that threatening, sonny."

"Fweaten," he repeated, pucking his brows a little. "I must never let people fweaten me."

"No, never," she said; "and you see, if you are always good and honest and truthful, and do not do things which you would be ashamed for others to know you had done, then no one could threaten you; because you would not be frightened of other people—you would be 'without fear,' as the noble French knight was."

"Yes, and now explain to me about wepwoach," he asked, nestling against her shoulder.

"Well, they are really rather like each other. To be 'without reproach' means that you have never done any cruel, dishonourable, petty thing; nor any unknightly action which you would blush over when you thought about it in bed at nighte You see, they follow each other, and you can hardly be one without being the other! If you never do anything wrong or degrading or unjust or cruel, you need never fear, and if you hav. no fear it is because you know yourself that you are doing your very best to lead a good, generous, honest, pure life. I think if you could try to say to yourself, 'Would I do this action, or say these words, or think these thoughts, if Jesus Christ were sitting in that chair or standing quite close to me, of if I were resting my head on His shoulder ? '—just as you are here with me now—if you could come to think of Him as your *personal* friend, then I think that you would begin to be able to be like your hero, Bayard the Knight—' without fear, and without reproach.'

"I will give you a little motto, my darling, and when you are a man and a knight you will live up to it, and think of me. These are the words ; they are really French words :

> " ' Mon sabre au Roi
> Mon cœur à ma Dame
> Mon honneur à moi
> A Dieu mon âme.'

"And this is what they mean in English :

> " ' To my King I give my sword ;
> My heart I give to my Love ;
> In honour I keep my word ;
> My soul to God above.' "

He flashed the great, dark eyes which she had given him warmly over her face.

"What does 'my Love' mean ? " he asked, and when she told him he said, "But I shall never love any lady except you, Mother ; never, never. I know I shan't."

Tears sprang to her eyes.

. . . .

When quite small Christian discovered one day how very easily he could hit anything, and from this inborn gift he developed into an extraordinarily good bowler ; he just couldn't miss a wicket, it seemed. Being strong, and having well-made limbs, he was well fitted for playing games.

Another of his gifts was music, which he had inherited from his mother, and he played the violin well for a child of his age. He was very happy at school, because everyone liked him, and he soon became champion boxer, and captain of the cricket eleven. How all the other little boys delighted to see him coming on to the playing fields ! He was a born leader among them, and he could make them do anything he liked. Whatever side he was on always won. He was victory's favourite. Added to these gifts, the other side of his character was conspicuous, and gave him an immense power over the boys, although perhaps they would have laughed at it had he not been such a oner at games. He was never cruel, never unjust. He never cribbed, and always took the side of the weakest. If any boy was ill,

Villancourt would sit by his bed, bringing him sweets, fruit, games, and books.

He loathed lying and all forms of insincerity, and he seemed to have a supreme wisdom which came from his pure and simple little heart, and this gave him a kind of secret knowledge, which later enabled him to pierce to the very core men's souls and all other things.

Once when bowling at cricket, the ball hit a boy a nasty cut under the eye ; Christian ran up, to find the wound was bleeding a good deal.   Putting one hand under the boy's chin, he was pulling out his handkerchief when someone called out, " Hullo, the blood has stopped, what a rum thing ! "

Christian, seeing that this was the case, got up off the ground, and by so doing removed his hand ; at that second, to everyone's astonishment, the blood, which had quite stopped, began to flow.   Christian looked astonished, but knelt down and tried once more to staunch it, when, marvellous to relate, at his touch the blood stopped again !   And then it dawned upon them all that when Christian touched the child the blood ceased to flow !

An intense look of awe came over the little boy's face as he realized what had happened, and for the rest of the day he was very quiet.

That night it was long before he slept.   Something had happened that he couldn't understand ; something extraordinary, and he was frightened.   When all the other children were in deep sleep, tired out by the natural efforts of the day, this child lay in bed amongst them in a high tremor of disquieting turmoil. His body was quivering uncontrollably, and his mind and heart were in a state of extreme mental and emotional agitation.

From under his pillow he took a worn and tiny Bible, one that Quendred had given him when he was seven.   It was much be-thumbed, and favourite bits had been underlined by this strange boy.   To-night he read them over once more.

" Go ye into all the world and preach . . . and these signs shall follow them that believe in My Name ; they shall cast out devils . . . if they drink of any deadly thing it shall not hurt them ; they shall lay their hands on the sick and they shall recover."

" If you have faith as a grain of mustard seed . . . nothing shall be impossible to you."

" And John said, ' Master, we saw one casting out devils

in Thy Name and we forbade him because he followed not with
us,' and Jesus said unto him, ' Forbid him not, for he that is not
against us is for us.' ' "

And after he had read these words to himself—words which
were fraught with such immense and profound meaning for him
—he prayed that his eyes might be opened yet more, and his
spirit touched, so that he might *know* the wonderful things of
God.

That night he dreamed a dream, and it was this :

He was travelling in every kind of way ; by foot, by carriage,
by ship, by aeroplane, by motor.   Through dark, interminable
forests ; along dusty country roads ; through busy cities ; by
smoking homesteads and gardens ; over rivers and oceans.   Then
at last he seemed to be flying up towards the top of a mountain,
through great jagged cavernous rocks, and in the end he found
himself looking out from the windows of a castle on to a fair,
green, smooth lawn, with two rows of tall, closely-clipped and
pointed yew-trees, making a path towards him.

Suddenly there fell upon his ear the sound of deep chanting,
and then there appeared in the pathway a procession of black-
garbed, black-hooded men, heads reverently bent, hands
devoutly clasped.

Soon they divided, and stood quite still facing each other,
while a strangely arresting figure appeared and walked slowly
between the men.

As the Figure drew near, all the others sank to their knees.
From Him emanated a shining, curious, and unearthly light ;
penetrating, but not dazzling ; clear and silvery like the moon.

Then—as is common in dreams—the scene disappeared, and
he was left sad and disappointed, feeling that he had been on
the verge of seeing or hearing something very wonderful, something of transcending importance.   But suddenly he heard footsteps coming slowly up the stairs.   He ran to the door and flung
it back, feeling quite sure that he would see the wonderful Figure
again, and he was right.

Floating rather than walking, the shining Figure—seemingly
made of light—was coming definitely towards him ; as he
threw open the door It held out both arms, and in a marvellous
voice—very low, yet vibrating with love and tenderness, a voice
which he felt would understand all the desires and passions, fears
and agonies, hates and ardours of the human heart—said :

" Come to Me, I have waited for you for a thousand years."

S

When he woke he was bathed in sweat.

.   .   .   .   .   .

It was New Year's Eve, 1913.

Quendred and her husband and son were at Ullcombe for the holidays, and the great hall was hung with ropes of evergreen and holly.

In the middle, opposite the picture of the ever-smiling ' Rosemouth," stood an enormous Christmas-tree beautifully decorated with shining baubles and chains, and quaint little silvery fireworks.

Among the other guests was Hugh Traquair—whose love for Quendred had prevented him marrying anyone else. He had left the Army for politics years ago, and was now a member of the Cabinet. On account of the old Duke's will, he would inherit—through his mother—most of the Fitz-Urse money. Maddalena was also there, and, of course, Patrick Fitz-Urse and his three pretty sisters.

Following an age-old custom, they were going to dine in the great hall that night. Huge logs blazed in the two stone fire-places at either end of the room, and all was brilliantly lit.

Dinner was over and the time for the New Year Toasts had come.

Anthony stood up, his poor sightless eyes giving a pathetic look to his suffering face, for he had never had real health again since the Boer War.

He held up the sparkling wine, and gave the first of the toasts which, for hundreds of years—had been given in that hall on the last day of the Old Year.

But since the Duke had left the world to enter a monastery his son had given yet another. It was to his father's memory.

Standing to-night at the top of the long, glittering table, laden with wine, fruit, and crackers gaily mingling with gold plate and shining glass, he said :

" To the honour of God."

It was drunk in silence.

" The King."

This was drunk with deafening cheers.

" My Father."

Quietly and sadly the glasses went up, and through the mist which dimmed Maddalena's eyes she saw once again the winding road to Santa Barbara and heard his eager, boyish voice asking her to be his wife.

And the last toast was now given :
" My House, may it live for ever."
As the words left his lips they were lost in a terrific crash.
The picture of Rosemouth lay prone ! In falling it had knocked over a large gilt chair, the legs of which had gone straight through the canvas, splitting the laughing, buoyant figure beyond repair.
They all rushed towards it.
" What's happened ? " called out the blind man. " What was that noise, and why is there all this confusion ? "
Christain, who, alone of the party, had not moved but had stayed with his uncle, told him what it was. Anthony called to Patrick, and between the two boys was led to the prostrate " Rosemouth," their goddess of good fortune, on whose well-being they all—perhaps unconsciously, and certainly unwillingly —based their belief in their luck and prosperity.
With photographic clearness the evening of the ball for his coming-of-age returned to him, and he remembered how he and the wild, attractive Patricia had—half in fun and half seriously —passed their hands behind the picture to make certain that it was secure.
" Lift it up," he now commanded hoarsely. " Don't leave it on the ground, I won't have it there. Prop her against the wall. She can easily be fastened up again ; quickly, help me to move her," and he bent down to the ground, groping to find the picture. In a second Patricia was at his side.
" It's no use, dearest," she said, " we can't move her to-night. Come away now, and let us go and finish dinner, and then the carol singers are coming."
She led him back to the table, sitting near him, and putting Patrick on the other side. But he wouldn't be comforted, and a gloom fell upon the party. As he went to rest that night— or, rather, the morning of the first day of 1914—the words of the doggerel rhyme beat through his mind :

> " If Rosemouth hang in the Castle Hall,
> No evil shall Fitz-Urse befall ;
> If Rosemouth fall, or movéd be,
> Fitz-Urse, Fitz-Urse shall surely die."

and lying in bed, with sightless eyes wide open, the disastrous words haunted him, and hunted away his peace of mind.

   .   .   .   .   .   .

Since the accident, Christian was possessed of an intense longing, which was to be able to restore in some way his uncle's eyesight to him.

He wondered if he could accomplish it ; he felt as though in some circumstances it might be possible.

For the next few nights he hardly slept, but spent the time in prayer. He ate almost nothing, and always prayed that his faith might be enough to do this thing.

Then on the fourth day, finding Anthony alone in his room, he asked him if he might touch his eyes. Anthony smiled tolerantly, but did not demur. It was a terrible moment for the boy.

In an agonising act of Faith and Love in the Master who had once said, " And greater things than these shall ye do," he groaned, and large drops stood upon his forehead.

" You promised, Lord, you promised," he whispered, almost fiercely. " Do not withhold your power. If You do, how can I ever trust You again ? "

All the while his strong young hands were pressing the sightless eyeballs, and his own eyes were closed. He was uplifted in prayer, and quite unconscious of his surroundings.

For a little time they both remained motionless, then very slowly Christian removed his hands, first his right and then his left. As he did so he looked at the left eye. It was sightless still !

Christian made a supreme effort of Love and Faith, then shudderingly he withdrew his left hand, at the same time falling to the ground. All the strength and power of his pure, child-like spirit had gone out of him, and his body, physically weak from fasting and prayer and loss of sleep, collapsed. Virtue had gone out of him, but he had achieved ! With his right eye Anthony Athelston saw the light of day once more ! He rang the bell, and the exhausted boy was tenderly carried to his bed.

Meanwhile, Anthony's occulist in London was telephoned for, and he arrived the same evening. He made a minute examintion of the eye, and after humming and hawing for a little he said that the blindness of this eye had always been somewhat of a nervous affection brought on more or less on account of the state of the other one, and he had sometimes thought that as time went on the sight might perhaps be restored to it and so on. But next day, on his way back to London, when cosily ensconced in a first-class carriage, fur rug over his knees, large cigar between his lips, and casting his eye over the ' Social Column ' in the *Times*—he thought to himself that it was not only in Old Testament days, nor in mediæval times, that miracles happened ! Miracle, that favourite child of Faith, as Goethe has it.

And now Christian—the outwardly ordinary, English schoolboy—found himself a sort of hero.

Patricia, whose nerves had entirely given way when the picture had fallen, couldn't make enough of him.

" Yes, indeed, our child is a wonderful being," said Simon to Quendred slowly, " but it is a frightfully dangerous power unless used properly. It makes me fear for him ; you don't know how much it makes me fear sometimes."

" Don't fear, Simon beloved," said Quendred, taking his hands and holding them fast in hers. " Please don't fear, just trust in God, and thank Him for the son which He has sent us. Having such a son must make us far more careful in our lives, lest anything we do or say might harm him, or dim the shining whiteness of his pure spirit."

.   .   .   .   .   .

Christian, recovered from his fearful fatigue, was now quite normal again ; happy and boyish as usual. But Quendred's eyes observed another look in her son's face ; a peculiar look of aloofness, of radiant tranquillity, of utter trust and peace. A look of perfect happiness, such as is seen on the face of one who is initiated into the secret bliss given by the deepest knowledge of love.

Many happy moments they passed together, and during one of their talks Christian had said :

" Mother, I must choose a profession like everyone else. Patrick is going into the Army, and is always talking about this war with Germany which he says is sure to come sooner or later. Hugh Traquair does nothing but plot politics, and the girls are always thinking of their dances and their parties. I must have an aim too, I must do something."

" What is your aim ? " asked Quendred.

" My aim," he said seriously, " is to get the highest I possibly can in spiritual and internal things. To do this I must, as the ' Imitation ' says, ' with Christ go aside from the crowd.' You gave me that book, Mother. I've had it as long as I remember ! "

" I gave it to you the day you were christened," she said lovingly.

" It is full of beautiful things, and has helped, and does help me so much," he said, " I love it when it says that we are lifted to God by two wings, and the wings are simplicity and purity ; and he says, too, that it is *not* an illusion when we are sometimes rapt in ecstasies, and then return suddenly to ordinary weakness.

" I was so glad to read that, Mother, because—well, I did feel so wonderfully light and exalted the other day when God cured Uncle Anthony through me ; and then, when it was all over, I felt horribly and utterly weak, both physically and spiritually, and I had dreadful thoughts that perhaps it was the devil and not God who had helped me. I am so afraid lest I let myself imagine things. Mother, it was awful, awful. No one can know what agony I suffered ! "

His face became deathly white, and a look of great wonderment came over it.

Quendred hardly knew what to do, for she felt that he was so far away from her, and that he heard, saw, and knew about things of which she was entirely ignorant.

" I prayed for a wonderful son," she thought ; " and now that I have one I must not grudge him to the God who answered my prayer," was her bitter-sweet thought.

" Yes," she said aloud, " I felt that the time would come when you could no longer live our life. But need it be just yet ? You are so young ! You are only sixteen ! You might get ill ! Besides, you must finish your schooling, and how and where would you live ? Stay with us till you are twenty. We love you so ! Think what it will be for us when you go ! Will you stay ? "

" Do you wish it very much, Mother ? "

" Yes, my darling, very, very much. When you are twenty we'll support you in all you desire."

So he stayed.

CHAPTER XIX

FRA GIOVANNI

" I'll be this abject thing no more,
Love—give me back my heart again."
—G. Granville (Lord Lansdowne), 1667-1735.

THE day had gone to evening, and a thin old man was slowly filling wooden pails with water from a pump in the middle of a fourteenth century courtyard. These he carried slowly away, disappearing behind a low, arched doorway, through which could be seen one of the most exquisite views in Italy.

Lazily the Arno wandered through the soft, billowing valley, and in the distance purple-blue hills rose into, and mingled with, the sky.

The day was July 13th, 1914, and the Duke of Seyntleger had been a monk now for just twenty-one years. No one but the Superior knew who he was, and to all the simple brethren of the Monastery of San Girolamo he was known as "Fra Giovanni."

To-day, then, he was busy carrying water to the oxen who were hot from their efforts of drawing in the hay-carts.

His thick, snow-white hair still had the ripple of its youth running through it, but his face was worn and lined and seemed shrunken, making his eyes look enormous. They were tragic eyes.

Was he happy? Ah, who can tell? Only he and God knew that. But the vision of Maddalena, youthful and desirable, on the road to Santa Barbara ; again, lying ill when her babies were born ; and, once more, standing at the station waving him farewell, would often appear before his eyes—at work, in the refectory, at recreation, and when he retired to rest.

And now he was again upset and distraught, for lately—on ooking at the old coat he had worn when he left England, and which he had stuffed away into the wooden box in which he kept

his meagre wardrobe—he had found—slipped between the lining
—the letter which Maddalena had given him the night before
he had left Ullcombe. It was the letter which his father had
written to Cardinal Costanzi forty-five years before.

With the indifference to mundane things born from leading
the life of a recluse, he slowly tore the letter open and read it
through to the end, but then indeed did the scales fall from his
eyes.

"Blind!" he groaned. "I was blind—and weak, weak!"

No eyes but the Cardinal's had read it, and now at last the
man most closely concerned in the conspiracy of Duke, Pope, and
Cardinal, knew the truth!

He now saw plainly how these three men—all convinced from
their own point of view that they were acting rightly—had, in
secret collusion with one another, tricked him and used his life
as their pawn. The meaning of the conversations which he had
had with them long years ago, and of which he now recalled every
word, came back to him most vividly, and he suddenly realized
what a plot the whole thing had been.

They had cheated him of a normal vocation and the priesthood ; they had cast Maddalena purposely in his path to fascinate
him away from giving himself to God—in order that each of the
three actors in the drama might get what he wanted ; while
he—poor, miserable puppet that he now saw he had always been—
never knew himself what he really wanted the most, Maddalena
di Santa Fiora, or the Roman Catholic priesthood!

They had tricked him.

The Duke, because unconsciously fearful lest the Fitz-Urses
should become extinct, as foretold upon Rosemouth's picture ;
the Cardinal, because he wished to conciliate his father, and inwardly regretted his treatment of him when he lapsed from
Rome ; the Pope because he well knew how much more valuable
he would be to the Church of Rome as a father of sons, than as
a priest vowed to celibacy.

To salve their own consciences these three had—perhaps unconsciously—played havoc with his soul, his heart, and his mind.
His life—the only one that he would ever have to live on this
earth—had been ruined. And for what ? That a great family
should be perpetuated ; that a great family should become
Catholic ! Hideous thought ! Ah, vile, abominable thought !

Thus he felt to-night when—in his tiny, moonlit cell—he held
the cruel, life-shattering letter between his trembling old fingers.

He sat on the edge of the boards which served him as a bed, and remembered with a shudder that his father had instigated the whole thing.

" That men *dare* so to play with another's being ! " he moaned, and tears trickled slowly between the rough fingers which had once been so fine.

Suddenly he pulled himself up, and his thin, slight figure became rigid ; his great dark eyes stared unblinking at the dreary, empty cell, and his fingers clenched and unclenched spasmodically.

" I shouldn't have let them rule me," he muttered. " I shouldn't have tried to please them ; I should have gone sternly forward in the way I thought best for myself. And yet—did I ever really know what I wanted most ? I did desire priesthood with all my strength and all my power, and yet the sweet toils of Maddalena were so strong that I believe I would have stayed with her for ever, after we were reunited that wonderful night in Berkeley Square, had it not been for Father Ignatius. He made me definitely see that it was sinful to stay with my wife. Had it not been for him I *would* have stayed.

" And now the horror of it all is that the priesthood hasn't given me what I thought it would ; and although I like saying my daily Mass the life has—on the whole—disappointed me.

" I had hoped for much more exalted things ; for satisfying communion with God ; for visions of Him perhaps ; even for powers of healing if only my faith could be made strong enough by prayer and supplication.

" All this was what I desired, and in my ardent youth I was convinced with absolute certainty that the Roman Catholic Church gave these consolations far away above and beyond what any other Church could ever possibly give, and that wonders could be wrought by her sons. But, alas, I find that it is not so. No priest, or monk, or friar whom I have ever met has had in the slightest degree any supernatural power of any kind.

" I see now what Cardinal Costanzi meant when he talked to me in the Forum the morning after I had met Maddalena. There *is* something greater than creeds. A passionate and pure love of God, and an overwhelming desire to know, love, and serve Him alone. *That* is what is greater. That is what Saints are made of. Not creeds, but faith. Not creeds, but love."

He sank down on the moon-flashed boards.

" Oh, that I might be allowed to do some great work before

I die," he prayed, " so that this useless, maimed, and thwarted existence of mine may be, at least, justified at the end."

   .   .   .   .   .   .

At the humble mid-day repast a packet was handed to him. It was from Maddalena. The letter was written from Ullcombe, and dated July 12th, 1914 :

" MY DEAREST,
      " I have told you before about Quendred and Simon's little son. He is such a wonderful child that we wish you to see him, for you—of all people in the world—would be attracted and drawn to him. He possesses qualities which I know would appeal to you. But, apart from this, he adores music and plays the violin so beautifully that we are taking him to Bayreuth especially to hear ' Parsifal.'
      " He has not been very well lately, and so has been allowed to remain away from school for a term. I have got a special permission from the Pope to bring him to visit you.
      " Quendred, too, is longing to see you again.
                      " Your devoted
                           " MADDALENA."

" My darling, my darlings, my children," whispered the married monk, the father.

A week later, on a warm July day, he sat with his erstwhile wife, his daughter, and his grandson in the peaceful, sunny monastery garden. It was a strange meeting—and no one quite knew what to say. Christian alone of the company seemed quite at ease. Knowing nothing of their past histories, and the intricacies made in their lives by man's laws, he took his monkish grandfather for granted, and chattered away to him with the spontaneity and the charm of youth.

Like most others, the old Duke was rather sceptical of the powers which he was told his grandson possessed.

As monk and boy wandered about the monastery, Christian talked with great simplicity to his grandfather.

" But what are you going to do ? " asked the monk. " What are your plans ? Unless you are a priest I think you will be useless. Those who have the power of healing are not men looked upon with much approval by the Churches. In the Catholic Church alone you would find a spiritual home."

" Before I do anything," answered Christian, " I want to obey the great command of God's to ' search the Scriptures,' because I want to be able to preach, you see. I want to be allowed by God to cure people of their spiritual and their bodily ills.

" He put on an equality the forgiving of sins and the curing of the sick, didn't He ? when He said ' Which is it easier to say ? " Go, thy sins are forgiven thee," or ' Arise, take up thy bed and walk ? " ' *He* knew both were possible, but even He—the Spirit of Perfection—even He had to *prove* He could cure their bodies before the people would believe that He could cure their souls. I can't really see why priesthood is so important. I can't believe that a man has those powers *just* and *only* because he's a priest, *just* and *only* because he belongs to Mother's Church ! It seems like trying to put the boundless oceans into a narrow canal. Such high and awe-inspiring forces cannot be handed down from one man to another merely by words being repeated over them, investing them with unseen might, in the way an official is handed the keys and insignia of office—it following that he becomes the possessor of great powers !

" It is all so different from that !

" Grandfather, St. John was right when he said, ' God *is* love,' and just and only because of that was He able to do the miracles. Nothing is of any value without love, and love means giving—that is why great love is so exhausting.

" Virtue was always going out of Jesus when He did miracles ; He was distinctly conscious of it. Does it go out of priests when they say Mass ? Could a priest—at the moment of Transubstantiation, when he claims to be effecting the most stupendous of all miracles—could he at that instant turn to the people and, with as much certainty as he says he is changing bread and wine into divine Body and Blood, cure them of their illnesses ? I don't think so.

" If a man is not burning with love and desire, spurred on by dynamic faith and will, he could do no miracle ; neither the one nor the other, neither Transubstantiate nor heal."

With the secret wisdom which was Christian's gift, he knew by instinct—while yet a child—things which it takes some of us a lifetime to find out, while others go to their graves without realizing anything about it.

In his bones he knew that achievement and success are the result of labour and will power. He knew that when these two are impelled forward by an ardent and an undying love, something will be accomplished. He knew that unless one believes a thing with mind and heart, and body and soul, one's words carry no weight, they have no power, they create nothing.

"Mother often takes me with her to Mass," he said. "Once I saw the Host shine like a silver sun. Then I knew the miracle had been done. But I only saw it once."

"Strange child," thought the old man ; "where does he get all his wisdom and knowledge from ? "

He felt that he had much to learn from this boy, whose spiritual development had never been moulded and hindered by credal teaching, and whom God had drawn straight to Himself by neither Sect, nor System, nor " Ism," nor Fear, nor Dogma, nor Threat—but only by Love.

.   .   .   .   .   .

Sitting with Maddalena on the evening before her departure, while Quendred and her son walked in the garden, Stephen made a supreme effort to tell his wife of the crowning tragedy of their lives as revealed in the fateful letter which he had lately read.

How he wished that he had never seen it ! But all such feelings were vain regrets.

During his years of silent monkhood, words had become difficult to him, and he had well-nigh lost the power of expression. This poignant situation was more than his negative nature could cope with, so, without a word, he laid the letter open upon Maddalena's knee ; then, sinking beside her, he buried his white head in his worn old hands.

Slowly she read the words—now faded to a pale golden shade —and slowly, slowly the cruel truth of the plot revealed itself to her mind. She gazed with the old infinity of love upon the figure of the man on the grass at her side.

"When will men cease meddling with God, I wonder ? " she thought. "And having meddled, who can teach them not to call the result of their meddling the will of God ? Some people imagine that their will and God's will are identical, and united in some mystical fashion. As a rule, all the troubles human beings suffer from are caused by themselves or by other human beings, and in reality very little can be laid at God's door, and yet we always call it 'God's will' if things go wrong."

Thus thinking, Maddalena sat with her crushed and broken-spirited husband kneeling silently at her feet.

Their lives flashed suddenly, quickly, and vividly before her, and she realized with an overpowering sense of impotent horror how a secret worm had been at work, night and day, day and night, destroying their happiness.

From the broken reed at her feet she lifted her swimming eyes to the hay-fields, and her gaze rested upon Quendred.

" My darling child," she whispered, " thank God I was true to my God and true to my mother love, and thus you and I are all the world to one another now, and we haven't let the teaching of the Church, masquerading as God's truth, come between us.

" My Quendred ! My pretty, tempestuous child, who hit the bland Jesuit's arm because natural justice flamed in your heart ; my lovely girl, whom Neiphausen's Catholicity didn't prevent him trying to seduce. Surely Christ meant religion to be something much greater and bigger and more blessed than these ignoble and petty squabbles about Creeds ?

" If we start with the demand that we must all agree in our views concerning Sacraments and Creeds, we are surely putting things in the wrong order ? Little Quendred ! Through fogs and mists, and lies and bigotry ; through cruelties and priest-craft ; through subtleties and hair-splitting, you have won through ! Won through to the all-sufficing, tender, comforting warmth of the personal love of God. We are always asking ' Do we agree with each other ? ' But you, Quendred, have taught me rather to ask ' Do we agree with Him ? '

" In looking on at your sufferings I have been taught to realize that the first and greatest question is, ' Do we agree in our obedi-ence to *Him* who is the source of our Faith ? ' ' What are the things about which *He* thought the most ? ' ' What condition did *He* lay down for discipleship and fellowship ? ' ' Where does *He* look for unity ? ' These are the searching and important questions, not the petty points raised in the Creeds by contro-versialists and dogmatists. To get into personal touch with the Infallible One is what we need, to study the works of fallible men is of only secondary importance. Faithful men must try to accept the mind of their Master as the law of their lives, and here is the first step in the attainment of a living union between Christians. But does my Church want a living union among Christians ? I don't think so, unless on her own lines, and with her at the head of affairs. She never has, and I fear she never will, lend herself to any sort of arrangement tending to union in the Churches."

The faded letter in her hand, and the broken man at her feet ;

her own thoughts and her daughter's difficulties, seemed proof enough of this.

Bending her head to her husband, she whispered :

" Stephen, come and sit by me, and let us try to forget." Yet even as she said the words, another omen flew across her mind, just as some black, evil, croaking bird haunts the steps of a traveller.

For suddenly she had visualized Lepantchine, and with a painful in-taking of her breath she closed her great dark eyes, grown so tragic and luminous through suffering.

Drawing her husband's hand within her own, she said :

" Listen, Stephen. As you have shared your secret with me, I, too, have one to share with you. You remember your friend, Father Ignatius ? "

" Indeed I do. What of him ? Is he dead ? "

" Not that I know of," said his wife. " But—do you realize who he is ? "

" Not at all. I never imagined there was anything to know," Stephen replied indifferently.

" He is Lepantchine," Maddalena said, " the man my father wished to kill years and years ago at Santa Fiora, on the day that you and I were betrothed, my Stephen ; on the day you told me you loved me, on the day you gave me this," and she pulled from round her neck the little bit of golden straw held together in a tiny case.

" Lepantchine ? " he whispered hoarsely. " Lepantchine ! Impossible ! Incredible ! Maddalena—it can't be true ? " and his dried-up, hot old hands sought hers feverishly.

" Yes, Lepantchine," said Maddalena, and then looking at Stephen steadily, with tense, unflinching eyes, she told him of their meeting in Berkeley Square the evening when he had left her for the heights of San Girolamo.

" But—but . . ." stammered the old monk, quite dazed by her story, " what did he do it for ? What was the object behind it all ? I can't understand."

" I think it was revenge, Stephen," she said.

" Revenge ? But revenge what for ? What harm had you ever done him ? " asked Stephen, trembling with horror at her words.

Maddalena wondered if she should tell this poor, harmless, spiritual old recluse—this wreck of manhood—the truth about the whole story ? Such a character as his would hardly be

able to imagine human passion taking so tight a hold on a man—
much less credit it, she thought. So she paused, but very eagerly
he prompted her to continue.

"Tell me," he muttered, while beads of sweat stood out upon
his forehead.

So, slowly and painfully, the Italian woman rehearsed carefully, word for word, her share of the drama at Santa Fiora so
many years ago, when he was her adoring lover and she his
passionate slave.

"And so you see, Stephen, Lepantchine hated me as he
hated no one else in that sordid story. The overwhelming
passion that he had for my mother was discovered—by me, and
its consummation frustrated—by me. I defrauded him of what
he was longing for ; *I* dashed the brimming coveted cup from his
lips so accustomed to sensual gratification that the miscarriage of
his desires nearly frenzied him ; I brought him—as it were—before
the tribunal of justice, yet I—in the end—gave him back his life.
I, a child of seventeen—'a chit of a girl,' as he called me in his
loathing sarcasm ! And so, instead of being obsessed with desire
for my mother, he became obsessed with desire to be revenged
upon me for having cheated him of my mother.

"Of this he made no secret when he came to see me in
London the night you left me, and he told me quite openly that an
overpowering wish to be revenged upon me for my treatment of
him had been the spur to his whole life since he had become a
priest. That you had dropped yourself into his power—entirely
unsought by him—seemed to him to be too strange not to be
used by him as the sign of God's will, and incidentally a cloak
under which to wreak his vengeance upon me.

"When he was quite certain that we still loved each other
deeply, he set to work—in satanic fashion—to take you away
from me so that, as he told me, he should make me suffer because
I had once made him suffer ! Revenge, and nothing but revenge,
was what Lepantchine wanted. He has dogged our lives, my
darling ; he has been our evil genius."

Stephen's face was shocking to look at. All expression seemed
to have been forced out of it. It was like the face of a
corpse.

"How damnable," said the old monk, trembling with sup-
pressed fury—"how loathesome and criminal and damnable."

Gently his wife drew him to her. His always slender form
was now reduced nearly to emaciation by constant fasting and the

ascetic life, and as she put her arms around him he felt almost like a boy to her strength and virility.

"Beloved," she said very tenderly, "please do not grieve. What is done, is done, and you and I have nearly run the course But—if you wish it—there surely could be a little future in store for us yet? Won't you come home with us, and live with me and Quendred?"

"No," he answered wistfully. "Oh no, dear wife, I can never do that."

"But you aren't happy here! I can see you aren't," she answered sadly.

"You are right," replied Stephen. "I am not really happy, but would I be happier anywhere else? No, no, this is the best place for me. I was always weak, uncertain, and changeable; seeking help from fallible sources; seeking help from that—that —devil! I am not fit to live in the world. This monastery is the best place for me.

"I am anchored here, and besides—you don't really want me! You've learnt to do without me! I would be an incubus. I would be like a ghost walking in your midst."

And deep down in her heart Maddalena knew that his words were true.

He took the slender chain of gold from round her neck, and kissed the little broken ring of straw which—in the transport of his boyish love—he had given her up there on the sunny road to Santa Barbara; which—in the ardour of his religious convictions—he had ruthlessly trodden upon, and which now —in the passion of his misery—he would fain make whole again.

But it was too late, too late! Too late, and the fateful words beat in his heart like the relentless and never-ceasing movement of the ocean.

"Faithful Maddalena," he whispered, "*you* are like God. *You* have never changed." And as he said the words a bandage seemed to be torn from his eyes, and he saw clearly that while God had always been there, unchanging, tireless, immutable, all-knowing, and waiting for him, he had stupidly sought advice and help from priests—men as fallible and as prone to evil as himself. And this was his retribution.

He had given God the go-by, and had set up priests—like the Pagans did of old—in His place.

"But I always believed that priests represented God, and they were so much easier to talk to than God, and you got an answer so much quicker," was his exceeding bitter cry, " and so I asked them, and not God."

Bending towards the broken, brown-garbed figure of her husband, so torn with impotent regret, so self-despising for the incurable weakness of his character which had ruined both their lives—she crooned to him almost the words with which she had comforted her poor, distraught mother at Santa Fiora forty-four years before.

" ' Sh, 'sh, my darling. Don't grieve. I understand, and I sympathize. I love you now as I have always loved you. ' For better for worse, for richer for poorer, in sickness and in health, till death us do part.' 'Sh, 'sh, darling."

And so, with his faithful wife's arms about him, he sank his weary head on to her breast, disillusioned with everything but her.

" He's like a child," thought Maddalena, " just like a poor, tired, lost child. Mother was like that too."

" But we cannot forget the past, Maddalena," he said at last, very low, " it's too deeply engraved with gall and vinegar upon our hearts."

" No, beloved," she answered, " we can't forget, but we can forgive."

With her face close to his she began the eternal prayer, in which he softly joined :

" . . . and forgive us our trespasses as we forgive them that trespass against us, and lead us not into temptation, but deliver us from evil. Amen."

.   .   .   .   .

The next morning they left for Florence, *en route* for Nürem-berg, meeting Simon by the way.

" Good-bye, my darling wife," Stephen said. " *You* have been true to your marriage vows. God bless you." When he came to Christian he pressed his withered lips on to the boy's forehead, long and slowly.

" Remember," he said, " that you will have much to bear. No one will believe that you are genuine. You will be mocked and shunned—nay, more ; they will call you a madman, a seducer ; and when you pass by, the world will cry out, ' Lo ! he hath a devil ! ' "

T

CHAPTER XX

PARSIFAL

" Music is the harmonious voice of creation, an echo of the invisible world,
one note of which the entire universe is destined one day to sound."
—Mazzini.

THE huge auditorium was crowded. Everything was silent and
in darkness.

Then from out of nothingness came a long-drawn, plaintive
air, deep and moving.

At last the dark curtain which hid the stage was gently drawn
apart, and the story of the Knights of the Grail began to unfold
itself. The Grail ; the *Sang Réal* ; the mystery of the cleansing
power of the Divine Blood, the Real Blood.

All this—Quendred had explained to her son—would be
shown with great respect upon the stage. He sat between her
and his father, motionless, enthralled.

Then Amfortas was brought in to offer the Chalice, but he was
not worthy ; he had sinned, and his wound left him no peace.
Who then was worthy amongst that company of knights ?—and
Parsifal stood there, knowing nothing, understanding nothing,
but just gazing, gazing. " Thou fool," said old Gurnemanz,
the master of the knights, roughly pushing him out of the
banqueting hall, " thou art not worthy to see such sights. Go ! "

Meanwhile, the celestial choir, mounting higher and higher,
sang :

" Blessed in love, blessed in faith."

And then years afterwards—his time of trial over—Parsifal returns, a " pure fool " and blameless ; worthy to offer the Chalice of the Blood of Christ. " The Chalice of My Blood, the Mystery of Faith ; which shall be shed for you and for many unto the remission of sins."

When the supernatural moment drew near a great quietness descended upon the Knights ; the air became cool, the hall grew dim, and, jewel-like, the tinted glass gleamed in the windows.

The unearthly music grew more and more gently exultant, and then !—in the Chalice the Blood glowed, for on to the blameless fool—*because he was blameless*—the Spirit of God had descended.

Overwhelmed, Quendred at that moment realised that the hero of this drama was what she had always longed vaguely for her son to be like. . . . Because Parsifal was sinless he could consummate the great change. Only perfection can achieve perfection.

A fool—a pure fool—Parsifal. He who, by remaining a pure fool, became beloved of God, because he was God-like, because he was able to do what God could do. Why ? Because he had faith and love, and no fear. A fool ! A pure fool ! Like God !

Gently, quietly, the curtain closed, and the great theatre silently became empty.

.   .   .   .   .   .

The four drove back through the pine-woods to their little romantic hotel, some way from the town. They were filled with the spirit of peace and love.

At the door of the hotel the servants ran towards them, hysterically crying :

" War is declared, oh, my ladies, there is war."

And sure enough, along the road beyond the garden could be heard the ominous rumble of gun carriages, the figures of men could be seen like shadows in the moonlight, marching, marching.

At four o'clock the next morning everyone was astir, and at half-past six the little party had got seats in the already crowded train.

Bustle, hurry, excitement, wonder, and the desire to get " home " as quickly as possible seemed to fill the people.

And at last they found themselves on Sunday night in London. Early on Monday they went to see the Seyntlegers. Patricia ran down the marble staircase to meet them as they

entered the house, answering the mute question in Maddalena's
eyes.

" Yes, it's war," she said, wild-eyed, " and everyone will have
to go.   The Declaration is being sent to the King to sign to-night,
and it will be in all the papers to-morrow morning.   " Oh !—my
Patrick, my darling boy," she sobbed, " I know that he'll never
come back."

" The Guards ? " whispered Maddalena.

" Yes, as soon as possible," answered Patricia, " they will be
amongst the first to go," and she squeezed her mother-in-law's
hand tightly.

Patrick was killed at the first battle of the Marne, and poor
Patricia never got over it ; she cried and cried, till her pretty
blue eyes lost all their lustre.   Her first-born !   Her only son !
Her darling !   Lying stark in France.

" How was he killed ?   Did he linger ?   Was it instantaneous ?
Did he suffer ?   Did he think of her at the last ? "   For months
she tormented herself.   Nothing comforted her ; neither friends,
children, nor religion.   She was abjectly miserable, and all joy
in life was gone.

About Christmas time the news came to Simon that the
young Duc de Chevernoix and his brother had both been killed
—and that in consequence everything, and all the estates in
Touraine, came to him and his heirs.   So thus, in the twentieth
century, he inherited a title from an ancestor who had lived three
hundred years before.   He was now known as Duc de Tréfontaines, and his son, Christian, became Marquis de Chevernoix.

The weary, dragging, bloody months went on, and daily the
holocaust of youth was offered willingly on European battlefields.   They just gave and gave their lives because they were
willing to die for what they loved, and they loved their homeland.

Every week reaped in more men as they reached the prescribed age, and so at last Christian's time came too.   It wasn't
what he had dreamt of, but he knew he had to go.

.   .   .   .   .   .

Even in the remoteness of San Girolamo there was some
excitement when Italy was drawn into the conflict.   When
Stephen was told of it, his heart was on fire with longing to help
in the great fight in some way.

" I cannot stay doing nothing while Europe is suffering, and my
very own flesh and blood are dying and dead," he had said one

day to the Superior. " Reverend Father, let me go with a few others ? Let us go down to the world of pain and struggle once more, and take our part in the strife of our brothers."

" But, my son," the venerable old Fra Lorenzo had answered, " priests may not fight. It is contrary to their sacred calling. You have come here to contemplate. Besides, you are too old to fight," and he smiled on the humble brother whom they all loved.

" I do not wish to fight," said Stephen. " All I want to do is to tend the sick ; to be allowed to bring them out of the firing line to safety, and there to minister to their bodily and spiritual needs. Give me leave, my Father," and he knelt at the other's feet, his splendid head bent over his hand. Duke pleading to peasant. In the spiritual life such things happen.

" Rise, my brother," said Fra Lorenzo, " I cannot refuse you. This war is unique in its demands on every kind of man power, and your position is yet more unique. Go with my blessing to the Front, and work for the wounded as you think well. But we are poor, you know ; we possess nothing, and without money little can be done."

Very humbly Fra Giovanni looked up, saying :

" My nephew is in the English Cabinet, and a rich man. If you give me leave to write to him, I know he will send me what would be necessary for our work."

So it was arranged. Money was sent and Stephen, with three other monks, started on their pilgrimage to the fighting line. For many weeks they worked hard at bringing in the wounded, and, despite his sixty-five years, Stephen's strength never flagged. He had always been healthy, and the frugal life and manual work which he had led for the last twenty years had made him hard and wiry.

It was the September night of the Italian *débâcle*, 1917, and the little band of monks knew no rest.

Fra Celano—a Tuscan Brother who adored Stephen and never left his side—was quite unnerved by the terribly swift and silent descent of the Germans. Everything was in confusion, and the regiments they were with suffered awful casualties. He was afraid to go under fire that night to do his work of love ; but the ardour of Fra Giovanni carried him through, and together they performed wonders.

Morning red was streaking the east when a shell burst near the two brown-garbed old men. Fra Celano was killed instantaneously, and the other lay for hours wounded, and unable to move. Part of his face had been shockingly scarred. September sun was shining on the plains when help came to Fra Giovanni.

"Look, there's someone lying in that hole," said an English voice, and a minute later Christian de Villancourt was gazing at the upturned, ruined, bloodless face.

Something attracted him to the dying monk, and he had him carried to his own tent to be cared for. As they passed by the General's quarters the latter saw Christian, and asked him who he had with him.

"A wounded monk, sir; I fear he's dying, he's in a terrible state."

"What!" said the General, "the Englishman from Florence?"

"Englishman!" said the other, "I don't understand."

"Yes, yes. An English Trappist was given special leave to come and do stretcher work here. I received notice of it from your cousin, Hugh Traquair. It was at his wish, apparently, that the monks were allowed to come."

Christian turned swiftly and left the General, without even saluting him.

In a moment he was kneeling at the camp bed.

"Grandfather!" he groaned, as he took the emaciated form in his arms as though to give it life from his own strong young body. "I'm Christian, your grandson," he whispered. "Oh, speak to me, just one word."

The old man opened his eyes and smiled.

"Christian!" he whispered—"how strange and wonderful that you should be with me now. I thought everything had been a failure, but it has—not been—a failure after all, because you have been sent to be with me here at the end. Ah, Christian, how I loved your grandmother! Tell her—tell her that to the end—I loved her! Dear—heart of mine. Faithful, loyal Maddalena."

There was a pause, and he swallowed painfully. Weakly he passed his thin fingers over Christian's face, and then said:

"You are so like your mother!—I send my love—tell her—I ask her forgiveness. I—was—unkind to her—and—bitter . . ." Here he turned his great, grey-blue, sunken eyes on to the boy's face with a far-off wandering look and, with a tremendous effort, he sat up, while his strange eyes seemed to be gazing through Christian away, away at something beyond.

Halting and panting, yet with an extraordinary calm, he said:

" I see—at last I see and know—creeds are nothing.. . .,
Ah! if I had—only known the God—with whom—I had to do. . . ."

His voice gradually sank, and became fainter and fainter, like
the sound of a bell being lost in the mountains. A wondrous look of recognition came over his face. He held out his
hands as though in greeting, then he fell gently backwards into
Christian's arms.

.   .   .   .   .   .

They laid his body to rest at Ullcombe, and over his grave
was written :

STEPHEN FITZ-URSE
7TH DUKE OF SEYNTLEGER
TRAPPIST MONK.
BELOVED HUSBAND OF
MADDALENA DI SANTA FIORA.
DIED UNDER FIRE
EUROPEAN WAR
1917
R. I. P.

And every night Maddalena would smile triumphantly to
herself, as, kissing his photograph, she murmured softly :
" He loved me to the end," for Christian had given her his
grandfather's dying message.

.   .   .   .   .   .

It was the March " push " of 1918. People at home spoke
about Channel ports in lowered tones, and seriously. Christian
wrote a letter of tender love and farewell to his mother, which was
to be given to her—in case . . .

Twenty-four hours later he was lying seriously wounded in
France.

It was pitch black, and desperately cold. First a garish
hideous noise, and a feeling as though millions of men and
guns had pounded over him, then absolute silence ; something
soft and warm trickling from his head ; something soft and cold
falling on to his face. Blood and snow. Life and Death.

He put out his parched tongue, and desperately licked the wet
stuff round his lips. Turning a little, he groaned aloud. Such
pain, such awful pain.

Then he heard a sound, and something moved and touched
him.

" *Wasser, um Gotteswillen, wasser,*" a weak voice said.
Christian fumbled for his water-bottle, and he remembered
some brandy which he had got the night before. Taking some
himself, he gave the rest to the German. The stuff revived them
both for a bit and they talked spasmodically.

" What a damned war this is," said the German in English.

" Who are you ? " Christian asked, moved to a faint interest,
and the pain was less at the moment.

" Borvin von Neiphausen," the other answered automatically.

At the name distant memories stirred Christian, then dimly
he remembered that his mother had a photograph of a man of
that name in one of her old albums at home. And remembering
by degrees still more, it came to his mind that when once they
had been looking at the pictures in the book together his father
had said of this man :

" He loved your mother once, long ago, Christian. He
might have been your father " : and that his mother had said
softly, " Poor Borvin."

" God ! How extraordinary," he now ejaculated aloud, and
the other man groaned :

" Nothing's extraordinary, except dying."

Christian painfully pushed the flask towards him, and
said, " We're both done for, aren't we ? All's over ; but—God
—remains. I want to pray ; will—you—also ? "

He reached out his hand, and, in the darkness, found the
other's.

Praying they said :

" Out of the depths have I cried unto Thee, O Lord. Lord
hear my voice. For with Thee there is propitiation. Let my
cry come unto Thee . . .." With the weakness and the strength
of agony they grasped and held hands, and then came oblivion.

Gently and purely the snow fell upon them, and lovingly
covered them with her soft white cloak.

.   .   .   .   .   .

And when the stretcher-bearers came, they found the hands
of these two soldiers locked together. Both were still alive,
but Borvin couldn't live for more than a few hours. With rum
and warmth Christian soon became much restored, and when he
once more realized who his companion was he asked that he
might look through the contents of the German's pockets.

" There might be something I could send to his wife," he told the nurse who was with him. " They used to be friends of my people's before the War."

Nothing of much interest, however, was found, but when they took off his tunic a very flat gold case slipped out of a breast-pocket, cunningly hidden in the lining.

" Ah," he thought, " this is what I'm looking for ; this will be something she will like to have," and he opened it.

But, to his great surprise, his eyes fell upon a faded old photograph of his own mother.

Quickly glancing at Prince Neiphausen, he found the dying man's eyes fixed upon the little case, and he tried to hold out his hand to take it, but it fell back weakly at his side, and a groan of pain escaped his twisted, discoloured lips.

Christian put it into his hand, and then, bending down to his ear, he said very slowly and distinctly :

" I am Quendred's son."

An extraordinary look of pleasure flitted across the man's face, and then—with a tremendous effort—he whispered :

" Then you can kiss her—kiss her for me—she would never kiss me—Ah-h-h . . ."

Quietly his head fell to one side, and Borvin's spirit passed.

. . . . . .

During the summer Princess di Santa Fiora had died. None of her English relations could get to her, and it had been a lonely death.

" We must go to France, Quendred," Simon said to his wife one gay May morning in 1919. " We are French now, you know, and there will be much to do at Chevernoix."

" Yes, we must, and I want Mother to live with us, Simon," she had answered. " You won't mind, will you ? To me she is the very best and dearest after you and Christian, and so much joy has gone out of her life now that my grandmother is dead."

" Mind ? I shall, on the contrary, be proud that she should honour my house," Simon had replied.

And so by the time September came they were all established at the historic castle on the Loire.

One soft yellow evening Quendred and her son were walking in the courtyard. A slender silver moon lay on its back in the dark sky. The sweet smell of stocks and tobacco plants rose fragrantly on the air, and from the castellated wall masses of autumn roses—tawny, cream, and scarlet—fell like a cascade to the gentle river beneath.

Together they stood by the wall and talked.

" You know, Mother," he was saying, " you said you would let me go and fulfil my desire."

He had grown into an extremely tall, slim-hipped, deep-chested youth. The military experience of the last two years had developed him very much, and, although he had been so dreadfully ill after his wound in France, health had once more begun to glow in his cheeks. His dark eyes were softer for the knowledge of men and things which had come to him during the War, and that which had found him a boy, unfamiliar in the practical knowledge of men, pain, and the world, left him deeply enlightened as to all three.

" What a lot there is to be done for the world," he would often think ; " great, glowing, mysterious, palpitating world ! —can I help you ? I wish to so much. Will you thank me ? No ! —that doesn't matter ; it's foolish to expect it, yet it's human to like gratitude ! But I am too weak yet to be of any use. To get strong I must work ; work in the world, and with the world, but not of it. A hermit's life is useless nowadays, I see that plainly. Besides, the Son of God didn't retire from the world : He lived in it, worked for it, loved it !

" Not to the world of the hundreds did He go, but to the world of the millions, and that is what I want to do, Mother."

Quendred didn't answer just at once.

She knew that she had promised, but where would he go ? And how ? Had he a plan ? What was the future of this son of hers to be ?

And then he told her that he wanted to go as a workman, and help to build up the people's homes again in the most ruined parts of Northern France.

" You see, now that you have given me some of my great-grandfather's money to do as I like with, I feel I really can be of some use in the world, Mother," he said.

" I want to go and live with the working people *as* a workman, and amongst the people ; and then, when I am fit for it, I want to help the men made blind by the War. As I cured Uncle Anthony's sight, I might be able to cure them ! I cannot hope to do more than this ; to believe in God's promises ; to try and do all that lies in my power to make others happy. And so you'll let me go ? "

" When, dearest ? "

" Now, Mother ; at once. Don't say you mind. I must go, I feel a power which never lets go of my soul, drawing and drawing me."

" You'll come back sometimes, darling, won't you ? " pleaded Quendred. " Don't desert us for ever."

When telling Maddalena of this conversation, Quendred reminded her of the night which they had spent together on the top of the Tyrolese mountain, when she had told her of her secret desire to have a son who, at some future time, might be great.

" And I think that your prayer has been answered," Maddalena said.

CHAPTER XXI

"... BUT THE SPIRIT GIVETH LIFE"

" From the death of the old, the new proceeds,
And the life of truth from the rot of creeds."
—JOHN GREENLEAF WHITTIER.

DURING the War Ullcombe had been used as a hospital, and since Patrick's death, Anthony—much aged—had lost all interest in it. He had bought a house in London, and nine-hundred-year-old Ullcombe was put on the market.

Impossible taxation was given as its excuse, but Patricia and Maddalena and Quendred all knew that it was because the race of the Fitz-Urses had come to an end.

It was bought for £300,000 by Lord McArmaghdale, a rich shipowner who had got a good deal richer during the War. He made great plans to modernize the old house, and central heating, the newest form of electric light, and twenty bathrooms were at once put in. When all was finished the new owner—delighted at the result—came down and entertained a large house-warming party.

No one ever knew how it happened—perhaps, as some thought, the spirit of Ullcombe rebelled against all these innovations—but early in the morning one of the guests noticed smoke coming out from under their bed, and, in five hours, stately Ullcombe lay a heap of smoking ruins.

When Maddalena was told of it, her father-in-law's words flashed back to her with great vividness.

" We have gone on for nine hundred years, but I see the end, I think I see the end," he had said.

" Poor old dear," she thought, " what a mercy he's dead. What would he have felt at the total extinction of his family and his house ?   Ullcombe burnt, and not a Fitz-Urse left in the world.   Rosemouth's sorry little ditty has indeed been fulfilled up to the hilt."

.   .   .   .   .

Maddalena was now an old woman, and she spent most of the day either quietly in the garden at Chevernoix, sitting by the window of her sitting-room overlooking the Loire, or driving through the country lanes.

The atmosphere in this old French house was one of perfect happiness and calm, because of its inmates. They all loved each other, and no one sought to label the other with a particular creed, the tenets of which had to be adhered to under pain of each thinking that the other's final salvation was a moot point !

These were wonderfully peaceful times, after the nervous religious strain of the last years, and the horrors of the War, and many were the talks they all had—drawn together by the outstanding personality of the old Duchess, and the calm happiness which radiated from Simon and Quendred.

Maddalena's eyes were as brilliant and as clear as when a young woman ; her voice was still liquid and youthful, and her body had taken on none of the disfigurements of age. She had never stopped behind, but had marched on bravely with the youth of the world in unfeigned sympathy and enthusiasm. Her spirit had never grown old, and, like some radiant, ageless plant, she seemed ever to be putting forth new branches. Always interested in new ideas, new schemes, and the evolution of thought, she was indeed a source of inspiration to men of the world who were " doing " things, and Chevernoix—because of Maddalena—became the high road between London, Paris, and Rome to all their friends. Thus Quendred's French home was a centre of all that was interesting and intellectual of the day. A continual stream of people passed under its portals ; coming in, hoping for much ; going out, entirely satisfied.

.   .   .   .   .

One hazy, lazy day in June, Christian and his grandmother sat under the lilacs talking, as was their wont.

She wanted to tell him something of the past, and of the great part which religion had played in the lives of his immediate ancestors. She knew that Quendred never mentioned creeds to him, either in praise or in depreciation, and knowing how her daughter had suffered from their decrees in the past, she loved her all the more for being loyal to the creed of her education in not defaming it to her son.

She told him of how his great-grandfather had turned to Rome, and then left it again.

" Your antecedents were all very religious, my Christian," she smiled gently, " and it is only very religious people who wish to change their religion, whether ' to ' or ' from.' I wish that you could have known him. He was the most remarkable man I have ever met, and he taught me so much—charity, toleration, sympathy, and breadth of view.

" He hated oppression, tyranny, and persecution. Those were the things which stirred his blood, and it was because he was not able—like so many good devout Catholics, who wouldn't hurt a fly—to agree that the evils of the Papal Curia and Ultramontanism were compatible with a divine Church, that he felt there was no other course open to him than to leave that Church.

" He could never forgive the Popes the things they (as Christ's vice-agents, and claiming to be God-like) had done, or had allowed to be done."

His grandmother patted his hand lovingly.

" You just follow the light that has been given you," she said tenderly, " and go straight on. I don't think you need Popes, Christian dear. You have the God-sent gift."

And now Christian felt once more the call of the voice, which would not be silent, and the boy felt impelled, in his humble way, to go out amongst men to tell them of the wondrous things which he had in his heart. And those who heard him speak, marvelled at his power.

When the news came that he was coming, the children ran to meet him, and the women brought their babies that he might only look upon them, for from the simplicity and purity of his heart came a passionate and consuming eloquence, and a supreme and secret wisdom which at once touched everyone's inmost being.

He always spoke with absolute sincerity and undeviating truthfulness, and his voice was eager, clear, sweet, and sonorous. To whatever house he came, peace seemed to come also, and many were the family feuds he mended. When he spoke, all kinds of people flocked to hear him.

He had no axes to grind, either credal, political, or social, and he seemed to move about among the people with a kind of entire aloofness from the things of this world, although his sympathy and love for them was one of his chief characteristics.

He had the most piercing insight into the core of things, and his advice on every matter was eagerly sought.

He always spoke on the Gospels, which he had grown to love with increasing strength ever since his mother had first filled his mind with the wonder of their beauty as a small child.

And as he spoke the people hung upon his words and closed in nearer to him, so that they might better see his noble, radiant face, and even touch his clothing. Every word he uttered was palpitating with feeling, and the reason was because he *knew*, because he had *experienced* that of which he told them. And the people, hearing him, also *knew* in some strange way that this was not empty talking. In the mysterious way that the uneducated masses are held in silent, breathless enthralment by a truly great actor, musician, or preacher, these people—unintellectual and unread—knew that they were in the presence of a man who was very great, and very rare. Just as a spurious gentleman can never be mistaken for a real one, so can spurious sanctity never be mistaken for true sanctity. Both are always found out in the end.

These people needn't have come to listen to him ; they weren't bound by a creed to do so, on a given day, under pain of mortal sin. They were not forced either by convention or religion to leave their cottages after work was over, to follow him. No law made the men eschew the public-house to go to hear Christian speak. If what he said had bored them, they would very soon have become inattentive and have drifted away. These people received no three-lined whip to attend his utterances. They just *came*. He *drew* them, for they knew that what was dropping hot from his lips had been forged, burning, in his heart.

Like Francis of Assisi he drew them, and some there were even who wondered if it were not the "holy little Man of God" come back once more after nearly seven hundred years to give a helping hand to the groping souls of twentieth century men and women.

Once Simon had told Quendred that he feared this preaching of their son's might not be allowed to go on.

" But why not ? " she had asked, surprised.

" He doesn't preach credal teaching, you see ! He's not offering the people one of the systems ! I wouldn't be surprised to hear that he is asked to stop."

" But, Simon, he's doing no harm ! I feel certain you are

wrong.   Remember that you *aren't* a Catholic, and I *am*, and that although I disagree on many points with the Church I do believe that Catholics want to make the world more spiritual ; I'm sure they want to teach the people more about God.   Don't get bigoted, Simon, I couldn't bear that ; I've had so much of it."

Simon smiled.   Quendred was so warm-hearted, and so generous ; she forgot injuries so quickly, and never thought of imputing evil to anyone.   She was so unreservedly unsuspicious in her whole outlook on life, that her husband hated even to have said what he had.

"All right, darling," he answered.   "Perhaps I'm wrong. Perhaps I'm too much inclined to be ' down ' on Rome.   But you see, in the past her actions haven't won my trust, and so I'm inclined to regard her with a good deal more suspicion than you are, even after all you've suffered at her hands !   I hope you think I am quite fair to our tenants here, though ?   Do you think I give enough money to the church and the schools, and M. le Curé ?   I sent him half a dozen bottles of port the other day, because he had a nasty cough, poor old chap.   You know I'm only anxious to treat our people with absolute justice and kindness, and I always remember that the money I get from the Chevernoix estate is won by Catholic toil and Catholic hands, and so must be returned to them in kind, and not used elsewhere.

"I should think it extremely wrong if I were to take the Chevernoix rents to keep up an Anglican monastery, or a Y.M.C.A. Club in the Western prairies !—although I honestly think the latter is doing more useful work than poor, harmless M. le Curé is here, with his ' tummy,' and his snuff, and his little drops of cheap cognac.

"That you are a Catholic, of course, also makes an enormous difference, and I hope I would never be either unjust or unkind to any institution or person of your Faith.   See, I haven't even closed the private chapel, although you know my feelings about Catholics since the trouble we had to get married ?   I wasn't bigoted before but I fear their behaviour has made me inclined to be so now.

"Yet, because your mother wants it so much, I allow Mass to be said—to please her—every day in my house !   Dearest, you must never call me bigoted again !   If the case were reversed, do you think a Catholic husband, inheriting a Protestant estate and a Protestant private Chapel, would do as I am doing for his Protestant mother-in-law ? "

"No, I'm afraid I don't ! " Quendred had to confess.   " But then, no other Protestant would behave as you are doing, would he ? Be honest ! "

" I'm only a Protestant, though, in so far as I protest against Rome," said Simon, smiling.

" You're the best, the cleverest, and the most darling creature that ever lived, bless you," said his wife, " and I never, never regret the day I heard you singing on the road to Santa Barbara, when you made me see the mistakes in the Catholic religion, and when you made me give you my heart."

" Do you think you'll never change ? " he asked rather wistfully, and this was the first time he had ever said the words to her.

" Would you like me to ? " she said.

" Yes."

" But what shall I change *to* ? " she asked. " What *is* there to change to ? "

" What is Christian ? " asked Simon. " What he is, we can be."

" You are right, darling," said his wife.

" Because you've taken off one coat, you needn't necessarily put on another," Simon said. " Sometimes underneath the coat will be found a very lovely garment, which has been crushed and ruined almost beyond recognition by the thick opaqueness of the other one."

" Yes, I see," said Quendred . . . " Would it please you for me not to be a Catholic ? "

" Not unless you are convinced it would be right," he said.

" I should so hate to grieve Mother," Quendred answered very softly. " That is the only thing which keeps me back I sometimes think."

" Darling," said Simon, taking both her hands in his, and kissing them, " I shall never try to influence you, and I shall never try to embitter your life because of any religious views you do, or do not, hold. Your mother, I feel sure, would feel exactly as I do."

" Thank God for you and my mother," she said. " Surely I am the happiest woman on earth to be blessed with you two, and Christian as well."

" But you've suffered to get that happiness, haven't you ? " said her husband, as his mind reviewed their courting days.

" Yes, I know," she answered. " But that's all gone and over now. I want to forget it, and I have forgiven them all ages ago. Oh, those naughty priests ! But now, you see, they're as nice to me as possible."

U

" You wonderful, generous, resilient woman ! You beloved Quendred," said he, smiling as though at a child. " I only hope you won't be again disillusioned."

.   .   .   .   .   .

It was Christian's custom when he was at Chevernoix to walk about amongst the people round his home, and talk to them on simple and touching themes. Nothing credal, however, ever passed his lips. One day he spoke on these words of the mystic Thomas à Kempis :

" With two wings a man is lifted up above earthly things : with simplicity and purity."

Without telling him of her intention, Quendred had—un-unknown to him—followed him, so that she might hear him speaking when he was unconscious of her presence. Quietly she sat behind a thick cluster of bushes where neither he, nor those who listened to him, could see her.

" To *seek* God," she heard him tell them, " in the simplicity of our hearts is the first, and the central, and the last step towards finding Him, and he who has found Him wants nothing else.

" But many of us seem to carry our devotion in our books and pictures ; in outward signs and figures ; many have God on their lips, but he is seldom in their lives.

" There are many teachers who are full of grand words, but they give not out the Spirit, yet Jesus Christ says over and over again :

" ' I come to bring you the *Spirit ;* my words they are Spirit ; the letter killeth, but it is the *Spirit* that has the life.'

" Many teachers do well and speak well, but if the love of Christ is not guiding their tongues they cannot set the heart on fire, they cannot move the mind of men to the inward comprehension of the high things of God. Then let us turn rather to God than to man for guidance and for help. . . ."

For about half an hour he spoke thus, and then his discourse was finished.

Throbbing, his pleading voice fell like gentle balm upon the cool, soft night breeze, upon the hearts of these rough toilers.

" ' Foxes have holes,' " said he, " ' and birds of the air have nests, but the Son of Man has nowhere to lay His Head ! ' "

His voice ceased and silence—the silence of intense emotion —came to those listeners in the dewy forest.

Deeply touched and moved by his passionate appeal, the

simple peasants dispersed, and walked back in happy silence to
their little homes, through the balmy, sweet-smelling darkness.

. . . . . .

Quendred was just going to move out of her secluded hiding-
place, when she heard footsteps, and from behind a large tree
the parish priest advanced towards her son.   She was extremely
surprised at his sudden appearance, so surprised indeed that—
almost against her will—she quickly withdrew behind the bushes
again !

He went up to Christian, who was sitting on the ground
reading his tattered little New Testament.

The priest touched the young man's shoulder.

" Good evening, M. le Marquis," he said rather nervously.
" I disturb you ?   You are reading ? "

Smiling, Christian rose, saying, " The Gospels.   I never tire
of them, do you ? "

The priest took the small, old, worn volume, and, glancing at
the title-page, he pursed his lips.

" The Protestant version !   That is not right, my son ! "
he said.   " You will never succeed if you insist on ignoring our
Holy Catholic interpretation !   And it is in reality about this
that I have come to speak to you to-night.   Of course, I realize,
Monseigneur, that you are not a Catholic—ah, the pity of it !—
and so, naturally, I have no jurisdiction over you.   I also know
that M. le Duc, your father, is our landlord, and a Frenchman, by
the inheriting of all these fair lands.   Never before have we had
a landlord who was not of our holy religion, and I do not wish
to be troublesome in any way, Monseigneur, but—but . . ." and
the man broke off even more nervously than he had begun.

" Please continue, M. le Curé," said Christian.   " You have
something which you feel it is important that you should say
to me ? "

" Yes, Monseigneur, indeed I have, and it is very unpleasant
for me also.   I have just been listening to you speaking to these
poor peasants, and I feel that it is my duty as a Catholic priest
of the Church of God to ask you in all gravity to refrain from—
doing so any more."

" Why ? " asked Christian.

" It is against our holy religion," said the priest.

" But is it against God ? " asked the youth.

" If it is against the Catholic religion, it cannot be for God,"
murmured the Curé.

" But *how* is it against your religion ? " asked Christian.
" I never even mentioned it ! "

" Yes, that's just it. He who is not with us is against us,"
the priest said, more excitedly.

" But Christ didn't teach that ! " said Christian. " On the
contrary, He said that ' He who is not against us is with us.' "

" But the Church teaches it," said the priest.

" Whom do you put first, then, M. le Curé ? "

The priest hedged.

" Christ speaks to us through the Church. If you don't
believe in her, you cannot believe in God," he said. " I am
sure that if you would only be fair to our Faith you would see
that it is the only religion which fulfils the words of the Bible
in the largest number of places."

" But when have I ever been unfair to Catholicism ? " asked
Christian quietly. " I have lived amongst it all my life. My
mother belongs to that Faith, and there is nothing I don't know
about it. I never preach any creed, I couldn't ; I don't know
how to ! But I feel that—I may be able to speak just about
God. Are you going to ask me to stop doing that in your
parish, which is, after all, my own home ? "

" I fear so, Monseigneur," said the priest. " I fear that is
the errand I came here for to-night, at the command of my
bishop. Apparently the fact of your going about amongst the
people has reached Rome. The Bishop of Montfleur—our bishop—
is there now, and has been much with the Holy Father. He
is likely to be the next French Cardinal. I am sorry that
it should have fallen to me, Monseigneur, to rebuke you in this
way. *I* see no fault in you but—the Church must be obeyed,
and is it not out of order that you should preach to my flock ? "

" I did not know that it was ' out of order,' M. le Curé ! "
Christian said. " In the Middle Ages the Friars walked preaching
all through Europe, and collected whom they could to listen to
them. The world was their parish, the broad highway their
pulpit, every man their flock ! To-day men of all creeds do not
hesitate to go amongst others and preach whatever they like in
religion and in politics in the public places of our great cities !
Why am I, alone, debarred from speaking about Jesus Christ ?
It seems to please and comfort the people. Why doesn't the
bishop wish it ? "

The Curé shrugged his shoulders slightly.

" When will all you good people understand the Catholic

religion ? " he said testily. " When will you realize that it is *impossible* for Catholics to agree that yours is anything but the weakest of makeshifts ? In fact, nothing more definite than a protest against Rome, and surely no spiritual person can agree that a ' protest ' is a Faith ? "

" All such things have no interest for me," Christian quietly answered the highly-excited priest. " I care for nothing but the sublime words in the New Testament. I love the Gospels, *les Evangiles ;* and I'm sure you do too ! You cannot frighten me as I think you do some of your followers. Do you teach your poor flock fear, M. le Curé ? "

" If it's necessary, we do," returned the priest restively.

" But there is no fear in love ! " Christian said very gently. " ' Perfect love casteth out fear,' because fear torments us. If we do not fear, we are made perfect in love."

But there was no appeasing M. le Curé.

" That's all rubbish," he said quickly. " I know all that way of talking ; it's as old as the hills, but it's useless. We've *got* to teach a creed, and the only creed worth teaching is Roman Catholicism. I must beg of you, M. le Marquis, from now onwards, to cease preaching."

" And what if I refuse ? " queried Christian. " This is my home—and my father owns the whole place. Besides, you have no jurisdiction over me. I am not one of your flock."

" I shall be forced to ruin your meetings if you continue, Monseigneur," said Père Lapetrie, with some heat. " As parish priest I have great power, and I warn you straight that I *shall* ruin them."

" By whose authority ? " said Christian slowly.

" By the Pope's authority, Monseigneur."

" Is this the fact ? " Christian asked, flushing, and very much surprised.

" Yes," the priest answered.

" Doesn't he wish God's words remembered then ? " pressed Christian.

" Only with the Catholic ' imprimatur,' " answered the priest.

" I can't believe it ! " sighed Christian.

The Curé once more shrugged his shoulders.

" I have given you the message, M. le Marquis, and now I must go. Good night, Monseigneur. I will pray for you that you may have light to see the truth of our holy religion."

" Good night," Christian answered.

The priest disappeared, and Quendred's son was left standing alone. His head drooped to his breast, his hands hung listlessly by his sides. He was terribly disappointed. He couldn't understand it ! Would he be treated like that in England, he wondered ? Should he go to England ? Would England give such teaching as he offered a better hearing ?

At that moment Quendred walked towards him.

" Darling," she said, " I couldn't help hearing it all ! I came out because I wanted to hear you speak without your knowing that I was here."

" Mother ! You here ? " he said, very much surprised. " I am sorry that you overheard that interview. I fear it may make you dislike that poor, harmless old man who, after all, is only obeying orders. Oh, Mother beloved, how I wish you weren't a Catholic," said Christian, with intense feeling. " I have never been angry with them before ; I've always treated them with the greatest respect and courtesy. I've never said a word against their creed or anyone else's. I'm not in the least bit interested in creeds ; they're so modern, so changing, and so evanescent when one thinks of the great words—' In the beginning, I am ! '

" Mother ! If I went to England, would I be told to hold my tongue ? I have never wanted to do more than tell people what I feel so strongly that I *know* about God—then why am I forbidden by the Pope to speak·? I am beginning to realize that I am being persecuted, although I had never dreamt of such a thing ! It sounds too silly and mediæval a word even to *think* of in these scientific, emancipated, and freedom-loving days of our century ! Yet it almost looks like it, doesn't it ? Doesn't the Pope love God ? Doesn't he want His truth and His alone, to be taught and preached ? "

While Christian had been talking, a sad determination had stolen into Quendred's face. Putting her hand into his, she said :

" Some creeds can exist very well without God, Christian ! Some creeds don't seem to need Him at all." (Her cheeks were still scarlet at the remembrance of the priest's words to her son.) " They are all completely mad about creeds," she thought to herself, " and dogmas, and rituals, and what theologians did, or did not, say. The fountain may not be drunk at, but must be collected into pipes bearing different names, and distributed, carefully edited, from taps marked High—Low—Latin—Anglican, to suit different varieties of mind and climate. Why can't the Church leave one alone ? Why can't one be left to pursue harmless, God-fearing lives, without for ever being interfered with by Rome, or from Rome, or through Rome ?

" By their way of teaching and carrying on their religion they have made me see that it is nothing after all but propaganda for the system evolved year by year in the Curia. Europe has been described as a lot of wicked old men covered with Orders, and I think the same description might apply to the Church as well. All the great Souls of all times and of all creeds have known this in the depths of their inmost being, and that is what has made the greatest ones go and live alone, apart from the world—so that they should no longer be tormented by fallible sinful men bleating out rules of their own invention, but instead fear the lovely voice of Christ, drawing them to Himself in His own way."

Yet even still—after all the suffering Quendred had been through—she was too loyal to tell these thoughts to her son.

He suddenly took her by the shoulders, and, gazing with calm intentness into her face, his shining dark eyes piercing right to her soul—he said :

" I don't think you believe in it yourself, Mother ? "

" I don't think I do," she answered, returning his gaze as frankly, and for a second these two souls were laid bare to each other.

" Then leave it," begged Christian, and his arms went round her, and his face was pressed to hers.

And thus they wandered homewards in the dusk of the summer evening ; heart to heart, and one in belief. Not belief in a creed, but belief in the all-sufficingness of God, and sincerely convinced through the pains—as it were—of a new birth that God has made us free in *Him*, and through *Him*, not in and through a dogmatic Church.

" Christian, dear son of mine," she whispered to him happily, as they lingered in the darkling woods, " largely through you I have been led to understand the Life which is the Light of men, the Light which shineth in the darkness ; the Word which was with God, the Word which *is* God, which was made Flesh and dwelt among us, full of grace and truth. How clearly I see now that we are not saved by Churches, or by nations, or by families, but as individuals through a personal knowledge in a personal Saviour."

So long had they wandered on the way home, that now the moon had appeared; and as Quendred looked at her son's face the moon's soft radiance lit it up and made it shine as though like silver. He seemed to her to be like some pure and valorous knight who had conquered all difficulties, and whose countenance even reflected some of Heaven's light.

"Mother darling," he said gently, "I am so glad that you have come to feel like this—come to know that God never made His work for men—Churchmen and theologians—to mend. God is complete and finished, but men seem to forget it. Men forget that He said, 'Let us make man in our image,' and insist on saying, 'Let us make God in our image.'

"In turning what was once simple and divine teaching into something distorted and undivine which they call 'religion,' men are in reality doing their best to set God's words at naught. His teaching was Godlike—so easy, so sincere, so straight, so noble—but men have contrived, with their un-Godlike minds, to make it so terribly difficult that *their* interpretation of His words again needs further interpretation which is then handed to the world as the only means of Salvation! And so at last, separated from our Shepherd, and harried hither and thither by wolves disguised as sheep, we find ourselves in the most pitiful plight.

"We have lost the fount and origin, the real cause of all our heart's peace and happiness, in the grey mist created by the human exposition of divine thoughts, and this mist has cast such a shadow over the world that it has left us in an eternal state of partial eclipse.

"Theology, dogma, creeds, are the Moon: God alone is the Sun. Do you remember how wonderful it all was in 'Parsifal,' Mother? There were no creeds there, were there?"

And that night he played to Maddalena and his father and mother the music that Quendred loved so well, and which meant so much to her down in the secret places of her soul. He played the tender, pathetic, and heart-clutching air of "Parsifal the Pure Fool."

Made wise by pi-ty, the blame-less fool.

THE END

PRINTED BY THE ANCHOR PRESS, LTD., TIPTREE, ESSEX, ENGLAND.